THE ROAD TO SECOND CHANCE

A Novel

TONI M. ANDREWS

THE PAPER HOUSE
PUBLISHING

CONTENTS

For Jim Dandy
and my parents Paul and Arlene
and my sister Edna
who taught me to always fight for underdogs.

PART ONE
BEFORE

"Hold dear to your parents for it is a
scary and confusing world without them."
- *Emily Dickinson*

CHAPTER 1

Death had been kind and had granted us more time than anyone expected. It had waited longer than the doctor had estimated. Had granted minutes that became hours and hours that blended into days. But the odd suspension of Death's arrival to claim the soul of my mother, Faye Martin, seemed wrong, like something stolen. As it drew closer with each unexpected day, I often found myself casting nervous looks over my shoulder. The little hairs on the back of my neck standing up. I expected to see the grim reaper holding its scythe, glowering at me.

Sometimes I would stand beside her bed as she slept, adrift in her medication–induced sleep. Staring down at her, a mantra in my brain: *Don't die. Don't die. Don't die. Not tonight. Not yet. I won't let you! You've got to talk to me! There isn't much time left.* I would stand like that in the darkened bedroom. Guilty for wanting to keep Death at bay not for her, but for my own sake. Some nights, my frustration and impatience that had accumulated for decades got the better of me and a deep-rooted anger would rise inside, its tentacles spreading throughout my body, burning in my chest like a hot liquid. In those moments I wanted to grab my mother by the shoulders, lift her off the bed, and shake her over and over again to make her wake up and talk to me.

Still, I would always kiss her goodnight. In all honesty, it was an insincere kiss that I planted on her forehead. Next, I would tilt my head to her ear and whisper gently, convinced that she could hear me, "Mama... please, please talk to me. Tomorrow. Please. We're running out of time." I wanted to scream, *how can you be so goddamn cruel to me, your own daughter? You will talk to me. I will make you!*

Instead, I would take deep breaths to calm myself and then simply tell her goodnight and insist that we *would* talk tomorrow. That it *must* be tomorrow, that I had waited long enough. On one of those nights as I stood by her bed and swayed wearily, waiting, and watching for some sign from her, unexpectedly, she moaned. A sudden excitement overcame me. *This is a sign!* She had heard me. She would not die. Not yet!

I had made an agreement with Death. Silently negotiated, I had promised Death that in exchange for giving my mother more time, it could take the equivalent time off my life. I convinced myself that this had been deemed acceptable because Death had not, despite all the grim predictions of immediacy, arrived.

No one knew about my agreement with Death, but others reminded me constantly that it was near. I knew the Hospice staff and some of the hired home health aides meant well when they whispered to me their warnings. The end was near and that Death, though delayed, could come at any time. Any time! I had confided in them my need to have an important conversation with my mother and they had expressed sympathy but lately, they would cast worrying glances at Mama then back at me as if they knew this would never happen.

Likewise, I am sure in his own way, my older brother Neal meant well even as he rolled his eyes at me when I shared my plan to persuade our mother into having a final conversation with me. For it to be about our father who had died nearly forty years ago when I was just two. Despite years pleading, she had refused to speak to me about him, never once uttering his name. Her stubborn defiance to share anything about the man who had given me life turned my interest in him to an unhealthy obsession and I needed some resolution before her hardened heart finally stopped.

"Mama isn't going to talk to you about Daddy so get over it," Neal had said to me the day after the visit to the oncologist's office where we had just received our mother's terrible diagnosis: Multiple Myeloma. The stage four cancer had spread from her skull to her feet. Terminal. She was given two weeks to live. Sitting in the doctor's office, Neal and I had burst into tears. But Mama, strikingly pale from anemia and rail thin having lost twenty pounds from her already slender body, had sat in quiet shock, staring straight ahead. Her mouth hung open as if it knew it should say something but could conjure nothing. It was a most unusual response from a woman so typically outspoken. I had reached over to hold her hand and she had roughly pulled it away from me. A moment later, she grabbed my hand with such a strong grip that I winced.

"No, Neal. It's different now. She's dying, and she knows it. This is when families resolve these things." We had been sipping beers and waving away mosquitos on the patio of Mama's house on the muggy August night, trying to come to terms with her fate. "It would be nice if you'd try to help get her to talk to me," I told him. "At least you can remember Daddy. I can't."

"You know I've tried. She's never gonna forgive him. And talking about him would be like forgiving him so I'd say it's a lost cause. Get over it."

The beer loosened my emotions and my simmering anger surfaced. "Get over it? She *owes* me this conversation. She *owes* me answers, while there's time."

"Well, there isn't much time left. Don't get your hopes up."

Hope is all I have, I wanted to scream. But instead, I nodded and planned.

◈

ASIDE FROM MY DETERMINATION TO HAVE A FINAL TALK WITH Mama about my father, it fell upon me to oversee her care. There was no other family living nearby. Mama's remaining siblings all lived in her hometown of Second Chance, a former coal-mining town, in West Virginia. They were all older and, due to health issues and economic hardship, did not travel. Neal couldn't afford to miss any more days at the printing company, plus he would need more time off and even more hours without pay when he took leave for the funeral in West Virginia.

I had the time, since I was working as a substitute teacher, and as it was summer, I was entirely free. The divorce two years ago from my ex-husband Phil meant that I would eventually go back to teaching full time to support myself and our ten-year-old son, Christopher. But for now, I was available. I readily agreed to leave my nearby apartment and move with Christopher back into my childhood home to help care for Mama. Her modest, three-bedroom house was in a neighborhood called Potomac Manor in Virginia just a few miles outside Washington, D.C. We moved there after my father was killed in 1962 when Mama decided to leave West Virginia and make a fresh start. She purchased the house with the life insurance money from my father's death claim and it proved to be a good location for Mama when she became a proud U.S. Civil Servant and took a secretarial job at the Pentagon.

As I settled into my old childhood bedroom and set Christopher up in Neal's old room across the hall, memories engulfed me. If the walls of the house could talk, I knew which stories about our family they would tell. Some stories contained laughter, music and happiness; some contained ugliness, anger and discord. And too many were composed of tragedy–heartbreaking events that occurred both to our family and to our country. News of these catastrophes came to us through the electrical wires running inside those very walls. The announcements, and our reactions, reverberated off the walls, leaving them untouched, but us forever changed.

I thought a lot about our family's story and my relationship with my mother when friends and relatives called to tell me what a good daughter I was. How they admired me taking on such a difficult role. *Was I a good daughter? What would she say?* These thoughts went through my mind as I stared at myself in the mirror above my old dresser. A woman I did not recognize stared back. My eyes were red from on and off crying and dull from sadness and they revealed my deep fatigue. My brown shoulder-length hair needed trimming. The golden highlights I had applied every few weeks had dulled and the gray roots atop my head betrayed my forty-one years. My face without make-up was pale. This made the dark circles beneath my eyes look stark. I forced myself to smile but frowned instantly as I noted my chubby cheeks. They had become fuller now from the weight I had gained caused by drinking too many glasses of wine each night. I turned away. I did not want to see any more of her.

If I hadn't been a good daughter up until this point, did moving in to care for her as she was dying make up for my past failings? I was tortured by both a sense of duty to Mama and equal amounts of anger toward her for many things, but mostly for withholding information about my father. Being Faye Martin's daughter had never been easy for me and having well-intentioned people praise me felt wrong, like I was wearing an ill-fitted coat that hung on me and dragged along the ground when I walked.

The truth? I was glad to have my mother to myself, needing me in a way she never really had and with me in control. Selfish? Maybe, but I believed that staring death in the face would cause her to do the right thing. She was a complicated person and often hypocritical to be sure, but she had sometimes revealed a steely courage and sense of purpose that I did not believe I had inherited. I was counting on that. As Death lurked, all I could do was hope she would find the courage to answer my questions. To share stories about my father only she could tell, and perhaps reveal if she had a photograph of him hidden somewhere since I had no memory of his face. I also needed her assurance that he had loved me and that I had mattered to him. If I knew better who he was, I reasoned, I would know better what I was made of and find the sense of purpose and courage I lacked.

And for her own sake, I needed my mother to tell me that she had at last forgiven my father and that, despite his final and fatal mistake, he had been a good man.

⚜

"Jesus H. Christ! I'm only sixty-nine years old!" Mama wailed, "This *cannot* be happening to me!"

But it was. I was distraught, trying to comprehend the fact that this woman who had so dominated my life would soon be gone. I scurried about in a daze, trying to comfort her, chart her medication schedule, care for Christopher, keep Neal posted, make meals, carry Mother, who was Mama's old and nearly deaf Welsh Terrier (named in honor of her own mother and purchased in honor of John F. Kennedy's Welsh Terrier, Charlie) outside for its business, get the mail, pay bills, run to the pharmacy and make all the phone calls for all the preparations dying at home required—all while looking for an opportunity to talk.

Soon after the diagnosis, Hospice sent a social worker to meet with us. Anne McClay immediately put us at ease with her gentle manner. Her voice was soothing with the trace of a Scottish accent. She gathered Mama, Neal, and I into the TV room off the kitchen for a conversation about death with dignity. The room was a time capsule from the late 1970s, with its shaggy brown wall-to-wall carpet, a sofa covered in a swirly floral pattern of orange and brown and a glass-topped coffee table. Next to the sofa, sat Mama's favorite recliner like a throne in all its faux leather glory. Directly across from that stood her 27" Sony TV, which was the newest item in the room (it had replaced our old 1969 RCA). The Sony sat regally on a quality wood cabinet. The remote controller, however, was always to be on the arm of Mama's recliner (and God help the last person who used it and failed to leave it there).

If the kitchen was the heart of most homes, the room with the television was the heart of ours. TV had always been central to our lives. In my earliest memories, it seemed always to be blaring. I think the endless banter from the TV comforted Mama and was an electronic replacement of the large, noisy family she had left behind in Second Chance.

Now the TV sat silent and seemed to be brooding over its exclusion from this most serious family gathering as Anne, seated on the sofa, explained how Hospice worked, what their role was and what would happen when death arrived. Mama, sitting in the recliner with the footrest out, kept shifting uncomfortably during the conversation, grimacing. "Just put me to sleep like a dog," she told Anne. "That's the humane thing to do. We put animals to sleep. We ought to let humans do the same. I don't want to feel nothing. I don't want to hurt! I don't want to know I'm dying. Give me as much drugs as you can!"

"But Mama," I interrupted before Anne could reply. "You don't *really* want that, do you? I mean, don't you want to be alert and able to talk and–"

"Hell no! I don't want to feel nothing! And who the hell do I need to talk to, Laney Mae? I'm done talking. I'm done... living."

"But Mama, what about Christopher?" I asked. I was seated close beside her on a chair I had dragged into the room from the kitchen table. "He needs you. He needs to see you and talk to you so that he can spend time with you and accept this. This is his first death." I reached over to stroke her arm just once (more than that and I think she would have slapped my hand away). And there it was: "the look"–the expression that Neal and I knew and dreaded. Her eyes narrowed into a glare, then one eyebrow arched upward, her lips forming a tight, angry line. It was the "what-the-hell-did-you-say-to-me" look; the look that stopped us in our tracks from the time we were kids.

"*His* first death?" Mama exclaimed. "Well, isn't that special? This is *my* first death, too!"

"Oh Mama, I–I didn't mean that–" I stammered.

Neal seemed to enjoy this. Seated next to Anne on the sofa, he rolled his eyes and shook his head. *Did I hear him chuckle?*

I spoke quickly. "Oh Mama! That's *not* what I meant. It's not just Christopher. Claudia and Frank and Harrie and everyone will want to be able to talk with you on the phone." I turned to Anne, "They're her siblings. Up in West Virginia." Anne nodded in understanding.

"And Mama," I continued, ignoring her scowl, "Gladys is planning to visit. You'll want to be able to visit with her and talk, won't you?" I turned again to Anne. "She's Mama's lifelong friend."

"That's wonderful that your friend is visiting," Anne said, coming to my rescue. She took Mama's hand. "Faye, listen, we'll keep you comfortable. I promise we'll manage your pain. And when you are to the point where you feel it's unbearable and what you're on now isn't working anymore, the Lorazepam and morphine will help manage the pain and yes, help you sleep easier. How does that sound?"

Mama's bony shoulders shrugged. She shook her head, her stead-fastly dyed blonde hair neatly coiffed, defying, the scourge of the cancer consuming her body in its fullness and shine. "What is that . . . Lorza–?"

"Lorazepam. It's usually called Ativan. It helps when patients are really anxious and scared."

Mama nodded. "Yeah. That stuff sounds like what I need. But I still say we treat dying dogs better than we do people! If I could put myself to sleep right now, I would. I mean, if I'm gonna die, let me die, you know?" She had shifted her eyes from Anne to Neal to me and then back to Anne. With resignation she said, "Oh hell. Your plan sounds okay to me Anne." Then she raised a finger and pointed at me. "For now," she said firmly. "For Christopher."

Next, Anne inquired about Mama's faith, "Are you religious, Faye? Do you belong to a particular church? Faith can be a great comfort."

Mama seemed taken aback. "I consider myself religious, Anne. I don't go to church no more but when I did, it was to the Methodist Church near here." She motioned toward me and Neal. "They went to Sunday School there."

Anne smiled. "So, Christian." She made a note on her paperwork.

"A *loving* Christian," Mama said.

Anne looked up and tilted her head to the side, quizzically.

Mama continued, "I don't like what some folks have done to Christianity! They use it to divide and to spread hate. The ones on TV? They're hypocrites! Raising all that money? For what? I'm not *that* kind of Christian!" I resisted the urge to ask her what kind of "loving Christian" would not forgive a husband who had died nearly forty years ago and would not speak his name or share anything about him with his daughter.

"And, Anne, I do believe in Heaven and a spiritual life after death," Mama offered. "I have faith I will see my mother and my father and all my brothers who have died and my sister who passed. And there are a lot of historical figures I look forward to meeting, too or seeing again, like President Kennedy."

I hesitated but could not resist this opening. "Mama," I said, bracing myself as she turned to look at me. "What about Daddy? Will you see him, too?" I heard Neal let out a groan, but I didn't care. Anne was my witness; maybe she could help me get Mama to talk and why not now? Again, I received "the look." I swallowed uncomfortably. Mama's voice was filled with contempt. "No, I will *not*. We have had this conversation before, Laney Mae. He. Is. Not. Up. There!"

I frowned and looked at the carpet. We had indeed had this conversation before, the first time was when I was eight. There had been so much upsetting news on TV that year about death: Martin Luther King, Jr. then Bobby Kennedy had been shot and killed. It seemed that every evening on TV there were more ghastly images of American troops and innocent people dying in the tragedy that was Vietnam—all this happening just a couple of years after my uncle Rob, Mama's brother, had been killed there. My young mind was consumed with death. This had triggered in me an urgent, new concern about my daddy: what had happened to his soul?

I decided to ask her in a round-about way one evening when I had her to myself. We were having popcorn and watching The Carol Burnett Show. During a commercial I turned to her and asked, "Mama, what happens when we die?"

"Why you asking me that? You're too young to worry about dying!"

"I just wanna know–"

Exasperated she replied, "If you're good, you go to Heaven. If you're bad you go to the devil and burn in hell." I had asked her if I was going to hell since she had often told me I was bad: bad for not cleaning my room, bad for not coming home when she called me when I was playing outside, bad for fighting with Neal. She scoffed. "That's not the kind of *bad* I mean, Laney Mae! I mean serious bad like people who do awful things like murder. And people who lie and cheat." She paused before adding, "Like your father."

I remember my mouth filled with saliva and I was sure I would throw up. I made quick excuses to run to my bedroom. I prayed to a God I did not know very well. *Please, oh please, allow my daddy out of hell and into Heaven.*

Mama turned to Anne, waving her hand at me. "Do you see what I have to put up with? She is always badgering me about her father, and I do not wish to talk about him."

That did it. "Badgering?" I stood and hovered above her. "That's a horrible thing for you to say, Mama! I'm not *badgering* you! I'm *asking* you like I have *asked* you for the last three decades to talk to me about my father. I have a right to know about him and from *you*!"

Anne tried to interject, "Many families have unresolved issues like this and—"

"It's *her* issue," Mama barked, "Not mine. I'm *resolved*!"

I huffed with anger but was emboldened by Anne's presence. My voice rose. "No! It is *your* issue, Mama. Always has been! You've refused to talk to me about him and now you're dying!" This harsh statement hung in the air. The "look" on Mama's face collapsed into a frown and her bottom lip trembled.

"Thanks for that news alert," Mama hissed, fighting a sob.

"Well, I'm sorry but it's true!" I took a deep breath to calm myself and lowered my voice. "But before you die, Mama, you owe me a conversation about him."

Her eyes widened in shock at the audacity of my demand. "I *owe* you? How dare you say such a thing? I don't *owe* you anything! I provided for you all your life! He sure as hell didn't! And let me tell you something, if I could stand up now, I'd slap you in the face for saying such a thing! You lean down here and let me slap your face!"

I laughed at her. "You want me to *let* you slap my face for asking about my father?"

Neal had had enough. "Stop!" He stood and put his body between mine and Mama's, always the peacekeeper and diplomat. "That's enough! Both of you knock it off," he said sharply. "Let Anne finish up what she needs to go over with us."

I sighed and sat on the dining chair but then quickly scooted myself back away from the recliner to be sure I was out of Mama's slapping range. We scowled at each other while Anne smiled at Neal and told us she had covered everything she needed to, and asked if we had anything to share or questions?

Neal frowned at me while Mama simmered in anger; "the look" had returned. She composed herself and turned to Anne and said, "I'm sorry you had to see that. My own daughter attacking me! But I do appreciate you going over everything."

Anne gave us a sympathetic smile. "Believe me, lots of families have issues."

Mama nodded. "Well, speaking of family, my family back home will handle all the—" She stopped, her voice breaking. She looked down at the floor, struggling to compose herself. She had never had patience for tears—"*Don't turn on the waterworks*"—she'd say to me when I was young and about to cry. "They'll handle all that. My nephew Jake works at the funeral home there."

"Thank you for sharing that, Faye. It's great that your family is able to help."

Mama bowed her head. She slumped in exhaustion and brought her hands up to cover her face, whimpering. Neal rose and knelt before her. He took her hand and leaned in close to her and murmured words of comfort.

Anne and I smiled politely at each other, but I could not hold her eyes very long due to my guilt over losing my temper and putting Anne in the middle. I looked back at Mama as Neal knelt beside her and felt a pang in my chest as I tried to imagine what it would feel like to be told I would soon die. I could not comprehend having such information handed to me. I bowed my head, feeling shame over my outburst and insistence that my mother talk to me about my father before Death's arrival, while I planned my next opportunity to do so.

CHAPTER 2

I knew more about how my father died than the life he lived. This was thanks to Neal, who, only once, told me the story. Prior to that, all that I knew about my father, Gilbert "Gil" Martin, could be summarized on a short list of facts. Some that I had cajoled out of Neal, a few from Mama's siblings who were brave enough to secretly tell me about him (swearing me to never reveal them), and Mama's best friend Gladys who hadn't known my father well, but shared some tidbits.

I had no idea what he looked like because, having been just two when he died, I had no memory of his face. In addition to throwing out all of his belongings, Mama had ripped up all photos of him or torn his face out of group photos in the days following his death. No one else had a photo to share. Most of Mama's relatives didn't own luxury items like cameras back then and even if they did, she would have demanded they get rid of anything to do with "that man" or risk her wrath.

Still, over time, I was able to assemble a list and of what I knew for sure:

- *He was born on May 15, 1925*
- *He had brown hair and brown eyes*
- *He smoked cigarettes*
- *He had taken some college courses*
- *He successfully sold insurance all over the state of West Virginia*
- *He drove a nice car*
- *He loved all sorts of music including Johnny Horton, Hank Williams, The Mills Brothers, Elvis, Jerry Lee Lewis, Guy Lombardo, Bing Crosby and Frank Sinatra*
- *He danced with me in his arms and sang songs like "Swinging On A Star" and "When the Red, Red Robin Comes Bob, Bob, Bobbin' Along."*
- *He was an only child. He was named after his father, Gilbert Sr.*
- *His mother's name was Kathleen Reid Martin*
- *His parents died within three years of his death*
- *He and my mother met when he came to Second Chance to sell insurance*
- *He purchased a new home for our family in River Mount, a town a half hour from Second Chance where we lived when I was born*
- *He was especially kind to my aunt Harrie, Mama's younger sister, who had Down syndrome at a time when few understood the condition, and many treated her cruelly*
- *He voted for John F. Kennedy in the West Virginia Primary and for President*
- *He liked to go out at night*
- *He liked to drink beer*
- *He died on an icy mountain road on January 27, 1962. He was not alone.*

His not being alone when he died was not fully understood by me until January 27, 1969, on the seventh anniversary of his death when I was nine. On that night, I waited until Mama was asleep then nervously knocked on Neal's bedroom door. He was thirteen which meant he was easily irritated and lately it seemed like he wanted nothing to do with me. Mama had noted Neal's edginess in the last few months, too, and attributed it to his becoming a teenager. But, I believed it had more to do with his growing discomfort with the man who would become our stepfather in a few months, Art McDaniel. Art never liked Neal and his cruelty to my brother and to me was one of those ugly stories the walls of our house would witness.

He did not respond to the knock, so I opened his door. My brother sat up in bed and switched on the light.

"What do you want?" he asked, annoyed.

"I want to talk to you." I closed the door softly and stood beside his bed.

"Do you know what time it is Laney Mae?"

"I know it's late."

"Did you have a bad dream or something?" His voice was kinder.

"No. I haven't even been asleep yet." I hesitated then said, "Neal, I know what today is. It's the date Daddy died."

"So?"

"So, I want to know what happened that night. No one has ever told me the whole story. You were there. I know you saw it all."

"Jesus, Laney Mae! I would just like to forget it, okay? It was an awful night. I'll tell you some other time. Now go to bed."

"No! I'm not leaving here until you tell me." I reached out and laid my hand on his arm. "Please?"

For a minute he did not answer then he said, "Well, I guess you're old enough now." He leaned in close to my face and said, "Don't you dare tell Mama!"

"I won't. I promise."

"Well, all right. But after I tell you, you're going to bed and if you have bad dreams, don't blame me."

I climbed on to the bed and sat, in front of him. Neal sighed and began his story. "That night, it was really cold, and everything was all icy. Daddy had gone out." He hesitated and looked at me sadly. "Look, Laney Mae. There's something you gotta know about Daddy. You already have an idea about him from the bad stuff Mama says. The thing is, he used to go out a lot at night. He loved to have a good time. He'd go have drinks and he hated being cooped up in the house. But if he didn't come home by a certain time, Mama would get really mad. She'd smoke and curse and drink. And if he was *really* late, she'd get you and me in the car and go hunting for him. And that night, Daddy had gone out after supper and hadn't come back. I had gone to bed and the next thing I knew, Mama was shaking me awake. Telling me to get out of bed and that we needed to go find Daddy. I didn't want to go. I was so comfortable and told her to please let me sleep. She told me to get up, pulled all the blankets off me and yanked me out of bed. It was so cold; I remember I started shivering right away.

Mama told me to get myself dressed then go to your room and get you dressed while she got the car ready. I remember begging her to not make us go. I said, 'Mama it's so darn cold and icy outside and I bet Daddy will be home soon.' She told me to hush and get you and be outside in three minutes while she got the car ready or else. I remember she had a cigarette hanging out of her mouth and the ash kept getting longer. I asked if I could just stay in the house with you while she went looking for him. Then she got even madder and said, 'I don't want to hear another word from you, Neal. Besides, I can't leave you all alone here. What if something happened like at the Wallace house a few years ago? They left the kids alone and the house burned down. You wanna die in a burning house?'

So, I got dressed and went into your room to get you dressed in your snowsuit. I remember you woke up—you had just turned two—and you looked like you were gonna cry so I started playing peek-a-boo with you and soon you were okay. I got you downstairs and you said, 'Go bye-bye?' and I was like, 'Yeah, we're going bye-bye all right.' I remember walking you down the front steps and I slipped on the last one and landed hard on my butt and it hurt. And you said, 'Uh-oh.'"

Neal allowed himself a chuckle and I smiled. He continued. "I saw Mama was scraping the windshield and I said, 'It's too icy. We shouldn't be driving in this, Mama.' Well, she stopped scraping and that's when I noticed that she only had on a light jacket and a sweater and pants and she was wearing her bedroom slippers! She didn't have a hat or gloves on and she was still smoking a cigarette. Her hair was blowing all over the place. I remember thinking that she looked like a dragon. I was scared of my own mom! She screamed at me, 'Is all you can do is complain, Neal? It ain't that bad out here! Why look: it's hardly even stuck two inches.' Well, I had a bad feeling something awful was gonna happen if we got in that car, so I tried one more time. I called out, 'Please, Mama. How come we gotta go hunt for Daddy anyways? He's probably just at Crystal's Palace having a few beers and he'll be home soon.'

Well, that did it. Mama ran over and grabbed my arm and your hand and pulled us hard to the car. She screamed, 'Get in the goddamn car!' And Laney Mae, your little legs couldn't keep up and you lost your footing. Mama just dragged your body along in the snow and you started crying and when we got to the car, Mama opened the back door, scooped you up, laid you down on the back seat and told you to go night-night. And you just laid flat because the snowsuit was so stiff you couldn't move. So of course, you cried, and Mama told you to hush up and she turned to me and said, 'Why didn't you bring her a bottle or her pacifier or something?' Before I could answer, she grabbed me by the arm and shoved me in the car so fast I didn't have time to duck, and I hit my head on the car doorframe. Did that hurt! I started crying even more. Mama told me that I got what I deserved for being so uncooperative."

Neal stopped. I waited, worried he had changed his mind and would not continue. He leaned back against the headboard and looked past me as though watching the story unfold like a movie. He said, "Mama drove crazy! The car was sliding all over the road. I was so scared. First, we went by Crystal's Palace. You know the place?"

I nodded. It was hardly a palace. It had been a simple restaurant with a bar, jukebox and a couple of pool tables. "The one that's all boarded up now?"

"Yeah. That's the one. So, she goes in there and comes storming out. Turns out someone told her daddy had been there and left. So, she sped outta there and we skidded, and I was sure we'd go off the road right down the mountain and die. We had driven only a couple of miles when... I heard the horn."

"The horn?"

"Yeah, a car horn. It was just blaring. When I heard it, I felt sick to my stomach. It was such strange sound. I knew it was a car horn, but it sounded like an animal, moaning... dying. I knew that sound was *wrong*, and it meant something *bad*. Then I saw the sheriff's car and a state trooper's car with lights flashing and the sound of the horn got louder and louder. I remember Mama looking back over at me with this weird look on her face.

She drove up really slow to the accident and pulled up behind a state trooper's car. I was sitting in the backseat but leaning forward holding on to the front seat and I remember saying to her, 'Mama, what's happening? Where is Daddy?' The sheriff saw us drive up and he ran over to the car. I remember seeing his face in the headlights and his expression when he saw it was Mama's car. He knew our family. I swear all the blood went out of his face. Mama rolled the window down and threw out her cigarette. The sheriff leaned down and looked in the car and he said, 'Faye, it's bad.'

I could see what happened. A coal truck had hit Dad's car head-on and had pushed his car off the road and into a ditch. But no one was doing anything, and I couldn't stand it! Knowing it was Daddy's car and that god-awful horn blaring and no one doing anything."

Neal stopped speaking and raised his hands to cover his face. I sat silent, anxiously wringing my hands until he looked up and I saw his tears. He wiped his face with the bedsheet and continued, "I couldn't stand it, so I slid over to the door and bolted out. I ran as fast as I could toward that ditch. I remember screaming, 'Dad! Dad!' and I heard Mama and the sheriff and the state trooper holler at me and tell me to stop but I wouldn't. At one point, I hit a patch of ice and fell hard but I just got back up and ran on before they could stop me.

I came to the edge of the road and looked down at Dad's car. I remember looking up at the truck cab and seeing the driver moving a bit and when I realized he was alive, I thought, well Daddy must be alive, too! I made my way down into the ditch, but I slid and had to crawl over to the car door. I grabbed the door handle and pulled myself up and . . . and . . . there was Dad's face. His eyes looking right at me. The headlights from the truck were shining right on him. Blood was running down his head. The crash caused his body to fall forward onto the steering wheel and that's why the horn was blaring. I guess his body and the dashboard were all crushed together. At first, I couldn't even get my breath. I moved my mouth, but nothing would come out. Then I started screaming, 'Dad, wake up! Wake up!' I heard the trooper and sheriff behind me and then I heard an ambulance come up. Next thing I know that state trooper grabbed me underneath my arms and pulled me out of the way and held me tight. He tried to take me out of the ditch but I screamed and elbowed him and so he just stopped and let me stay but he kept his arms on me tight. I watched as the sheriff tried to open the driver's door, but it was stuck. He had to really pull and lean his foot against the car to get the door open. He reached in with both hands and pushed Dad's body off the horn. And just like that"–Neal snapped his fingers–"there was silence. It was *so* quiet without that horn. I felt like everything was going in slow motion. I just stood there with snot running down my face, freezing on my skin and then . . . I saw *her*. In the seat next to Dad, there was this lady. She had been slammed into the windshield and her hair was all bloody, but I didn't realize it was blood at first. I thought, who has that color of red hair? Then I realized that it was blood. Some of her hair was stuck in the windshield glass. She was dead, too. I could tell, even though her eyes weren't open like Daddy's."

I gasped and clapped my hand over my mouth, "But who was she, Neal?"

"I don't know. I never did know. No one told me, and I knew better than to ask."

"Then what happened?"

"The sheriff pulled me up to the road and took me to stand next to Mama and I'll never, as long as I live, forget her face. She looked insane! If I thought she looked crazy before, now she was *really* crazy! Her eyes were wild. I know now that she was in shock. She stared in the car and kept looking from Daddy to that dead woman and back at Daddy. She kept running her hands through her hair. She was muttering and her whole body was shaking. She must have been half frozen standing there with no coat and in her slippers! Finally, the sheriff came over and told her we had to go home, that there was nothing we could do and that she had to get outta the cold while they took care of things. He took hold of her arm and took me by the hand and he walked us back to the car where you had been the whole time, Laney Mae. You were asleep on the back seat. The sheriff offered to drive us home, but Mama said no, that she was fine to drive. I was just crying and crying and got in the front with Mama. I couldn't believe Daddy was dead. I kept thinking it was some sick joke and that he would all of a sudden get out of the car, laughing, saying, 'I fooled you all!'

Then the sheriff leaned in the window and he said to Mama, 'I'm so sorry about your husband, Faye.' And Mama? Well, she turned to him and said, 'Husband? He is *not* my husband anymore. I am no longer married to *that man*.' The sheriff looked like she had slapped him. He said something like, 'Faye, you're upset and this is a horrible shock, but we'll sort all this out tomorrow. I'm so sorry. Gil was a friend of mine.' Mama just glared at him and said, 'Your friend. *Really?* What about his girlfriend there? Was she your friend, too?' The sheriff shook his head and told Mama he didn't know who the woman was but before he even finished talking, Mama rolled the window up and we spun out of there. I'm still surprised we got home alive ourselves, the crazy way she was driving.

That night was the only night I remember her letting you and me sleep in her bed with her. I don't know how, but I fell asleep pretty quick. When I woke up, Mama and you were still asleep. I remember thinking I had dreamed it all but, then it all came back.

The next few days were just awful. You don't remember our house there in River Mount but that's where we lived then. I don't remember everything. Only that everyone was crying all the time. Mama stayed in her bedroom a lot. I could hear her wailing, then I'd hear her screaming and then she'd get quiet again. Aunt Claudia and Uncle Luke kept going in trying to calm her down. I remember Mama gathered up all Dad's things and threw them outside the bedroom window. Straight out the window! At one point, when she was throwing his stuff out, I remember she said something like, 'I'm glad that bastard and his whore are dead!' Aunt Claudia told her not to say such things. Said that she'd go to hell and Mama said, 'I'm already in hell!'"

"I don't remember any of that," I said in a whisper.

"Well, be glad you don't! One of the worst things was the day before the funeral when Dad's parents, Grandma and Grandpa Martin, came to see us. Can you imagine how awful this was for them? Daddy was their only child! As they pulled up in front of the house, Mama came flying outta her bedroom and told them to get out! Grandma Martin started crying and hugging me tighter and Grandpa Martin kept trying to get Mama to calm down. She just told them to leave, that she couldn't stand to be reminded of *that man*.

The day of the funeral, I got up early and got dressed in what Aunt Claudia had laid out for me and I was helping with you. I remember Uncle Luke, Uncle Frank, Aunt Harrie and Aunt Ruth were there, planning to go. But then Mama came out and said that none of us was going to the service. Uncle Luke was like, 'Faye, you can't mean that!' and Mama was like, 'Oh really? The hell I can't.'"

Neal shook his head at the memory. "So, we didn't go to the funeral. I think Mama was ashamed that he was out with that woman and, just couldn't bring herself to sit through a service for him. But I think Uncle Luke went anyway without telling Mama. Sort of representing our family. And, not long after that, Mama moved us away from Second Chance down here to Virginia. She said it was a fresh start."

He sighed. "And that's what happened, Laney Mae. That's the story. Now go to bed."

I remained still, trying to comprehend all my brother told me. I thought about what my brother had been through, seeing our dead father. I also felt pity for Mama; no wonder she had been hurt and angry. Why wasn't Daddy home where he belonged? Did he love this other woman more than us?

As if reading my mind, Neal leaned over and took both of my hands, a gesture of kindness that touched me. "Listen to me, Laney

Mae. What Daddy did–being out with that other woman–that was wrong. But no matter what Mama says now, I'm sure he loved us. And I know he loved Mama, too. That I can remember for sure."

"But I can't remember anything," I said and the tears I had tried to hold in, began to stream down my face. "I don't even know what he looks like! And if he was bad, does that mean part of me is bad too? Mama always says he was a liar and a cheat and is burning in hell. But was he all bad? He was still our dad!" I punched the mattress with my fist. "I just want Mama to talk to me about him. She loved him once, didn't she?"

"I don't understand it either. But when someone you love hurts you, it's a hard thing to get over."

I slid off the bed and used the sleeve of my nightgown to wipe my tears. I started to leave but turned back. "Neal, don't you think that if that car crash had never happened and Daddy had lived, things would be better? Maybe bad things wouldn't have happened?"

"What are you talking about? Bad things happen all the time. Just watch the news on TV."

"But his dying changed Mama. So, it changed us, too. She took us away from our home. She brought us here where people are mean and nasty and call us hillbillies; people like Mrs. Clarke! If we hadn't moved here, she wouldn't have ever been our babysitter. She was so mean! And even Uncle Rob dying in Vietnam. I feel like that wouldn't have happened, if Daddy hadn't died. Don't you see?"

Neal shook his head. "That doesn't make any sense. Things happen the way they're supposed to whether we like it or not."

I stared at him, struggling to find the words to sum up my anguish. "But Neal, if Daddy hadn't died, he would be here to protect us, to keep us safe. To save us from all the bad stuff."

"How could he save us, Laney Mae," Neal said, "when he couldn't even save himself?"

CHAPTER 3

Sleep became a challenge, and I don't mean falling asleep, I mean *staying* asleep. The toll of caring for Mama left me physically and emotionally exhausted. I was so relieved every day at seven p.m. when one of the hired health aides arrived, freeing me from endless tasks and continuous worry. I would help the aide walk Mama from her recliner in the TV room to use the bathroom, get her into bed (wearing adult diapers which she despised), and then give her pain and anti-anxiety medication which helped her sleep. She was not yet on morphine, but the Hospice workers told me it would be necessary very soon.

Mama would sometimes hold my hand as she drifted off to sleep but, we spoke little. Once, I tried to sing to her and the look on her face stopped me cold, "Well, now I know why you didn't make the school chorus," she said, eyes closed. We both laughed. Ribbing each other and moments of humor were rare, and I treasured them. Propped up on pillows to help her breathing, I would watch over her until her eyelids grew heavy and I was sure she was asleep.

Tiptoeing from her bedroom, I would whisper thanks to the

health aide and make my way through the living room, slowly climbing the stairs to my childhood room where I would find Christopher waiting, snuggled in the bed. He would have already completed his goodnight ritual with his grandmother which took place right after his nightly bath and was to be reading until I came to bed. He had not slept in Neal's old room a single night since we had moved in. I did not mind. I wanted him near.

After reading a story to Christopher, I would turn out the light, kiss him on the forehead and, at last, lay my weary head on my pillow. I would then allow myself to begin the comforting drift into blissful sleep. But then, what I called the night panics would begin. These were ominous voices in my head that mocked me with taunts that Death was coming, that my so-called agreement was a joke and, that Mama would soon be gone. The voices goaded me about other things, too. They reminded me that I was 41 years old and told me that the best years of my life were behind me. They testified that I was a failure—*just look at your divorce!*—and promised me I would never find love—*Phil had found someone younger, prettier, better!*—and never have another child, despite the two I had hoped for. They offered me only the grim prospect of a lonely life in an apartment I could barely afford with a son who would be forever traumatized by his parents' divorce and the pain of his father's rejection.

I would bolt up, crying out, "No!" then force myself to take slow, deep breaths until the panic subsided and my heartbeat returned to normal. I fought back against their prophesies, reassuring myself that I was *not* used up, that I *could* find love and, that I had Christopher and a brother who loved me, friends who cared and family, although we were not especially close, but whose blood I shared. And through them I had a history. Which always brought me back to the mystery of my father. I could accept his death but not the execution of his memory. Was this to be my mother's legacy?

Sometimes, I would slip out of bed and tiptoe downstairs to

make sure Mama was still alive and see for myself that Death had not arrived. Many of the home health aides who rotated in service were used to this and they would motion that Mama was okay. Relieved, I would slowly make my way back to bed. Often, I would take another Xanax, roll onto my side and stare at Christopher until sleep at last found me.

I often marveled that Christopher, wrapped in a bundle of blankets even on those hot summer nights, usually slept through my disruptions. Though he was not unfamiliar with pain and loss and the inevitability of his grandmother's death, he managed to sleep peacefully next to me, his tormented mother.

⁂

I ROSE EARLY TWO DAYS AHEAD OF GLADYS'S ARRIVAL. I WANTED to straighten the house, run errands, get groceries, and plan a special dinner. Christopher had spent the night at his friend's house and would spend the day with them at the neighborhood pool, a much needed respite from the sadness of watching his grandmother's slow progression toward death.

Mama was still sleeping when I crept downstairs at six-thirty and the health aide, an older woman named Helen, dozed on the sofa in the living room. I walked past her to Mama's bedroom and pushed the door open. There she slept, without her dentures, her thin lips hugging her gums, her mouth hanging open and head tilted to the side. I found Mother curled up on the floor, picked her up and carried her outside to do her business.

When I came back in, I fed the dog then brewed coffee and made a bowl of yogurt with berries for myself. The smell of coffee roused Helen who joined me in the kitchen to report a mostly uneventful night. "She moaned a bit and I went in a couple of times, but she slept okay," she told me, "I just checked and she's still sleep-

ing. I'll get her up soon and help her to the bathroom before I go."
She took a steaming cup of coffee from me.

"Helen, I scheduled someone to be here from ten to three. I
have to go out. Do you know who's coming?"

Helen shook her head, "Not sure. But good for you. You need
time away from all this." She paused and then asked, "Has she talked
to you yet? About your father?"

"No, I keep looking for the right moment." Helen nodded and
then we heard Mama calling. She took another gulp of coffee,
"Coming Miss Faye," she called out. "Duty calls," she said to me.
"Good luck. Maybe today will be the day." She winked as she left the
kitchen.

Mama's appetite was better in the morning, so I prepared a bowl
of raisin bran with sliced banana, coffee and some orange juice and
put it all on a tray with her medication. I watched as Helen guided
her slowly through the kitchen to the TV room. Leaning on the
walker she had vowed to never use, Mama's face grimaced with each
step. Her physical demise was startling, even to me, someone who
saw her daily. Before the cancer let its presence be known with pain
in her back and hips that was so sudden and severe that she could
hardly stand, Mama had been a boundless bundle of energy that
defied her age. She had exercised daily, lifted hand weights, gardened
and, taken Mother on regular walks. "If you rest, you'll rust and I
ain't gonna rust," she would say. Now she could no longer stand or
walk unaided. My once fit and vibrant mother now resembled a
walking skeleton.

Helen helped position her in front of the recliner. Mama
moaned as she sat and closed her eyes, exhausted. "You take care,
Miss Faye," Helen said, patting Mama's hand and moving the walker
to the side of the chair. "I'm not sure who will be here tonight, but
I'll see you again soon."

I stood beside the recliner holding the tray and watched as

Mama forced a smile. "Thank you... Helen," she said weakly in the halting manner that was now normal. "Go on... home... and get some... sleep."

Helen laughed, "Sleep? Ha! I'll be doing my laundry then grabbing a nap before heading to my other job." She left with a cheery farewell.

"Helen's situation ... is a perfect example... of what is... wrong with... this country," Mama lamented. Each word required effort, but she had much to say, "Hard working folks... never get a break. I'm telling you... the rich get richer and the poor get... poorer... all the time." I dared not engage her on the issue of trickle-down economics and remind her that she had voted for Ronald Regan and his tax cuts for the wealthy over Jimmy Carter in 1980.

I put the tray on Mama's lap. She frowned at it. "Good God! Why . . . did you . . . give me so . . . much food? I'm not . . . hungry." She waved the pain pill in the air. "This ain't . . . cutting it anymore." She downed the juice. "It hardly helps . . . and . . . constipates me."

"The Senokat's there, too. You gotta take that, Mama. It will help."

"And I need this fentanyl patch on my back changed. It's been three days."

"I know, I have it all written down on the schedule and I'll do that after breakfast. Now try to eat some," I encouraged. "Anne is bringing the morphine today, remember? The ones you let dissolve under your tongue? She said they work for twelve hours. I'm sure that will be a great help."

Mama shook her head and looked confused. "I thought she . . . said . . . liquid?"

"Well, they will provide that when—" I caught myself and frowned.

Mama cocked her head. "When . . . I can't . . . swallow anymore?"

I sighed and nodded. "At least there are options for—"

She rolled her eyes, "How about . . . the option . . . of *not* . . . dying? Can they give . . . me that? I'll . . . take that." She spooned a bit of cereal and banana out of the bowl and slowly raised it to her mouth, her hand shaking.

Changing the subject, I reminded her that I had scheduled another health aide to come during the day so that I could run errands and go to the grocery store. "Christopher spent the night at Josh's house. They're going to the pool. He'll be home later."

Mama swallowed with some difficulty and made a face. "I miss . . . him when he's . . . not here." She frowned then pointed the spoon at me and said, "I hope that aide you scheduled . . . it's not that . . . one gal. What's her name?"

"You mean Sissy?"

Mama grunted. "Oh God! Yes . . . Sissy! All . . . she does . . . is that endless . . . whistling. That is, unless she's talking. She cannot . . . be quiet . . . to save . . . her soul."

"She's really nice, though."

Mama scowled, "I hate . . . having . . . all these . . . strangers . . . in my house."

I decided to change the subject, "Mama, we do have something special to look forward to: Gladys comes day after tomorrow!"

Mama smiled weakly, "She . . . coming . . . alone?"

"Far as I know."

Mama shook her head, "I guess . . . I'm too . . . much trouble for . . . anyone in *my* family . . . to drive down with her to come . . . see me."

"Oh, Mama. They care. It's just not that easy for them to travel." I made excuses for them but I, too, shared Mama's disappointment that none of her siblings were coming.

She scoffed, "Well, they won't . . . have to . . . worry about me . . . much longer."

"Oh Mama," I said sadly.

"It's true." Her face crumpled, "I guess I'll never see . . . my sisters and . . . brother again. Not in this life." Two tears spilled from her blue eyes.

I saw an opportunity and stepped over to sit on the sofa next to her recliner, "Mama, you know, you're right. I hate to say it, but you will be going soon." She frowned but I continued, "So Mama . . . please . . . *please* talk to me about Daddy." I held my hands before her, clasped as if in prayer.

She gave me "the look" again as I had come to expect. With effort, she swallowed the cereal she had been chewing and threw her spoon down on the tray, "Don't . . . you . . . do it! Do not start in . . . on me."

I unclasped my hands and stood, "Then when, Mama? We've *got* to talk and soon. You're getting weaker. It's hard for you to speak now! Isn't there something you want to tell me about Daddy before it's too late?"

"Goddamn it, Laney Mae!" Her voice was suddenly strong, and she shook her head, struggling to control her anger. "I want you . . . to . . . stop! How many times . . . have we been through this? Why are you . . . tormenting me?"

My face grew hot, "Mama! All I want you to do is talk to me. I've asked you and asked you and you *are* running out of time. This is one of the cruelest things you could do to me! Your own daughter! He was *my father*. I have a right to know about him. Why can't you understand that?"

"Enough!" Mama yelled. She lifted the tray from her lap and threw it onto the floor, displaying physical strength neither of us thought she had. My mouth dropped open. I looked from her angry face to the tray on the floor. The raisin bran, banana slices and milk splattered on the carpet, the coffee and juice spilled over, running off the tray and forming ugly puddles.

"Really Mama?! I can't believe you just did that!" I stormed to the kitchen and grabbed paper towels. When I returned, the dog was sniffing around the tray and lapping up the milk. "Move Mother!" I snapped, knowing full well she could not hear me. I pushed the dog away and knelt down and began to clean up.

"You . . . take it easy . . . with my . . . dog," Mama said evenly.

I glared at her, "Right! Let's not be mean to the dog. It's okay to be mean and cruel to your daughter but, God forbid we hurt that dog's feelings!"

Mama had had enough. She began to try to rise up from the recliner but did not have the strength. She pushed against the arms and pressed her legs against the chair's leg rest and grimaced as she tried to lower it down to a seating position. I watched as she struggled, enjoying her frustration, knowing full well she needed my help.

"You look like a turtle on its back," I said and began to laugh.

"Goddamnit . . . Get me out . . . of this . . . chair!" She leaned back and pushed again but nothing budged. Mama stopped her struggle and stared at me as I convulsed in laughter and, unexpectedly, she too began to laugh. She laughed like I had not seen her laugh in months, so much so that she actually snorted. This only made us convulse further, tears running down our faces. When the moment was over, I picked the tray up from the floor and we stared at each other in silence.

"Do you want more breakfast?"

"Just . . . coffee."

"Would you like some carpet strands with that?"

"Oh . . . but . . . of course," she returned the sarcasm.

I stared at her, waiting. "I shouldn't . . . have thrown . . . the tray," she said softly.

I knew better than to expect her to say, "I'm sorry." Those two words were not in her vocabulary. Still, I nodded, hoping she might also say she shouldn't have refused to speak to me about my father for nearly four decades, but she was saved by the phone ringing.

Sighing, I carried the tray to the kitchen and grabbed the handset. It was Claudia, Mama's closest sister, calling from Second Chance.

"Oh! Laney Mae, how are you all doing, sweetheart?"

"Oh, we're okay," I told her as I walked back into the TV room with the phone. "Mama just finished breakfast."

"Oh! That's good. How's she feeling?" Claudia's voice was edgy and filled with apprehension, but it seemed to always be when it came to her relationship with her older sister. When they were young, Claudia and Mama had been very close and nearly inseparable but, in later years a tension had developed between them that lingered still. I always attributed this to my father's death. To my thinking, Claudia never forgave Mama for fleeing the scandalous circumstances of his death and in doing so, abandoning her own family and Second Chance in the process. In Virginia, Mama had a steady paying job, a three-bedroom home, a color TV set and all the trappings of suburban life. Meanwhile Claudia and the other siblings on the mountain were left to scrape by in a town that was dying, with limited income, health issues and few prospects of anything getting better. Between my five aunts (one of whom was wheelchair-bound) and my depressed, alcoholic uncle, they had little money, one (barely) working car, and no inclination to come down off the mountain.

Even to see their dying sister.

"She's in some pain but she's doing okay," I replied. "She's looking forward to Gladys coming to visit."

"I'm sure she is. That'll be nice."

I hesitated, "Any of you all coming with her?" Mama's eyes widen as she listened.

My face fell with Claudia's reply. "Oh honey, I wish. It's just not possible." Claudia's voice faded.

I shook my head and resisted the urge hang up. I paused to allow her discomfort to grow. I said tersely, "Well, that's too bad."

Mama's head dropped.

"Can I talk to her?" Claudia's voice was filled with guilt, and I could tell she hoped I would say that Mama was resting and could not be disturbed.

"Sure, she's right here." I held the handset out to Mama who shook her head and waved her hand and mouthed "no," clearly indicating she did not want to talk. But I put the phone into her hand and the sisters began an uncomfortable conversation that I knew would be brief.

⁂

MAMA ALWAYS JOKED THAT HER FAMILY WAS LIKE A POOR VERSION of the Kennedys. Like the Kennedy clan, the Hartman family was large. There had been thirteen Hartman offspring to the Kennedy's nine "hostages to fortune" as Joseph P. Kennedy had once referred to his children. Like the Kennedys, the Hartman family had featured an ambitious patriarch and a supportive matriarch who was devoted to her religion and her wifely role, producing babies one after the other. Both had deaths in service to their nation or tragic accidents, and even a sibling with an intellectual disability.

The similarities stopped there.

The Hartman family had established itself in the beautiful mountains of West Virginia in the town of Second Chance (known by many as just "Chance") in the late 19th century when my great-grandparents, James and Anna Hartman, German immigrants, arrived. They purchased some land and set up a timber business. They started their family but within a generation, coal mining became the leading industry. James' son and my grandfather, Luther "Pop" Hartman (who died of lung disease a few years before I was born) and most of his sons and sons-in-law became coal miners. Mama always made certain that Neal and I understood just how grueling coal mining was and how hard things were for her family, particularly during the years of the Great Depression.

I have never set foot in a coal mine, but I am certain that my great-grandfather James could not possibly have foreseen the impact the national demand for coal would have on his own children and grandchildren; one of whom would die in a mine explosion. "Poor Henry," Mama had said of her brother as she recounted the sad story to Neal and me on one of our car trips back home to Virginia from Chance. "He died crouching down after the explosion, trying not to breathe in all the bad air and his legs got stuck like that. They couldn't straighten him out." I remember how I had cringed when she described what happened next. "They had to go and break his legs, just to lay him out on a stretcher and get his poor body out of there." Pop Hartman, she told us, was never the same after that. Well, no wonder, I had thought. For days, I could not get the image of my poor dead uncle—whom I had never known—out of my mind. He had been just thirty-three. He had survived World War II only to perish under a mountain just miles from his home.

Like the Kennedy's compound in Hyannis Port, Luther Hartman created a compound for his family, too. Though limited in time and money, over the course of several years, Pop constructed three homes on the plot of Hartman-owned land on the mountain which came to be called "Hartman Hill." Two of them were modest two-story structures, smaller than the main house in which he, my grandmother, Nettie, and Mama with all her siblings resided. These homes were narrow in design but were constructed with decent materials that remarkably stood the test of time given the harsh weather on the mountain. The third house he built was larger and more elaborate. It had been intended for his oldest son to reside there and carry on the next generation, but Mama's brother Luke hated coal mining and eventually fled to the warm sunshine of Florida.

Initially, Pop had rented the two smaller houses out while Mama and her siblings were young, a nice source of badly needed income. According to Mama, he had endured some backlash because he had rented one of the homes to a Black coal miner–the father of Gladys Johnson–Mama's childhood friend. Gladys's father Bernie had relocated to West Virginia from South Carolina looking for work and he found it deep under the ground mining coal. Facing racial hostility from some at first, the Johnsons were forever grateful for Pop's willingness to give them a place to live at a reasonable rent. The proximity the families shared forged a bond that lasted three generations–long after old Bernie and Pop died. And as for the original hostility, after a while it seemed not to matter to anyone in Second Chance. According to Mama, "The men all came home from working in the mines covered with coal dust, so everyone was black."

Neal and I often heard Mama and her siblings joke that the town of Second Chance should be renamed "No Chance" for its best days had long passed. Where once it had been a vibrant timber town and later a busy mining town, Chance now lay hollowed out with many of its residents, especially the elders, idle and poor. Those who remained, that is. The population had dwindled significantly and, with the people went much of the town's soul.

When we were kids, Neal and I would stare out the car window as we drove to West Virginia for family visits and wonder why everything looked at least a decade or more behind the times compared to our surroundings back in Northern Virginia. With each mile, affluence gave way to poverty. Newer houses, office buildings and busy shopping centers in Virginia dissolved into an endless vista of mostly dilapidated and vacant homes and trailers that were plucked here and there among rolling hills, tall trees and gentle valleys resting between mountains. Many of the small towns like Second Chance seemed ancient to us, as if time had come and decided to sit and stay. The cars that people drove, the clothing they wore, the hairstyles on the women, and the old signs on buildings that had been there since even before Mama was born. It all symbolized the hard fact of economics, which as children we did not yet understand: the people living here didn't have the luxury of getting a new car every few years, new clothes every season, the latest hairstyle or bright new signage. By then, coal mining had come and gone so the people had no choice but to leave or make do. And the hardworking, mostly older souls who were left in towns like Second Chance–many of whom had been coal miners–coughed a lot, nursed aching arthritic bodies and stared at the world with apathetic eyes. To me, they seemed to accept the condition of their town and their lives. They seemed to accept all the circumstances fate handed them, as if they collectively shrugged their shoulders and said in a most pragmatic way, "Well, what can I do about it?"

All this troubled me about my home state, especially when I was young and primarily for one simple reason: it provided mean people with ammunition to fire at will about West Virginians in general and my family, in particular. At an early age I came to understand that, to the rest of the world, it didn't matter who you were, what you did or how hard you worked. If you were from West Virginia you were fair game for ugly comments and humiliation, and no one would ever forgive you for being from there.

I did not personally know most of my Hartman aunts and uncles. Many of them died before I was born but I came to know all about them thanks to Mama who was steadfastly loyal to her siblings–despite periodic family tensions. She taught Neal and I all about them which, was an ironic twist to the fact that I knew so little about my own father. I knew the thirteen names and brief biographies by heart, in the order of their birth:

Luke–*The oldest child, born in 1917. He served in WWII and he died of cancer in 1965 after moving to Florida.*

Harold–*Born in 1919, he also served in WWII. He was killed in battle in 1943.*

Hilda–*Born in 1921, she still lived in the Hartman house in Second Chance. She had a stroke several years ago that left her paralyzed and unable to speak. Her life has been sad: she lost a daughter years ago in a car accident. Her son, my cousin Donnie, rarely visits her.*

Henry–*Born in 1923, served his country in WWII then died in the mining accident in 1948.*

Louise–*Had the shortest life of all: she was born in 1925 and died at age 12 from pneumonia.*

Kurt–*Born 1927, served and gave his life in the Korean War in 1952.*

Frank–*Born in 1929. Uncle Frank still lived on Hartman Hill like Hilda. He served in Korea but returned wounded both physically and emotionally. He is the last surviving son.*

Margaret–*Born in 1931. Her husband died in a coal mining accident. She still lived on Hartman Hill. She has two grown daughters who live nearby, my cousins, but I hardly know them.*

Faye–*Mama was born in 1932.*

Claudia–*Born in 1933, she is closest to Mama and she is the glue holding what's left of the family together.*

Ruth–*Born in 1935 she, too, resides in Second Chance having fled an abusive marriage.*

Harriet "Harrie"–*Born with Down syndrome in 1938, Harrie still lived her life much as she always had under the careful eye of her sisters, especially Claudia.*

Robert–*The baby of the family, born in 1940 he would be the third son to die for his country in another war: Vietnam. His middle name was Christopher. I named my son after him.*

The Hartman family members that remained had something in common that mattered to me: they had all known my father. Over the years, they had secretly shared stories about him with me or added facts to my list and for that I was grateful. But now, like

Mama, they were growing old and closer to death, and I thought of them as relics. I had been closer to them when I was younger but hardly saw them anymore, save the one time a year–Memorial Day– when I used to accompany Mama to Chance to lay plastic flowers on the graves of the departed Hartman family members and little American flags on the graves of the brothers who had served in the military.

The fact that none who remained would venture down off that mountain to see their dying sister bothered me more than I would admit, and I was uncomfortable knowing that Mama's death would soon reunite us. I was not sure what we could offer each other or if we even cared to offer each other anything at all.

CHAPTER 4

When we were children, I would sometimes take my brother's face into both of my hands and study him. He would only allow this on rare occasions when he was in a very good mood or after he had retold a story from his library of memories about our father to me, which I regularly begged him to do. He knew his stories triggered a need in me to try to summon some memory my brain might have of our father's face. I would examine Neal closely to discern something familiar but also to determine what parts of his features were inherited from Mama and which had to be from our father.

Neal's eyes fascinated me. I was certain his brown eyes were from Daddy as Mama's eyes were blue, (as were mine). But more than that, I was convinced that my brother's eyes held a magical connection to our father's soul and that if I just looked hard enough, I would catch sight of him. Neal would dismiss this as nonsense and promptly revert to being an annoyed big brother. "You're creepy," he'd say. "Daddy's not in my eyes. I just have the same color as him."

My quest for information about my father was endless. When I could find no physical clues of him such as a photograph, I tried to imagine his face. I formed a rough composite in my head and when that didn't work, I assigned him a face. A handsome man in a magazine advertisement, a news reporter, or a TV actor became the face of my father. Andy Griffith was a natural for this due to his warmth, wisdom, and unconditional fatherly love for Opie. In my mind, my father did all the things fathers like Andy Taylor did: he assigned me chores, taught me how to fly a kite and how to climb a tree. He took me camping and showed me how to fish, would let me win at checkers and demonstrate the proper follow-through in bowling. I would imagine him coming home from work and spreading his arms wide as I flew into his embrace. He would attend school functions where all my classmates and their parents and the teachers would look at him admirably, noting how handsome and funny he was. Sometimes I would scan the audience during a school play or choir and imagine him winking approvingly at me. Each night, he would make sure I did my homework and tuck me in with a story and kiss on my forehead.

I would talk to my imaginary father too, especially before I went to sleep. Of course, I did this in a whisper, lest Neal or Mama hear me. Even though they did often hear me and ask who I was talking to. To which I would tell them no one, and quickly explain that I was just reading aloud with a flashlight or practicing something for school like the multiplication table or a poem. My "father" and I would discuss many things and laugh often. He would praise me or scold me (*You didn't do your homework*) and offer me advice about life (*Ignore that boy in class, he has no class*). Whenever I was worried or afraid (which seemed like all the time) I would urgently summon him in a whisper using my special name for him which was "Dandy." He would appear as if a genie summoned from a bottle, listen to all my woes, comfort and assure me all would work out and, sometimes sing to me (this was especially true when Christopher Plummer's face temporarily replaced Andy Griffith as that of my imaginary father after "The Sound of Music" film was released).

Not having a father meant Neal assumed a role larger in my life than that of an ordinary big brother. Although I irritated him regularly and we quarreled often, I think he decided early on that he had to try to do for me all the things a father would do; things my imaginary father could not. He read me stories, taught me to ride a bike, helped me with homework, threw ball after ball to perfect my softball pitch, blasted albums on our stereo console in the living room to ensure I developed good musical taste (The Beatles and Motown mostly) and, demonstrated how to dance without looking dorky. He put band aids on my scuffed knees and seemed to delight in yanking out my loose teeth. Later, he would walk me down the aisle when I wed Phil and comfort me when my marriage ended. He would then take on yet another fatherly role, this time for my son. I knew I could run to him when afraid, rely on his sympathy when I was hurting and count on him when I was in trouble.

One afternoon he found me curled into a pathetic little ball of misery on the lower bunk bed in the bedroom we shared for a time when Mama slept in the other upstairs bedroom. We had more visitors back then and Mama wanted to keep the first-floor bedroom for them, including my aunt Harrie who would stay with us sometimes in the summer to attend a special school in Arlington for adults with Down syndrome and other intellectual disabilities.

Neal had come to get his baseball mitt and heard me whispering to myself and noticed I was crying. I had just gotten home from my third day of fourth grade at Robert E. Lee Elementary School, an institution where I had never felt comfortable no matter how I tried. I don't think many of my classmates did, either. But how could we? There we sat, White students and a few Black students, in classrooms in buildings where, just a few years before, we would not have been permitted to sit together at all, as Virginia defied integration. We eyed each other nervously, trying our best to make this going to school together work and sometimes we did, allowing ourselves to be what we were: young children. Young children who were standing for the Pledge of Allegiance that promised liberty and justice for all, learning to add and subtract, laughing as we chased each other in a game of tag and pushing each other higher and higher on the swings on the playground at recess. Until someone called another an ugly name, using a word they had heard at home or at the store or almost anywhere. A word that caused us all to freeze with an awkward silence enveloping us. Then we went home to parents who contended with, and in some cases, perpetuated the barriers that their parents and many generations before them, had erected to keep us apart. These were walls of distrust both seen, and unseen and they surrounded us. Tension followed us everywhere and caused us great confusion over what we were told and what we saw. This fueled a torment in us that we could not articulate; that compounded the usual angst of kids our age.

Alone on my bunk bed that afternoon, I faced the wall and would have crawled right into it if I could as I lamented the day's events to Dandy. The day had been so awful for me that I had made up my mind I would never go back to school. I planned to run away that night after I was sure Mama and Neal were asleep. Dandy was trying to talk me out of running away but I was determined.

"What's wrong with you?" Neal stood next to the bunk holding his mitt.

"Kids at school were mean to me today." I rolled over onto my back, wiping tears off my face.

He sat beside me. "What happened?"

I scooted up to sit beside him. "Neal," I began. "Are we hillbillies?"

"Who said that?"

"Some kids in my class. We had to give talks about ourselves and stand up in front of the room and when I said I was born in West Virginia one of the boys yelled 'hillbilly' and a lot of the kids started laughing. Then, at recess, a bunch of them came up to me and kept calling me 'silly hillbilly' and saying mean stuff and they were all laughing at me!" I began to cry again.

Neal shook his head and patted my leg. "Now listen Laney Mae. This happened to me too. You just have to stand up to them and defend yourself like I had to do. The first time someone made fun of West Virginia and wouldn't stop, I let 'em have it." He punched his fist into his mitt.

I sat up, eyes-wide, "Can't I just go to a different school?"

"Of course you can't! Listen, I'm gonna tell you what Mama told me. You have to stand up for West Virginia! You tell them that without West Virginia, John F. Kennedy would never have been elected president and who would've saved us during the Cuban Missile Crisis?"

"The what?"

"And you tell them that West Virginia was part of Virginia until the Civil War. We left Virginia because we were the good guys! We were against slavery. We were on the winning side!" My thirteen-year-old brother was on a roll. He stood and caught sight of my Easy-Bake Oven. "Are any girls calling you names?"

I nodded, "Especially Melanie Gibbons, the mean prissy girl."

"Well, you ask Miss Prissy and her friends where they think the electricity comes from to power their damn Easy-Bake Ovens. From coal! That's right! And where does coal come from?"

"West Virginia?"

"That's right! You gotta grow thick skin and ignore them or give it back to them!" He sat back down on the bed. "If it gets worse, though, just have Mama call the school. They won't want to mess with her!" He chuckled.

This thought horrified me, "No! Don't tell Mama. If she calls, that will just make it worse."

"Well, if they don't stop, you take your little hillbilly fist and punch 'em in the mouth!"

I gasped, "I'll get in trouble."

Neal shook his head. "You gotta hold your head up Laney Mae. Like Mama told me when we first moved here, don't ever be ashamed of who you are or where you come from." He paused and leaned closer to me and said, "If Daddy were here, that's what he'd tell you to do, too. Stand up for yourself!"

"He would?"

"Yep. That's what he'd expect of you."

Just behind Neal my imaginary Dandy nodded and gave me a confident grin and a wink. That settled the matter. I would not let my daddy—real or imagined—down.

The next day, to my relief, my classmates did not bother me during school but walking home that afternoon a group of the "prissy girls"—including Melanie—started to follow me home and taunted me, calling out, "hey hillbilly girl" and, "hey retard from West Virginia." They also added a particular insult that cut me to the core. One of them yelled, "She doesn't even have a father!" to which Melanie replied, "Yes, she does! Her mother's brother! That's what they do in West Virginia!" This was followed by laughter and a chorus of, "eww" and, "gross" and one of the girls decided that was the perfect time to pick up a rock the size of an apple and throw it at me, striking me in the back. I froze but only for a moment, doing my best to shake off the assault while summoning Dandy to arrest them all. I walked faster, my stomach in an awful knot as I clutched my Monkees lunchbox tightly to my chest. I decided that if they didn't stop, I would have to do what Neal had advised and stand up for myself, my family and West Virginia. I quickened my pace and ran around the corner where a six-foot tall hedge bordered the side-walk and hid.

I heard the prissy girls coming, shouting "silly hillbilly" and then, when they rounded the corner, and I was out of sight, I heard Melanie's voice. 'Hey, where'd she go?' She sounded disappointed. As they came around the corner I jumped from behind the hedge. I grabbed Melanie in a bear hug and, with all my strength, pulled her off the sidewalk and shoved her on to the grassy yard of the house whose owner I did not know. Melanie shrieked. As she put her hands up to defend herself, her lunch box and her school papers fell to the ground. I moved slowly toward her with an expression that I bet was close to Mama's "look." Before she could get too far from me, I rushed forward, my hand balled into a fist, and landed a blow right on her cheek. Melanie grabbed her face in shock. I watched as a red spot formed where my fist had landed. The other girls also watched; mouths open.

"Don't you call me a hillbilly anymore," I raged, recalling what Neal told me to say, "I am *not* a hillbilly. West Virginia is a great state! Without West Virginia we would not have had John F. Kennedy for President and we'd all be dead! And West Virginia used to be part of Virginia, but we were the good guys in the Civil War! You dumb people from Virginia were the losers!"

As I ranted this, I moved one step at a time toward Melanie. She backed away from me and I felt great satisfaction shoving her as she did. Her arms were outstretched, her head shaking side-to-side, her long blonde hair sashaying back and forth. "Leave me alone," she whined. I noticed a small bush, only about two feet high, right behind her and as I hoped, Melanie unknowingly backed into it and tumbled over, landing flat on her back. Her dress was hiked up so that her underpants showed, and her pretty hair was spread out beneath her. Her eyes were wide in fear. She was helpless.

I sprang and sat astride her, forcing her arms to either side of her head, pinning her in place. "You got an Easy-Bake Oven?" I hissed.

"Huh? What? Why?" Melanie stared up at me, confused.

I bent over and got as close as I could to her perfect pug nose. "Where do you think the electricity comes from to power your damn Easy-Bake Oven, huh? It comes from coal and that comes from West Virginia! Don't you ever make fun of me or my state again! You hear me?"

Melanie nodded, "Okay, okay. Now get offa me!" She pushed but I held her down firmly.

"Not 'til you say West Virginia is a great state and I'm not a hillbilly."

By now a small crowd of students from school surrounded us. I felt powerful and energized. Neal had been right!

Melanie frowned at me and shook her head, so I squeezed her hands harder. "Say it," I hissed. "And say it loud!"

"Okay, okay! West Virginia is a great state and you're not a hillbilly. Now get off!"

Satisfied, I pushed off her and stood, panting, grinning broadly. Then I turned and gave the crowd of kids from school my best rendition of Mama's "look." They stared at me, dumbfounded, then began to move away. I tilted my head back to gaze at the sky. Somehow, somewhere I believed my real daddy had surely witnessed this momentous event and was proud of me. I couldn't wait to tell Neal. Score one for the Mountain State!

Unfortunately, my trials as a girl without a father from West Virginia continued. In middle school, where a host of new faces greeted me, I took the chance to reinvent myself. Many of these were kids from other elementary schools who knew nothing about me or my origins, hillbilly or otherwise. In the new biography I created, my father (with the face of Sean Connery) was a very important official at The White House; he was sort of part Secret

Service, part right-hand man to the President and had served every president since Eisenhower, joining that administration straight out of Harvard. I told all the new girls I met this, and they all believed me. Until my lie came crashing down at a school event in eighth grade when some of their mothers cornered Mama and me wanting to know what, *"Mr. Martin does at the White House? It's so exciting that he works there!"* One girl's mother had begged Mama to help her take her in-laws to the White House for a tour. *"Can he get us a tour? You know, behind-the-scenes? My mother-in-law would be tickled pink!"* I stood frozen with dread; my make-believe persona destroyed.

Mama had given me "the look" and I cowardly slipped away and fled the building, running all the way home wondering how much stuff I could cram into one suitcase as I planned to run away that night while my imaginary Sean Connery father followed me home, scolding me for lying.

When Mama arrived at the house a short time later, we got into a terrible fight, and she put me on restriction from both TV (*"Your imagination has gone wild"* and, *"you watch too much TV"*) and girlfriends for a week (*"How dare you lie to those nice girls and embarrass me in front of their mothers"*). She need not have. None of my new "friends" wanted anything to do with me after that and I continued to be ostracized well into high school. I had railed at Mama that it was all her fault for not telling me about my real father and as I sobbed, she had told me to, *"Stop crying or I'll give you something to cry about!"*

Of course, she didn't need to give me anything to cry about. Ever. I already had plenty.

CHAPTER 5

That evening, Neal arrived after a long day of work at the print shop with hamburgers, fries, and a tray of milkshakes from McDonalds. He still wore his work shirt with his name embroidered above the right pocket. Knowing my neat and tidy brother, he had started the day with a clean, pressed shirt but now the shirt told the story of a typical shift with ink stains smeared on the front, sleeves rolled up and the tail untucked slightly in the back from his constant movement. My brother was a blue-collar working man with an unfulfilled artistic spirit. The printing process excited him with all the inks and the tantalizing fresh-off-the-press aromas. He never tired of watching plain sheets of paper stock become *something*, a creation in which he could take some tangible satisfaction. Seeing him, I felt a wave of love and admiration for my ruggedly handsome, hardworking brown-eyed brother.

Christopher jumped off the couch where he had been playing Nintendo and let out a happy yelp for the food, the shakes and, the presence of his uncle. I loved to watch the two of them together.

Whenever Neal visited, Christopher followed him around like a puppy, sat beside him as they watched TV, begged him to play video games, shoot basketball and take him places, even the most routine errands, anything to be near him. Christopher had started forming this intense attachment to Neal when Phil left over two years ago.

I dragged a chair from the kitchen table into the room and sat beside Mama in her recliner. Unfortunately, even the aroma of the food from McDonalds had not triggered any appetite in her. She refused the half of cheeseburger and a few fries I offered and instead sipped her vanilla milkshake while I sipped a glass of red wine. We sat together and watched a cartoon show with Christopher and Neal who both ate while laughing, talking about the video game and bantering about who was the better player. I smiled, pleased to see Christopher happy. Since Phil left, I had witnessed my formerly carefree son transform into an unhappy soul, withdrawing from others; his confidence eaten up by his father's rejection. It was as if little parts of him had begun to fold inward, blocking others out, including me. I reminded myself and others who noticed this change in him (including his teachers) that Phil had not just left *me* for another woman, he had left Christopher too. Phil had promised to always be there for our son, he was not. Christopher soon became an inconvenience. This was shown especially after Phil remarried and got a nice promotion that transferred him to New Jersey where the happy couple purchased a home in an exclusive community with a pool in their backyard. *A pool!* Phil and Amanda's first child was now almost two years old (the timing of Phil's leaving was not lost on me or anyone who knew us) and they had announced their second was on the way. The second child I would never have. Another little half-brother or half-sister Christopher would have, but likely rarely see.

As we sat there, Mama hardly spoke, but because she had started the morphine, I was not totally surprised. She seemed to be in less pain but too weak even to hold the milk shake so I reached over and held it for her as she took a final, long sip from the straw then waved her hand for me to take it away. She laid her head back on the recliner and closed her eyes. I watched her with growing unease as she tried to fight the sleepiness brought on by the medication and something else that I knew was happening; her body was shutting down. The Hospice nurses had prepared me for this. As I watched her bat her eyes and shake herself to keep from nodding off, I understood Death was a step closer.

With this cheery thought, I downed the last of my wine and found myself thinking that there was something seriously wrong in the universe. Our lives were falling apart while Phil and his new wife were thriving, decorating a nursery and splashing around in their swimming pool. I knew the anger I carried toward Phil was unhealthy, but I could not seem to let it go and move on with my life. *What did I have to look forward to anyway?* I stared at Mama, asleep now, her mouth opened slightly, drool on her chin, and shook my head. Death, I thought; that's what I have to look forward to. I raised my wine glass in a mock cheer and went to the kitchen to pour another, ignoring Dandy (now older, often resembling Andy Griffith in his later years when he starred as Matlock) telling me, *Now I think you've had enough of that red wine there.* I knew he was right but lately the guilt about my having too much to drink was easier to ignore.

I returned to my chair and watched Neal and Christopher as they played the video game. Despite their laughter and the shrill video game music and irritating sounds blaring from the TV, Mama dozed. The room felt cold due to the air conditioning and I grabbed a light throw off the couch and draped it across her chest. Suddenly, I imagined her dead. I stared at her gaunt face, spindly arms, thin legs and pale feet on the leg rest and thought how surely, in just a matter of days, her body would lie rigid and flat on a cold, metal table at the funeral home, blood drained with embalming fluid pumping inside. The grim visions of what awaited Mama's body made me shiver but what alarmed me more, I realized, was my sudden awareness of her impending *absence*. Until now, I had given only vague thought to her actually, physically *dying*. Looking down at her I knew with certainty that when Death finally did arrive, I would be lost. Her dying would be as though all the lights in the universe suddenly went out. I would be stranded in a darkness so complete I would be unable to see where I was going. I would have to feel my way along. I would have trouble knowing where to step next. I would have no one to tell me which way to go. For the first time in my life, I would be free of her control but, that meant I would have to make decisions without her instruction and suffer any repercussions without her guidance. I would, in other words, have to become an adult.

And this thought scared me to death.

⚜

PROMPTLY AT SEVEN O'CLOCK, SISSY, THE WHISTLING HEALTH aide, arrived. Mama had catnapped on and off since we had dinner and I was bringing her a cup of tea when the doorbell rang.

"Oh God . . . it's her," Mama moaned.

I went through the kitchen to the living room and let her in, leading her back to Mama in her recliner.

"Helloooo all! Helloooo Ms. Faye," Sissy sang out with great cheer. She whistled absentmindedly as she sat her tote bag on a table in the corner, patted the dog's head and came to stand next to Mama in her recliner. "It's hot as you know where out there," she said, laughing. "Hey! That rhymes!" She cackled.

Mama rolled her eyes and said nothing.

Sissy felt Mama's forehead and gently brushed her hair with her hand. "How you feeling? I thought tonight I'd give you a nice refreshing wash. Ready to head back for that soon?"

Mama shook her head with effort. "Sissy," she began, speaking in a low and raspy voice, "Why don't you . . . go get that ready but . . . I was about to . . . have a . . . talk with my children. How about . . . in a . . . half hour?"

Sissy's eyebrows arched upward, and she grinned, casting a quick, hopeful look in my direction. "Why sure! Anything you want." She turned, resumed her whistling and left the room.

"What I *want* . . . is her to stop . . . that damn whistling!" Mama said, slapping the arm of her recliner. This seemed to exhaust her, and she laid her head back and sighed heavily.

Neal and I looked at each other, both wondering the same thing: what was this talk Mama wanted to have? In a snap I decided it was going to be my long-desired conversation about my father. *It had to be!* I was instantly thrilled, and my heart raced in my chest. It was finally happening, I thought excitedly. I briefly wondered why she wanted to speak to both Neal *and* me at the same time but decided that was fine. My brother had his own unresolved issues to settle with our mother. We could cover a lot of ground in one conversation; two wrongs righted.

"Christopher, time for your bath," I playfully clapped my hands as I sometimes did to get him moving, eager to get him up to bed so Mama could have her talk with us. "Spit spot!" I added in my best Mary Poppins voice.

"When I'm done with this game," he said with annoyance, never taking his eyes off the TV.

Edgy and impatient, I grew angry. This conversation with Mama could not wait. "Christopher! You heard me. Let's go!"

"In a minute. I want to finish this level."

Perhaps it was the wine or my anxiety or my eagerness to talk to Mama before she changed her mind or all the above but something in me snapped and I raged, "I said *now*!" I stormed across the room and switched off the TV.

An uncomfortable silence followed. Even Mother the dog struggled up from the floor, sensing the tension in the room. Christopher leapt up, "Mom! I was playing that! You messed me up!"

"I messed you up? Oh really? Well, I don't care!" I seethed, "Get. Upstairs. *Now!*"

Christopher's eyes widened in shock. His face crumpled, and I thought he might cry. I felt instantly ashamed. My reliable conscience, Dandy, admonished me. *Don't take your anger out on him. That's just not fair. That boy doesn't understand what's really happening. Yelling at him ain't gonna help.* Christopher set the game controller on the coffee table. "Okay," he said in a low voice, "you don't have to yell at me."

Neal watched this unfold and said, "Come on now, Laney Mae. What's wrong with you?"

"It's time for his bath," I snapped, "He's been playing that damn video game all day."

Mama spoke, "He . . . has . . . not! Why . . . are you raising . . . your . . . voice like that?"

I spun around and glared at her. Of all people, who was she to tell me not to raise my voice? My childhood had been filled with the sound of raised, angry voices. "Mama, please, let me handle this." I turned back to my son. I bowed my head, my hair falling in front of my face, concealing me. I was glad to be hidden from the three of them for a moment. I looked up, tucking my hair behind my ears and said, "I'm sorry Christopher. I shouldn't have snapped like that." At least I can tell my child I'm sorry, unlike my own mother, I thought.

He shifted his eyes from me to the floor then looked over at Neal. "You're not leaving yet, are you?"

Neal gave him a half smile, "Nah, I'll stick around. We'll play another game after your bath."

Christopher recovered his joy. He beamed. "Get ready to lose," he told Neal.

"Ain't happening," Neal replied with a laugh.

Casting me a hurt look, my son walked out of the room to go upstairs. I called out, "Want me to come up and get you started?"

He did not answer.

❀

MAMA DIRECTED US TO SIT BEFORE HER. THE HOUSE WAS QUIET now that the TV was off and only the distant sound of Christopher's running bath upstairs and Cindy's whistling as she busied herself in the living room disturbed the silence. I was literally on the edge of my seat.

"I've got . . . some things . . . to . . . go over with you," Mama began, each few words requiring a breath. She looked at me and I smiled warmly, leaning toward her eagerly. "Laney Mae . . . you and Christopher . . . you live here after I'm gone."

This was a pleasant instruction, but I immediately felt guilty and looked at Neal and back at Mama. "Thank you, Mama. That will be wonderful. But Neal—"

She interrupted me, "Let . . . me finish . . . Later, when Christopher is . . . done college . . . you and Neal settle up. This house is . . . paid for. I want you each to have . . . equal halves. I already . . . worked it out in my Will."

We knew Mama had a Will but never were brave enough to ask for its details. Neal and I nodded respectfully at her. "Okay, Mama," Neal said.

"The lawyer's card is in . . . my dresser drawer . . . where I keep all the paperwork and stuff. And Neal . . . you still got the safety deposit box key?"

He nodded.

Shifting her gaze to me, Mama said, "You . . . take care . . . of this house. The yard, too. Christopher . . . can . . . help." She paused, the effort to converse wearing her out. She leaned her head back and closed her eyes for a moment. Then she pointed her index finger at me and said, "And you fly . . . the flag . . . every day . . . like I do. You hear me?"

"Yes, Mama. I know that's important to you." Mama had installed a flagpole in the center of our front yard in 1962 and flown the flag faithfully since then. "Don't worry," I said hoping she would now get on with telling me about my father. I kept a smile frozen on my face, but my impatience was growing.

She arched an eyebrow. "Did you . . . raise the flag . . . today?"

I swallowed hard. Of course, I hadn't. I hesitated. "Uh, well . . ." Dandy appeared behind Mama's recliner and shook his head at me. *There ain't no use lying to her.* I lowered my head and stared at my flip-flops. "No, I forgot." I looked back up. "I'm sorry. I'll do it tomorrow morning."

She shook her head and frowned and gave me the "look." "How . . . much . . . do I ask? Can't you do this . . . one thing?"

"I'm sorry."

Neal spoke, "Mama, Laney Mae's had a lot going on but don't worry, your flag will fly. We promise."

Mama shifted her eyes back and forth at Neal then me. She motioned for the cup of tea and Neal helped her sip then she pushed the cup away. She turned and gazed at me and said, "Now, one . . . other thing, Laney Mae . . . and . . . it's important."

Here it was, I thought, my heart pounding. I leaned closer.

"I've . . . made up . . . my mind. Mother . . . is going to . . . live with Claudia. She shouldn't stay here. We . . . worked . . . it all out.

THE ROAD TO SECOND CHANCE

Laney Mae, you drive Mother up there . . . when Jake comes and . . . you all take . . . me . . . home." Her face crumpled, and she closed her eyes. Tears rolled ran down her cheeks.

I was incredulous, "What? *Mother*? That's the important thing you want to talk to me about?" My mouth dropped open. I rose from my chair. "The damn dog? That's it? What about Daddy? I thought you were going to finally talk to me about him!"

She scowled, "Well, you . . . thought . . . wrong."

Enraged, I clenched my fists but before I could reply, Neal stood in a rush. He grabbed a tissue and knelt in front of Mama and patted her cheeks. "Mama, it's okay, it's okay," he murmured, "We'll take care of Mother and the flag and everything. Promise. Now you just rest."

Mama took the tissue and blew her nose lightly. She made a face at me then shifted her gaze lovingly at Neal. "And Neal . . . you . . . need . . . to get . . . married. Settle down. Have . . . a kid. And you know *who* I'm . . . talking . . . about."

Neal forced himself to smile but shook his head, "Now, Mama, don't worry about me–"

"But I *do* worry!" She said with an intensity that exhausted her, and she closed her eyes.

Neal looked up at me and shook his head. He stood and held his hands up to stop me from saying anything more. "Let it go," he whispered, "I told you and told you. Leave her alone."

He turned and called Sissy, summoning her to come and take Mama and get her bathed and ready for bed. Sissy arrived and with Neal's help, got Mama out of the recliner and to the walker then guided her out of the room.

When my brother returned, I was waiting for him. "Neal," I hissed, "What the hell was that? Why didn't you help me get Mama to talk? This was my chance! I may not get another! You saw how she could hardly stay alert."

He shook his head, his face reddened with sudden anger, "Oh my God, Laney Mae! Our mother is *dying*! Do you hear me? You need to stop this and the sooner you accept this, the better for everyone. I told you she wouldn't talk to you about dad so accept it. And I am sorry. Really. But life is full of disappointments. Let it go."

❦

I SIPPED MY THIRD GLASS OF WINE SITTING IN MAMA'S RECLINER as Christopher and Neal played one last video game. Neal let Christopher win and they agreed on a rematch next time. On his way to bed, Christopher came over to me tentatively. I set the wine down and stood. We stared at each other wordlessly for a moment. "I'm so sorry I snapped at you," I told him. He stepped over to me and wrapped his arms around my waist. I pulled him into a tight embrace and buried my face in his freshly washed hair. I breathed in his soapy scent. I gently lifted his face up and held it in my hands. "I'll be up in a few minutes. Pick out what book you want to read." I kissed his forehead.

He nodded, told Neal goodnight and scampered through the kitchen and up the stairs.

Neal switched the TV off and faced me. I could tell he was trying to read my mood after our confrontation earlier. He eyed the nearly empty glass of wine on the table but chose to ignore it. "I'm beat," he said. "Gladys comes day after tomorrow, right? What time you want me here?"

"Just plan on dinnertime. I got stuff to grill if you can do that." He nodded. I reached out to touch his arm. "Before you go, I have a draft of Mama's obituary. Can I read it to you?"

He sighed wearily, "Now?"

"Now." I motioned for him to sit on the couch, I pulled the sheet of paper from the pocket of my shorts and unfolded it. "Obviously, the date is to be determined." My effort at dark humor failed. He frowned at me.

"Okay, here's what I have," I cleared my voice and read aloud:

"Faye Rose Hartman Martin McDaniel, entered into eternal rest on September (to be determined), 2001. Beloved daughter of Nettie and Luther Hartman, cherished sister of Luke, Harold, Hilda, Henry, Louise, Kurt, Frank, Margaret, Claudia, Ruth, Harriet and, Robert Hartman. Beloved mother of Neal Luther Martin and Elaine Mae Martin Langston.

Cherished grandmother of Robert Christopher Langston. Former civil servant. Proud American. Owner of a beloved dog named after her own beloved Mother.

Widow to two men, one who she deemed never existed and whose memory must be kept as dead as he is and the other, one of the meanest sons-of-bitches to ever walk the earth."

I looked up at my brother and saw that his face had darkened with anger. The wine had made me bold enough for sarcasm and the mention of our stepfather. Dandy frowned at me. *You ought not to have gone and done that. Why are you trying to provoke your brother?*

Neal stood and looked down at me, glaring. "Oh, that's *really* nice, Laney Mae. I'm sure Mama will *love* that." I could almost see steam coming from his nostrils. "And why would you bring *him* up?"

I rose too, standing a good four inches shorter than my brother. "Why not? His ghost is here too. He haunts all of us, especially *you.*

The funny thing is, we can say *his* name out loud. We have pictures of him."

Neal shook his head, trying to control his anger and I could tell he was struggling with what to say to his intoxicated sister. "Mama *never* talks about him," he scoffed. "She doesn't even use his last name anymore."

"Yeah, well of course she doesn't! Especially because that might mean she'd have to *apologize* to you about him! That would require mentioning his name."

He rolled his eyes. "I have long since gotten over expecting any apology from her about Art. Unlike you, I have moved on."

I laughed, "I don't think so, Neal. Actually, I think I'm *not* the only one who needs to have a final talk with Faye Rose Hartman Martin McDaniel!" I poked him in the chest. Tipsy from the wine, I swayed slightly.

Neal started to reply then turned his back to me. For a moment, I thought he was going to storm out the back door. I watched as he clenched and unclenched his hands and imagined he was counting to ten silently to calm himself. He turned to face me again, his expression neutral. He tilted his head to one side. "I think, Laney Mae," he said evenly, "when this is all over, and Mama has passed, that you ought to get some help."

I snickered. "Help? Really? A therapist? Okay, sure. I'll do that! But Neal, we *all* need help."

He stepped closer to me. "You're tired. You had too much wine tonight." He took the paper with Mama's draft obituary on it from my hand, balled it up and shoved it in the pocket of his pants. He gently took my shoulders and guided me backward to the couch. He sat, pulling me down beside him. Tenderly, he held both of my hands while I tried to decide if he was being kind or patronizing. The wine inhibited clear thinking.

"Try to do what I do," he told me. "Put things you have to deal with in little mental piles. I figure, if there's a beginning and an end, I know I can get through anything. So, all this?" He waved his hand in the air. "In a few days, Mama will pass. And a few days after that, we'll have her viewing and the funeral and bury her back in Chance and it will all be over. And then, we'll be back here, and this will all be behind us." With obvious weariness, he stood, ready to depart. He managed to give me a half smile as he looked down and said, "That's what I do. It helps me get through things. Try it. Break things down. Soon, this will all be over and behind us."

I returned his half smile but mine was insincere. "And then what, Neal?"

My question seemed to confuse him. His brows furrowed together. "What do you mean, 'then what'?"

"What happens after that?"

He looked at me blankly, hesitated then said, "We just . . . we . . . just—"

"Come on, Neal! We just do *what*?" I stood quickly and moved closer, so he could smell my wine-laced breath. "We get through all this, so we can go on living our *happy* lives, right? Me, so happily divorced! You so happily alone! Both of us fucked-up! My son, soon-to-be fucked-up if he isn't already because of his father. Is that what we're supposed to do? We just keep living our fucked-up lives but we do it without Mama now like we did without Daddy and with nothing to show for it! Is that what we do when this is all behind us?"

He stared at me intently for a moment and then suddenly his face crumpled. His brown eyes filled with tears. *Oh, now look what you've gone and done,* Dandy moaned. I was filled with regret and my heart ached at how weary and beaten my brother looked. *Now you go on and apologize and give him a hug,* Dandy urged. *Take back all your angry words and that silly draft obituary, mentioning your stepfather.* But I was weary and beaten, too and I did not have the generosity these acts required so I said nothing. Dandy bowed his head in sadness then faded away.

My brother seemed to accept my inability to recant. He quickly wiped the tears off his face and pursed his lips together. He took in a deep breath and, somewhat composed, he nodded his head. "Yeah, Laney Mae. That's what we do. We just keep going." He leaned in very close to me and added, "What else *can* we do?"

CHAPTER 6

My mother was a woman of conviction and contradiction. There were many times when her proclamations of right and wrong compared to her actual behavior, like turning a convenient blind eye to situations, confounded me. As long as I can remember, she was never too shy to let it be known to anyone who cared to listen (or had to) that she would not condone lying, cheating, prejudice or cowardly behavior of any kind. She believed in hard work, discipline and self-sufficiency. She believed in doing unto others as she wished to have done to her; equal treatment of all people, fairness, respect, and doing things right the first time. She was resolute in her belief that individuals are responsible for their own decisions and actions. I wish I had a dollar for every time she said, "We make decisions and we have to live with them."

But there was one decision she made that I wished with all my heart, she had allowed herself to change her mind about and reverse: the decision to marry Arthur "Art" McDaniel in the summer of 1969. It was an act based on poor judgement, blind love and a refusal to acknowledge the cruelty of the man who became our stepfather. In fact, I'd say Art turned out to be the antithesis of all Mama *claimed* to stand for, but it took her years to see this. By then, the damage was done, and Art was dead. Her decision was made without any consultation or warning and it ruined several years of our lives; especially Neal's. Coming not long after our father's death, it shook us to the core like an earthquake after a hurricane and left permanent damage to our family infrastructure. Just a few years later, Mama would make another irreversible decision which felt like a final blow: to choose Art over her son.

Mama met Art shopping for a new car. By an awful twist of fate, he ended up as her salesman. Neal was thirteen and I was eight when we accompanied her on this expedition. I remember vividly how Art seemed to glide across the showroom floor like Fred Astaire to greet our pretty mother. She was dressed in a flattering blue sheath that hit above her knee, a lovely scarf tied beneath her chin with pearls like Jackie Kennedy jingling on her chest. The other salesmen seemed chagrined that Art had so deftly beat them out of yet another walk-in prospect. None of us could have known that day that Art would get much more than a sale. He would end up with a wife, two instant children, a home that was paid for and a chunk of money he would manipulate from his new wife to start his own used car dealership; which would inevitably fail a few years later.

Art was a good-looking man and Mama warmed to him instantly. I found out later that he was ten years older than her and concealed his age quite well. Tall, attired in a well-fitted suit and tie and clean-shaven with a nice head of dark hair (that later we discovered he colored), Art presented a professional image. A whiff of cologne floated around him that I actually found pleasant at the time; later that smell would nauseate me whenever he entered my airspace. He wooed Mama during the process of looking at the different cars, taking test drives and completing all the paperwork. He made small talk, smiled a lot and stared at her in a way that made her blush. By the time we left the dealership she had a sparkling new green Plymouth Fury and a handsome new suitor. I had never seen Mama so excited and giggly.

At first, Art was indifferent toward Neal and me. He'd swoop into our house mostly on weekends, pick Mama up and off they'd go on a date to dinner or a movie. This went on for a few weeks but soon his visits increased. I discovered him one early morning in the kitchen when I came downstairs to get breakfast before school, knowing full well that Mama had already left for work. It was confusing to me but infuriated Neal who, teenager that he was, knew exactly why the car salesman was "visiting" so early. "Mama and Art had a sleepover again," I'd tell my brother if he was still upstairs on a weekend morning. Neal would scowl, pull the blankets over his head and refuse to come down until he knew Art had left.

Art soon began to reveal an edginess laced with ready anger that made us increasingly uncomfortable. There was no small talk for us kids. No, "how you doing?" No, "how is school?" No, "need help with your homework?" No, "want to toss the softball?" No, "let's watch a movie and have popcorn." If he paid us any attention, it was usually with an icy stare that made me shiver or to bark orders at us. So, we learned to avoid Art.

One time he and Mama were sitting around our living room having cocktails and chatting with another couple that would be joining them for dinner out. I was sitting on the floor in front of Art playing a board game with a friend from school when I felt his foot hit my back. I thought nothing of it, figuring he was crossing his legs. But then it happened again... and again. He was purposefully kicking my back—not hard, but not soft either—with his shoe, safely out of Mama's view. I scooted around to face him, expecting perhaps he would be laughing or thinking it was a joke; but instead, he stared coldly. Dandy stood behind Art, sadly shaking his head, frowning sternly at Art, and warning me to keep quiet. I sensed this was not the time to speak up. I held Art's eyes despite my uneasiness. He was testing me, daring me to say something about the kicks. I finally looked away, but I later wished I had stood up calmly and then screamed as loudly as I could, "You kicked me!" *Would Mama have rushed to my defense? Would that have been the end of Art?*

Neal's encounters with Art were not so benign. The more frequently Art visited and became embedded in our lives, the more the tension between them grew. Everything Neal did seemed to irritate Art: Neal's shoulder length hair made him a hippie, the music he listened to was trash, his anti-Vietnam war opinions made him a communist, and his friends—especially those who were not White—prompted Art to call my brother a name using that word that began with "N" to which he added "lover." This was a particular favorite phrase of his but, bully that he was, Art would only say these things when Mama was not present. The "N-word" was an ugly term she claimed she would not tolerate, and I always admired her for admonishing anyone who used it in her presence. But Art was sly, and knew to dish out his hatred when she was out of earshot or out of the house. Neal would erupt in anger and he and Art would rage at each other with increasing animosity. When we filled her in later, Mama would refuse to believe Art would speak in such a way, waving it off and telling us to be respectful to each other. Nothing Neal seemed to say could convince her of the depth of the man's cruel animosity toward him.

All this got worse when Mama and Art got married in July 1969. Without warning, she ordered me and Neal to pack for a week's stay in Second Chance while she and Art went off to get married and enjoy a honeymoon in Florida. I remember being in Second Chance then because it was the week Neal Armstrong walked on the moon. By then I had developed a new theory that Daddy's soul had not gone to hell as Mama suggested but instead, resided on the moon, between hell and heaven. It made sense to my nine-year-old brain. The night of Neal Armstrong's giant leap for mankind, I had slipped outside when everyone was asleep and stared up at the moon, willing Daddy who lived there to say hello to Armstrong and somehow intervene to stop our mother from marrying Art. Dandy watched me, his eyes bright with excitement. *Ain't that something? People being up on the moon? Hot dog!* I nodded happily, grinning in awe and we kept our eyes on the sky. Me hoping in vain that the real Gil Martin could somehow change our fate.

AFTER THE HONEYMOON, ART MOVED IN AND ASSUMED COMPLETE control. If we thought he was difficult before, we were taken to a new level of meanness. He told us he was now our father and we were to answer to him. He was the man of the house. "You're not my father," Neal had said, his voice dripping with disgust. I remember the sick feeling in my stomach as I watched this conversation but still slightly excited about the indirect mention of our father. Art had downed his Scotch and put his cigarette out in the ashtray on the coffee table, grinding it over and over again. His cold eyes locked with Neal's. He told him, "I would advise you to speak to me with respect or not at all. Or things are going to get unpleasant around here." Neal had folded his arms across his chest and looked at Mama who sat next to Art, her head bowed down. "Mama? Say something!" Neal had pleaded. Mama had forced a smile and said, "Now, now, you all. Let's try to get along. All Art wants is for us to be a family, right Art?" Art had smiled smugly and nodded, "That's right Faye. I'm the daddy and you're the mommy." Neal shook his head, astonished by Mama's unusual demure behavior. He had scowled and stormed from the room. Before Art could follow him, I decided to deflect the attention from Neal. "You're not my daddy!

My real daddy died," I told Art defiantly, as I stood and put my hands on my hips. "I only need *one* Daddy." Art had shifted his eyes from Mama to me and said coldly, "Well, your *real* daddy was a bad man. Why would you want him as a daddy when you can have me?" He smirked and held up his glass, "Now go get your real daddy another Scotch." I looked to Dandy standing behind Art for help, but he looked at me sadly, telling me, *You best do as he tells you for now.* He and I would discuss this at length later that night while I clutched a pillow and tears flowed but we came up with no good solution to the situation.

Neal began to spend less time at home, and I suffered in his absence. Being five years younger gave me limited options of escape. Neal would run off to the home of his best friend, Greg Smith, as often as he could. Greg and Neal were in the same grade. He lived just a few streets over from us with his dad and older sister, Susie. He and Neal had met at Robert E. Lee Elementary in the third grade the year after Mama had moved us from Chance. They had remained friends ever since. Early on, they had discovered that they shared an unfortunate common bond: both had lost a parent. Greg's mother had taken her own life when he was just six, a year younger than Neal had been when our daddy had been killed. Like Neal, Greg's young eyes had seen too much. He had been the one that found his mother's lifeless body in the garage early one morning after his father had left for work; a hose running from the exhaust pipe into the driver's side window. He thought she was just sleeping. The Smith's weekly housekeeper had noticed the door to the garage open in the kitchen and went to investigate, discovering the dead woman and her terribly confused son trying to shake her awake. The woman screamed so loud the mailman two houses away had come running.

Mama had heard about Mrs. Smith's suicide before we even met the Smith family. It was whispered around Potomac Manor like the sound of wind whistling beneath a door during a storm. Everyone knew about it, everyone shivered from the fact of it, but no one felt the need to openly address it and help the family heal. Neal, Greg and I became comrades in sorrow, half-orphaned, and half-parented. I think this was the main reason that I developed such an enduring crush and emotional reliance on Greg, one that would plague me, and him to a degree, into adulthood. This was not just a school-girl crush made up of daydreams and fantasies with songs by the Carpenters in my head; it was so much more than that. I had great expectations of my brother's friend. I believed only Greg could save me from my sadness and love me unconditionally since my father wasn't here to do so. That together, we could help each other mend from our losses. Even years later, floundering in a failing marriage, the thought of Greg was not far from my mind although I had not seen him in decades. Somehow, I expected Greg to reenter my life and rescue me. What I failed to understand was that Greg was too lost to find me, let alone, himself.

⚜

LIFE WITH ART STEADILY WORSENED. NEAL AND I LIVED IN A world of softly cracking eggshells as we tried to tip-toe around him. His moods and his edginess, all heightened by his increased drinking. I came to despise Mama's Plymouth Fury and the man who sold it to her. My hatred for Art reached a climax on my twelfth birthday when he discovered I had invited all the girls in my sixth-grade class, including Carole who was Black, to my party. He cornered me about it on his day off while I was watching TV after school and Mama was at work. He told me to uninvite her. Appalled, I refused. I looked past his shoulder to Dandy. He shook his head. *Well, that just ain't right,* he said. *That little girl is a friend of yours. Her skin color ought to make no difference at all.* Dandy's eyes narrowed and his frown deepened. For the first time I could recall, he looked angry. *Your mama won't like him saying this. Don't you worry. Stand up to him!* Emboldened, I put my hands on my hips and told Art that wasn't right, that Carole was my friend, and she would be hurt to be left out. I continued and said that he was discriminating against her, and that Mama would be on my side about this. I'll never forget how he sneered at me, how his lips curled into a smile as though I had complimented him. "This has nothing to do with me," Art scoffed. "It's the neighbors. What will they think seeing a colored kid coming to our house? You need to think, young lady! And your mother will see my point on this, don't you even think twice about that!" I had laughed at him, told him he was wrong, that we had Black guests at our house before: Gladys and her daughter and some of Neal's school friends.

"Ah, yes, well that was before," he had replied.

"Before what?"

"Before me. I'm in charge now. This is my home. I determine who comes into it."

As soon as Mama came home that evening, I ran to tell her. She finally seemed torn and facing a moment of truth. Assuring me she would handle it, I followed behind her as she found Art in front of the TV sipping a beer. "Art, honey, now I don't want to argue with you, but Laney Mae can invite her friend to our house. That girl's color has no bearing on that." Art's cold eyes shifted from Mama to me. He told me to leave the room while they discussed the situation. The result? I got to invite Carole to my birthday party but *not* to the house and my party was moved offsite to the local bowling alley. I remember Art had the nerve to come to my party, acting like a jolly good step-father. He ate pizza, drank beer and bowled with Mama. Many of my friends watched him, taken in by his good looks; this only made me angrier. Later, it was Art who carried the pretty sheet cake created at my favorite bakery to the table where I sat, surrounded by my friends. Carole, who was standing just behind me, was unaware of the ugliness that had preceded the party. I stared down at the pretty pink rosebuds with green icing stems and "*Happy 12th Birthday Laney Mae*" on top. I counted the twelve pink candles plus one to grow on as I watched Mama light each. I smiled at my friends as they sang happy birthday to me. As I leaned over the cake to make my wish, I sought and found Art's eyes. He stood beside Mama, a smirk on his handsome face. I closed my eyes, leaned forward, and blew the candles out. My wish? That Art McDaniel would die. Dandy frowned sternly and shook his head. *You ought not to be wishing for someone to die,* he said. *Even someone as mean as him. It ain't right.* I hated to disappoint Dandy, but I let my wish stand. I glared at Art who sneered as he tilted his head back and downed his third bottle of beer.

LOOKING BACK, I'M SURPRISED THAT NEAL SURVIVED FOUR YEARS of Art, even though inevitably, the ongoing hostility and tension would explode. All it needed was a match tossed onto the emotional gasoline.

It was a mild evening in April, a few months after my bowling alley birthday party. The sun was out longer, the air was filled with the sweet aroma of blooming hyacinths. I had been walking quickly and half running home from a friend's house because we had downed two sodas and I had to pee. As I skipped along, daydreaming about Greg, Art pulled up to the curb in the Plymouth and ordered me to get in the car. He was headed to the Dixie Stop-N-Shop, a local convenience store. I begged off but he ordered me to get in, so I obliged. I always obliged. I told him I had to pee and that I'd just wait in the car. "Like hell you will," he snapped as he took a final drag on his cigarette. He tossed it past my face and out my window. I cringed as bits of ash fell on my shirt. "We need a bunch of things and you need to help carry it all."

I squirmed uncomfortably. "But I can't hold it. I swear!"

"Don't give me a hard time, Laney Mae. Now come on. I'll even let you get some candy, but only one, of whatever you want. Now let's go."

I opened the door, the need to urinate making me whimper. I remember standing very still to ensure I could hold the pee. Dandy encouraged me as he often did when my will was tested. *You can hold it, honey. I know you can. Don't you let him get to you! Let's show him!* I grimaced and slowly walked into the store, trying to ignore the fullness of my bladder, and went to the candy aisle but Art ordered me to grab coffee, paper towels and dish soap. "I'll get the milk," he told me, breezily. He was in a good mood, but I knew why: he had already started drinking. This was the happiest Art ever got: early drunk. I also knew the real reason we were at the store was because he was out of beer.

As I was reaching for the dish soap, the store doors opened, and music blared from a transistor radio. I heard voices singing along with the song, "*Treat Her Like a Lady.*" I moved to the end of the aisle and peeked around and was surprised to see Neal with three friends. I recognized Rodney, a Black kid Neal's age, and his younger sister, Michelle, who I guessed was a year younger. I had seen them around the house listening to music with Neal and other friends but never when Art was there for the same reason Carole was not allowed. The other boy in the group was Billy who, like Rodney and Neal, was a senior. Billy lived around the block from us and was White, so he could visit the house anytime. Neal, Rodney and Billy were all seniors in high school—all part of the "too cool for school" group Neal had jokingly referred to as his clique of friends. I watched as the four of them came into the store, laughing and dancing to the song. Neal twirled to the music and nearly fell, cracking up. I laughed and was just about to call out to my brother when the store clerk yelled and startled everyone.

"Hey! You kids knock it off! I don't want that music playing in my store," he bellowed. He was short and muscular. His clean-shaven face was pale. He had closely cropped gray hair. I had seen him before and could never recall him saying hello, let alone smiling.

Neal and his friends stopped and gawked at him for a moment, the radio still playing, then they burst out laughing. Billy, who held the radio, grinned and kept his eye on the clerk while he turned the volume up even higher. He sang along loudly.

The clerk moved quickly from behind the counter. He pointed at them, his face reddening, a vein in his neck pulsing. "Hey! What did I say? Get the hell out of the store if you're not going to behave and act respectful. Now turn that radio off or I'm calling the police!"

Neal and his friends cast each other quick glances, then moved defiantly further into the store, all singing loudly with the song. I stared at my normally obedient brother and wondered what had gotten in to him. It was at that moment that Art appeared at the other side of the store. He held the milk and two six packs of beer with a look of disgust on his face. My body went cold with dread. I knew in that instant that the stage was set for a showdown with the store's bright fluorescent lights, the blaring music and a small audience of shoppers in the store. It felt like I was watching things unfold in slow motion as Art advanced toward Neal and his friends and the shocked expression on Neal's face when he spotted Art. I silently willed my brother to leave and to usher his friends out of the store. But instead, he made one of those decisions Mama would say he had to live with: he stepped *toward* Art. He would meet his enemy there on the battlefield of a suburban convenience store named in honor of the Old South, his Black and White friends standing with him, all emboldened.

"Neal!" Art yelled over the music. "You and your *friends–*" he sneered at Rodney and Michelle with hate-filled scorn reserved just for them on account their skin color, paying scant attention to Billy, "—need to take that radio and get your asses out of this store. Now!"

Feeling sure I would throw up, I gasped and raised my hand to cover my mouth. I saw Neal's face redden and knew the long-simmering anger he held inside for so long had no place else to go and would explode. I look frantically from Neal and his friends to Art. The tension grew heavier and I felt a sudden need to stop whatever was going to happen. I stepped forward and that was when Neal noticed me. His face lost its color, and the brother I knew, anxious and paternal, returned. He pointed at me and told me to get out of the store. I shook my head. I was about to say something when I saw Art set the milk carton and the six-packs of beer on the counter and begin to walk toward the group, spit flying from his mouth as he spoke. "Something wrong with your ears? I said turn that goddamn music off!" He roughly grabbed the radio out of Billy's hand, switched it off then shoved it into the front pocket of Billy's jeans which seemed a brazenly forward and intimate act to my 12-year-old eyes. I remember how unsettling the sudden silence was and I noticed, from the corner of my eye, people rushing to leave the store. I felt panic as I saw them escape and knew my brother and I were trapped. The store clerk stood wide-eyed, mouth hanging open, as Art took control.

Neal stepped over to stand between Billy and Art, keeping about a foot of space between them. I remember realizing how tall my brother had become; he was nearly as tall as Art. I noticed, too, how his face was unfamiliar to me, contorted with an anger I had never seen before. I saw, too, that his hands were clenched into tight fists. He raged, "I heard you and I *hate* you!"

Having delivered his message, he turned back toward his friends to leave but Art grabbed Neal by his shoulders and dragged him back. He swung him around and began to roughly shake him. I felt sickened as I watched Neal's head bobble with the force of Art shaking him. Art screamed, "You hate me? *Really?* You hate the food I put in your stomach? You hate the clothes I put on your back?"

Neal twisted and struggled but could not quite free himself from Art's grasp. He swung his arms wildly but could not raise his arms high enough to strike a blow. I watched as Neal paused and then, with all the force he could muster, he brought his knee up and landed a blow directly on Art's crotch. Art let out an animal-like howl and released Neal's shoulders. He doubled-over in pain. Neal advanced and started shoving Art back toward the store counter. Art managed to recover slightly and landed a punch on Neal's shoulder. I remember the dazed look on my brother's face and how he then put up his dukes, bobbing and weaving around our stepfather like a nimble prize fighter. He was young, light and quick. Art, once slender and fit was chunky, slower and now slightly drunk.

"Come on you drunk!" Neal screamed. His eyes were wide, his hair a mess from the tussle. "Come on you bastard! I hate you!" Neal paused then yelled, "And I hate this goddamn store!" I watched as his eyes wildly darted around looking for something. He spotted a tall stack of soda cases that had just been delivered. Neal grabbed the top case. With great effort, he lifted it above his head and then heaved it onto the floor toward the door. I jumped back as it shattered, glass, soda and foam flowing across the store. Billy, Michelle and Rodney also jumped out of the way. I turned to see Art staring at Neal. Suddenly, he stormed at my brother who lowered his body and they ran toward each other like raging bulls. I remember the sickening thud their bodies made when they collided. Neal had the advantage and his impact knocked Art back. He fell to the floor and slid across the store on the floor tiles in the flood of soda and shattered glass. The look of shock on his face filled me with a brief, bittersweet moment of revenge. Neal turned to me and started to say something but then shook his head and bolted past me, past Art on the floor and out the door. His friends followed.

I stood frozen, unable to move and began to shake uncontrollably when I heard the store clerk on the phone with the police. "That's right. A riot! A goddamn riot! We have a man down. Bunch of teenagers, including coloreds, caused it all!" I watched as Art, grunting and cursing, pushed himself first to all-fours and then, to standing. His shorts were stained with cola and little streams of blood trickled down his legs, arms, and hands from the small cuts he had received caused by the broken glass. He glowered at me and that is when I felt it: the warm sensation of urine as it ran down my leg. I looked up and Dandy pointed at the door for me to leave. *Go! Now! Get home!* he told me. Horrified, I bolted from the store and ran home.

That night I remember lying in bed as Art had raged to Mama about the incident. Dandy tried to calm me. *It'll be alright. This will all blow over.* But the police had come, and I knew my brother was in trouble. "That boy needs to learn!" I heard Art yell. "A little time in jail is what he deserves. He destroyed property! He assaulted me!" I could not hear clearly what Mama said in reply, but the tone of her voice suggested she was trying to coax Art out of his anger.

The next morning, I crept downstairs and found Mama and Art sitting in the kitchen in heavy silence, cups of coffee in front of them, their cigarettes burning in the ashtray at the center of the table. "Where's Neal?" I asked. Mama only murmured that she was not sure. Art had then leapt up from the table. "Not sure? Really, Faye? I know where he is! He's over at his pal Greg's house. You are letting him get away with murder, Faye!" Art shoved his chair under the table and went to the sink where he dumped his coffee. "I know what you've planned. You're going to sneak him up to live with those hillbilly relatives of yours, if you haven't already. Well, you know what? Go ahead! As long as he never sets foot in this house again, I don't care."

Mama did not speak. Instead, she rose, moved to the sink and began to wash dishes. I waited for her to say something, to defend her son, to tell Art to get the hell out of our house. But she said nothing. Art sneered at me then walked from the kitchen, slamming the front door as he left the house.

I stepped over to Mama and grabbed her arm. "Mama! What is going to happen to Neal?"

Mama pulled her arm from my grasp. "Now don't you get involved with this, Laney Mae," she told me. "Neal will be alright. Greg's dad is driving him up to Chance as we speak. He will be out of state and safe. We'll just wait until things die down and see what happens."

I felt dizzy with exasperation. "But Mama when is he *coming home*? He graduates soon. What's going to happen if he isn't here to finish school?"

"I do not know."

"What do you mean you don't know?"

She swung around to face me. "Damn it! I can't think about that Laney Mae! All I know is Neal will be safe up there. Frank or your uncle Pete will help him find a job. He can finish school later."

"Later? But Mama, when can he come home?"

"Home?" She said this as though referring to some distant, unknown place. She sighed heavily. "I don't know Laney Mae. I just don't know."

I shrieked at her and began to wail hysterically even as Dandy shook his head and motioned for me to stop. *Now keep calm. Don't push your mama.* "What do you mean you don't know? How can you let this happen, Mama? What happened at the store was Art's fault! He was awful! He's so mean to us. He always has been and especially to Neal!" I was sobbing so hard I felt that I was going to hyperventilate. "How can you choose Art over your own son? What kind of mother are you?" Dandy's eyes widened in shock. *Uh-oh.*

Mama threw the washcloth onto the counter. She turned, raised her hand and slapped me hard across the face. I remember thinking that I understood what "seeing stars" meant as I swayed, my vision blurred. I worried that she had knocked out some of my teeth because I tasted blood. She raged at me, her face contorted with anger. "Your brother made a very bad decision, Laney Mae! He assaulted Art! He destroyed that store's property! We'll have to pay for the damage or we're going to probably get sued! Don't you lecture me about what kind of mother I am!"

I raised my hand to lightly touch my cheek where she had slapped me, running my tongue inside my mouth over my teeth, relieved that all appeared to still be in place. Dandy's face was red with anger, something I had never seen before. He said, *She's the one that made the bad decision. Not Neal!* Shaking off the shock of her striking me, I repeated what Dandy said. "No! You are the one who made a very bad decision! You! Not Neal!" Dandy motioned to me. *Get out of her way, she's gonna hit you again!* Before she could, I ran from the kitchen and fled upstairs to Neal's bedroom. I stood in his doorway and sobbed. My knees crumpled beneath me and I slid down onto the floor, the ache of his absence consuming me. Dandy knelt beside me. *This is just an awful mess. She ought not to have hit you like that! If I was here, none of this would have happened. Remember when I told you that you shouldn't have wished for Art to die when you blew out those candles?* I nodded. *Well, I've changed my mind! I sure wish it would come true. I've never seen a meaner man than Art.* Then my imaginary father began to cry. *I should have never gone out that night!* He pounded his fist into his thigh. *I wish I could turn back time and stay home, home where I belonged. I'd be here to protect you and Neal. If only . . .* He wept softly as I sat beside him whimpering until I was all cried-out. I crawled into the room, across the hardwood floor and climbed into

Neal's bed. I wrapped his sheets and blankets tightly around me and breathed in his scent. As I lay there, I talked to Dandy about where he thought Neal was and discussed whether I should run away to join my brother up in Chance. I suggested that maybe Mr. Smith would drive me there. Aunt Claudia would protect us, I told my imaginary father but we both knew she was no match against Mama's wrath. *Your mama will just come find you,* Dandy said. Awful images ran through my mind of police going to West Virginia and bringing Neal back to jail. I shook thoughts from my head and, exhausted, fell asleep with Dandy sitting forlornly beside me.

When I awoke, the daylight was fading into evening. I was surprised Mama had left me alone all day and not forced me to go to school. That was to be the only concession she would grant me that day or in the days ahead. I rose, I carefully made Neal's bed and straighten the room. I saw a pile of dirty clothes he had left on the floor near his closet from the day before. I picked them up and clutched them, wishing I could somehow reverse all that had happened as easily as rewinding a film to land at the very moment he had tossed the clothes down. I would freeze him in that split second and then find some way to keep him safe there in his bedroom, safe from Art, safe from making his fateful, but justified, decision. Standing in his doorway, I looked back and felt some satisfaction with how nice the bedroom looked. Dandy said *You did a right good job. You're a good sister to your brother.* I vowed to him that I would keep it neat and ready for Neal's homecoming. He nodded but his face was sad.

If I had known then that it would be five years until he could return, I am not sure what I would have done.

CHAPTER 7

The living room had become the dying room. All the furniture had been pushed aside and into corners to accommodate a rented hospital bed. That morning one of the Hospice nurses, Jane, had coordinated her visit to help me oversee the delivery and placement of the bed, along with an oxygen concentrator, a wheelchair, and a portable commode. This was done covertly while Mama napped in the TV room in her recliner with Mother curled up on the floor next to her, oblivious to all the activity. Helen, the health aide, sat nearby as Christopher watched cartoons.

I dreaded the moment when Mama saw her new "dying room." I envisioned her, even in her weakened state, cursing and refusing to use the bed and certainly not the commode. I was overwhelmed by the delivery of the equipment and with it, a clear sign of Death's advancement but Jane insisted it was past time. The bed would help elevate Mama's upper body she told me, making it easier for her to breathe. "And now that she's on both the comfort meds—the morphine and Ativan—we won't want her moving around because she could fall. She'll be getting more and more out of it and will sleep most of the time. You'll be glad we have this bed and this equipment. It's for the best."

None of it was for the best if you wanted to have a meaningful conversation with someone, my mind screamed. I watched with growing unease but listened politely as Jane busied herself readying the bed, showing me how to use the oxygen concentrator and offering tips on use of the commode. She had me find a folding tray table and directed me to set it near the bed. From her bag of supplies, she whipped out a clipboard with a pre-printed chart clipped in place. This was meant to more carefully track the doses of the morphine and Ativan. Mama had started on the extended-release morphine pill that dissolved beneath her tongue and was given it every twelve hours. I had easily tracked the doses on a message pad by the kitchen phone, but Jane insisted I now use the chart since Mama would begin using the faster-acting liquid morphine and a liquid Ativan and both could be given more frequently. "It's getting harder for her to swallow. Thank goodness for the liquids. They go to work quicker so it helps us stay ahead and gives them relief."

Edgy from too much coffee, I wanted to pause all the activity. Just last night I had awakened twice in panic and the voices in my head berated me about how close we were to the end. I knew I sounded insensitive when I replied to Jane that I thought Mama was *already* sleeping a lot. "Plus, her best friend is coming to visit, and I know Mama will want to be able to be alert and visit with her and . . ."

"And what?" Jane asked, glancing at me quickly while she leaned over the bed, tucking sheet corners.

"And . . . well . . . I haven't had a chance to have that talk with her yet. You know, about my father. It hasn't happened, and I'm just worried with the heavy meds, all she'll do is sleep."

Jane stopped smoothing the sheets out with her palms and

turned to face me. We locked eyes for a moment. To my relief, she smiled with understanding. I knew she had taken pity on me and I genuinely liked her. *Who wouldn't?* She was so grandmotherly, with short gray hair and smile lines around her eyes and mouth. She was a compassionate woman, quick to offer a reassuring hug and soothing words. I admired how tenderly she had attended to Mama on her past visits, giving even the most routine tasks an extra measure of comfort. Jane would gently stroke Mama's face, squeeze her hand and whisper gentle murmurings to her, words that I could not quite hear although I had leaned closer trying. Now I felt ashamed and wondered what this good woman thought of my selfish desire to keep Mama alert and able to talk to me in spite of her pain.

"Oh dear, Laney Mae, regular doses help us stay ahead of the pain." She stepped over to me and took my hand and held it in her warm, doughy palm. "Try to understand: dying is hard work. Your mother's meds will cause her to sleep but it's not like she's in a coma. It's more drifting in and out."

"But Jane, she's so out of it. I've tried sitting with her and talking to her and the next thing I know, she's asleep. I don't know what to do. I want to talk to her, but of course, I don't want her to be in pain." Dandy raised a knowing eyebrow. *You sure about that? Seems to me that getting your mama to talk is the most important thing to you, not her pain.* I bowed my head.

Jane squeezed my hand. "Don't be so hard on yourself. You've never been through this, honey. *Of course* you want to talk to her! But I can't stress enough how important it is that we stay ahead of the pain. Thank goodness we have these meds! I cannot imagine how we would help patients cope without them. Imagine the old days? They probably used liquor."

I thought of my nightly glasses of wine as I told her I understood all that. "I just need a little more time," I said as if I were back in high school asking a teacher to allow me to finish an essay.

Jane shook her head. "I wish I could give it to you, I really do. Look, I know this is hard to hear, Laney Mae but for your sake, I'm going to be honest with you. Okay?" She studied me, her smile gone. Reluctantly I shrugged my shoulders and nodded, a fresh bout of dread coursing through me.

"I have observed enough cases over the years to be able to say this to you: your mother doesn't *want* to talk to you. It's really that simple. I'm very sorry. But you need to accept that."

I stiffened and pulled my hand away. "No, Jane." I struggled to keep my voice polite. "It's just that she's waited *too* long. I think she realizes that now but can't stay alert." Dandy said, *Now Laney Mae, you know that's not exactly true. Don't you?*

Jane sighed. "I don't think so, honey. Your mother has had opportunities to speak with you. She has been very clear that she doesn't want to. And, since you brought up needing time, I have to tell you. It's my estimation, based on her symptoms, that she's got about three, maybe four days left, if that. Of course, no one knows for certain, but I want you to be prepared. Her body is shutting down. This time next week? She won't be with us."

This was not what I wanted to hear. I resisted the urge to slap my hands on my ears, refusing to acknowledge Jane's truth. Instead, I clenched my fists at my sides and forced my voice to sound calm. "Well, as I said, her friend is coming. Maybe she can coax her into talking. That's what I'm hoping for. If Mama can stay awake, that is." I frowned and looked at the hospital bed as though it held some solution.

Jane put her hands on my shoulders. "Maybe her friend can encourage her. We can hope, right? Look, I know this is hard. Unresolved issues all come to a head with death one way or the other. But no matter what, just find comfort in the fact that soon your mother will be at peace. You'll find peace too, knowing you were here for her."

Peace? I almost laughed but caught myself. I couldn't recall ever feeling a real sense of peace in this house. A ghost lived here with us; the ghost of my father and the circumstances of his death. It kept us frozen in another time neatly divided into before and after. Before his death there was peace, hope and stability; of which I recalled nothing. After there was conflict, despair, and turmoil; which I knew all too well. *Now you show this fine lady some respect. She's just trying to help you*, Dandy told me. "Thank you, Jane, for everything you are doing to help us," I said, putting an end to the conversation. She pulled me into her arms and I allowed myself to savor the warm, unconditional comfort there, comfort I could rarely recall receiving from my own mother.

⁂

As predicted, Mama was not at all happy with her re-arranged living room. After Jane departed, I had tried to brighten it up a bit by opening the floor-length curtains on the large picture window, allowing the late August sunshine to fill the otherwise drab room. Outside the flag fluttered on the pole, something Mama could see from the hospital bed. I had gone outside and clipped several blossoms of blue Hydrangea. I placed them in a vase on the tray table next to the clipboard. I had arranged her own bed pillows and an afghan Claudia had made for Mama years ago on the sterile bed to cozy it up. For myself, I had dragged one of the dining table chairs across the room and placed it near the bed, anticipating the minutes, hours and remaining days that I would sit beside her, hoping until the end, that she would talk.

She had dozed off and on all morning in her recliner and seemed content to remain there, watching Christopher play his video games, with the dog lying next to her, Helen trying to tempt her with some applesauce. Around noon, Mama began complaining of pain and wanted to go to her bedroom to lie down. Helen and I helped her up and Mama leaned on the walker, swaying slightly. She began her slow shuffle forward and if we tried to assist or guide her she would bark that she could handle it. So, we allowed her, step-by-slow-step, to make her way into the kitchen and then turn the corner into the living room. Behind her, I braced myself. She stopped, and I watched as her head slowly rotated left-to-right to take it all in. "What . . . the hell . . . is all this?"

I scooted past her and stood in the center of the room, facing her. I rambled as I explained everything to her as positively as I could, pointing out the benefits of the bed and having the oxygen, (hoping that she had not yet noticed the commode). I waved my hand to draw attention to the sunny view from the window and the lovely Hydrangeas from her yard, but it was Christopher who appeased her. He hopped up on the bed and began to raise and lower it, announcing how cool it was and asking if he could sleep there. Then he spotted the wheelchair and pushed it over to where she stood, "Grandma, this is cool! I can push you and we can go on nice walks!"

She stared at him in silence for a moment then allowed a smile to push up the corners of her mouth. "Well, that . . . might . . . be nice, Christopher," she managed to say, her breathing shallow.

I stepped over to the bed. "And Mama it's actually really good that the bed arrived today because I was going to wash your bedding and let Gladys sleep in your room while she's here and you can start using this bed."

Mama frowned, unconvinced. Her eyes darted around the room and she spotted the commode. "Well . . . I can tell you . . . right now . . . I am . . . *not* . . . using that thing!" She looked at me as if readying for battle.

Helen rescued me, "Oh Ms. Faye, don't worry! That's just for backup! We'll do our best to get you to your own toilet. In fact, let's go do that now then we'll give that fancy bed a try. What do you say?"

Mama closed her eyes and swayed but Helen and I caught her. She grumbled and straightened herself. Ignoring us, she shuffled and pushed the walker until she was closer to the window. She looked out and saw the flag. I stepped over and said, "See Mama, the flag is up and flying, just like you want. And you can see it from the bed."

Mama looked at me sideways. "Did you . . . raise it up . . . this morning?"

I had not. I had just left it flying all night. My face told her this.

"You just left . . . it out there all night, . . . didn't you?" She scowled.

I lowered my head and nodded slightly, "But Mama I—"

"Was the floodlight on? Shining . . . on it . . . like it's . . . supposed to . . . in the dark?"

I shook my head. "I couldn't find the floodlight Mama. I had a lot going on—"

"Well, you . . . either take that flag down at dusk . . . or get a goddamn floodlight . . . you hear . . . me?"

Christopher had been listening and came over to stand beside me. "Grandma, you're being mean to my mom." He frowned at her and put his hands on his hips.

Mama's eyes widened, and her mouth fell open. She stared at him and said haltingly, "Christopher . . . I am *not*. I'm . . . just . . . asking her—"

"No, you're being mean!" He came to me and wrapped his arms around my waist. I was overcome by his courage to defend me. My face crumpled. I could not stop the tears. I hugged him to me and kissed the top of his head.

Mama swayed again, gripping the walker tightly, but managed to steady herself. "I am not . . . being mean, Christopher. You . . . have to . . . . understand that . . . ." She had to stop speaking in order to catch her breath. Christopher, concerned, twisted around to face her. She struggled to continue, swallowing with some difficulty. Helen moved closer to her. Mama tilted her head down to look Christopher in the eye and said, "The. . . flag . . . is important . . . to me." She pursed her lips together then slowly moved her head in my direction and looked me in the face. I was shocked to see tears welled in her blue eyes. "I'm . . . sorry," she whispered, the two words so historic in their rarity that my mouth dropped open. She cleared her throat then added, "I . . . do . . . appreciate . . . all you . . . are doing, Laney Mae. You . . . know that."

The tears in my eyes blurred my vision of her and for a moment, I did not recognize my mother.

☙❧

CHRISTOPHER HOVERED AROUND ME LIKE A PROTECTIVE SHADOW the rest of the morning. In confronting Mama, he had proved again that he was my small prince of courage, my protector and my guardian since Phil had left us. At just ten, he had developed a firm moral compass grounded in an unambiguous sense of right and wrong. I saw no contradiction in him. Not for the first time, I silently thanked whatever God was listening to me, for giving me my son. Despite my brooding nature and an unhappy aura of loss and sorrow, I could at least claim him, my prodigy, my hope.

Helen got Mama to the bathroom, freshened her up, and dressed her in new clothes. Mama was sufficiently exhausted from her expedition to the living/dying room and decided not to use the hospital bed for now (but agreed to sleep in it that night) and returned to her recliner to await the arrival of Gladys. With the TV on low and Helen beside her, she slept on and off, and I was grateful for the calm. While she napped, Christopher helped me tackle Mama's bed. We stripped the sheets and ran the laundry. I showed him how to measure the detergent and start the wash and then, when the bedding was dry, he helped me make the bed, smooth the sheets and fluff the pillows. We talked not about death and sadness but about school starting in a few days, who his new teacher would be, how much homework he would have, and which friends he hoped would be in his class. We went outside and cut more Hydrangea blossoms then put a simple glass vase brimming with the flowers beside the lamp on the nightstand. Satisfied, my son announced he would like to go to the pool with his friend but promised to be home by four o'clock to greet Gladys (who he said he had no memory ever meeting) and help Uncle Neal grill dinner.

Alone and suddenly overcome with fatigue, I sat down on the edge of the bed and stared at the Hydrangeas. They were full and beautiful but, I realized with sudden sadness, they were dying now that I had cut them. The blossoms had begun their journey toward Death at my hand. Irrational a thought as it was, my eyes filled, and I let tears roll down my face. We were all on this journey to meet Death, I thought, only our departure times vary. "Please let her have more time," I whispered to the room, the Hydrangeas, the bedspread and to Death, lurking impatiently, in the TV room near my mother as she dozed in the recliner.

I turned my thoughts to Gladys and in my mind, traced the times she had visited over the years. Her visits that were often more like rescue missions, many of them following some major, life-altering event. Although I was too young to recall, I know that her first visit was a few months after my dad had been killed and Mama, still reeling from the shock of it all, had fled Second Chance to Virginia and this house. Gladys had suffered her own horrible loss the year before my father died when her second child, a boy she named Frederick, died of crib death at just two months old. This happened when Gladys lived in Delaware with her husband, Darryl and her daughter Francine, who was four.

Mama had been the one to go to the rescue that time. Little Frederick's death shattered the already fragile marriage they had and Gladys and Darryl divorced not long after (but they remained friends). Gladys began a decade of dividing her time between extended visits to Delaware to see her brother Charles and his family as well as Darryl, so Francine had time with her father and then returning home to Chance to help care for her parents as they aged.

The next time Gladys visited was in August 1963 when she and Mama attended the March on Washington for Jobs and Freedom along with two hundred fifty-thousand others, and this was where they heard Martin Luther King, Jr.'s iconic speech. Mama would later tell me how hopeful she was to be part of that day, especially when Mahalia Jackson sang "*How I Got Over*" and thousands clapped and sang joyfully together. "I tell you I had chills," she shared with me later when I was doing a school report on the historic March. Neal told me that he, Francine and I watched the King speech on live TV at home with Greg's sister Susie babysitting us, but I have no memory of it and there were no photos of Mama and Gladys from that day.

I do recall Gladys' next visit only a few months later. It was the week before Thanksgiving in 1963 when Mama found herself in between caretakers for me and Neal. My aunt Margaret came and helped out for one week, and Gladys came the following week with Francine who was six. Mama had hired a new woman–Betty Clarke– (who would become my worst nightmare) to start the weekday job on the Monday after the holiday. And so, Gladys was here on Friday, November 22. I was only three-and-a-half, but I have never forgotten the shocking moment when Gladys suddenly cried out, "Oh my God!" and brought her hands to her mouth when the news bulletin announced that President Kennedy had been shot. Neal was at school and Mama at work at the Pentagon. I remember how

Francine and I, at play on the floor in front of the TV with an assortment of dolls and stuff animals, sat in incomprehension.

I know that Gladys came a few years after that, when my uncle Rob died in Vietnam. I could vaguely recall the service at Arlington National Cemetery, but I do remember Gladys and Francine staying with us. After that, it would be a decade before Gladys visited again. When Art died in 1977 from a sudden heart attack. It had taken five years for my birthday wish to come true. Five years of more cruelty, discord and misery. Five years without Neal at home. Truth be told, when Art died, Gladys' visit represented a joyful celebration because she brought Neal home with her. There were no tears for Art.

And the last time I could recall her being here had been for Christopher's baptism in 1991. I knew there were photographs of that, so I rose and went to Mama's closet. I pulled one of the photo albums she kept there from the shelf and flipped through until I found pictures from the baptism. There was little Christopher in his white gown (which had been worn by Phil at his baptism) being held by the Priest; Mama in a lovely blue suit that matched her eyes, Gladys in a pretty green floral dress next to her, and me, trying to imitate Princess Diana by wearing a hat that looked ridiculous to me now. Francine was not there; by then she had married and moved from Second Chance to River Mount where she started her new life with her new husband, Bruce. Neal was there, alone as always, handsome in a suit and tie. Phil's family members and some of our assorted friends celebrated the occasion and their faces smiled at me, frozen in a time that seemed more like fifty years ago and not ten years ago. I peered closely at Phil's face in one of the photos, trying to discern some evidence of unhappiness with his life and found none. I could never have predicted the end of my marriage then; it all seemed content, and *normal*. Looking at the photos I realized this was probably the last time we as a group of people were all together. I also recalled that Gladys had planned to stay a with us for a week but had to leave suddenly: her older brother George, in Delaware, had fallen and he died two days later. Mama had gone with Gladys to help her. As I stared at Gladys in the photo, wide smile on her face, (possibly taken at the very moment her brother was falling) it occurred to me that for every happy event, fate seemed to deal us a tragic one. I closed the album and hugged it to my body as I considered something else: each time Gladys had visited us (except once, to attend the March in August 1963), death had accompanied her in one way or another. And now, she would visit us again. As would death.

CHAPTER 8

On Christmas Day in 1971, I received a special gift from Mama. We were in Second Chance surrounded by Hartman family members, all of us were spread out between the living and dining room and the kitchen of my grandparents' home. Pop Hartman had been dead for years but my grandmother, Nettie, was alive. She had suffered a stroke and was confined to a wheelchair. She could no longer speak but her eyes sparkled as she sat in the middle of the holiday festivities; happy to be surrounded by family. I remember that it had snowed most of the day and outside looked like a soft blanket of glittering cotton candy and this added to the celebratory atmosphere. We had exchanged gifts and had just finished an early dinner, with Christmas music playing on the radio and so many bodies crowded into the house, it was warm and snug.

I was sitting at the dining table playing a new board game with Neal and two of my cousins when Mama switched off the radio and announced that she had a special surprise. From behind her she revealed a small box wrapped in gold paper with a green bow. She smiled at me and said, "This is for you, Laney Mae." I remember the shock I felt at being singled-out by my mother, and then realizing it wasn't because I was in trouble. Eyes-wide, I looked over at Neal for some clue, but he also seemed just as surprised. I walked over to where Mama stood, eyeing the interesting little box.

At that moment, my uncle Frank, who had slept through most of the earlier festivities on the living room couch, appeared in the doorway of the dining room and said with mock irritation, "Jesus H. Christ! I know I slept a while but ain't Christmas over yet?" He grinned devilishly as he scratched his belly. Outside observers to this scene might have taken one look at Mama's older brother and shaken their heads sadly. He was hardly the best representative of the industrious Hartman stock established by my great-grandfather James, especially as the last surviving son. He was, put simply, a mess. He was disheveled and unkempt with his pants unbuttoned at the top and the round paunch of his stomach pressing impolitely against the zipper. His thinning hair stuck up in every direction and his face was dark with beard growth, evidence of the fact that he had spent most the last two days on the couch sleeping off the effects of his gin drinking. He was only forty-three then but looked twenty years older. He had no home of his own. He lived either at my grandmother's house or nearby with one of his sisters. On occasion, he made his way to live with Claudia and her husband Pete. Like a hermit crab he was completely portable, slinking from one house to the other and wherever he ended up, that was home. If you asked him where he was going, Frank would always say, "Until I stop" and he meant it. He had never married, had no children and had never held a steady job, except for his time in the U.S. Army.

Even at eleven years old and as fond as I was of him, I knew something was terribly sad about him. Mama told me and Neal that

Frank was the way he was because he was, "damaged in the Korean war." She said when he had joined the Army, he was an energetic and healthy young man, excited to see the world. But, returned from the war a wounded, silent and perpetually tired man who stared into space, drank, and slept a lot. Whatever his physical wounds, including being shot in the shoulder, the mental wounds and heartache were the ones that would not heal. These injuries to our uncle's soul were largely from guilt: Frank had come home alive from Korea but his older brother, Kurt, who served in the Marines, had not.

Aunt Claudia stood at the sink washing dishes and put her hands on her hips and mocked her brother. "Frank, you goat! You slept through everything, including dinner. I kept a plate warm for you, and Faye is just giving Laney Mae an extra little gift, that's all." She tossed the dishtowel over her shoulder and folded her arms across her chest. She scowled and rolled her eyes, but I knew this was all banter.

Frank started to reply but Art, who was seated away from everyone in the corner of the kitchen and drinking his fourth beer, said sarcastically, "Well, if it isn't Frank Hartman! You've been on that couch so long I forgot what you looked like."

I remember how quiet and uncomfortable the room became for us all but not, I noticed, for Frank. He shifted his eyes lazily and gazed at Art the way someone might look at a fly that has landed on a plate of food; disgusted, and contemplating how to strike and not miss. Frank moved from the doorway to stand closer to the dining table. He turned to face Art, leaned back slightly, opened his mouth wide (which revealed several missing teeth in the back), and let out an enormous belch. "There," Frank told Art, "in case you forgot what I sounded like, too."

We erupted in laughter, but I quickly clamped my hand over my mouth trying to stifle myself. All I needed was Art to see me laughing at him. Mama stomped her foot and said, "Stop it! It's Christmas Day. No bickering!" She waited until everyone quieted down and then she turned her attention back to me. "Now back to this gift, Laney Mae. I was going to wait and give it to you on your birthday in a few days, but I decided to do it today." She handed me the box. "Now, don't get too excited; it's nothing brand new but it's something you've wanted to have as your own."

"It's a picture," my aunt Harrie blurted out.

"Harrie!" Mama snapped. "Don't tell her!"

I swung around to my aunt Harrie who stood with her hands covering her mouth to suppress her giggles; her eyes dancing with merriment. A stocky woman of thirty-four, boyish with short hair, Harriet Jean Hartman was the youngest Hartman daughter. Spirited and bold, she was a force to be reckoned with, a vibrant soul that the challenge of Down syndrome could not suppress, although unkind people had. Harrie had been born during a time and in a place where her condition was misunderstood, and assistance practically nonexistent. She had endured being called, "retard" and, "Mongoloid" since she was a child. While the Hartman clan had always tried to shelter her, the truth was they were ill-equipped to contend with her special needs and did what they were told to do by the doctor from the moment she deemed, "different" at birth. Mama told us later that there was no school for her kind and instead, Harrie spent her days by Grandma Nettie's side or roaming the hills around the houses, with all the siblings taking turns keeping an eye on her. Harrie had been, according to Mama, happy and active. She was loved unconditionally. And while strangers stared curiously or mocked her slightly slanted eyes, flat nose and small chin, her facial expressions and joy at the simplest things made her adored by her family and the friends who came to know her.

Things got more challenging when Harrie turned thirteen. For one thing, she had been sterilized. The doctor assured Pop and Grandma Nettie it was necessary, and they never questioned it. Mama told me and Neal that it was a frightening and confusing experience for Harrie to be taken away for the procedure. For a while my poor aunt had become sullen and angry but over time, with the ongoing support of her family, she recovered. Later, thanks to Mama, Harrie got to experience a whole other world. Mama discovered a special school in Arlington, Virginia near her job at the Pentagon for people with intellectual disabilities. For two weeks in the summertime, Harrie would come stay with us and Mama would drive her each day to the school where she got to learn new things and make friends. She learned about music and got to do crafts. I remember how proud she was when, at the age of twenty-eight, she learned to sign her name with an X. I always admired Mama's dedication to her sister.

"Sorry Faye!" Harrie told Mama. "I won't tell her *what* picture!"

I stared at the little gold box with its green bow and felt my heart beat faster. This was it! Mama was finally giving me a photograph of my father. At the exact moment I had that wonderful thought, I caught sight of Art's scowling face and knew it could not possibly be. Mama would never bring up my father in front of Art let alone a photograph of him.

"Go ahead and open it," Mama told me, lighting a cigarette.

I pulled the ribbon and ripped the paper and lifted the lid of the box and folded back the tissue paper. I saw the back of a photograph and something about it was familiar. I glanced up at Mama then lifted the picture out of the box and turned it over. I felt a simultaneous rush of happiness and sting of disappointment. I struggled to not let Mama see my mixed emotions. My eyes filled with tears and I looked up at her and said, "Thank you Mama. I'll treasure it forever."

"Well, what is it a picture of?" My aunt Ruth asked in her usual grumpy tone as she leaned toward me. I held it up for everyone to see. "It's me. And John F. Kennedy. You know? From when he came to West Virginia and Mama made us all go meet him."

"Now you take care of that photo little Missy," Mama said. "It's a piece of history."

I had held the photograph before and yet I still found it incredible that I was the small baby in the picture and that John F. Kennedy was holding me. *Me!* I was gazing at the image when Art came over to me. I tried to step away from him but was not quick enough. He pulled the photograph roughly from my hand and peered at it. "What's the story behind this?" His words were beginning to slur. His mouth smiled but his eyes did not. I reached to get the photograph back from him, but he raised it up, above his head and out of my reach.

"Give it back," I pleaded with him and jumped up to try to take it from him.

"You'll get it back," he sneered at me. "How the hell did you all meet JFK?"

Claudia hesitated, looking around the room in case anyone else wanted to tell the story. When no one else spoke, she said, "Well, Art, it was when he was campaigning in the West Virginia Primary. It was May, 1960. He came through River Mount and Faye just thought he was the greatest thing and sure to be president. So, she rounded us all up to go see him and got her a new camera to get some photos." She looked over at Mama and said wryly, "Faye, why you entrusted me to get a photo, I'll never know! I didn't know how to operate that newfangled thing!" She redirected her conversation to Art. "So, I was supposed to get in a good position and take a photo of Faye and Neal and Little Laney Mae and Gi–" Claudia caught herself and my heart skipped. She had been about to say "Gil." I felt my father's memory hovering and braced myself, hoping someone would say his name. But no one did. Claudia

THE ROAD TO SECOND CHANCE

looked at her shoes, sighing with relief that she had caught herself, then continued. "Anyway, I was supposed to snap a nice family picture of them with JFK, but it didn't turn out quite right. Which, I insist to this day, was not my fault! There was a crazy rush of people and I got pushed back and had to snap fast but at least I got that picture!"

Mama snorted, "Of the back of my head. Thanks a lot!" The Hartmans laughed. Art did not.

"Well, it is what it is! You can see Laney Mae and JFK and that's worth something!" Claudia insisted.

Art still held the photo above my reach. He snickered and said, "I will never understand why people supported him. He was a communist and a n–" he caught himself before he said what I could only imagine was the ugly word he called Black people with the word "lover" at the end

"He was a great man and president," I said to Art, surprised at my own boldness. "Give me back my picture!" Dandy appeared behind Art, his face grave. *Careful there, he's not of his right mind, not one bit. Step away from him. Let it go.*

"Art, please!" Mama pleaded.

Art sneered at me then handed me the photo. "Read your history, young lady. Old man Kennedy was a bootlegger and a crook. All the Kennedys are corrupt. And you West Virginians fell for it. That's because he poured so much money into this state back then. Well, where are they now? How's all that money old man Kennedy spent helping you now?" Smug, Art strode back to the stool where he had left his fifth bottle of beer waiting. He titled the bottle toward Mama then took a long drink.

"We admired him, Art," Claudia's replied. "It was something to see him in person. He was what you call charismatic. And besides, Faye here is the one who gave him the idea for his most famous line."

"What are you talking about?" Art smirked, still slurring his words.

Mama spoke sharply, "Claudia, stop! Art doesn't want to hear this. You heard him; he doesn't like the Kennedys."

Ruth, always ready to tangle with Mama, said, "Don't you get on Claudia, Faye. He asked!"

Mama sighed and gave Ruth "the look." She inhaled deeply as she eyed her husband. She said, "Okay, Art. You want to hear what I said to Kennedy? Really?"

Art nodded, sneering. "Of course."

She blew out smoke and roughly jammed her cigarette out in the ashtray on the table. "Okay. Since you asked. First, when he came up to shake hands with people, I told him I wanted him to meet my little Democrat, so I held Laney Mae up and he took her. I was hoping he'd kiss her, but I found out later that he wasn't like other politicians, he didn't kiss babies–"

"Not ugly ones," Frank said in a serious voice and everyone howled, Neal the loudest of all.

Mama said, "Frank Hartman! My baby girl was *not* ugly. She was a skinny little tadpole, but she was *not* ugly!" This lightened the atmosphere and Mama grinned, seeming to forget Art, and continued, "Well, Kennedy said, 'She's sweet. I wish she were old enough to vote.' And, of course, that is the picture Claudia got: JFK holding Laney Mae, looking like he was worried he'd drop her, and the back of my head. Not my face! No one would know that was me! And just the back of little Laney Mae's head in her bonnet. And it was too far out! Claudia got the whole crowd instead of getting close in on me and JFK."

"I will never live this down," Claudia laughed.

Uncle Pete said, "And right after the picture, that's when you gave him his famous line."

Mama nodded, "Yes, Pete, I did. I said, 'Senator Kennedy, you're going to win West Virginia big. I just know it!' And he said, 'Well I certainly hope so.' Now, I knew he was being moved along and everyone was pushing and trying to shake his hand, but I wouldn't let go."

"Poor man," Ruth said. "He didn't know who he was messing with!"

"Oh, shut up Ruth!" Mama snapped but she laughed. "So, then I spoke the words that just came to me from my heart. I said, 'Senator Kennedy, people need to start asking what they can do for this country, don't you think? And not what this country can do for them!'"

We whooped and applauded, and Mama basked in the memory, but it did not last. Art began to bellow. "What! What did you say?" He rose from his chair too quickly and swayed slightly. He waved his arms about, the now empty bottle of beer dangerously close to slipping from his grasp and flying across the room. "Are you kidding me? Are you actually telling me that that you–" he pointed the bottle at Mama, "a hillbilly gal from this godforsaken town of nowhere, gave JFK that line? His most *famous* line? Now I've heard everything!" He roared with laughter.

Like a quickly drawn shade, a silence fell. I looked at Mama. Her face was red with anger. I heard the sound of shuffling feet and saw Frank and Pete move toward Art who backed away from them, his hands held up in mock surrender, rambling. "What? What did I say? You're upset because I used the word hillbilly?" He looked around at the unhappy faces surrounding him and decided to go for broke. He called JFK a communist, a traitor and the particularly nasty name he had almost said earlier that began with N and had the word "lover" added.

That did it for me; I snapped. I bolted from my chair and raged, "Shut up! Shut up! I hate you!" I pounded on the table. "You are *not* going to ruin my Christmas gift! You are not going to ruin Mama's story and say that awful word and those things about President

Kennedy." I heard Mama gasp. Dandy shook his head and held up his hands for me to stop, *No, Laney Mae. Let it go!* But I ignored him and began to move toward Art. I heard Mama say, "No, Laney Mae, stop!" But I continued toward him and felt the hands of my relatives reaching out to restrain me. On my way to do whatever it was that I was going to do to my stepfather I dropped the photo of JFK and me on the floor but by then I had reached Art and I began take swings at him only to be held back by Neal, Pete and Frank.

Art was furious. "You watch yourself young lady," he growled, the smell of beer strong in my face. "Don't do something you'll regret."

By now I was sobbing. I wanted to reach his face, scratch him with my nails and punch his ugly mouth. From the corner of my eye, I saw Harrie coming toward me. On the way, she bent and picked the photo off the floor and handed it to me. Then she turned to face Art. "You are mean Art! You say mean words." Then my aunt made a fist, drew her chubby arm back and gave Arthur McDaniel a solid right punch directly in his mouth. Art buckled over, grimacing. Frank, Pete and Neal dropped their hold on me and rushed to Art before he could punch Harrie back. They wrapped him in their collective arms and hustled him, with great commotion, outside.

Claudia rushed to guide Harrie out of the kitchen. "I *had* to punch him, Claudia! I had to! Art said mean words and he made Laney Mae cry!" Claudia cooed gently to Harrie to calm her down and led her out of the kitchen. That was when I turned back to locate Mama only to discover that she was gone. She had fled the room, fled the confrontation and, in a manner completely atypical to my pre-Art mother, cowardly left it to others to clean up the mess. Dandy hovered in the background. He shook his head sadly and shrugged. There was nothing to be done.

WHEN I WAS AROUND TEN, I BECAME OBSESSED WITH A PHOTO IN LIFE magazine in the issue published a week after JFK was assassinated. Mama kept the magazine on the top shelf of our coat closet (this was where she would continue to keep copies of newspapers and magazines to document major historical events of our lifetime). I would carefully take the magazine down, lay on my stomach on the living room floor and study it cover-to-cover. The photo I obsessed over was of JFK and Jackie as they walk together having just descended the steps of Air Force One in Dallas at Love Field on that brilliantly sunny day. They are larger than life in the full-page photograph. He, dashing and handsome, toying with the button of his suit jacket. She, lovely in her pink suit, red roses cradled in her arms, with a shy smile on her face. It was a moment frozen in time, a moment just before they stepped into the presidential limousine to begin the motorcade through Dallas that would end with his brutal death. I would stare at this photo, mesmerized with the knowledge of what was going to happen next. I would fantasize that I had magical time-travel powers and could somehow step into the photograph and stop them. "No! Don't get in that car!" I would tell them. They would listen to me, heed my warning, and get back on Air Force One, safely returning to Washington. He would live. None of the bad things that happened after he died would happen. Our country would be spared the shocking loss, we would be safe, and everyone would be happy.

Of course, I had these same ideas about my father's death, although I had to imagine what he looked like. I fantasized that my magical powers of time travel would allow me, his daughter from the future, to go back to that terrible January night in 1962. I would stop him from leaving the house, warn him what would happen, throw myself at his feet and grab hold of his legs to keep him home. He would never get into his car, never pick up the other woman and their rendezvous with a coal truck and subsequential death on the icy mountain road would never happen. Instead, he would stay home, play records and dance with me in his arms. And as with JFK, none of the bad things that happened after my daddy died would happen. Our family would be spared the shocking loss, we would be safe, and everyone would be happy.

❧

ONE DOES NOT FORGET THEIR FORMAL INTRODUCTION TO DEATH; it stays imprinted in the memory forever. For me, that happened on November 22, 1963. The events of that day are the first actual memories I consciously recall. And even though my young ears had heard people speak about others "dying" or "passing away" (including in reference to my father), before that day I was too young to understand but Kennedy's murder changed that. As I watched TV like a zombie over that long, sad weekend, and the images and sounds beamed from the screen into my eyes. I learned that a person could be smiling and waving one minute, shot dead the next, be put into a box draped beneath the flag and rolled to a place where a large hole would be dug; then put in the ground forever. To put it in the simplicity of my three-year-old mind: Kennedy was *all gone*. I understood then that my daddy was all gone, too. As I got older, I came to the tragic realization that without my own memories of him, he wasn't just *all gone*. Instead, it was as though my father had *never been*.

When Mama got home from her job at the Pentagon that day, Gladys, Francine, Neal and I hurried from the TV room to greet her and stopped when we saw her coming in the front door, her face streaked with tears mixed with mascara, struggling to carry a most unusual item: a large, framed picture. I understood later that it was one of the official portraits of President Kennedy that had, until that afternoon, hung on the wall in her department at the Pentagon.

I remember that it looked enormous to me, how curious I was about it and that I was immediately drawn to the face of the man in the picture.

Mama stepped into the living room, gently set the portrait on the floor and leaned it against the couch. I walked over and stood before it. I stared at John F. Kennedy, who stared back at me and then realized that his was the same face I had seen flashed on TV all afternoon. Later I would learn that this was a very famous portrait of Kennedy taken shortly after he was elected by Fabian Bachrach Jr. Dressed in a pinstriped suit with a thin, dark tie and the hint of a smile, Kennedy gazed straight into the camera with undeniable confidence. Beneath the president's black-and-white image on cream-colored matting was the famous excerpt from his inaugural address that Mama had suggested to him:

> *"–ask not what your country can do for you–*
> *ask what you can do for your country."*

"Colonel Baxter said I could have this," Mama told us, pulling a hankie from her purse and blowing her nose. "He knew how much I loved the President. Can you believe they were taking his pictures down already?" She turned to Gladys, unable to continue. The two most important adults in my life at that moment fell into each other's arms, sobbing. I wrung my little hands together with worry. Mama wailed, "I can't believe someone shot him! I can't believe he's dead! It's like we just met him in West Virginia yesterday! Oh, dear God!"

Tears running down her face Gladys said, "How could this happen? In broad daylight? Nothing will ever be the same. God help us!"

I remember feeling afraid, nudging my way in between Mama and Gladys and wrapping my arms around my mother as tightly as I could. She stroked my hair and we stood like that, with Francine and Neal joining in the group hug for a brief time before Mama broke us up ordering Neal to go and get a hammer. "I'm going to hang this in a place of honor." She kicked off her high heels and stood on the couch. She removed two small paintings she had bought at a flea market and, taking the hammer from Neal, pulled out the picture holder hooks. We watched as she lifted JFK's portrait and eyeballed its placement then, carefully centering it, she hammered the picture hook into the wall. Gladys handed her Kennedy's picture and Mama slid it into place, adjusting it so it was straight. She stepped off the couch and the four of us stood silently staring at the dead president. Gladys said solemnly, "I feel like his eyes are looking right into my heart."

Mama replied, "I know. I guess it's my imagination, but I feel it too, but never before today. I'm so glad I got to bring this home. I know Colonel Baxter wanted it, but I cried and begged him, and he said, 'Oh for goodness's sake, take it! I voted for Nixon anyway.'"

Neal had been quiet but now asked, "Mama, are they going to get whoever shot him?"

"Oh yes, they are little mister! Whoever did this is going to get caught. Maybe they have already! I'm going back to watch the TV."

Everyone returned to the TV room to watch more of the dreadful news except me. I remember staring up at JFK for several minutes, drawn to the sad aura that surrounded his image. And then, for what would be the first of many, many times, I climbed up onto the couch, turned myself around and sat on its back next to the picture. In that instant, JFK became the first of my imaginary fathers. I would come to realize who he really had been, of course, and this would require me to create a new pretend father (that would be Dandy later). But for now, JFK, with his kind eyes, was all the pretend daddy I needed on that most sad day. I leaned my head over Kennedy's shoulder and ever so gently, rested my head on the glass. I remember contentment filling my soul because this important man was now mine and I felt safe. I don't know how long I sat like that, alternately leaning my head on his shoulder then tilting back to look into his eyes. I remember that I talked to him and told him in a quiet voice that I was very sorry about what had happened to him; but that I was glad he lived with us now. I told him all about me, about Mama and Neal, my toys, my swing set and who Gladys and Francine were. I told him what scared me at night and how I worried about everything. I told him I used to have a daddy but that he was gone, and I didn't know where he was or what he looked like.

Sometime a little later Mama called me to come to dinner, but I did not want to leave the spot where I sat next to JFK, so I ignored her, even when her voice got louder, and she barked, "Get your little behind in here!" Next, I heard Mama tell Neal to get me and I heard him push his chair back, scraping the kitchen floor, and stomp his way to the living room. He gasped when he saw me sitting beside JFK. "You better get down off there, Laney Mae," he whispered. "If you knock that picture off the wall, Mama's gonna be really mad." But I refused, telling him this was my daddy, and I could sit there if I wanted. He told me JFK was not my daddy and pleaded with me to get down, but I refused. "Don't say I didn't warn you," he told me. He called out, "Mama, you better come in here." I braced myself as she made her way to the living room, Gladys and Francine following her. Mama was muttering under her breath about what happens to children who do not listen but when she saw me, she stopped abruptly, and her mouth fell open. "Laney Mae!" Her voice was sharp. "What are you doing up there? Get down right *now!*"

"She thinks that he's her daddy," Neal said.

Mama gasped. "What? Jesus Christ! Laney Mae, he is *not* your daddy! For crying out loud, that is President Kennedy! He died today! That is just a picture I brought that home from work. Now get down!"

I folded my arms across my chest and shook my head, but my defiance began to wither, and I felt the heavy crush of sadness because I knew this was a battle I could not win. I always lost to Mama; everyone did. I began to sob helplessly. I turned to look at Kennedy up close one last time and his eyes were so calm and confident that I suddenly decided I didn't care what Mama said, I would not move until I wanted to! All that mattered to me was that he was here and that I could look into his eyes and see him looking back and lay my head upon his shoulder anytime that I wanted. If Mama made me get down, I would sneak back up later.

"Did you hear what I said, Laney Mae?" Mama's voice had reached shrill. She moved toward the couch to yank me off, but at that moment, Gladys took a hold of Mama's arm and stopped her. "Faye, leave her alone," she said firmly. "She's not hurting anything."

Mama spun around and stared at Gladys, dumbfounded, unaccustomed to anyone standing in her way or stopping her. "What? Not hurting anything? How can you say that, Gladys?" She pointed at me. "Look at her! Sitting up there, talking to that picture, thinking he's her daddy—that is crazy! It's *not* normal!"

Gladys focused her eyes on me. I stared back at her, wringing my hands. She tilted her head to the side and her expression was one of sadness and pity. Keeping her hold on Mama, she said, "And what is *normal* about anything that has happened on this awful day, Faye? Tell me that." She pulled Mama's arm gently. "Now come on. Leave her alone. Leave the child alone." Mama shook her head slowly as she stared at me then bowed her head and mumbled something I could not hear and then Gladys led her back to the kitchen followed by Neal and Francine.

Amazed, my tears dried instantly. I wiped my face with my hands. I looked back at JFK to confirm he had seen the whole thing, too. Allowing myself a small smile of triumph, I once again laid my head on his shoulder and sighed in relief. Gladys had stood up for me, she had taken my side against Mama and we had won. In that consecrated moment, as the sun began to set on that mournful day and our house filled with a mix of dim light and ghostly shadows, somehow I knew Gladys was the only adult in the world who ever would.

CHAPTER 9

I used my palm to wipe the steam off the bathroom mirror and stared with discontent at my sad reflection; my freshly washed hair wrapped tightly in a towel. The hot shower had done me good, but I still looked tired, dejected and old. I was becoming someone I never thought I would be but could not yet name who that was.

I pulled the towel off my head and ran it briskly through my hair, then combed it out, battling some tangles. I grabbed the blow dryer and worked the hot air quickly through my hair, bending at my waist to dry the underside. Rising back up, I switched to a round brush to try to smooth my thick locks and again noticed the gray roots. I frowned at the top of my head, wondering if the appearance of the gray was there when my marriage had begun to fail. *Was that the reason Phil had chosen someone younger?* I peered at the small lines beneath my eyes and noticed for the first time, the faint appearance of two vertical wrinkles between my eyebrows. I traced one with the tip of my index finger. That's from all the frowning, I thought; all the sadness. Dandy appeared in the reflection standing behind me.

He said, *I don't think you look old at all. Why you could pass for thirty-one, not forty-one!* I rolled my eyes forlornly and opened the medicine cabinet. I found a jar of facial cream and smeared it over my face. "Yes, I'm just the picture of youthful radiance," I said aloud. I stared at myself for a moment and, although still quite dissatisfied, there was nothing more I could do except put on make-up, but I lacked the ambition to do so. I could not remember the last time I had worn any. *Probably when we went to the doctor's office and received Mama's death sentence.*

I returned to the bedroom and rummaged in the suitcase I had brought from the apartment. I came across a sundress I had absent-mindedly packed and decided to wear it, though it seemed too festive. How did one dress for a pre-death dinner party? I chortled and silently scolded myself for such morbid humor but, truth be told, I did feel somewhat festive knowing Gladys was on the way and would arrive any minute. I was filled with anticipation and hoped that her presence would finally help break down the emotional walls my mother hid behind.

I had just tossed the dress over my head and was sliding my feet into my flip flops when I heard Helen from downstairs, screaming my name and yelling for me to come quickly. Heart racing, I bolted downstairs and arrived in the TV room to find Mama on her back, spread eagle the floor, Helen kneeling behind her, her arms beneath Mama's armpits, straining to lift her. Mother the terrier was hovering by them, panting in distress.

"Oh Laney Mae," Helen cried. "I went to the bathroom for just a quick minute and she must have tried to get up. I'm so sorry. I thought she was asleep! Can you help me? I can't lift her alone."

I rushed over and dropped to the floor. Mama seemed in a daze, her arms flaying about, her legs limp like a ragdoll's. She seemed unable or unwilling to help us get her back up. I crouched on one side and Helen shifted to the other and she told Mama to help on the count of three but when we got to three we barely managed to lift her a few inches from the floor. Her body, which probably weighed barely a hundred pounds, seemed immovable. "Mama, work with us," I pleaded but then she began to flay her arms about defiantly.

"No . . . not . . . going to . . . that bed!"

"Ms. Faye, we aren't taking you to the bed now," Helen said. She was out of breath from the struggle. "We're just trying to get you in the recliner."

"No . . . you . . . are not!"

I took Mama's face into my hands and made her look at me. "Mama! Listen to me. We have to get you back in the chair, okay? *Not* the bed, the chair. Please don't resist us, Mama. We don't want to hurt you."

Mama stared at me. "I . . . can't . . . too weak."

Helen and I stared helplessly at each other. I told her, "Neal can't get here quick enough. I better call 9-1-1—"

"Looks like you could use some help."

I looked up to see Gladys standing in the doorway leading from the kitchen. She displayed a calm and confident air and, I thought, a somewhat amused expression considering the chaotic predicament that greeted her. Nearly six feet tall and solidly built, she stood before me as she always had in my memory, with a reliable self-assurance that lived up to her height and defied her age. Her face appeared youthful and smooth with only a few trace wrinkles, her eyebrows dark and carefully shaped. She held herself erect, hands on her hips, no slight bow at her waist to stave off any invisible arthritis pain, no old person's bend to accommodate an aching back. Only her chalk white hair pulled back in a bun at the nape of her neck in any way betrayed her as a woman nearly seven decades old.

Overcome with emotion, I ran to her, flung my body into her

arms and began to sob. "Oh Gladys! Oh Gladys," I cried. "Please help us! She fell. We can't lift her."

Gladys allowed me a short embrace then abruptly released me and moved to where Mama lay. She lowered herself onto her knees and took Mama's face into her hands.

"Faye, I'm here."

The transformation of Mama's face was nothing short of miraculous. Gone was her grimace of pain with her eyes narrowed into small slits of agony. Now she stared eyes-wide in happy surprise and reached out to clutch her friend's arm. Smiling broadly, Mama declared, "Look who's here! Oh . . . look who's here . . . look who's here . . ." She began to sob, tears of happiness wetting her pale cheeks.

"I'm here alright," Gladys said. Winking at me she added, "And just in time from what I can see."

"Gladys to the rescue," I exclaimed happily. I knelt beside her and introduced her to Helen.

"I'm sure glad you came when you did," Helen said, her face red, sweat on her brow.

Gladys nodded then focused on Mama. "Faye," she said in a calm but commanding voice. "We need to lift you back into your recliner. Okay? Are you ready?"

Mama gazed at Gladys and nodded agreeably. "Yes, I'm ready," she said more clearly than I had heard her speak in days.

"One . . . two . . . three," said Gladys and she and Helen lifted Mama off the floor and eased her back into the safety of her recliner. I thought Helen was going to collapse from the stress of it all. She kept apologizing but I assured her I was not angry, that I forgave her, and that all was well that ended well.

"You go home now," I told her. "It's been a long day."

Helen sighed and hugged me. "I'll see you tomorrow." As she

said this she looked nervously at Mama, her uncertainty of there being a tomorrow for Mama written on her face.

"Yes, we *will* see you tomorrow," I replied. I was certain: Gladys was here.

❦

ONCE WE HAD MAMA RESTING SAFELY IN THE RECLINER WITH Mother nestled on her lap, I led Gladys through the living/dying room to Mama's bedroom and left her alone to unpack and shower. While she did, I returned with a glass of wine to sit beside Mama who dozed, her hand on the dog's back. I was in awe over the effect Gladys had on Mama and feeling happily expectant. Mama would do whatever Gladys asked her to do. All I had to do was get Gladys to ask her.

"What's a woman got to do to get a beer in this house?" Gladys said grinning as she stepped into the TV room and plopped beside me on the couch.

"Help lift a hundred-pound woman off the floor," I joked.

"Hahaha, very funny. Were you *really* going to call 9-1-1?"

"What else were we going to do?"

She rolled her eyes and shifted her gaze to Mama. "Is she sleeping most of the time now?"

"Off and on. She gets her next morphine at seven so I'm hoping before then she'll come around a bit." I went to the kitchen and returned with a bottle of beer. I sat beside Gladys and watched as she took a long sip and stared with sadness at Mama. I told her Neal would arrive soon to grill chicken for dinner and that Christopher would be here soon after spending the afternoon at the pool with his friends.

Gladys looked sideways at me and chuckled. "They let Black people in that pool now?"

"Yes, Gladys. What, do you think this is 1967 or something?" We smiled knowingly at each other, recalling the time she and Francine visited us after my uncle Rob died. The day after we had laid him to rest at Arlington National Cemetery, Mama, Neal, me, Gladys and Francine had walked together to our neighborhood pool and tennis park and were stopped before we ever got inside the entrance gate. Gladys and Francine, though they were our guests, were not allowed to accompany us because of the color of their skin. Mama had erupted, yelling at the kid working at the gate, the pool manger, the head lifeguard and half the people present about how unconstitutional this was and that her brother had just been killed in Vietnam fighting for democracy and Jesus H. Christ, look at the hypocrisy of this situation! This was a private pool, they said. They had the right to determine who came in and who did not. Gladys told Mama and everyone within earshot that she had no interest in dipping even one of her "beautiful black toes in that pool." Instead, she convinced Mama that they should go to the store and purchase one. Within hours, Gladys and Mama had erected and filled a large wading pool in the backyard. I remember that they had spread towels on the grass and sipped cocktails while we kids splashed happily. "Can't do this at that damn community pool," Gladys had said, raising a toast to Mama.

Gladys seemed lost in memories. "We sure had times together." Suddenly her face crumpled. "I cannot believe this is happening to her. I feel so bad! How could I let so much time go by without seeing her? My God! How can she be dying? How can she be leaving this world?" She let out a sob and took a long drink of the beer, tilting her head back, wet tears running down her face. I was a bit alarmed at her emotion. Where was my tower of strength?

"I know. It's hard to believe. I can't imagine the world without her."

We sat in silence then Gladys said, "How's it been for you? Awful, right?"

I nodded. "Well, it's been hard because Mama won't accept that this is the end. What I mean is, I think she always thought she had more time to take care of *things*."

Gladys nodded. "I'm no nurse but I can tell she's not got much time left. I'm glad I got here when I did."

"I'm so glad you're here." I hesitated then said, "Gladys, I've been trying and trying to get Mama to talk to me before . . . well, you know, before she . . . goes." I lowered my voice when I said this.

Gladys tilted her head to the side and look at me like she did the day JFK died. "About your dad, right?"

"Yes. I've tried and tried to get her to talk about him, all my life, as you know, but since she was diagnosed, I've tried whenever I've had a chance, but she gets so mad and won't. Do you know I've never heard her say his name? In my whole life?" I waited while she considered this. "I just want her to tell me about him. If she does, that means that in a way, she forgives him. I think it will help her. I think it will bring her peace."

Gladys nodded but one of her eyebrows arched like a truth detector. I shifted a bit uncomfortably, fear growing that she would not agree to help me. She said, "You know Laney Mae, I agree she needs to forgive Gil." I sighed and felt grateful tears welling in my eyes. Then she said, "But I know it's not just *her* peace you are concerned about. I know that you need peace, too. And to get that, well, *you* also need to forgive *her*."

I recoiled, nearly spilling wine on myself. "What do you mean? *Me*? Forgive *her*?"

"Yes, forgive her for not being able to forgive him."

I shook my head. "That doesn't make sense!"

"Think about it."

"Gladys, all I'm asking is that you encourage her talk to me before it's too late."

"And I will, Laney Mae. I'll speak to her and see if we can get her to talk this evening. I've always thought she should. I didn't know your daddy that well. I lived in Delaware most of those years including when he died." She grew solemn and she looked down at the floor. I knew she was thinking about her baby son and that awful time.

Unexpectedly, Mama's creaky voice said, "What . . . are . . . you two . . . talking about?"

Without missing a beat, Gladys turned to her and said, "About how ornery you are."

Mama grinned and looked from Gladys to me. Surprising us both she said, "I'd like a beer."

I jumped up happily. "One beer coming up!"

This was going exactly as I hoped.

❦

AFTER DINNER, NEAL AND GLADYS HELPED MAMA OUT ON TO THE patio. This was one of her favorite places. Due to her illness and the heat and humidity, she had not had the chance to sit outside for many days. Now, in the early evening of that first day of September, it was refreshingly cooler, and we all reveled in this fact though we could not help but notice that a breeze had picked up and ominous clouds were making their way toward us.

We were in for a storm.

The patio was a rectangle patchwork of flagstones that Mama had installed as a gift to herself after she retired from the Pentagon. It had become a pet project and she had been involved with every aspect from the layout of the patio and the selection of the stones to the purchase of a matching patio set complete with coordinating cushions, an umbrella table with four chairs, two roomy lounge chairs and a comfortable chaise.

Directly in front of the patio was an oval-shaped fish pond that was about eight feet wide. This had been my pet project. I had begged Mama to allow me (with Neal's help) to install it two years earlier after Phil had left and Christopher and I had moved in to the dreary apartment where we had no such thing as our own backyard. The pond was bordered by carefully-placed rocks sitting obediently along the perimeter. It was stocked with assorted floating plants, a small waterfall, a silly frog statue that squirted water and colorful goldfish. Despite Mama's regular complaints that the waterfall was too noisy, I knew she had come to enjoy the pond as much as I did.

Just beyond the pond, our gently sloping backyard lay before us, seemingly unchanged despite the decades. Although the yard was bumpy with rough patches where grass would not grow due to the shade of the trees, it provided an unexpected tranquil setting uncommon to most suburban tract homes. Tall trees, a variety of shrubs and even the rusty old swing set that Neal and I had played on and that Christopher now enjoyed, occupied the area near the back fence where I had spent many hours of my childhood.

After getting Mama and Gladys seated, Neal and I returned inside to finish cleaning up the kitchen while Christopher agreed to carry Mother out into the yard to allow the dog to stretch its legs and do its business. I was headed back outside to the patio with another beer for Gladys, a fresh glass of wine for myself and a plastic cup with a little beer for Mama when I stopped at the screen door to listen, silent and unnoticed. I strained to hear what Gladys was saying then suddenly heard Mama let out a mournful sob. She wailed, "This . . . is the . . . last time . . . I'll be on my . . . patio! It's the . . . last time . . . I'll ever . . . sit out here with my family . . . my dog . . . with you!" She turned her face to Gladys and raised her shaking hands to cover her face.

Gladys leaned closer to Mama and laid a hand on her shoulder. "Now you listen to me Faye. That's *not* true! In the next life, you'll be able to go *wherever* you want and *do* whatever you want and *see* whatever you want to see."

Mama sniffed a few times then said, "I . . . pray . . . you're . . . right."

"Well, sure I'm right!" Gladys exclaimed with a reassuring grin and confidence. But with sudden seriousness her smile fell away. She said, "But *not* if your soul is weighed down, Faye. Not if your soul is weighed down heavy." She leaned closer to Mama. "Do you understand what I'm saying Faye? Your soul is heavy right now. And that's not good."

Mama let her hands drop from her face to her lap. She struggled to sit straighter, she seemed instantly more alert "What?"

Gladys made her eyes wide and she gave Mama a knowing look. "Faye, you know what I'm talking about. You need to talk to Laney Mae about her daddy."

My heart fluttered with hope, but before Mama could respond the moment was interrupted when Christopher ran up from the yard carrying Mother, telling Mama and Gladys what a good a dog she was and how she had done all her business and gotten the ball twice too. "She can't hear, but she can still see," he remarked happily.

This was followed by Neal coming up behind me from the kitchen. "Why are you just standing here in the door?" He pushed past me and went out to the patio. He pulled a couple of chairs closer to Mama and Gladys and motioned for me to join them. I handed Gladys her beer and stared at her with wide eyes. She gave me only a slight, uncertain shrug. Mama's head was tilted down, her chin resting on her chest. She appeared to be staring at one of the flagstones. I sat down with my glass of wine and held onto the cup with a few sips of beer for Mama. Dreading the silence, I decided to take us all down Memory Lane. "Mama, what year did we move here?"

She raised her head slowly and eyed me suspiciously. "Nineteen-sixty-two. You . . . know . . . that."

"Well, I don't remember it. I was only two."

Gladys said, "I can't believe it's almost forty years ago since you left West Virginia."

Mama grinned. "The . . . neighbors . . . remember . . . us hillbillies moving into . . . their . . . neighborhood."

Neal laughed. "We sure caused a stir! I can remember all the names they called us, won't repeat some of them. Folks were pretty mean to us. Hillbillies get no respect!" He chuckled.

Gladys playfully arched her eyebrows and deadpanned, "Try being a Black Hillbilly."

Neal, who was taking a sip of beer, laughed so hard it sprayed from his mouth. He said, "No thanks, Gladys. Being a White hillbilly is bad enough!"

Mama laughed, a sound I had not heard for days. "Oh they . . . didn't like you Gladys . . . visiting here in their White neighborhood . . . not one bit!"

Christopher had been listening as he sat on the patio next to Mother. "What are you guys talking about?"

Neal said, "How some people treat others bad because of where they came from or because of their skin color. People were mean."

"Were?" Gladys arched an eyebrow, frowning. "Still are." Neal nodded sadly and tilted his beer toward her in agreement.

Christopher said, "I don't get it. What does it matter if you're Black or White or something else? I'm not *White*."

Gladys chuckled. "You're not?"

Mama said, "Christopher . . . some . . . are White like us . . . and some have darker skin–"

"No, Grandma," he cut her off, turning to face her. He held his

127

arm up for us all to see. "No, my skin is not white. Paper is white. Clouds are white. I'm–" he considered his skin, rotating his arm as if modeling a wristwatch. "I'm peach!" He grinned at us, and we gawked at him as we contemplated his matter-of-fact assessment of race.

Gladys said, "Well, you know what Christopher? I never really thought about it like that but, now that I look at you more closely, I think you're right: you are more peach than white."

My son nodded and with the most eloquent simplicity he said, "We're all colored, Gladys."

We adults eyed each other and, for a moment, were silent. Mama shifted her eyes to Neal and I saw something pass between them. Images of Art flashed in my brain along with Francine's face. She had been Neal's first and only love but race and all the pressures to not marry from family and society proved too great an obstacle for them. It wore them down and apart. I looked at my brother and my heart ached for him as I considered how different all of our lives would have been. If only the color of one's skin had been viewed as something unique and beautiful: each person's color part of the biggest box of crayons ever assembled and each as loved and respected as the other.

Neal rose. "And with that philosophical statement . . ." he paused, unable to continue and I was surprised to see that he was close to tears. He cast his eyes down and swallowed over a lump in his throat. He gave his body a shake to settle his emotions. Recovered, he looked up at us. "I have to get going. I got to be at work early, but I'll be back tomorrow afternoon. I'm taking half a day off." He leaned over Mama and kissed the top of her head, murmuring that he loved her and turned to lean over and kiss Gladys on the cheek. They held each other's eyes. Did I see sadness and regret silently conveyed? My brother turned and ruffled Christopher's hair, promising to play video games the next day.

"No, Uncle Neal! Don't go!" Christopher cried, suddenly upset. "Stay! Let's play some video games. Please!"

"Tomorrow. I promise," Neal said. He began to walk away, but Christopher grabbed his arm. He was near tears. "Please! I don't want you to go!" He used both hands to hold Neal's arm.

Neal knelt down to be eye-level. "Chris, I'll be here all afternoon tomorrow, okay? Now come on, I got to go."

My dejected son turned away, folding his arms across his chest.

"Christopher, go on and play your games now and practice," I said as brightly as I could. I downed the last of my wine and sat the glass beneath my chair on the patio. "You can play an extra hour tonight!" This seemed to ease my son's disappointment. He spun around and gave Neal a quick hug and ran into the house, the screen door slamming. Neal shook his head and gave me a sad look. He turned to walk through the yard and leave by the side gate.

I turned back to Mama and Gladys, at last alone and was suddenly aware that I was running out of time. It was nearly seven o'clock. I knew the health aide would arrive soon and it would be time for Mama's Morphine and Ativan and then the battle to get her into the dreaded hospital bed. I looked at Gladys expectantly but before she could speak and try to guide the conversation to the topic of my father, Mama spoke. "That boy . . . needs his . . . father."

The irony of her words insisting a child needed a father caused me to sputter and my anger, suppressed like a caged beast and fueled by wine, filled my chest with a suddenness that shocked me. I bolted from my chair, dropping the plastic cup with Mama's beer. I struggled to keep the rage from my voice. "He *has* a father. He just doesn't get to see him very often."

Mama rolled her eyes and scoffed. I looked to Gladys who shook her head in uncertainty. A clap of thunder in the distance startled us. The dark clouds had moved closer. I stepped over to stand in front of Mama and looked down at her, deciding in that instant that all was hopeless anyway and that I may as well go for broke. "And you know what Mama," I hissed. "I would have preferred a *sometime* father to no father at all." The wind around us picked up, swirling dead Crape Myrtle blossoms into a mini cyclone above the patio and blew the plastic cup around, the beer seeping onto the flagstones. Dandy stood behind Mama motioning for me to stop. *Take it easy, now. Don't push her buttons! You don't wanna get her all worked up.*

Mama tilted her head back and glared at me. "Don't you do it . . . Don't . . . bring him . . . up. You not having . . . a father was . . . his fault, not . . . mine!"

"His fault? You are blaming *him*? For dying?" I railed. "Really? I have never understood how you could you just wipe him away, like dirt on your hands! Why won't you talk to me about him? He was *my father*. You just erased him as though he never existed. I want to know about him from *you*! I want to see his face. Is there a photo of him somewhere? Tell me!"

Gladys tried to intervene, "Now, Laney Mae, let's take it easy—" but I ignored her.

Mama said, "You . . . are . . . obsessed about . . . a man who . . . cheated . . . on me!" She raised her thin arm and pointed her bony index finger at me, her voice rising over wind. "Think of all the time . . . you have wasted on him! If . . . you had spent . . . half that time . . . paying attention to . . . your . . . husband . . . he'd still be here!"

Our raised voices brought Christopher from the house. He positioned his body between us while Mother the terrier went to stand beside Mama, displaying its loyalty, tail between its legs. Christopher said, "Grandma, what's wrong? Why are you yelling?" He turned to me and frowned when he noticed tears running down my face. "Mom? Why are you crying?"

Mama said, "Don't . . . worry . . . Christopher. Listen to me. I want . . . you to . . . tell Gladys . . . the names of . . . them . . . fish in the . . . pond."

Confused, he looked at me, but I could not speak as I sobbed.

"I asked . . . you . . . to do . . . something." Mama's voice was stern, and Christopher looked afraid. He could not disobey her any more than I ever could. Mama told Gladys, "You will . . . recognize . . . the names."

My son stepped to the edge of the pond and peered down at the fish. I could tell he was trying to remember all their names as my tears fell like raindrops onto the patio. Another clap of thunder made all of us jump and I cast nervous eyes to the sky.

Christopher pointed to the largest goldfish. "That is Luke. He was your oldest brother, Grandma. He died when my mom was a little girl."

Mama's face instantly softened. "Go on," she told him.

He named them all: Harold, who died in World War II. Henry who died in the mining accident. Next was a small white fish with orange spots. This was Kurt who died Korea. He pointed to a black fish she had named after Rob who perished in Vietnam. Finally, the fish named Louise. She was the sister who died at twelve of pneumonia.

"That's . . . good . . . son." Mama paused to collect herself, obviously fatigued. "Now . . . why did I . . . name them after . . . my brothers . . . and my sister?"

"Because they were special to you?"

"That's right," Mama said, struggling to raise her body straighter in the chair. "Unlike . . . *some* people . . . they are . . . worth remembering."

I groaned and cried, "Who are you to decide that? For God's sake! Who are you to decide who is and isn't worth remembering?" As if on cue, a bright lightning lit up the sky. Frightened, Christopher rushed over to me and wrapped his arms around my waist.

Gladys had had enough. "Stop this! Both of you! We got to get inside!" She rose and stepped over to Mama then looked over at me for help to lift her out of the chair, up the stairs and into the house. My body shaking, I contemplated instead fleeing down the path Neal had taken, bolting out the gate and never, ever returning.

At that moment the screen door opened, and a young man appeared. He smiled and gave a quick wave. "Well, hello there! I'm Dennis. Your aide tonight. I hope you don't mind but I let myself in when no one answered. The front door was unlocked." He bounded down the steps to the patio, keeping a smile frozen on his face even as he nervously observed me crying, Christopher clinging to me, Mama hunched over in the chair, her breathing struggled, and Gladys wringing her hands. With forced cheerfulness he bent over Mama and said, "Ms. Faye? Let's get you inside and ready for bed. Time for meds, right? How about a little oxygen?" He looked up at me with wide eyes and I nodded cooperatively. We moved inside just as the rain began to fall.

◈

LATER, AFTER THE HOUSE WAS STILL AND EVERYONE WAS SETTLED, including Mama sleeping in the hospital bed, oxygen tube in her nose, Dennis beside her reading a paperback, I returned to the patio with another glass of wine and stood before the pond. The rain had passed and washed the air clean and I inhaled deeply. I retraced what had happened earlier. Despair and anger collided and simmered in my chest. Who was she to decide my father was not worth remembering? Why was she, so close to death, so unforgiving? I admitted to myself that I understood the pain my mother had expressed over a husband who had been unfaithful, but my empathy ended there. My father had paid for his "crime," but I was the one suffering. I would never allow Christopher to suffer in such a way, I told myself, no matter what Phil had done.

Dandy was beside me. He asked, *do you remember what happened to that first batch of fish?* I nodded. The first batch had died. The original Luke, Harold, Henry, Kurt, Rob and Louise had not survived when the pond surface had frozen over that first winter. Mama had discovered them in awful stillness beneath the ice. She knew the fish needed an air hole and she went into action. She ran back into the house and found the hammer, the same hammer she used to hang JFK's portrait. Returning to the pond, she desperately whacked the surface repeatedly trying to open an air hole which, we learned later, was exactly the wrong thing to do. The shock waves from Mama's futile pounding killed all the fish. They were suspended in terror, unable to surface. Louise was partially trapped in the ice and could not move. By the time I got there, expecting to find the house burned down after my mother had phoned me to "Come over here! Now! Oh God, it's awful," I discovered her, in her bathrobe, kneeling by the pond, the hammer next to her, sobbing and shivering in the cold. She insisted that we remove all the little fish bodies and bury them in the yard; the dearly departed fish, worth remembering.

Before the next winter, I had purchased a floating de-icer and this second batch of fish survived but a hard lesson had to be learned and a loss endured. Thinking about this as I sipped my wine, I realized how typical Mama's actions had been that morning. Dandy agreed, *your mother's first reaction to any problem was always to come out swinging or, as was the case with them little pond fish, hammering.* He was right. Mama hammered me about my divorce and other failings; she pounded Neal about never having found a spouse and never having children; and when my father died that night with the other woman, Mama had, without pause, pounded his memory away. Losing his life wasn't enough. His crime documented before her eyes, my mother's choice of punishment was to erase him, to figuratively pound his very existence shut in the coffin in which he was buried. And now I knew why: if Gil Martin hadn't existed, if no trace of him remained, if his children forgot him or couldn't remember him and carried only his last name, if no one ever spoke of him again as the person he was, then the pain couldn't exist either.

But I knew Mama had miscalculated. So did Dandy. *She could pound and pound away and think she had nailed the pain shut but those nails? Well, nails like that have a way of popping off, allowing what's buried deep, to come out.* I nodded, downed the remainder of my wine and went back inside.

CHAPTER 10

L ooking at photos of myself between the age of three and eight saddens me. An aura of fear haunts my little face. In many photos, I clutch my hands tightly together in worry, (no doubt I was wringing them the way I always did and often still do). In nearly every photograph (except for school portraits), I am frowning and looking away from the camera, eyes cast to my right or to my left. In a few, I have turned my head around just as the camera snaps as if to see if someone was lurking behind me.

That was because someone was, and her name was Betty Jean Clarke.

The woman who would become my source of torment entered our lives the week after JFK was assassinated which was appropriate given the gloomy pall that had befallen our home and our country. When several babysitters hadn't worked out and experiences at different nursery schools left me bewildered and Neal alone at home after school, Mama ran a classified ad in the local paper searching for someone she hoped would be like Mary Poppins. A more complete opposite of Miss Poppins could not have been found but nonetheless, Mama hired Betty Jean Clarke on the spot. A short, slightly overweight woman with pale doughy skin the color of an eggshell, she epitomized the word bland. She wore the same thing every day: a tight gray shirtdress over which she would tie a white apron around her waist. Below her fleshy ankles she wore what looked like men's work shoes. These had soft soles that were sound-less and allowed her to creep up on me which she often did. She wore her dull black hair, streaked with gray, pulled back into a tight bun. Her face was round and the harsh red lipstick on her mouth did nothing to brighten her appearance. Even the gold crucifix she wore failed to soften any of her hard edge.

Although Mrs. Clarke was ten years Mama's senior (and looked even older), they discovered they were both widows and seemed compatible from the start. Mama was won over by how Mrs. Clarke spoke during her interview for the position. "Madam, it will be a privilege to work for you and care for these adorable children." Mama was sufficiently buttered-up, but I sensed danger from the moment I encountered Mrs. Clarke and had clung to Mama's arm during the interview until she became annoyed and peeled me off. Neal was also leery. After Mrs. Clarke left my brother said our new babysitter smelled too perfume-y, like she was covering up a stink and, he noted, she didn't smile with her eyes. Mama told Neal to keep his opinions to himself.

And so it was arranged that Mrs. Clarke would come to our house Monday through Friday and provide housekeeping, food preparation and childcare. She lived less than ten minutes away and would arrive before Mama left for the Pentagon and would depart each evening when she returned, leaving dinner ready. From the start, she impressed Mama with her reliability and her prowess at running a smooth household which she did by utilizing a most effec-tive tool: fear. But Mama did not know this. It was Mrs. Clarke's little operational secret. Everything was spic-and-span (or I felt the sting of a pinch on my ear). Everything had its place (or I was strapped to a chair with a belt to restrain me from making a mess). Toys were to be picked up (or they vanished). My clothes were to be kept neat and I was to endure her brushing my long hair into a pony tail no matter how tangled it was nor how roughly she yanked the brush (or I felt the smack of the back of the brush on my butt). Every bite of food was eaten (or I sat at the table for hours until it was). These things occurred mostly while Neal was a school and she had me to herself. Her tactics included shoving me, slapping my body (never my face) or pulling my hair until my eyes watered.

By the end of the first week, I had learned to be quiet, obey her without question and stay out of her way. I often escaped by crawling up on the couch to sit beside JFK where I would cower and whisper to him about how awful she was and beg him to help me. At first, my sitting next to JFK's portrait and talking to myself greatly annoyed her. She told me what a terrible man he had been, called him awful names and said November 22, 1963 was the happiest day of her life. But soon she didn't mind as it kept me occupied and out of her way.

Neal offered me some comfort and protection when he was home. Although Mrs. Clarke was hard on Neal and subjected him to ridicule ("Hillbilly boy" was her favorite nickname for him), I was the one she delighted in torturing.

In those early days of Betty Jean Clarke's rule, I tried to tell Mama how mean she was. I cried when Mama left in the morning, clinging to her and ran to her with relief when she returned each evening. If Mama was even a few minutes late, I would panic and stare out the big front window, wringing my hands until she pulled into the driveway. But Mama said I was being too clingy and had to give Mrs. Clarke a chance. Was I behaving nicely, she asked? What had I done to upset Mrs. Clarke? Why wasn't I a good girl? After all, Mrs. Clarke was *so* polite, and *so* professional. What was the matter with me? It was only for a few hours a day, she told me when I complained, lip trembling, eyes filling. "Don't turn on the waterworks!"

As bad as it was, it would get worse for into her arsenal, Betty Jean King would add a new weapon: blackmail.

❦

IN THE SUMMER OF 1966 WHEN I WAS SIX AND NEAL WAS ELEVEN, Aunt Harrie came to stay with us for two weeks to attend the special summer school program in Arlington that Mama had arranged. Each weekday morning, she and Mama would rise early, have a quick breakfast, and depart, two sisters off on their daily adventure. Mama would drop Harrie off at the school on her way to work and pick her up at the end of the day on her way home. Harrie loved going to school. It made her feel important and gave her a sense of belonging. One day when they returned home, Harrie came through the door carrying a huge rag doll, as big as I was, telling me she had made it just for me. I squealed with delight. The doll was Raggedy-Anne style with a fabric body and floral dress. Its head was adorned with stringy brown yarn for hair to match mine. Its face had been crafted with colorful thread embroidered in an imperfect manner so that one of its eyes laid crooked, next to the nose. Its smile was jack-o-lantern-like and jagged, but the overall expression was silly and sweet. I loved it instantly.

"What you gonna name her?" Neal asked.

Mama said, "Why don't you call it "MeMe" since it's a little you-you?" We all laughed and agreed "MeMe" was the perfect name. From the corner of my eye, I saw Mrs. Clarke watching us, arms folded across her chest, her red lips curled into an insincere smile. Somehow my life-size doll, made with love by my aunt, emboldened me and I sneered at Mrs. Clarke, tempted to stick out my tongue, but wisely decided not to. After hugging Harrie, I announced that I was going to introduce MeMe to my other toys and I headed upstairs to my bedroom, dragging my doll behind me. Like JFK, and then Dandy later, MeMe would become a confidant. She became a constant companion and my mute witness the atrocities of Betty Jean Clarke. And one dreadful day, MeMe would be given up in a most unholy sacrifice and lay down her fluffy life for me.

❧

A FEW WEEKS AFTER HARRIE HAD RETURNED TO SECOND CHANCE, the front door opened and in walked my uncle Rob, Mama's youngest brother, yelling "How-Dee!" He was surprising us with a visit before his deployment to Vietnam where, in less than a year, he would give his life for his country. Mama was at work. School had not yet started so Neal was home. Rob strode into the living room with a large duffle bag, dumped it on the floor and dropped to a knee, throwing his arms open wide as Neal and I rushed forward to greet him. I clung to him and he lifted me off the ground and twirled me around. As he did, I saw Mrs. Clarke's cheerless face with each rotation. She lurked near the kitchen but instead of my usual apprehension, I felt happy and brave in the protective arms of my dashing uncle.

"And you *are?*" she asked, frowning at Rob.

"Well, howdy there, you must be Mrs. Clarke." Rob stepped over to her, carrying me on his hip. "I'm Robert Hartman. Call me Rob. I'm Faye's brother. I'm surprising her with a visit. She never mentioned me? I'm the handsome one!" He laughed and winked at her and held out his hand. Mrs. Clarke frowned, then reluctantly took his hand, her red lips curling down with distaste. She pulled her hand away quickly and wiped it on the front of her apron as though she had just touched something dirty.

Rob arched an eyebrow and smirked at her, "Something wrong?"

Betty Jean Clarke scowled but said nothing.

Rob said, "Lady, you just shook hands with one of Uncle Sam's fighting soldiers. Nothing you need to wipe off of me!" He put me down, but I held onto him, clutching his waist. Rob continued, "Yep! On my way to Nam, oh yes, I am! Lord knows, I don't really want to go but it's either waste away in Chance or head to glory in Vietnam. You know?"

Mrs. Clarke raised an eyebrow and muttered, "Now I know why we're losing."

Rob's face changed. His cheeks reddened. He moved closer to her and leaned in so far that his face nearly touched hers. I hoped he would hit her. Silent for a moment but breathing heavily, he said, "That's not a very nice thing to say, now, is it?"

Neal and I looked at each other each hoping our uncle would put this awful woman in her place. Instead, Mrs. Clarke stepped back, seeming to be at an unusual loss for words. Rob stepped toward her again and said with mock seriousness, "So, I got one question for you lady." The tension rose. He paused for effect then said, "Anything to eat in this house?" He howled and scooped me back into his arms, twirling and singing the little jingle he composed, "Going to Nam, oh yes, I am! Going to Nam oh yes, I am!" Mrs. Clarke grunted, turned on her heel and retreated to the kitchen.

⚜

LATER THAT AFTERNOON, ROB APPEARED IN THE DOORWAY OF OUR bedroom. "I got a little surprise for you two," he told us, dropping his duffle bag into the middle of the room. He opened it and pulled out a handful record albums.

"What albums you got Uncle Rob?" Neal asked, scooting closer.

"These are special ones." He looked from Neal to me and

winked. "They belonged to your daddy." My brother and I gasped, and I clapped my hands together in delight. We stared at six record albums laying on the round braided run on the floor as though they were treasure from a sunken ship. Before us lay Elvis Presley's "Blue Hawaii," "Johnny Horton's Greatest Hits," "Hank Williams Memorial Album," "Sinatra and Swingin' Brass," "Meet the Mills Brothers," and Bing Crosby's "Going My Way."

Neal was ecstatic. "Daddy's? Really?! Where did you get them? I thought Mama threw all his stuff out."

"Harrie had 'em. I guess she got 'em after your daddy died. Maybe Faye gave 'em to her. Or maybe Harrie just took 'em figuring Faye didn't want 'em anymore. But don't worry, Harrie won't miss these. She's got other records; she's always collecting stuff!" He chuckled but then grew serious. "Now listen, don't tell Harrie, okay? I just felt like since they were your daddy's, you two ought to have a few of them."

Neal frowned and shook his head. "We better not let Mama know we got these either. She'll be really mad and throw them away!"

"You got that right Neal! Keep 'em out of sight and don't play 'em when she's around or she'll take 'em and throw 'em away and be mad as heck at me!"

"I wanna play Daddy's albums now!" I said, picking the album with a smiling man with curly golden-brown hair on its cover. "Is this Daddy?" I asked, confused.

Rob laughed. "Ah, heck no, Laney Mae. That's good 'ol Johnny Horton. May his soul rest in peace." Rob picked up "Going My Way" and told us it contained our daddy's favorite song. He slid the album out and nodded to Neal to move his portable record player closer. I rose up to my knees and held my hands prayer-like with anticipation. Carefully, Rob placed the record on the turntable and set the needle on the album. The deep baritone of Bing Crosby began to sing about swinging on a star, mules, fish, monkeys, and moonbeams in a jar.

Neal grinned, "I remember Daddy singing this all the time!" We listened to it a few more times along with tracks from the other albums. But when Uncle Rob placed the needle on to the haunting "Whispering Pines" by Johnny Horton, I was mesmerized. I could imagine Mama playing the woeful song about a love that was gone forever. Sighing, Neal said, "I remember Mama playing this all the time when Daddy would go on one of his business trips. She must have known one day he wouldn't come back."

Rob nodded, "Sometimes I still can't believe 'ol Gil is gone." We sat silently for a moment then Rob added, "I'm just glad you have these now. Take good care of 'em."

The song ended, and Rob lifted the stylus off the record when, unexpectedly, the bedroom door swung open and Mrs. Clarke stood before us, frowning. "What's going on in here?"

Slightly rattled, Rob stood and tried to act cool. "We're just listening to records."

She looked intrigued and came into the room. She bent over and picked up two of the albums and sneered. I cringed. I did not want her touching anything as special as something that belonged to my daddy. "Where did these come from?"

Neal jumped up. "My uncle brought them. They were–" He clamped his hand over his mouth.

"Were what?" Mrs. Clarke raised an eyebrow. She smiled wickedly. "Oh, for Heaven's sake Neal. I already know. I heard you all talking. You can't keep things from me! They're albums that belonged to your father that you don't want your mother to know you have." She waited. "Isn't that right?"

I began to wring my hands. Rob leaned toward her, "You were listening to us outside that door? That's eavesdropping." She said nothing but offered him a smile of satisfaction, her red lips curling up. He stomped his foot. "Now listen here! I brought the kids these albums and it's none of your business. This is a family matter so you can just keep quiet about them. You hear? These are all they have left of their daddy. No need to mention it to my sister, okay? It would just upset her." He paused. "Please?"

Mrs. Clarke eyed him coldly. She looked down at me, still sitting on the floor then shifted her gaze to Neal. She made her face appear sad in false sympathy and she made a tut-tut sound. With an exaggerated sigh she said, "Well, now that you've explained, I see it really is none of my concern, is it?" She smiled at Rob, revealing yellowish teeth, the top front ones smeared with red lipstick.

Rob no longer smiled but his face showed, relief. "Thank you for being understanding."

Neal and I looked nervously at each other. I had been holding my breath and at last exhaled in relief. But Mrs. Clarke was not finished yet. "Laney Mae, my dear," she said, turning her full attention to me. "What did I say would happen the next time you didn't flush the toilet?"

My eyes grew wide. I bowed my head, "I'm sorry, I forgot."

"What did I say would happen, *dear*?"

"You said I would have to scrub it clean."

Rob interrupted. "Oh come on! Really? My six-year-old sweet little niece forgot to flush, and you are going to punish her?"

Mrs. Clarke turned from me to glare Rob. "Stay out of this," she hissed at him. "I will not let some hillbilly tell *me* how to discipline these children."

Rob's mouth fell open. "What'd you call me?"

"You heard me."

"Why you mean old—" But he stopped. He pursed his lips together and looked down at the albums and back at Mrs. Clarke. I could see he was calculating the cost and benefit of appeasing this awful woman. "Okay Laney Mae. If that's the rule, then come on. Let's go get scrubbing. I'll help you."

Mrs. Clarke held up her hand. "No, she'll do it. Alone."

Pouting, I followed Mrs. Clarke downstairs, flushed the toilet, sprinkled Comet in and scrubbed to her satisfaction, eager to return upstairs to listen to my father's record albums then find the most perfect hiding spot for them that I could.

❧

WHEN I RETURNED TO OUR ROOM, NEAL WAS LISTENING TO THE records, but Uncle Rob was not there. Assuming he was downstairs unpacking in the guest bedroom, I lowered myself to the floor and laid on my belly, my head resting in my hands as I listened to the music. We sat there like that lost in the songs, thinking about the last time our daddy had played the albums. I gently traced my fingers over the covers happily imagining my hands touching them as his hands had.

Suddenly, Uncle Rob burst in the room, grinning ear-to-ear. "Well, I got us a plan!" He rubbed his hands together and laughed.

"Plan for what?" Neal asked, sitting up, turning the volume down on the record player.

"To hopefully get that old battle-axe fired," Uncle Rob said. "Here's what we're gonna do." He told us that he had been doing reconnaissance like a good Army man and discovered that Mrs. Clarke was pulling clean clothes out of the washer into the laundry basket and heading outside to the backyard to hang them on the clothesline. "What do you say we give the old grump a scare?"

"How?" Neal asked.

Uncle Rob chuckled. "You'll see. Now hide those albums where your mama won't find 'em and come with me." He started to leave the room then turned and pointed at MeMe laying on my bunk bed. "And Laney Mae? Bring your big doll. Hurry up!"

We giggled with anticipation and followed our uncle down the hall into Mama's bedroom; by now, we would have followed him to Vietnam. Once in the room, Rob dropped to his knees and motioned for us to do the same. Together we crawled over to the window that faced the backyard. From there, the three of us peered over the windowsill where we saw Mrs. Clarke below, hanging laundry on the clothesline.

"Now Laney Mae," Uncle Rob said in a low voice. "Take off the shirt and shorts you're wearing." Though confused, I decided that I would do anything my wonderful uncle told me to do. I took off my top and my red shorts and handed them to Rob who quickly took MeMe's dress off and put on my shorts and top instead. I watched him, in my undies and t-shirt, mystified.

"Okay, now listen," Rob told us. "I'm gonna open that window up really quiet. Then, when I count to three, I'm gonna toss MeMe out and when I do, Laney Mae you scream really loud, and I mean really loud, okay? Like you would if you were really falling out of this window!"

My mouth dropped open. "But Uncle Rob, I don't want MeMe to get hurt." I trembled at the thought of anything happening to my doll.

"Ah honey, no! Don't worry! Old MeMe here is made of fluff. She'll be just fine!"

Neal covered his mouth, laughing. "Mrs. Clarke is gonna pee her pants when she sees that doll come flying out of the window thinking it's Laney Mae!" He rolled onto his back and cackled, cupping his hand over his mouth.

Uncle Rob arched his eyebrows. "Yeah, pee her pants or—" he said, taking the doll in his hands. "Have a heart attack!"

Neal stopped laughing. He sat up, a look of worry on his face. "Uncle Rob, I don't think we should kill her. We'll go to jail!"

Rob laughed. "Oh hell, Neal. It won't kill her. You all aren't *that* lucky. She'll get spooked is all. We'll have a good laugh and maybe she'll be upset enough to quit!"

"We're gonna get in big trouble," Neal moaned. I looked worriedly from my brother to Rob.

Rob said, "Well, guess what, Neal? Who cares? Don't you worry. I'll take the blame. Hell, I'm going to Vietnam. What's Faye gonna do to me that's worse than that?"

"Okay," Neal said. "Let's do it. I hate that woman."

"Atta boy!" Rob stood up and quietly opened the window all the time watching to make sure Mrs. Clarke did not look up and spot him. Next, he slowly raised the screen. We cringed when it made a slight noise. We held our breath and waited. Below, Mrs. Clarke continued to hang laundry. Rob exhaled and crouched down. "We're set! Are you ready Laney Mae?"

I looked at Neal who gave me a thumbs-up. "Yes, I'm ready, Uncle Rob. Let's scare that battle-axe!"

Rob chuckled and began the countdown. "One." He positioned MeMe, face forward, on the ledge. "Two." He motioned me to move closer to the window. "Three!" He hurled MeMe off the ledge and on cue I leaned forward and screamed as loudly as I could. I'm proud to say it was a shrill, piercing, and high-pitched scream and I felt great satisfaction as it left my body. We watched as MeMe sailed from the window down, down, down to the ground where she landed with the softest thud.

Mrs. Clarke turned quickly at the sound of my scream. She looked up and her eyes saw a small form falling from the window. Her mouth formed a huge O. She dropped the pillowcase she was about to hang on the clothesline. Her eyes stared in horror as she saw what she believed was my little body hurling toward the ground.

Her hands fluttered up to her face and her legs buckled beneath her. She wavered a moment and then fell backward, collapsing on the ground into a large heap, completely still.

Rob gasped. "Uh-oh."

"Is she dead?" asked Neal.

Rob seemed unsure. "Nah. Bet she just fainted. Now come on, we got to get down there."

When we reached her body Rob crouched and leaned over her mouth. "She's breathing," he whispered. An idea came to him. He snapped his fingers. "Quick! Laney Mae go take the doll back inside and put your clothes back on and go and get it back in its dress." I grabbed MeMe and scampered into the house. As I left, I heard Rob ask Neal, "Where does your mama keep the liquor? Go grab me a bottle of something!"

I know from many retellings of this story that my brother's face instantly changed from fear to confusion, but he did not question our uncle. He ran into the house and carried back a bottle whiskey. Eager to see what was happening, I quickly pulled my clothes off MeMe, put them on and then tossed the doll onto the couch in the living room. I ran back outside where I knelt on the ground beside Neal, Uncle Robb and the splayed body of our babysitter.

"What are you gonna do, Uncle Rob?" Neal whispered.

Rob took the bottle and opened it. He poured almost all of it out in the grass. Next, he poured a little on to his fingertips and spread it around Mrs. Clarke's lips.

"I see what you're doing," Neal whispered, grinning. "You're gonna make Mama think she's a drunk!"

Mrs. Clarke sputtered and moaned. Her eyes fluttered slightly but did not open. Uncle Rob put the nearly empty bottle in the clothes basket, tucked beneath some of the laundry.

"Come on! Let's get out of here! Get back inside now!" he ordered.

We ran into the house and went back to the bedroom. "Let's just play a game and act like nothing happened. You hear?" Rob said. "What time does your mom get home?"

Neal looked at the clock on the nightstand. "Usually by five."

"Well, it's almost that time. You all just gotta act cool when she gets here. And besides," he said with a grin, "I'm Faye's surprise today! She'll be focused on me being here. Don't you worry."

A short time later we heard Mama coming in the door. We ran downstairs excitedly and when she saw Rob bound down the stairs, she yelped happily and hugged him, and they twirled around, laughing. "I cannot believe you are really here Robert!" she told him. "What time did you get here?"

"Oh, a little earlier today. Me and the kids were just visiting together."

"Well, let me go change then let's have super," she told him. "Maybe we can go out for ice cream after dinner!" She walked into the kitchen. "Where is Betty Jean?"

"She was outside hanging clothes," Neal told her, his voice shaking slightly. "We were upstairs. We haven't seen her in a while."

Mama walked through the kitchen to the TV room calling for Mrs. Clarke. Suddenly she shrieked, "Oh my Lord! Betty Jean is just sitting on the ground outside! She must have fallen! She's trying to get up. Rob! Help!"

Mama flew out the back door with Rob, Neal and I following. We stood over Mrs. Clarke who was awake but disoriented. She was sitting upright, teetering slightly. Her hair had fallen from the tight bun and hung about her face. She looked up in confusion at us. Mama squatted beside her and took her hand. "Betty Jean, what happened? Are you alright?" Then she suddenly stopped speaking as she caught the aroma of whiskey. "Oh! Do I smell whiskey? My Lord! Have you been drinking?"

Rob knelt down and pretended to notice something in the

laundry basket. He pulled out the bottle of whiskey and held it up. "Well, look-ey here."

Mama gasped, speechless.

Mrs. Clarke began to sputter. She looked up at us and shook her head defiantly but was at a loss for words until suddenly she pointed at me and screamed, "You! You're all right! But you fell! I saw you fall from that window!"

Mama's eyes follow Mrs. Clarke's outstretched arm and she looked from the window to me, then at Neal and then at Rob. "Why are the window and the screen open in my bedroom?"

"I was taking a little nap in there, Faye," Rob replied coolly. "It was hot, so I just opened up the window."

"Why'd you open the screen? You're letting all the damn bugs in." Mama looked back to Mrs. Clarke who struggled to get up. Rob reached to help her, but she jerked her arm away from him, scowling. She managed to stand but wobbled. "I tell you I know what I saw! I saw Laney Mae fall from *that* window. Scared me nearly to death! I fainted!" She smoothed out her dress and tried to pull her hair back into a bun.

"Mrs. Clarke, how in the world could Laney Mae have fallen from that window and be standing here now without a scratch or broken neck or anything? You are seeing things because you were drinking!"

"I most certainly was not drinking, and I don't know *how* it happened, but I'm telling you, she fell from that window!"

Mama shook her head and said, "That's enough! Let's get back in the house. I'm getting to the bottom of this!" She snapped her fingers. "Neal, carry that laundry basket in. Let's go!"

Back inside, Mama walked into the living room and suddenly stopped. There on the sofa was the MeMe doll, in all its naked glory, its dress in a crumpled ball next to it. In my rush to get back outside, I had failed to redress the doll as Uncle Rob told me to do, let alone, return it to my bedroom. Mama swung around and gave us "the look" In a low voice she demanded, "What in the world have you all been up to?"

"Shit." Rob muttered. He knew we were caught. Neal and I cowered.

Betty Jean Clarke had not caught on and continued to profess her innocence regarding drinking. She stood next to Mama imploring her to believe her. "Mrs. Martin. I cannot work for an employer who doesn't trust me. I think the time has come for me to get my things and be on my way."

Mama turned to her. "You don't need to do that Betty Jean. I'm not exactly sure what happened here today but if you say you weren't drinking, I believe you. And if you say you saw Laney Mae—or what you thought was Laney Mae—come flying out my bedroom window—" she stepped over and picked up my naked MeMe doll. "Well, I might just be inclined to believe you about that too."

Mrs. Clarke looked at my doll and her eyes grew wide. She spun around to Rob and her pale face reddened. "You! You dressed that doll up like Laney Mae and threw it out of the window, didn't you? My God! Scared me half to death."

"Yeah. Really sorry about that," Rob said. To us, clinging to him, he leaned down and whispered, "Sorry it was only *half*." We couldn't help it; we giggled.

"What did you say?" Mrs. Clarke moved toward him, but Mama stepped in between them. She told Mrs. Clarke to go home, take the next day off with pay and that we would see her Monday. Mrs. Clarke removed her apron and went to the kitchen. She returned with her pocketbook on her arm. With one last disdainful sniff toward Rob, and a terrible glare at Neal and me, she told Mama, "I'll need to think about this, Mrs. Martin. I don't know if I can work here anymore. What I ought to do is call the police!" She pointed at

Uncle Rob and said, "What he did, and those kids did, was attempted murder!"

Mama cooed, "Oh now, they didn't mean to murder you. Really. It was just a stupid prank. I'll take care of them. Nothing like this will ever happen again."

Mrs. Clarke stepped over to where I stood next to Rob and Neal. She bent down and curled her lips back into a smile. "I'm sure sweet little Laney Mae had nothing to do with this. Did you?" I stared at her, my stomach churning. Mrs. Clarke waited expectantly but I stood silent, fear racing through me. Coyly she said, "Laney Mae and I have an understanding, don't we? She knows to behave and not get Mrs. Clarke upset, don't you?" Her back to Mama, she glared at me. I could only nod meekly, terrified that at any moment she would tell Mama about Daddy's record albums now hidden under clothing in the bottom drawer of my bedroom dresser. To my great relief (and to Neal's as well) she said nothing. With a final sneer, she marched across the living room and left, slamming the door.

Mama stood simmering in front of us, muttering to herself and I suppose trying to decide the appropriate punishment for our crime. She strode over to the sofa and grabbed MeMe. Panicked, I ran over to her and took hold of MeMe's legs, trying to wrest her from Mama's grasp. "Mama, no! Please don't hurt MeMe!"

Mama ripped the doll away from me and held it high above her head, well out of my reach. "Hurt it? You threw it out the window! Say goodbye to this damn doll!"

I began to wail but Mama would not give in. Despite Uncle Rob and Neal telling her to blame them, that it had all been their idea and begging her to let me keep my doll, she refused. "We make decisions and we have to live with them, little missy! You all could have caused Mrs. Clarke to have a heart attack! You have to learn a lesson." She turned to Neal and said, "I will determine your punishment and inform you by this evening. And you . . ." she stepped up to Rob. "I don't know what I should do about you! I guess going to Vietnam is punishment enough!"

✤

LATER THAT NIGHT, I WAS NUDGED AWAKE BY UNCLE ROB. HE knelt beside my bunk and I could just make out his sad face in the dim glow of my nightlight. "Honey, I'm so sorry about your doll," he whispered so to not awaken Neal in the top bunk. "I'm gonna write to Harrie and ask her to make you a new one, okay?"

I shook my head. "No, no, no!" I sobbed. "I want *my* MeMe! Not some other doll! I want her!" I punched the mattress. He assured me Mama would cool down and return MeMe to me. He promised to talk to her before he left the next day. I reached out and rubbed his cheek, rough with beard stubble. "Please stay here, Uncle Rob. I don't want you to go away."

"Oh honey, don't worry. Everything will be okay, and I'll be back before you know it."

Even decades later, I could still hear the animal-like wail that came from my mother when she answered the phone on a Saturday afternoon in June 1967. Aunt Claudia called with the news that Rob had been killed in combat. I was in the kitchen with her putting away groceries and watched as Mama's legs collapsed and she slid down the wall to floor, clutching the handset, sobbing. "No! Please not Robert! Oh God! Oh God! No . . ." over and over. Neal and Greg had been listening to the new "Sgt. Pepper's Lonely Hearts Club Band" album in the living room. They ran to the kitchen and Neal rushed over and knelt beside Mama. She dropped the phone and grabbed him and pulled him to her and they sobbed together. I stood, frozen, wringing my hands, in tears. Greg came to me and put his arm on my shoulder in comfort. Dandy covered his face with his hands in sadness as he stood near me. The music still played on the stereo. It floated into the kitchen and ironically, "A Day in the Life" played next. We remained there as the song played, trying and failing to comprehend the news about a lucky man whose luck had run out.

⚜

MRS. CLARKE CONTINUED TO USE THE SECRET OF OUR FATHER'S record albums to coerce us into doing her bidding for another two years. Even Uncle Rob's death did not soften her cruelty; all she had to do was raise an eyebrow and give a warning look and my brother and I would surrender to every whim. The heavy burden of coercion and blackmail wore us down and simply could not be sustained and finally came to a climatic end on a hot August night in 1968.

Mama had a dinner date with Art and had asked Mrs. Clarke to stay late one evening to watch us. Neal and I rarely had to endure Mrs. Clarke past dinnertime and so we tiptoed around her like soldiers walking through a minefield. It blew up when Neal, who had become quite the young anti-war activist, and Mrs. Clarke, who saw everyone left of Barry Goldwater as a communist, got into a heated argument watching the brutal chaos unfold on TV that night outside the Democratic National Convention between protestors and the Chicago Police. The disagreement between my brother and our babysitter escalated–like the protests–and became physical–like the protests–when she grabbed my thirteen-year-old brother for saying something she deemed "smartass." She raged that Neal was communist (among other awful names) and that he needed to learn a lesson. She pushed him across the room and slammed him against the wall, her fat fingers squeezing his neck. Dandy appeared, *I do believe she is trying to choke him. Do something Laney Mae!* I ran full speed at her back and hurled my little body onto hers only to ricochet off. Regaining my bearings, I attacked again and pounded her rump with my fists and tried to tug her dress and pull her off Neal or otherwise distract her. Then, she raised her leg and kicked me hard in the stomach, causing me to release my hold on her instantly and I stood dazed, the breath knocked out me. I fell to the floor and rolled around trying to breathe. I gazed up at Dandy who murmured it would be all right. *You got the air knocked out of you is all. Now just sit up and breathe really slow like through your mouth.*

Suddenly Mama's voice rang out. "What in the world is going on here?" I was never more relieved to hear her voice. She had walked into the TV room after Art dropped her off just in time to see Mrs. Clarke plant her foot in my stomach. Neal broke free from Mrs. Clarke and ran to Mama, sobbing, "Look at my neck, Mama! She tried to strangle me!" He pulled his shoulder-length hair back and revealed the ugly red marks left there by Mrs. Clarke's claws.

Before Mama could respond, Mrs. Clarke began to bellow, "That's not true! Neal is the one who caused this, Mrs. Martin. He became violent! He was worked up watching the riots on TV! I had to defend myself!" She moved closer to Mama and said, "There are things you don't know. Things I must tell you about these children!"

Mama stared aghast at Mrs. Clarke, but my moaning needed her attention and she rushed over to help me stand. I struggled to regain my breathing, agony on my face and fear in my eyes and in that moment, Mama finally understood. I had *not* been exaggerating. This woman, this awful woman, in whom she had entrusted our care, was indeed a monster. Mama's face transformed and her expression was so fierce I thought she was going to kill Mrs. Clarke. Dandy grimaced. *Oh, that woman's in for it now! Faye's madder than a hornet!* Mama turned and charged toward Mrs. Clarke and got to within an inch of her face. Pointing a finger in the woman's face, Mama raged, "No one puts their hands—or feet—on my children! No one! I saw what you did! Now you get your things and leave this house immediately and if you don't, I'm calling the police!"

At the mention of the police, Mrs. Clarke's eyes-widened. Her eyes darted from Mama to Neal to me and I could tell she knew her reign of terror was over. Dandy said, *Well, look at that. Told you she was nothing but a bully. Picks on others to make herself feel bigger.*

And just like that, my five-year-long nightmare picked up her pocketbook, smoothed out her hair and stomped out the door never to be seen by us again. I thought it impossible that our ordeal could end so easily. But it did. *I told you, what goes around comes around,* Dandy said happily later that night as I sat in my bunk discussing the eventful evening and Mrs. Clarke's sudden departure. I nodded contentedly and drifted off into the most peaceful sleep I had had in a long time. And Daddy's albums? They stayed my and Neal's secret and Mama never knew we had them. Until over three decades later.

CHAPTER 11

G ladys took pity on me and agreed to stay one more day. Instead of leaving on Monday, which was Labor Day, she planned to get on the road early Tuesday.

Mama had become increasingly agitated, and the nighttime seemed worse, and more frightening to me. Confined to the hospital bed and mentally adrift in a steady flow of morphine and Ativan, she mostly slept but, when roused, panic sometimes seized her. More than once she tried to pull the oxygen tube from her nose and heave herself from the bed, only the bed rail keeping her from tumbling out. Watching her in these panicked states with her eyes wide in desperation and fear, I thought that she must have spotted Death lurking in the corner of the room, biding its time in the way a man might glance at his wristwatch waiting for his date to stop primping; the way I often had felt its nearness myself as I watched over her. She would become frantic, cursing and, with amazing strength, lash her arms and kick her legs, trying to propel herself from the bed so that she could run as fast and as far as her thin, weakened legs would take her. The previous evening, Gladys, the health aide, and I had to hold her down and try to calm her as I gave her more of the liquid Ativan; we were, after all, at the "as needed" stage. We held her tightly until calm overtook her.

Afterwards, Gladys took me aside and told me she'd stay but, when she did leave, she thought it best to just go without any theatrical final farewell to her best friend.

"You know she's barely aware of things going on around her and I don't think she'll notice I'm gone," she told me. "If I do some big dramatic goodbye, it will upset her and rile her up and then we'll both start crying like babies; and then what? I just go? Leave you here to handle it? No! I need to slip out quietly. That's the best way for me to leave. Once I'm gone, if she should ask for me, you can distract her, or just tell her I'm napping, or in the bathroom, or gone to the store."

"You can't do that," I replied flatly. "You need to tell her goodbye or you'll be sorry if you don't. All of our truths are out in the open now, Gladys. Pretending otherwise won't do of us any good."

My more realistic view of the situation seemed to surprise her, but the ugly scene at the fishpond convinced me that my chance to have my longed-for conversation with Mama was all but done for. Might as well face it.

Gladys stared at me in silence, her eyes wide with uncertainty and her lips pressed tightly together. *Why, she's afraid*, I thought. My superhero, my rescuer, our wise old friend, was human after all; sometimes brave, sometimes scared. Just like me. Our eyes locked as we each contemplated the other's move. Then her eyebrow arched upward, and a shrewd smile began to form. "Okay," she said, putting her hands on her hips, the plucky Gladys resurfacing, "I'll say my last goodbye to her. But you–" she lowered her chin and pointed her index finger at me, "You have to tell her you forgive her. Before she dies. That's what *you* have to do."

GLADYS HAD SAID A FINAL FAREWELL TO MAMA BEFORE SHE departed early Tuesday morning. She had quietly dressed, had coffee, and then loaded her suitcase into her car, carefully catching the screen door as she did so that its slamming did not hasten Mama's awakening. Helen had stayed overnight again, and she tiptoed about preparing to rouse Mama, change her diaper and lightly wash her before she would depart when her shift ended at seven a.m. When it came time, the three of us stepped up to the bed, with Mother the terrier keeping a careful watch. Gladys leaned over and lightly traced Mama's face with her fingertips. Mama opened her eyes. It took her a moment to focus. Gladys told Mama matter-of-factly that she had to go back home, told her that she loved her, and told her that she would see her again in the next life. Mama's eyes had widened as she absorbed this information and a tear trickled down her cheek. With one hand she reached and laid her palm against Gladys' face. She managed to say, "I . . . love . . . you . . . I will . . . see . . . you." Then, exhausted, her hand dropped to the bed. Gladys leaned over and kissed Mama ever so gently on her forehead. With that, she took one long last look at her friend, turned to face me, and pulled me into a tight embrace. "Tell her. Like we agreed. Before it's too late," she whispered in my ear.

Alone in the house for the first time in weeks, I sat beside Mama and cringed at the horrible and more frequent "death rattle" sound coming from her throat. My eyes followed the tubing in her nose down her body, over the side of the bed and across the floor to where the oxygen concentrator sat, irritatingly loud in my newfound solitude. Equally irritating was the drone of the central air conditioning running nearly constantly, as it attempted to ward off the heat and humidity, even though it was barely past ten o'clock in the morning. I sighed and considered that at least there was silence throughout the rest of the house. Christopher had happily departed for the first day of fifth grade over an hour before and so the TV stood silent in the back room. No hum of cartoon characters, no obnoxious cereal and toy commercials blaring.

Mama stirred slightly, and I rose from the chair, which caused Mother to struggle to rise from the hardwood floor beside the hospital bed. Of late, the dog always seemed to be under my feet and had nearly caused me to trip more than once. When I rose, she rose, when I sat, she would sit or lay nearby as though she did not trust me to be alone with her mistress and I had to concede a certain admiration for Mother over her distress at the current condition of her owner. The dog sensed death; of this I was certain. I took a step toward the bed and Mother lowered her head and peered with great seriousness from beneath her bushy, wire-haired eyebrows. "What?" I asked loudly, "I'm just going to step over to the bed. Is that alright with you?" The dog opened her mouth in a yawn that ended with a pathetic whine filled with human-like resignation. "Thank you, Mother," I said as I stepped past her. Mama moaned slightly and rolled her head to the side away from me, eyes closed. I took her hand and leaned in but hesitated, uncertain. *Should I just tell her I understood and forgave her, or should I wait until she was, hopefully, more alert? Would that even happen?* As I was contemplating this, she rolled her head toward me, eyes open. She moaned, "Please . . . please–"

"What Mama? What do you need?"

"Please . . . don't . . . want–" Her eyes closed.

"Don't want what?" I pleaded, but she had drifted away. Renewed disappointment filled me. I stepped back to sit on the chair and when I did, I tripped over the dog and nearly fell. "Damn it, Mother!" I snapped. Mother scuttled away, circled the chair and came to sit in front of me, lowering its head. Feeling a sharp pang of pity and unexpected tenderness, I knelt and took the dog's friendly face into my hands. "You don't understand, do you, girl?" Mother's eyes were mournful. "But you know, don't you? You know." I kissed the top of her head, and the dog seemed to relax. I returned to the chair and, once again, I focused on Mama's chest, silently willing it to rise, to give us just a little more time. Dandy leaned beside me and with great sadness said, *I hate to say it, but I do believe this will be her last day. I surely do.*

❦

THE HOME HEALTH AIDE ARRIVED AT EXACTLY SEVEN O'CLOCK AND knocked softly. I was rarely certain who, among the rotating aides, would be on the other side of the door, I was just grateful for their arrival. But now, I could not decide if I hoped for a familiar face, or a stranger to spend this night with us. I had not yet honored my agreement with Gladys to express forgiveness and understanding to Mama. I had allowed the afternoon to slip by without doing so, I knew that I needed to soon and wanted whoever was here to have some understanding of the situation.

I opened the door and found a young woman smiling warmly. I did not recognize her. I pushed the storm door open and she stepped inside. She was petite and appeared to be in her twenties, with long dark hair pulled back into a ponytail. "Ms. Martin? Good evening. I am Theresa Rodriguez. Your health aide? For this evening?" She spoke in questions with the slight trace of an accent. Light from the small overhead fixture above the entryway reflected off the gold crucifix hanging simply around her neck. I stared at it longer that I should have and thought of Betty Jean Clarke. Theresa noticed my stare and raised her hand and wrapped her fingers protectively around the small cross. Mother had lumbered over to investigate, and I waited as the woman endured Mother's inquiry. She patted the dog's head and then walked over to the hospital bed to do an initial check on Mama. I waited for her near the dining table and when she was done, motioned for her to come sit with me. I briefed her about Mama's condition, our family, the Hospice care, and how we had accepted the end was near. I also told her that I had longed to speak to my mother about something important, but that conversation had not happened and now, it appeared, it was too late despite many attempts. Without thinking, I added, intending it as sarcasm, "The only thing I haven't tried is *not* giving her the medication to keep her awake and less groggy so she can talk to me."

My attempt at dark humor did not go over well. Theresa clutched at the gold crucifix hanging from her neck and her eyebrows furrowed together in consternation. "Oh, I don't think that is a good idea." She waved her arm in Mama's direction. "You, see? She's resting fairly well, right? Her breathing is labored but that is to be expected. The medicine is important to keep her comfortable. I would not suggest that!" She shook her head decisively and her ponytail swayed back and forth in agreement.

I laughed softly and shook my head. "Oh, no, Ms. Rodriguez, I'm not serious. I was kidding." Or was I? Truth be told, the idea *had* occurred to me days ago when I watched helplessly as Mama slipped away from me when the Ativan took hold. "I know that it wouldn't really help; she'd only get more agitated. I've pretty well accepted that she can't talk, even if she wanted to."

Theresa offered a smile to show her relief and released her grasp on the crucifix. "Well, I'm glad to hear that." She allowed a small chuckle, "What is it that you want your mother to talk to you about?"

Christopher rescued me. He came down the stairs freshly scrubbed from his bath, smelling of soap, his hair wetted down, in boxers and a t-shirt. "Mom," he announced, standing at the foot of the stairs, "I'm done with my bath."

Theresa turned to him and smiled warmly, "Well, hello there. You must be Christopher. Your mom told me about you."

Christopher turned from me to regard her. I knew that he had gotten used to having strangers in the house, people who talked in hushed voices and smiled at him with eyes that were sad. He looked at this newest face and nodded shyly. Then he stepped over to me and wrapped his arms around me. He turned his head toward Theresa and eyed her with an expression of resignation over not just her presence, but the circumstances that required her to be here. When another moment passed, he stepped away, releasing me from his embrace. "I wanna say goodnight to Grandma now."

I nodded and told Theresa, "I'll let him say goodnight then I'll go up and read to him and get him settled. Come upstairs and get me if you need me, okay? I'll be back down to give her the next dose of the meds." I winked and added, "I promise."

"Okay. I'll come get you if I need you. Don't worry."

"Help yourself to a soft drink or there's coffee or tea in the kitchen."

Christopher and I walked into the living room. Mother lay next to the hospital bed and as we got closer, the dog rose to greet us, and Christopher patted her head. Then he turned to me and took my hand, leading me away from Mama and back over to the dining table. He whispered, "Mom... is Grandma . . . is she . . . is she going to die tonight?" Tears welled in his eyes.

I said, "Honey, you know that she could die any time now."

"No!" he cried. He raised his small hands and rubbed his eyes. "I don't want her to die, Mom!" He stomped his food then grabbed me at the waist, gripping me tightly. I wrapped my arms around him and buried my face into his hair and inhaled the sweetness of his clean scent. I felt the wetness of his tears as they seeped through to my t-shirt. I lifted his face up and gently held it in my hands. "I know. I don't want her to die either."

"What if I pray? Will God let her not die?"

"God's already decided it's time for Grandma. No amount of praying is going to change His mind."

"I'm still gonna try, though."

I smiled and tapped the end of his nose with my finger. "Say your goodnight first. We'll do your reading, and then you can pray all you want."

He nodded, wiped his nose on his shirt and we returned to the bed. He reached over the rail and placed his hand lightly on her arm. I positioned myself slightly behind him, my hands resting on his shoulders. "Can she hear me?" he asked, casting a glance over his shoulder at me, his eyes wide. "Even if her eyes are closed like this and she's sleeping? I always wonder if she can hear me."

"Sure she can. Her ears still work."

He nodded, relieved. He clutched the rail with both hands and leaned over the bed. "Grandma? It's me, Christopher." He paused and seemed to struggle with what to say. "I . . . I'm . . . going to bed now. Please don't . . . I don't want you to . . ." He stopped and let out a whimper then said simply, "I'll see you in the morning. Okay?"

Mama moaned softly once, then again. Christopher looked back at me. "Did you hear that?" he said excitedly. "She made a sound! Like she heard me!" She moaned again and reached her hand out toward Christopher and he took it. "Grandma, you can hear me, can't you? I love you, Grandma."

With great effort, Mama managed to reply, "I . . . love . . . you . . . too." She pressed her dry lips together then added, "Don't you . . . ever . . . forget that." Her eyes opened, and the corners of her mouth curved upward into a smile. Then her eyelids fell, and she was still except for the awful rattling sound in her throat that rudely interrupted the moment. Christopher did not allow this to dampen his joy. He turned to me, delighted, "Mom! She smiled! And she talked!"

"It's great, honey," I told him. I squeezed his shoulders gently as

I contemplated Mama's ability to converse now, even in a limited capacity, as I considered the hours and days and nights I had sat beside her hoping for *something*. My old frustration building, I told Christopher it was time for him to go up to bed, to pick out a book and that I would be up soon. I waited until he was gone before I allowed my forced smile to fall but I did not cry. I told myself I was done crying even as I knew that was untrue. I gritted my teeth and tried to suppress the familiar return of hurt as it took hold. I stared at Mama and suddenly it seemed to me that she was already dead. A shell of flesh and bones that would soon be buried in the ground, taking with her all the answers to all the questions I had about my father. Taking with her the gentle comfort she could have provided in telling her daughter that her father had loved her; and most of all, forever withholding the generous assurance that I needed so badly to simply know that my father had been a good man and that she forgave him.

I placed my hands on the bed rail as my son had done, resisting the urge to shake the bed and scream. Ashamed, I wondered what Theresa Rodriguez would think if I shook the bed and raged. I smiled grimly and decided I did not care what she thought, or what Gladys's thought, or what my son thought, or what my brother thought. I was at last, *done*. I bowed to the acceptance of a situation I was never, ever going to win. But, forgive her? Tell her I understood? No.

I leaned over and put my mouth next to her ear. Dandy appeared on the other side of the bed. *Now don't you forget what you promised Gladys. You promised that you'd tell your mama you forgive her.* He was solemn, one of his gray eyebrows raised in appraisal. A flash of guilt coursed through me, but I shook it off and, for the first time I defied my imaginary father. Instead, I said simply, "Rest Mama." But not in peace, I thought silently; I did not dare say this aloud for it was too harsh to utter into my dying mother's ear. But not saying the words aloud made the fact no less true: my mother, bitter, stubborn, and defiant to the end, would never rest in peace. Of this I was now certain, and I must admit that I felt at least a small bit of satisfaction over this fact.

Dandy's face fell in disappointment, and he shook his head sadly.

⚜

JANE ARRIVED BEFORE NINE O'CLOCK AND EXAMINED MAMA carefully as I watched. Theresa stood nearby, ready to help. I held my breath as Jane listened to Mama's chest, her eyes avoiding mine, looking up at the ceiling then at the floor. Removing the stethoscope, she frowned then allowed her sad eyes to find mine. "She's near the end," she said. "I expect it may be tonight." She looked to Theresa. "I'm glad you're here." Theresa nodded. Jane turned her attention back to me. "And I want to tell you something that's important, Laney Mae. At some point, you're going to give her the last dose of medication, only you won't know that it's the last. But you cannot think that the medication that you give her is what causes death. Okay? I just want you to understand that it's *not*. Some people feel guilt, like they had a hand in the end by giving the meds."

"I understand."

"Good. And I'd like to make a couple of suggestions. First, get a fan and put it on a table near the bed and let it blow on her, gently. It helps with the agitation when they feel like they can't breathe."

"Okay, I have one upstairs."

"Good. And something else that I've seen others do that may help is to play music." She tilted her head in the direction of the stereo console pushed against the opposite wall. "Does that thing still work? It looks as old as me." She smiled and winked.

"Yes, it works."

"Well, play some of your mom's favorite albums. Any kind of music she liked or maybe just some classical music on the radio. My last patient was retired Army and his family played military music for him and it was amazing how it comforted him."

Dandy appeared next to me and said, *I sure would like to hear those old records you got hidden upstairs and I bet your mama would too. You know? The albums that Rob brought you kids before he went to Vietnam.* I gasped. The record albums were stashed in boxes in my old bedroom closet with items I had no room for in the apartment. I looked at Mama, coma-like, and wondered if playing them would comfort her or upset her or she was too far gone to even be aware. Would it be too late? *You'll never know unless you try,* Dandy said grinning.

Jane smiled. "I think I've given you a useful idea."

"You have." Dandy raised his eyebrows and chuckled. *Well, I'd like some credit for this.* I told Jane, "There are some old albums she hasn't heard in years."

"Well, there you go. It's time she got to hear them once more."

⌘

AFTER JANE DEPARTED, I GOT CHRISTOPHER INTO BED AND I shooed Theresa to the TV room, telling her I wanted to be alone with my mother. I had rummaged through the box in my old bedroom and found the albums safely wrapped in sheets of tissue paper, tied with ribbon. I tiptoed downstairs, hugging them to my chest, and carried them to the stereo console. I panicked when I switched the stereo on. Dandy pointed at the cord on the floor and grinned. *Would help if you plugged it in.* I selected "Whispering Pines" to play first. I lowered the stylus on to the album and stepped over to the bed. The mournful and haunting "ooooo-u-ooooo" refrain by the background singers at the song's opening floated from the stereo, enveloping Mama and me as Johnny Horton's melancholy voice began to sing. *Oh that's fine, mighty fine music* Dandy said, closing his eyes. My body tingled with sentimental memories stirred by the song, and I watched, my excitement growing, as Mama's eyelids flickered. She rolled her head toward me and suddenly her blue eyes were open wide, fully alert. I stood beside her, clutching the bedrail, and watched as her mouth moved, but no words came out. "Mama, do you remember this song?" Dandy said, *Tell her, tell her all about Rob bringing 'em.* I leaned over and spoke into her ear and told her everything. She could not keep her eyes open long but for an instant, I am certain I saw the trace of a smile forming on her mouth but then, her head slumped again to the side and she was still. I played a few songs from each of the six albums—Elvis, The Mills Brothers, Sinatra, Bing, Hank Williams and Johnny Horton—and though sometimes she would moan, or her eyes would open then close, she did not speak, or I realized with despair, she could not.

I was playing a "Cold Cold Heart" from the Hank Williams album (hoping something would melt my mother's cold, cold heart) when Christopher came down the stairs slowly, groggy with sleep, rubbing his yes. "Mom, what are you doing? Why are you playing that music? It woke me up."

"I'm sorry, honey. I didn't mean to wake you. I'm just playing some old records I thought Mama would like." I sighed, my spirit defeated, my body suddenly heavy with tiredness.

"I was just going to turn it off. You need to go back to bed. You have school tomorrow."

He stood by the hospital bed and peered at Mama. "She looks like he's having a nice dream," he said. He asked me about the fan blowing on her and I explained how Jane said it would help then he walked over to the stereo and I watched as he picked up each album and examined the covers. "These are old, aren't they?"

"Older than me."

"That's old." He grinned. "Can you tell if she likes hearing them?"

I turned to look at Mama and was contemplating how to answer when Christopher said, "Hey, what's this? This little record?"

I turned around and was startled to see what he held: an old 45 in its original sleeve "Where did you get that?" I asked, walking over to him.

"It just fell out of this," he said, holding up The Mills Brothers' album.

"Let me see that." I took the 45 from him and gasped when I saw the title, "*Daddy's Little Girl*" by The Mills Brothers. Dandy said, *Well, look at that! You ever see this before? Now I wonder how it stayed lodged inside this album cover all these years.* "I don't know how we ever missed seeing this," I said, staring at the record, dumbfounded.

"Are you gonna play it?" Christopher asked, yawning.

I nodded eagerly as I fished through a cubby in the stereo and found an adapter and placed the record on the turntable. The song began and the soothing harmony of the Mills Brothers' voices filled the room. Dandy began to sing along. I recognized the song and knew I had heard some version of it before. It was popular at weddings for the father-daughter dance. But now the words and melody wrapped around me and seemed to squeeze my heart and I stood there in a magical state of wonder at the thought that my father had played this for *me*, his little girl. My face crumpled and tears ran. How could I have overlooked the record before? What if I hadn't gotten the albums out tonight? I might never have found it and now it was worth more to me than almost any other item I owned. Christopher reached over to comfort me, placing his arm around me, "Don't cry, Mom, don't cry. It's a nice song. I bet your dad sang it to you, didn't he?"

From the hospital bed, Mama moaned loudly. We stepped over saw that her eyes were open. A single tear made its way down her face. She struggled to speak. "Mom! She's trying to talk," Christopher said. "Grandma, we're here. Do you like that song?" We watched as she raised her hand, and I grasped it tightly and for one brief moment, our eyes locked and I knew . . . *I knew* she would speak to me, *knew* she would tell me what I longed to hear, *knew* that she had found a way to forgive my father. I knew all this for sure as well as I knew she *could not* speak to me, *could not* tell me what I longed to hear and *would not* be able to verbalize forgiveness. It was too late. Though she resisted, finally her eyes closed, her head dropped to the side and her hand fell limp in mine.

I leaned over and kissed her forehead. And ever so quietly, so quietly that Christopher could not hear, I whispered into her ear that I loved her, that I was sorry about the pain I had caused her and that I forgave her and asked her to forgive me for not understanding her pain.

Then, I rose and turned away from her and walked over to the stereo. The song had ended anyway, and the stylus was stuck at the end and the little record went round-and-round silently. I lifted the needle and switched off the console. I carefully slid the 45 back into its sleeve. Dandy watched; his face forlorn. *Honey, you did the right thing. You sure did. Now you go rest.* I took Christopher's hand, and we slowly climbed upstairs and to bed where I fell asleep almost immediately.

I FELT SOMEONE SHAKING ME AND WHEN I OPENED MY EYES Theresa was standing above me, her gold crucifix dangling above my face, directly over above my nose. I sat up in the bed, alarmed.

"Has she passed?"

"No. She's calling out for you."

"What? Asking for me? Time for meds?"

"Yes, it is time, but she's asking for you, too. Please, just come! Now! She's very agitated."

Groggy, I glanced at Christopher sleeping next to me then rose and made my way downstairs to the living room to find Mama writhing, moving her head from side to side in agitation. Her hands clenching the bed sheets tightly. Her face grimaced and her eyes squeezed shut. Deep lines distorted her features. Her breathing was quite struggled. She moaned and was mumbling, but I could not make out what she was saying. I noticed Mother pacing nervously beside the hospital bed, panting, her tail down in distress. The dog stopped pacing and then rushed over to me and managed to jump up and put her front paws on my legs and then ran back to the bed as though to say, *Come here! Help her!*

Suddenly, to my amazement, Mama grabbed the bed rail and pulled herself up to a sitting position. She leaned dangerously near the edge as she tried to get out of the bed. Theresa and I rushed over to stop her. I positioned myself at the top of the bed holding her shoulders, Theresa at the bottom, grasping Mama's shins.

"Let . . . me . . . up!" Mama roared, loud and clearer than she had sounded in days. "I . . . want out . . . of this goddamn . . . bed!"

I was shocked at both how alert she seemed and how much strength she had. "No Mama! You have to stay in bed!" I managed to force her back down, but she fought me with amazing force.

"God . . . damn . . . it . . . let me up!" She thrashed and kicked. One kick from her foot hit Theresa in her stomach. I watched helpless as she crumpled over, keeping my grip on Mama's shoulders. Recovering, Theresa rose and took a firmer grasp and said, "Mrs. Martin, you cannot be kicking, okay? You need to stay in bed!"

"I . . . need . . ." Mama struggled now to talk, her voice fading.

"Need what?" I asked.

"Need . . . need . . . Laney Mae." Exhausted now, she stopped resisting.

I moved around to the side of the bed so Mama could see me. I leaned over the rail and with both hands, gently took her face to hold her head still. "Mama, it's me. I'm here. I'm *right* here."

"My mouth . . . dry."

I told Theresa to get the medicine and to call Neal. I took the oral swab in a jug of water on the table and ran it over her lips. This seemed to relieve her, and she began to move her mouth to speak. "I saw . . . do you . . . see . . . them?" Her eyes were wide, and she managed to raise her arm to point. "Mother and Pop. They're here. They want . . . me . . . to . . . come." Her arm dropped back down to the bed.

I turned but saw nothing. "You saw Grandma and Pop? Saw their spirits from Heaven?"

Mama closed her eyes and smiled. I gazed with wonder at her face and saw no fear there, no agitation. She opened her eyes again and said, "I'm not . . . afraid since . . . I saw them."

"That's good, Mama. I'm glad you're not afraid." From the shadows of the room, Theresa rushed over to stand across from me on the other side of the hospital bed. She held the medications. "What's happening?"

"She says she sees her parents, that she's not afraid."

Theresa smiled at this. She held up the droppers containing the meds. I took the eye-dropper of liquid morphine and said, "Mama, here is your medicine. It will make you feel better." I slid the dropper into her mouth. Next, Theresa handed me the Ativan. "Rest now, Mama," I said as she eased the dropper into her mouth.

Suddenly Mama's eyes opened again, and she struggled to focus. "I should . . . have . . . told you."

"What?"

Mama swallowed with difficulty, trying to speak, her breathing raspy. "Told . . . you . . . that you . . . have–" She stopped and shook her head slightly as if wanting to rephrase her words but not having the strength to do so. Her eyes opened wide; she looked confused and disoriented. I could practically see words racing through her mind, words she did not have the ability to say. She said, "Go. See." Then a look of panic showed on her face as she realized her ability to speak was ending. She pursed her lips together and tried again. "There . . . are . . ." but she could not finish. The meds were taking over.

"There are what, Mama? What are you trying to say? Go see who?"

Mama's mouth moved and she reached out, trying to touch me. Her hand found my hair. She pulled it roughly and drew me to her. Then she spoke just one word; in a whisper it floated from her mouth and hung in the air between us, a magical, one-syllable utterance.

"Gil," she said.

My father's name! My heart jumped in my chest and I could feel the rush of blood pounding in my body forced by a sudden burst of adrenaline. "Mama! You said his name! You said Daddy's name!" I rose, ignoring the pain in my scalp as I pulled my hair from Mama's grip. I looked over at Theresa, elated and cried, "She said his name! She's never said his name to me."

Theresa smiled warily but nodded encouragement.

I turned back to Mama. "What are you trying to tell me?" But she was silent, and her eyes again closed. "Mama?"

Barely audible she said, "The picture—"

"The picture? What picture? Mama! I don't understand! Is there a picture of him?" I looked at Theresa as if she could help interpret but the aide shook her head helplessly. "She's trying to tell me something! Oh, help me!"

Theresa moved around to stand next to me. I turned back to Mama and squeezed her hands and gently shook them. "Mama! Don't stop talking. Tell me what you mean."

Mama opened her eyes briefly. "Can't." Then she mumbled, "Tomorrow."

"No, Mama! Now! Please! Talk to me now!"

Her eyes closed, and her chin dropped, and her head rolled to the side. The medication had taken her back. "Don't go back to sleep, Mama! Please! Don't go back to sleep!" I began to sob.

Theresa grabbed took me by the shoulders and pulled me away from the bed. "Please! You need to stop. She can't talk anymore. Let her rest."

I stared at Mama, trying to comprehend what had happened. Dandy stood beside me. *Now, honey, it's okay. She'll talk to you tomorrow. Let her rest.*

Theresa said, "Well, at least you got to speak with her, right?" She stepped closer and put her hands on my shoulders in comfort. "You can try again tomorrow, okay? Let her rest now and maybe by morning–"

That's when I began to laugh. It was a hollow, ugly sound.

Teresa frowned, "Why are you laughing?"

I turned to face her, a tragic grin on my face. "Why? Because there's *not* going to be any tomorrow for her. She's not going to last the night. You heard the Hospice nurse! You can see her condition!" Dandy bowed his head. *Don't give up. She might have more time. No one knows.*

"You don't know that" Theresa whispered, "Wait. Just wait. And pray."

☙❧

NEAL ARRIVED ABOUT FIFTEEN MINUTES LATER. THERESA GREETED him and he rushed over to me. I had abandoned the chair and was now on the couch, clutching a throw pillow to my chest, eyes swollen from sobbing. Neal was relieved to discover that Mama had not died. He stood near the bed, but I would not look directly at him. "You okay? The aide made it sound like Mama was passing when she called me."

I shrugged. I had nothing more to say. What was the point? Death was here with us. I wondered why my brother did not notice it hovering so closely as he stroked Mama's hair. My eyes darted about so I would be sure to see Death when it came. I found solace in focusing again on Mama's chest, silently marking each labored breath, waiting to record her last.

PART TWO

AFTER

"Dying is a wild night and new road."
- *Emily Dickinson*

CHAPTER 12

Mama did not die that night as I expected. Instead, she died early the next morning as darkness gave way to light and the small birds in the bushes near the house began their song of greeting to the new day, replacing stillness with the growing disquiet of sunrise. At that hushed moment, between the past and what was to be, Death captured her weary soul and lifted it up from her wasted body.

Neal and I had slept nearby; me curled up on the couch and Neal had brought pillows and a blanket from the bedroom and slept on the floor, the dog snuggled against his back. Theresa had spent most of the night in the TV room and had last awakened me at around two a.m. to give Mama what turned out to be her final dose of the meds. After that, we had all gone back to sleep.

It was Christopher who woke me and informed me that Mama had passed. It was just after six a.m., an hour at which he was rarely awake. He stood before me and gently shook my shoulder. I opened my eyes, struggling against the pull of deep sleep to focus on his face. I smiled, not yet recalling exactly where I was or the awful night that had passed.

"Mom," he whispered. "Grandma's gone." His head nodded in a calm and tearless affirmation.

I struggled to comprehend his message then gasped when I realized what he was saying. I bolted up and looked past him to the hospital bed. Mama's head was slumped, her eyes closed. She appeared to be sleeping. I listened for the struggled breathing and watched her chest. There was no sound and no movement. I leapt off the couch, my legs stiff and unsteady. I walked to the hospital bed and lifted my hand with trepidation, then reached over to touch her forehead but she did not respond and when I raised my hand, my motion caused her head to roll further to the side. I cried out and recoiled at her corpse. I stared at her face, grateful that her eyes were not open.

My cry startled Neal. Disoriented, he struggled up from the floor. The dog rose with him and walked, head low and tail down, toward the bed. Neal looked from Mama's still body to me. I gave him a nod. We held each other's eyes and then he lunged toward me and pulled me into his arms. He began to sob which both moved and alarmed me. After a moment he noticed Christopher.

"Are you alright, buddy?" Neal swallowed hard, struggling to contain his tears.

Christopher nodded, calmly, "Yeah. I'm okay, Uncle Neal." He smiled and said, "And I know Grandma's okay, too. Really. She is. Don't cry."

Neal seemed not to hear him. He glanced quickly around the room. "Where's the aide?" He called out, "Theresa! We need you!" Theresa rushed in, took one look at us and rushed over to the bed. She felt for a pulse that wasn't there. We watched her bow her head for a moment and then she turned to us. "I'm sorry. She's gone."

Neal's face crumpled and again he wept, but I remained dry-eyed, wondering how I could have sobbed so easily before but could not now shed a single tear. I watched as Theresa switched off the oxygen concentrator and its sudden silence caused me to shiver. I stood in the embrace of my brother and felt grief but, oddly, *not* for my mother. My sense of loss was for Death itself; I felt a most irrational longing for its invisible presence. The house was noticeably empty without it hovering about and I missed it; I missed the days *before* when it was nearby, and Mama still had time. My long battle was over and I had lost.

Of course I immediately felt guilty for having these thoughts and, to distract myself, I turned back to my son. I stepped over to him and hugged him. I sat on the chair near the bed and held my arms out, beckoning him. He stepped to me and I took his hands in mine. "I'm sorry you had to be the one to find her gone. I'm sure that was scary for you." His face conveyed seriousness but there were no tears.

"I didn't find her," he told me. "She came to me in my dream." He pointed upstairs indicating the bedroom.

I shook my head and stared at him, trying to grasp what he was saying.

Neal looked at him quizzically and stepped over to him. "What do you mean, Chris? Grandma came to you in a dream?"

"Well, I guess it was her spirit. But she visited me while I was up in bed asleep. She told me she loved me but that she was going and for me not to worry, that she was fine. And she told me to tell you both something." He stopped speaking and tilted his head to the side, seemingly trying to recall what Mama had told him.

I sighed. I dropped his hands and rubbed my temples. I was glad Christopher was so calm and so accepting but I could not begin to process any more other than the fact that Death and come and Mama was gone. I said, "Christopher, honey, I don't understand but if you dreamed about Grandma and that helps you accept–"

"No!" Christopher stomped his foot. "It wasn't *just* a dream. She came to me *in* the dream. It was real, like she was really talking to me."

Neal said, "It's okay, Christopher. Go ahead, tell us what Grandma said to you when she came to see you in your dream."

"That's what I'm trying to remember exactly." He thought for a moment, frowning then suddenly brightened. "I know! Uncle Neal, she told me to tell you that she was sorry." He looked pleased with himself. "She said that she was sorry about . . . art? Or something like that." He shrugged with uncertainty.

I gasped. "Oh my God."

Neal's face lost color. His eyes widened. "What? That's what she said? To tell me she was sorry about . . . *Art?*" His mouth slowly formed a smile, and a look of amazement transformed his face. He looked at me. "Did you hear that?" I stared blankly at him, my mind racing trying to recall if I ever had mentioned our former stepfather to my son.

Neal asked, "Anything else?"

"Not about you." He turned to me and smiled. "She told me to tell you something, though."

I held my breath. Dandy stood behind my son. *Now hold on. Let's just hear him out.* I scoffed. I had barely time to comprehend my mother's death and now I was being asked to believe she left secret messages for Neal and me in my son's dreams. Stories I had read or heard on TV talk shows about life after death, about spirits and ghosts and near-death experiences raced through my brain. Had Mama's spirit really visited Christopher in his sleep? Had she told Christopher something she couldn't, in the end, tell me herself? I swallowed hard. Like a butterfly, hope fluttered inside my chest and landed lightly on my heart. Recalling her strained efforts to tell me something just hours earlier, I reached out to my son. He stepped toward me and I took hold of his hands again, gently rubbing them.

"I'm glad Grandma visited you, Christopher, but I just am having a hard time understanding all this." I looked past him to watch as Neal moved closer to the hospital bed. He stared down at Mama with an odd combination of bewilderment and contentment on his face. *I'd say your brother believes*, Dandy said. I shook my head. This was more a case of him *needing* to believe that Mama had finally apologized for a past wrong than any certainty that she had. I managed a smile and said, "I just don't know what to believe, Christopher, it's all so strange."

Christopher nodded and smiled knowingly, and I felt as if I was the child, and he the parent. He said, "It's okay, Mom, but I swear, I'm not making this up." He paused for a moment to collect his thoughts then said, "Grandma told me, 'Tell your mom she's already got what she's looking for.'" He nodded; obviously proud he had gotten the message right. I stared at him, expecting more but he said, "That was it. She said you've already got what you're looking for." He cocked his head and looked at me quizzically. "What'd she mean by that? What are you looking for?"

I sucked in air and held my breath. Aghast, I cried, "Is that *all*? That's *all* she said?"

Christopher nodded uneasily.

I shot up from the chair. My disappointment was intense. "What does that mean?" I raged angrily at Mama's body, waving my arms in the air. "I don't know what that's supposed to mean! I've already got what I'm looking for?"

Christopher cowered and backed away from me, but I ignored him and stomped past him to hospital bed. My anger was back with a vengeance. My nostrils flared and my breathing came in short huffs. I clenched and unclenched my hands. I had a wicked urge to reach out and grab Mama's lifeless body and shake it, as though if I shook her hard enough, she would awaken from death and explain her post-mortem message for me. "What does that even mean,

Mama?" I demanded from her body. "For Christ's sake! If you're going to send me a message, why does it have to be a riddle?"

"Stop it!" Neal's voice was harsh.

Dandy scolded me. He leaned close to me. *You need to stop and get a hold of yourself. Your mama is dead. Show some respect!* I caught sight of one of her hands, slightly open, lying so still. As quickly as it came, my anger vanished, replaced by the awful, full awareness that my mother was really dead. A whimper escaped me, and I reached for Mama's hand. I lifted it, to my face and at last I wept. None of this is real, I thought. It isn't real.

⚜

THE LOCAL FUNERAL HOME SENT MEN WHO TOOK AWAY MAMA'S body later that morning. Christopher and I had gone upstairs to try to sleep and had not heard Neal let the men in, nor had we heard any sounds of the swift and quiet removal of her body. When I came downstairs later after a few hours of troubled sleep, (leaving Christopher still in bed), the sight of the now empty hospital bed hit me. Mama had really died. I cried out, standing at the foot of the stairs, and Neal, who was preparing a late breakfast in the kitchen, came and wrapped his arms around me and held me. Staring over his shoulder I noticed Mother laying forlornly by the front door and wondered what the poor animal had thought when Mama's body had been taken away. I resolved in that moment to be kinder to the dog.

Neal led me into the kitchen. He got me seated at the table and put a cup of coffee in front of me and began to try to put my mind on other things. He went to the counter and pulled out two slices of bread to make toast.

"I called Claudia. She took it pretty hard."

"Not hard enough to be here with her."

"Laney Mae, she loved Mama. Give her a break."

"Claudia was Mama's closest sister and should have been here."

He turned to face me and frowned, "Come on. She's older now, too. They all are. And she's got to take care of Harrie and Hilda, don't forget."

"I know. I'm just mad they never once came to see her after she got diagnosed."

"You know how they are. They don't like coming down off that mountain anymore."

"Well, maybe I don't want to go back up that mountain and see any of them!" I slammed my hand on the table.

Neal's eyes widened, "You got to do something with all your anger."

I frowned, "I have a right to be angry at them. I don't want to bury her up there! Why should we? Back up on the mountain she escaped?"

"Because it's what she wanted. It's full circle."

"Right. How philosophical," I scoffed.

He grinned. "That's me. Mr. Philosophical." He turned and put the bread in the toaster. "Claudia said Jake will get here later today. She guessed about three or four o'clock. They've got everything else covered up there with the funeral home and cemetery and all."

I sat forward in my chair, putting my elbows on the table, resting my head in my hands. "Oh my God. Jake! I still don't know if this is a good idea, Neal." I lifted the coffee cup and took a sip. It was hot and strong.

"What else are we gonna do?" Neal snapped, impatient with my grumbling. "Jake is as good an undertaker assistant as any so just deal with it."

I stared at Neal with wide eyes and then we both burst into laughter which seemed out of place. The sound bounced off the floor and ceiling and the metal cabinets and echoed back at us, but it could not be helped, even on this sad morning. Our cousin Jake,

Claudia's youngest, with his assorted job history (coal miner, truck driver, gas station attendant, convenience store employee and now, his latest profession, funeral director's assistant) was comical without even trying to be. He was lovable and optimistic but at the same time, capable of making even the most patient person develop a great urge to shake common sense into him. With Jake involved, Mama's funeral would be anything but typical.

"You know what they say, Neal," I said, trying to keep a straight face. "Don't mix family with business. I smell disaster."

Neal pulled the slices of bread from the toaster. "No," he said, "what you smell is burnt toast." He chuckled and tossed the blackened pieces of bread into the trash can and reloaded the toaster, adjusting the timer. He turned back to me, "Look, all he's doing is driving her body back to West Virginia. How much trouble can that be? He can drive. We'll be driving right behind him."

"Neal, we *are* talking about Jake."

"Yeah, well you need to give him a break, too. He will be just fine."

"I have my doubts about Jake getting us there. I don't quite share your faith in our dear cousin, but we'll see."

The plan was simple enough. Jake would arrive later in the official Final Rest Mortuary hearse. Tomorrow, Christopher, Mother the dog and I in our car, and Neal in his, would accompany Jake to the local funeral home which would prepare her body for burial and load her casket into the hearse. From there, we would follow the hearse up and down the mountains, returning her back home to West Virginia. A viewing would be held Friday evening with the funeral on Saturday. Neal would return home Sunday for work on Monday. Christopher and I would probably stay Sunday and drive home Monday.

There were still many details to work out and they begged for discussion as we picked at our breakfast. I was drained and nauseated, and I found I had great difficulty swallowing the toast and could hardly force small bites down. I felt Mama hovering all around us and I kept thinking I'd look up and see her standing over by the sink, still in her robe, smoking her morning cigarette.

Mama had left few instructions about her funeral and Neal and I mulled over options and wondered who would attend, how religious the service should be and whether or not to have an open casket. This last item left us sorely reminded of the sight of Mama's lifeless body earlier and neither of us spoke for a few minutes. Finally, to move the conversation on, Neal cleared his throat. "One of us needs to get up and say something at the service," he said, chewing on a last bite of toast. "You're the one that went to college," he grinned. "I think you're the automatic nominee." He leaned back in the chair, folding his arms, looking quite satisfied with himself.

"Me? Talk about Mama?" I frowned. I could not imagine what I would say, how I would keep myself composed, or how I could possibly sort out the ambivalent feelings I held for her in time to prepare a proper eulogy. "That would be too hard. I've got too many mixed up feelings about her. I wouldn't know what to say."

Neal scoffed. "There's plenty to say. You could say something like 'She was a hardworking woman who provided for us.' And you could say she was determined, she was independent—"

I cut him off. "And she was bitter, she was stubborn, she carried a big 'ole grudge on her shoulders."

He waved me off. "Oh, come on. Think about some good memories. You know, like things she did that stand out. Maybe a funny story? How about how she helped take care of Harrie? That says a lot. Or how about how she stood up against bigots around here?"

"Oh yeah? Like Art? Like Mrs. Clarke?"

He frowned at my sarcasm and continued, "Well, okay, she wasn't consistent. So, how about how patriotic she was? She voted in every election, she flew her flag and . . . you know."

I sipped my coffee, but it had grown cold. I set the cup down and pushed it away. I was suddenly fatigued and yawned. "I'll talk to Gladys. Maybe she's the one who ought to speak."

Neal considered this. "Yeah, that's an idea. Maybe she can say something, too, but I just think one of us has got to say something, Laney Mae. Between the two of us we should be able to come up with something good to say about our own mother."

Abruptly, I stood. I did not want to discuss this for my anger had returned; anger with Mama for dying, anger for her waiting until it was too late to do more than speak my father's name to me. "Well," I said bitterly, "One thing's for sure. We won't have to talk long. There isn't that much good to say."

Neal's mouth dropped open, "Oh, come on Laney Mae! You're just mad she never told you anything about Dad."

I sat down and tried to read his face. There was no way he knew that Mama had tried to speak to me unless Theresa had pulled him aside, but I decided that was unlikely. I told him, "I'll admit I'm disappointed about that. I had hoped Mama would finally break down and offer me something. But it's not just that. You know how she could be. You're awfully generous after the way she let you down. How she stayed with Art after what happened."

He opened his mouth as though to argue but then held his hands up in surrender. He sighed and tried humor again. "Hey, you heard Christopher this morning: Mama apologized to me about 'ole Art, remember? On her way to Heaven in his dream. So, I'm all square with her now." He grinned but his eyes were sad.

"All is forgiven?"

Neal's face flashed anger. He leaned toward me and put his hands on the table. "Isn't that what we're supposed to do when someone dies? Forgive them?"

I held my breath and weighed how to respond. *Should I tell him about playing the records and my last encounters with Mama or would it just annoy him?* I settled on telling him one thing, "I told her I forgave her. Last night. Before she died. Gladys had told me I needed to, so I did."

My brother's face transformed. He smiled with relief. "I'm glad to hear that. What did you say to her? Did she hear you?"

"I told her that I was sorry and asked her to forgive me for not understanding her pain. I hope she heard me. I think she did. Later . . . she tried to talk to me, but she couldn't."

He reached over and squeezed my hand.

"The sad thing is, I think she *did* want to tell me something, but she was so damn stubborn that she waited until it was too late." My anger was making a comeback.

He took his hand away, "So you *don't* forgive her?"

I frowned at him. "I'm doing the best I can, okay?" I changed the subject, "And speaking of her dying, what was all that about with Christopher saying she stopped by his dream to tell him she was leaving? Telling him to tell us things? And he's so calm about Mama dying when last night he was so upset just telling her goodnight. He couldn't have made it all up, could he?"

Neal sighed. "I don't know. Did you ever tell Christopher about Art?"

"Not specifically. I might have mentioned him in passing but, no, he wouldn't have known enough about that bastard to come up with what he said this morning."

"Well, it is weird. And what was all that about you already having what you're looking for?"

I took a bite of toast and shrugged. "How am I supposed to know what our mother's spirit meant in my son's dream?"

"Well, it's got to be about Dad."

"Guess I'll never know!" I scoffed. "She had years to talk to me. Years! She dies and, lo and behold, her spirit visits my son's dream and tells him to tell me I have what I'm looking for. A damn mystery case to solve! And you wonder why I carry around all this anger at her?"

"Okay, that's enough!" He slapped his hand on the table. "I don't know why she did that to you. She was a hard person. She was difficult. She wasn't June Cleaver. Hell, she wouldn't win awards for mother of the year. But I know she loved us." His voice cracked. He bowed his head and used his thumb and index finger to try to plug his tears. He wiped his nose roughly with a paper napkin. "I know she tried. She just let her anger get in the way some of the time."

"Some of the time?" I said, unmoved by my brother's emotional display. "Being mad at the world will do that to you."

"She wasn't mad at the world, Laney Mae. She was mad at Dad."

"Yes! Our long dead father! I'd say it takes a special kind of person to hold on to anger for nearly forty years, don't you?"

Now Neal smiled, "Well, little sister, I'd say you're holding on to some anger yourself, aren't you? And until you let it go, you haven't forgiven her."

Dandy appeared behind my brother. *He's got a point there.*

I shook my head. "Well, big brother, glad you have this all figured out. Angry? Yeah, I'm angry. But what I really am, right now, is *tired*. I'm really, tired, Neal. Tired of every goddamn thing." With that, I rose, let my dishes fall with a clatter into the sink and left my brother and Dandy and the ghost of my mother alone in the kitchen.

⚜

LATER THAT MORNING I SAT ON MAMA'S BED IN HER BATHROBE, my hair twisted up in a towel after a shower. I stared at the closed doors to her closet. I knew I had to open those doors soon. I needed to select the clothing in which to dress her for burial and have it ready to go with us on the ride back to Second Chance. A vision of my mother in a coffin flashed in my mind. The thought caused me to shiver, and I hugged my arms tightly around myself.

Besides selecting Mama's burial attire, I needed to check on my apartment, water plants and pack what Christopher and I would take. Which reminded me that I had to call his school. Which then reminded me I had to arrange for a neighbor or one of Christopher's friends to watch the house and feed the pond fish and also bring the newspaper up. Which also reminded me that I must finish writing Mama's obituary (omitting the angry references to Art and my father). It would be official now; we had her date of death: September 5, 2001.

When I could put it off no longer, I went to the closet and stood before it, staring at the plain bi-fold doors. I had opened them many times before, but she had still been alive. Inhaling deeply to brace myself, I grabbed the handles, closed my eyes and pulled the closet open. I was met with the scent of my mother in the gust of air. The smell of her perfume—Dune by Christian Dior—was intense and my face crumpled into tears. I blinked and stared at the suits and dresses that hung forlornly, crammed into the small closet, its shelves piled high with assorted handbags, shoes, shoeboxes and a few hats. I stepped forward and, with both arms, gathered several of the garments together and brought them to my face. I breathed in deeply and began sob, the sound muffled by the clothing. I wailed, "Come back! Please come back. Oh Mama! Please come back," over and over. The reality of her death now assaulted me, and I thought how nice it would be to just give into it, to allow my legs to collapse, to fall down and lay on the closet floor and just sleep and sleep and sleep until time healed me; sleep until the sadness dissipated. I thought about closing myself inside and hiding so as to avoid it all: the long car ride to West Virginia, the tedious encounters with relatives, the funeral service, and the long drive back to the empty house and my empty future.

I waited until the worst of the despair passed then steadied myself and let the garments drop from my arms. I used the sleeve of the robe to wipe my nose and with a sudden energy fueled by another bout of anger, I began going through the clothes quickly, like a mad shopper at a bargain basement clearance sale. *Deal with the task*, I thought, pausing only to wipe my nose again. *You're just picking out a dress,* I told myself. *Just focus on that.* But none of the dresses seemed appropriate and I began to feel overwhelmed. *Why did I have to make this decision? Should I pick something black?* Mama liked bright colors and the only black dress in her closet was an old cocktail dress from the mid-seventies. Dandy appeared beside me as I continued going through the clothing. *What about that pretty suit she wore at Christopher's baptism? You know that light blue one?* I nodded and found it hanging inside a clear plastic dry cleaning bag. I held it up. "It's just right," I said to Dandy. "Not too somber, not too frilly. Plus, it has sentimental value. Mama had admired herself in it and she even had shoes dyed to match." This thought caused me to look up to the shelves for the shoes. "Do you bury people with shoes?" I said this out loud and something that passed as a laugh escaped me. Dandy chuckled. *They just might. May as well bring 'em.*

I scanned the shelves and noticed several shoe boxes on the highest shelf. I took the suit and walked back over to the bed where I laid it out neatly. I crossed the bedroom and brought a small wooden side chair Mama kept by the bed over to the closet. I stepped upon it carefully and reached up to the shoeboxes. I peeked in a couple before I found the shoes that matched the suit. I pulled the box off the shelf and stopped. Behind it was Mama's keepsake box. It was a simple shoebox covered in wrapping paper with little red and pink roses. It had always been known as Mama's "rose box." I pulled this off the shelf with the shoes, stepped carefully down off the chair and carried the boxes over to the bed. I took the shoes out and laid them next to the suit. They were like new. I wondered about hosiery and laughed again. It all seemed ridiculous, and I wished Mama had chosen to be cremated, sparing me this morbid task. "How about the matching handbag?" I asked the suit, "And we mustn't forget to accessorize with jewelry," I said aloud, chuckling. Dandy said, *The right accessories make the dead woman's outfit!* This caused me to laugh, my fatigue making me slaphappy.

"Mom!" Christopher's voice was sharp. He stood in the doorway, still in his pajamas, hands on his hips. He frowned, "What are you laughing about? It's a sad day."

"Oh! Christopher, it's not what you think. Come here."

He stayed put, frowning. "What's so funny?" He pouted then added, "And I'm hungry!"

"Then go downstairs and tell Neal to fix you a sandwich or something."

"What are you doing?" He nodded his head in the direction of the bed and the clothing.

"I'm putting together what Grandma will be dressed in." I looked away from him and mumbled quietly, "What she'll be buried in." I looked back to see his reaction and saw that he seemed to absorb this without any sign of upset. I motioned at the suit. "See? This is a special outfit. This is what Grandma wore when you were baptized."

Curious, he entered the room. He stood beside me and considered the suit. He said, "When I was a baby? She wore that?"

"Yes. I think she would be happy with this. She liked it."

"Yeah. I guess." He paused then asked, "But why were you laughing?"

I sighed. "Because I was thinking about whether or not they bury people with shoes on and it just seemed funny to me. I mean, they hardly need them." I chuckled.

Christopher smiled and grunted out a laugh. "Yeah, I guess not." He pointed to the rose box. "What's that?"

"That's Grandma's keepsake box. It's a place where she kept stuff that was special to her." I lifted the lid off the rose box. There were a few old photographs, some handwritten letters and greeting cards that were yellowed and torn, two envelopes that contained hair clippings of mine and Neal's, an old locket without a chain that I knew had no photo inside, a John F. Kennedy inaugural button, and a few other items.

"What is all this stuff?"

"I told you. Things that meant something special to Mama. Like your Matchbox cars? You know how you keep them all together? Special—like that."

Christopher nodded.

I opened the envelope on which was written:

Laney Mae - 1960

I reached inside and pulled out a small clipping of light brown hair. "See this? This was my baby hair." I held it up and as I did, I thought to myself that when Mama clipped my baby hair, Daddy was still alive, we were still a family, John F. Kennedy was about to become our President, and everything was alright. I replaced the hair clipping in the envelope and continued sorting through the contents. I found the photo I was looking for.

"Have I ever showed you this?"

Christopher took it and looked at it closely before handing it back to me. "Isn't that Grandma and Aunt Harrie?"

"Yes. That's Grandma and Harrie and . . . " I ran my finger along one side of the photo which was jagged from having been roughly torn by Mama. "See this part? This was where your grandfather *was* standing."

"My grandfather? You mean your dad?"

"One in the same." I waved the snapshot in the air. "This was taken the day they got married. That's why they're all dressed up. Mama was twenty-two. Harrie would have been—" I paused to calculate, "only sixteen years old. Just six years older than you are now."

"Was Harrie, you know, like she is now, then, too?"

"Yes, a person is born with Down syndrome. It's genetic. We've talked about it, remember?"

"Yeah. I know. You've told me." He pointed to the photograph. "Why is he torn out of the picture?"

I gave him a surprised look. "I've told you about it."

"Oh yeah. Grandma was mad at him for being out with another woman and getting killed in the car wreck." Suddenly serious, he put his hand on my arm. "Mom? Do you believe me? About Grandma coming to see me in my dream? Because I swear, I didn't make it up. Do you believe me?"

I looked into his eyes and felt a rush of love for my son. "Well, I don't know what I believe Christopher. Before she died, Grandma was able to speak to me a little. She really didn't have much strength, but she said something sort of like what you said she told you."

His face brightened, "She did?"

I nodded, "She said something about a picture. But I don't know what picture. I don't know what she meant."

"See!" Christopher said, elated. He jumped up and down. "She was trying to tell you something! Maybe she meant *this* picture?"

I shook my head. "Christopher, I've seen this photo and every single photograph in this house. I've searched it from top to bottom since I was a kid. I don't know what she meant but I know there's no picture of my father anywhere here. See, she tore him out!"

"Well, at least you believe me." He stared at the rose box, then became excited. "I know! She wanted you to find this photo with Harrie in it. It's a clue!"

I sighed wearily. "Like I said, I've seen this picture. Now, I have a lot to do, and I'm done talking about this."

"Yeah, but when's the last time you saw it? Something made you find it again today." He looked quite pleased with himself. "Grandma is sending you clues!" He turned and headed to the door. "I'm going downstairs to get something to eat." He darted out of the room, and I frowned as I listened to his footsteps pound down the stairs. I looked at the photograph of Mama and Harrie and once again gently traced my finger over the torn part where my father should have been. Then I tossed the photograph onto the bed.

It landed on the blue suit.

CHAPTER 13

The apartment smelled musty. It had been several days since I had been by and now, in the stagnant heat, my plants were wilted. All the stale smells that come from a small spaced being closed too long greeted me as I stood in the doorway. To add insult, the building's air conditioning, never reliable, must have been out of service for a few days. Christopher wrinkled his noise. "Yuck," he said. "It smells in here." He raced past me to his room to his games and toys and the stuffed animals he still played with, although no one was supposed to know that.

I stood for a moment in the doorway. I swayed slightly with fatigue and leaned against the doorframe. My shoulders slumped, my eyes burned, and my temples ached from a brewing headache. I moved slowly into the apartment I had come to hate for it represented, in its austerity and shabbiness, my failed marriage and my failed life. I had lived here for the two years since the divorce. At first, I had tried to force myself into being excited about having my own place with elaborate plans to decorate and buy new furniture.

But those feelings of a fresh start had been short-lived as the dreary reality of my new life was realized.

The six rooms of the second-floor garden apartment were claustrophobic and ugly. My landlord would not allow me to paint the dingy off-white walls. All the rooms, except my bedroom, were too small. The place had cockroaches. The plumbing was unreliable. The utilities were inefficient but costly. I physically ached for more space and often longed for the house Phil and I had shared with all its space and highbrow decorator touches my mother-in-law had insisted upon (and paid for). With its custom wainscoting, hardwood floors, Ethan Allen furniture, tasteful antiques and perfectly manicured lawn, Judith Langston no doubt hoped the exquisite décor of her son's home would somehow make up for what her daughter-in-law from West Virginia lacked in pedigree.

I made my way down a short hallway to the large bedroom in which I had placed a beautiful iron bed with a canopy frame from which I had hung delicate lace curtains. At night, I would often pull them closed for they helped me feel sheltered from the new world I inhabited. I had splurged to purchase the bed, convincing myself that I deserved the luxury, the almost selfish decadence of it and being surrounded by fluffy down pillows and pricey bedding. I refused to sleep on the bed I had shared with Phil, even though he had offered me the first pick of our possessions and it would have saved me money to have taken the old bed. I bought myself all this to commemorate a fresh start, but it had not taken long for me to realize that a new bed could not compensate for the fact that each night I slept alone.

A chair and ottoman, salvaged from the division of marital property sat in one corner. Near that, a desk and two dressers stood neutrally; they were purchased after the divorce and had no previous knowledge of my failed marriage. They had not heard the shouting, the accusations, the final confession. On the dull white wall in front of the bed I had hung three charming oil paintings by a local, little-known artist from the Eastern Shore in Maryland, whose art I had begun collecting even as I knew my marriage was ending. Above the bed I had placed an antique round mirror, the only other item in the room from my married life. It had reflected some joy but in recent years, mostly despair.

The room was dark. I walked around the bed to the windows, pulled the curtains open and raised the shades. I noticed the red light flashing on the answering machine. There were two messages. The first was from one of Christopher's friends, innocently unaware of Mama's death, wanting him to play. As I listened, I walked back around the bed to the closet and opened the doors. I stared at my clothes trying to decide what to wear to the wake and the funeral. As I went through the clothes, the second message began, and I stopped pushing the hangers and listened. It was Phil. His message had come two days ago.

"Elaine . . . I . . . uh . . . I'm just checking in to speak to Christopher." He had started calling me "Elaine" after he left me. I turned to face the machine, my eyes narrowing into angry slits. If he had really wanted to reach me or Christopher, he could have called Mama's house. He knew that. His message continued with long, uncomfortable pauses. "I . . . guess you are with your mom. I . . . uh . . . hope she's . . . not in great pain. I'm sure you're taking good care of her."

I walked over to stand before the desk staring at the answering machine as he droned on. My breathing changed and the air I exhaled felt hot in my nostrils as my anger burned. Then, from the corner of my eye I saw movement and sensed Christopher. I turned quickly to find him standing in the doorway. He must have heard his father's voice from his room and come to listen. His face was blank, his eyes avoiding mine as he prepared to hear his father rejecting him once again. It was part of a pattern that had begun after the divorce. Once, so close they seemed inseparable, and now they were like strangers.

Phil's message continued, "Tell Christopher hi for me and that I'm really sorry we didn't . . . get together this summer . . . but . . . we'll . . . see each other . . . sometime."

Sometime? Sometime! What was that supposed to mean? Despite Christopher standing there, and my efforts to be neutral and not speak badly of Phil in front of our son, I snorted sarcastically. The whole summer had come and was now gone, and Phil had kept postponing Christopher's two weeks with him. It was one excuse after another. Work. The new baby was sick. The two-year-old was sick. Then came his new family's vacation. Work again. Amanda, the new wife, had to have dental work done. He had to travel unexpectedly for work. Then suddenly, conveniently, summer was over and promises of a long weekend or perhaps, Thanksgiving, together with our son were now being made.

And would likely be broken.

Phil's message came to its conclusion. "I'll talk to you about plans soon. Take care of your mom and take care of yourself. Bye." I reached out with my index finger and stabbed the stop button. I looked at my son. "Christopher." That was all I could say: his name. Words of excuse for his father would ring hollow. His face seemed ready to crumple into tears, but he gave himself a little shake and put up his now standard response, "I don't care. I didn't want go see them anyway." The hurt in his eyes betrayed him. I forced a half-hearted smile and held my arms out to him, but he did not want sympathy. He backed away and shook his head again, "It's not a big deal. She doesn't want me there."

My smile fell away, "Well, you know he loves you, Christopher—" I stopped. This is what I always said and now the words hung in the air; they had lost the comfort they might once have held. Why did I continue to defend a man who had chosen to leave us? I was tired of making excuses but when I looked into my son's eyes, how could I not? So, what could I say? What truth could I find to take the edge off this rejection? What else? I resorted to the standard line, "You're right. It's not him. It's *her*." There. It was easier to blame the other woman, the evil stepmother. I moved toward him, but again he backed away. He shook his head at me to not come closer, as though instead of a source of comfort, I was a threat, and I guess I was. I knew perfectly well what he thought: if he let me hold him, he would cry. My arms around him would make him sob and reveal that truth: his father's rejection really was a big deal. He really did care.

"I got to get my stuff ready." His voice cracked and he turned and ran back to his room.

I stood, my arms reaching out into the emptiness where my son had been. I wasn't sure whether to follow him or not and then decided not to. I looked at the answering machine. "You bastard," I said under my breath. I stomped over to the desk and pounded the machine, "You only call him to ease your guilt!" And once again the scene played in my mind of the night three years ago when I rolled over and saw it was 4:15 a.m. and realized Phil was not in bed. I gasped and ran downstairs. I saw his car was not in the driveway and I called his office. The security guard answered and told me no one was there. I called Mama, who seemed to know what I pretended not to, and who told me to call my in-laws and to tell them their son had not come home. But when I did, my mother-in-law, whom I had woken from a sound sleep, patronizingly assured me there must be a good explanation and for Heaven's sake, "boys will be boys" and if there had been an accident the police would have called. But of course by then I knew this and so I envisioned him with her. Amanda. The Barbie Doll-perfect woman I had first met at Phil's office holiday party and whom I had watched the whole evening as she and Phil seemed unable to stay apart from each other, leaving me alone at the table. I was feeling frumpy with an extra ten pounds

I couldn't lose and with my hair chopped short in a pathetic attempt to imitate Princess Diana. I had hung up on my mother-in-law and gone to sit in my perfectly decorated living room to wait and wait until at last, at five-fifteen a.m. he entered, carrying his shoes to not make noise on the rich hardwood floor, and I demanded to know where he had been. To which he told me, "working." I raged at him to not lie to me and then I bolted across the room. I shoved him back out the door and told him to leave. He yelled and pushed against me and told me I was crazy. He warned me that if he left, he would *never* come back.

Then, from the stairway came Christopher's voice, his scream like a glass shattering on stone, telling us to *stop*, tears on his face, as he ran over to us and placed his body between us and begged his father not to go away and asked us both why we fought all the time, why we hated each other and why we ever got married. Later that morning, while Christopher was at school, Phil told me loved me once, but no longer, and I slapped him and then he was gone.

Agitated, I returned to the closet and pulled a lightweight, short-sleeved black suit out and wondered if it still fit. I slid the jacket off the hanger and was pleased that it did. I kicked off my flip-flops, slid my shorts down and stepped out of them and pulled on the skirt. It was a little tight but would do. Dandy appeared beside me. *How about that pearl necklace? You always wore that with this suit. That would be nice.* I walked over to my dresser and opened my jewelry box. I lifted the top tray out to the compartment underneath where I kept the pearls and there I saw the old photograph, wrapped protectively in a plastic sandwich bag. Dandy saw it too. *Well, look at that. There it is. Your greatest treasure.* For the first time in a long time, I felt the unfamiliar tug upward on the corners of my mouth and I smiled with genuine joy. "Oh," I whispered as I lifted the photo of JFK holding me that Mama had given me so many years ago.

Suddenly Christopher called, "Mom! Help!" I hurried to his

room to find him standing on tiptoes on a chair in front of his closet, precariously balancing a pile of board games above his head which threatened, at any moment, to come crashing down. "Uh, I kind of need some help here, Mom," he said with a sheepish grin.

"Yes, I guess you kind of do." I stepped over to help him and at that moment I absentmindedly placed the photograph of me with JFK into the pocket of the jacket of my suit. And there it would remain until I would find it again.

৶৶৶

DRIVING BACK FROM THE APARTMENT, I FIGURED WORD HAD spread in Potomac Manor about Mama's death. I was certain some neighbors must have seen the men from the funeral home wheel her body out of the house that morning. The neighbors, although watchful, tended to keep to themselves, living quiet lives on the tree-lined street named for Martha Custis Washington, wife of George Washington. All the streets in Potomac Manor were named for famous women. The criteria seemed to have been that the women so honored had to have either been the wife of one of Virginia's Founding Fathers, or the wife of other great Southerners, or were great Southerners in their own right. There was Madison Street for Dolly Madison. There was Randolph Road, where Greg and his family lived, to honor Mary Anna Randolph Lee, wife of the Civil War general. Not many residents actually knew that Howell Court, which was a cul-de-sac around the block from Custis Drive, was named after Varnia Howell, Mrs. Jefferson Davis, the former and only, Confederate First Lady.

The homes in Potomac Manor were nearly identical in their simple design and their inhabitants were consistently Caucasian, but, in 1971 a White military family moved away and decided to rent their house. They had the audacity, (in the opinion of many residents, except Mama and a few others) to rent to the neighborhood's first Black family. I remember the uproar as residents of Potomac Manor watched the Thomas family pull up to the house on Loreta Lane (which was named for Loreta Velázquez, a daring woman who, disguised as a man, fought on battlefields for the Confederacy). Several turned on their heels, went back into their homes and called Realtors. "For Sale" signs appeared practically overnight and for the next fifteen years, Potomac Manner became a community of renters made up mostly of Black and Hispanic families for whom the neighborhood was a move up, poorer White families for whom the neighborhood kept them from living in a run-down apartment on the highway, and a handful of long-time owners (like Mama) who loved their homes and would never consider leaving. Mixed in periodically were transients, including a motorcycle gang who, one hot summer night, shot out nearly every one of the streetlights on Howell Court, just for entertainment. And I still remember the house of hippies on Randolph Lane over which a permanent haze floated from endless pot smoking in the mid-1970s, and to which the police made frequent visits.

The neighborhood had made somewhat of a comeback in the late eighties and early nineties as property values rose and younger and more diverse families began to buy homes there; but by then, Mama had little interest in her neighbors. She was not particularly close to any of them and preferred to be left alone, but she'd exchange a wave or share a brief conversation. I think most of the old timers in Potomac Manor who were left, who knew her, and had gotten over her West Virginia hillbilly roots, had come to hold a quiet admiration for her love of her home and her yard. They had watched her puttering in her garden in recent years, talking to squirrels, throwing cracker crumbs to birds. Watched her sitting with Mother, alone on the front stoop in an old lawn chair and surveying her world as the stars and stripes flapped on the pole, while she took long, slow drags on her cigarettes.

Her neighbor across the street, Clive Alexander, who was an original owner in Potomac Manor and who almost put his home up for sale when he saw West Virginia license plates on our family's car when we moved in back in '62, was one of those who had come to respect Mama. He was the first person I informed about her terminal illness. His wife Phyllis had jumped on the phone to spread the news. Soon after, a handful of neighbors phoned us to express their concern, and some dropped off baked goods and casseroles.

By the afternoon of the day she died, I had no doubt that the word had spread that Mama had indeed passed. But, there would soon be something new for Phyllis to report: the arrival of the hearse driven by my cousin Jake now parked in Mama's driveway. And not just any hearse. A pink hearse.

"OH MY GOD!" I EXCLAIMED WHILE I TRIED TO ABSORB THE reality of a bright pink hearse parked in Mama's driveway. I blinked my eyes and yet, somewhere in the back of my mind I was not totally, one hundred percent surprised. I had expected something like this. After all, Jake was involved.

I eased the Suburban in front of the driveway apron to hopefully block the hearse from direct view, but it would be difficult to miss. The hearse seemed enormous to me or maybe it was the bright, bumper-to-bumper pink color that made it seem so immense. It was a sort of a Pepto-Bismal pink, a pink not unlike the color I had insisted my bedroom be painted when I was eleven years old. A Marsha, Jan and Cindy Brady pink. Except pinker.

"Mom! What is that thing?" Christopher cried out, pointing. "Is that a hearse? Is that Jake's? Is that what he's gonna drive Grandma back home in? I thought hearses were supposed to be black."

"They *are* supposed to be black."

"Well, how come it's pink?"

I drew in a breath, my shock converting to anger. "Well, Christopher, because it's *Jake's hearse*! That's why! That's why it's pink!" I shrieked and pounded on the steering wheel, "I knew! I knew it!"

"Knew what?"

"I knew Jake coming down here and driving Mama's body back to West Virginia was a mistake." I put the Suburban in park, opened the door and jumped out, slamming the door. I stomped up the driveway and stood at the driver's side of the hearse, near its back bumper, with my hands on my hips, shaking my head and mumbling expletives under my breath. Christopher followed and we stood together gawking at it, as though a closer proximity would enable us to believe such an oddity could exist. I heard female voices and laughter. I spun around and saw two women I did not recognize across the street, one pushing a baby stroller. They stared at the pink hearse as they pointed and giggled. Without thinking, I barked at them, "What are you looking at?" I waved a hand toward the hearse, "Haven't you ever seen a hearse before?"

The women stopped laughing and looked insulted. One of them put her hands on her hips in a defiant stance and replied, "Not one like *that* we haven't!" They burst into laughter and continued on their way, glancing over their shoulders and shaking their heads as they moved up the street.

Christopher stepped over for a closer look. "Mom, what does the license plate mean?" He stood pointing. I stepped over and looked at the license plate, bearing the West Virginia state motto: *Wild and Wonderful* at the top that been personalized to read:

HEV'NUP

I snorted, "I guess it means, Heaven Up."

Christopher smiled. "Oh. I get it. Like the soda. Seven-Up. Heaven-Up. Cuz Heaven's up." He pointed to the sky as he nodded admirably. "Yeah. I get it."

I stared at him and was certain I would laugh like a lunatic or cry like one, or both. The pink hearse, the soda pop tagline license plate, the nasty women across the street—it was too much. With sarcasm I said, "You do, Christopher? You get it, huh? I wish I did. I wish I understood this . . . this *thing*. Whatever it is." I waved my arms wildly, and my voice became shrill. "For Christ's sake! It's pink!"

At that moment, the front door opened and Jacob Peter Hall, Aunt Claudia's second born son, Mama's nephew and my cousin, emerged. "Laney Mae!" he bellowed. Dressed in jean shorts that hung to his knees, hiking boots and a T-shirt adorned with a cartoon character's image, he leapt off the two front steps onto the walkway and, with his arms spread wide, ran toward me. I tried to back away and find something to hide behind; I even considered running around to the other side of the hearse, but there was no escape. Jake, all two hundred twenty-five-plus pounds of him, lumbered toward me. I braced myself as he rushed up and wrapped his large arms around me and lifted me off the ground. "Laney, Laney, Laney," he said, "Poor Laney Mae! I'm so sorry about your mama." Christopher grinned as he watched.

"Okay Jake," I told him. "Put me down."

But he did not seem to hear me and continued to hug me, my feet dangling, as he muttered sympathies, squeezing me tightly in a bear hug, like a rag doll, several inches off the ground.

"Jake!" I pushed my arms against his chest. "I said put me down. Now!"

He sat me down gently and when I stepped back, I was surprised and touched to see tears streaming down his face. He sobbed, "I can't believe Aunt Faye is gone! I just can't believe it. I mean, I knew it was gonna happen. We *all* did. But when it finally does–" he shook his head and could not continue. He brought his large hands up to his face and sobbed. I stared at him and was struck by how much older he looked even though I had seen him just a few months earlier over the Memorial Day weekend during Mama's annual trip to lay flowers on family graves and what had turned out to be her last time home. I had always thought of Jake as young and kid-like, even though he was a year older than me. He was so energetic and so boyish. His big, round, baby face only added to his youthfulness but now, when he lowered his hands, I noticed lines around his eyes and I noticed, too, that his hairline was receding. Soon, I thought, he would probably be bald on top, just like his father, my uncle Pete, had been. His dark hair had traces of gray streaks, especially on his beard which was, at least, neatly trimmed.

"Thanks, Jake. It is hard." I put a hand on his shoulder. It felt bulky and my hand felt small against it, lost.

He took hold of the hem of his t-shirt, stretched it up and wiped away his tears then blew his nose on it. I made a face and Jake shrugged and grinned. "It needs to be washed anyway." He turned his attention to Christopher and brightened. "Chris-Toe-Fur!" he whooped and wrapped his arms around him and lifted him off the ground as he had me, but unlike me, Christopher seemed to enjoy the attention. Jake told my son, "I'm really sorry about your grandma. I know she loved you. You were everything to her." He gently set my son back on the ground.

"Thanks, Jake," Christopher said. He pointed to the hearse. "Where'd you get a pink hearse? Aren't they supposed to be black?"

Jake's mouth fell open as though Christopher had just said the most outlandish thing. He threw his hands up and he feigned shock. "Pink? *Pink*! A pink hearse? Where?"

Christopher broke into giggles. "Right there! In the driveway!"

Jake turned and looked at the hearse and jumped back, as though he was seeing it for the first time. "Good God almighty! It is *pink*! Would you look at that!" He wiggled his eyebrows up and down playfully and laughed. He moved over to the hearse and ran a hand lovingly down its side. I noticed for the first time that white lilies-of-the-valley were painted on the doors. Jake stroked the hearse in all its glorious pinkness and said, "Now tell me this is not the most beautiful hearse you've ever seen? And it's a Cadillac, too! I call her The Pink Lady." He grinned proudly. He said, "The pink was my idea. I went and had it done a couple months ago. Remember my girlfriend's niece, Nicole? The one that got Leukemia?"

I remembered hearing about her, and I nodded.

"Well, she died a couple of months ago. She was only ten."

"Oh my God! I'm so sorry, Jake," I told him. "But what does that have to do with–"

"Anyhow, I told Chet, you know, my boss, the guy that owns the funeral home–'Let's get rid of the black! Eliminate it from funerals as much as possible. It's too depressing.' This little girl, Nicole, she loved pink. So, I went and had it painted pink, just for her. So now all we have is a white hearse and this pink one. You know why?" We stared at him. Jake waited for us to guess, his head cocked to the side, but we said nothing. "Don't you get it? The pink? The white hearse back home? They're supposed to be like *clouds*. White clouds and pink clouds. You know how they look pink sometimes when the sun's setting?" He motioned at the sky majestically and said, "Nicole's family loved the pink hearse. Made her mama cry."

"I'll bet it did," I said, barely containing my sarcasm.

But my cousin didn't seem to hear. He turned his palms up toward the sky and turned his gaze upward. He said, with great seriousness, "Transporting souls. Even little ones. That's my job. It's the best job I ever had."

"So how did it get to be pink?" Christopher asked.

"Oh, well, that took a little work," Jake chuckled. "Chet gave me the okay to do it. He thinks death is too dark and dreary to most folks. So, I had to drive it over to Maryland for the custom paint job. I got it done in time for little Nicole's funeral and knew I'd have it for Faye, too. Wouldn't Faye love it, Laney Mae?" Before I could answer he said, "Wait! Here's the best part." He dug keys out of the pocket, opened the driver's side door and slid in. He grinned and said, "Wait until you hear this."

My stomach tightened into a knot as I watched Jake turn the key and then I saw him push in a cassette tape. Suddenly, Bruce Springsteen's voice blared, singing, of course, *Pink Cadillac.*" Jake grinned, whooped loudly and began singing along. He drummed the dashboard to the passionate sound of Clarence Clemons' saxophone.

It was too much. I began to cry. I collapsed into sobs, holding my hands up to cover my face. Christopher stepped over to me. "It's all right, Mom. Don't cry." This just made me cry harder. When Jake noticed me crying, he turned off the music, slid out of the hearse, and came to me.

"Oh, Laney Mae," he put a hand on each of my shoulders. "I know! It's so hard. I felt the very same way when my daddy died! I can't even imagine losing my mama. But honey, we all got to face it someday. But I'm here for you! You hear? I'm gonna help you. We're gonna send Aunt Faye off right! She would have loved this! No boring black limos for Faye, no sir!"

I dropped my hands from my face and began to laugh uncontrollably. So, this is what it's like to go crazy, I thought. I couldn't catch my breath. I wrapped my arms around myself and laughed so hard I could barely stand. I bent over and stared at my feet and red flip-flops and felt dizzy. Little flecks of light danced before my eyes, the same little warning lights I got before a migraine headache.

Jake became silent. He looked worriedly at Christopher who stood helplessly. Jake spoke softly, "Uh, Laney Mae, you all right?"

He nervously stepped closer and leaned over me. "Honey. What's wrong with you?"

I abruptly stopped my laugh-crying. I stared hard at him, my eyes wild, my face red and tear-streaked and raged, "All right? Am I all right? Sure! Sure, I'm just great! How could I not be, Jake? I mean, just look at this—" I waved my hand in the direction of the hearse, "This . . . this . . hearse! It's *pink* for Christ's sake! *Pink!* How could I be all right? I'm sorry about little Nicole and all but Jesus H. Christ! A pink hearse!" I shrieked then began the uncontrollable laugh-crying again.

Jake's eyes widened. He cocked his head to the side and arched his eyebrows. He said, "Uh, yeah. I know it's *pink* Laney Mae," he forced a laugh, and playfully punching my arm. "I just explained all about that. Remember? I told you how I had the custom paint job done in Maryland and all."

"Jake! It's crazy! It's ridiculous! It's . . . it's . . . People are laughing at it!"

Jake's eyebrows burrowed in confusion. He glanced around the yard, then in front of the house and saw no one, certain that I had not only lost my mind, but I was seeing things, too. "Who's laughing at it?"

"Who's laughing? Everybody!"

"Uh, Laney Mae, I don't see nobody laughing."

"Well, they *were*. There were these two women walking by with a baby stroller. Christopher saw them! And I can't believe you drove that damn thing all the way down here and that no one looked twice at you?"

Now Jake frowned, "Well, folks was looking at it. But they were admiring it."

"Admiring it?" I snorted. "Oh sure. Sure, they were *admiring* it. Yeah!"

Jake bowed his head and when he looked up again his smile was gone, and his eyes were damp with fresh tears. He said, "I am sorry that you don't like it. I thought you'd think it was something special, but I guess I was wrong."

"Mom," Christopher said, nudging my arm, "You hurt Jake's feelings."

I looked at my son. I took a deep breath and held it, willing myself to calm down. I said, "I'm sure Jake's intentions were good but–"

Jake cut me off. "Well, there's nothing we can do about it now. Is there? I mean, I would have brought the white hearse, but it's broken down right now. So, what do you want? For me to paint it black again?"

I scoffed. "Yes! Sure! Paint it black again, Jake! That's what I want. You drive this damn thing back to Maryland or wherever the hell you need to and have it painted *black*! A nice, respectful, *black*! I want a simple, goddamn black hearse, here, in this driveway by the time we leave tomorrow."

"Mom! Stop it!" Christopher scolded.

Jake lowered his head. His shoulders slumped. I looked from Christopher to Jake and back to my son again. I closed my eyes and rotated my head around to ease some of the tension in my neck. I counted to ten silently as they watched, warily. When I opened my eyes, I looked at Jake and said in a low, steady voice, "Just once in my life Jake, I would like something to be *normal*. Just once!"

Jake grinned. "Ha! Hell, Laney Mae. Nothing's ever normal in our family."

"That's the problem! Don't you think it's time we started trying to be normal?" I turned and stomped away from them and as I did, I heard Christopher tell Jake, "It's okay. She'll get over it. It's just Grandma dying and all. She's always in a bad mood, but now she's all emotional. You know?" Then I heard him ask, "Hey. Can I see the inside of it?"

Jake recovered instantly. "Oh yeah! Hell, you can get in. It's all soft and white. Like a cloud."

I stood on the front steps and watched as Jake swung open the back of the hearse. I was about to protest my son climbing in when a group of four boys rode up on bikes. Word of the pink hearse had indeed spread through Potomac Manor. One of the boys, who lived around the block and had been in third grade with Christopher called out, "Hey Chris. What's with the pink hearse, dude?"

"It's for my grandma," Christopher told him. "She died. It's my cousin's hearse." He motioned at Jake who waved to the boys. "He's gonna drive her body back home tomorrow."

"Y'all wanna see it?" Jake asked.

The boys looked at each other and snickered.

Jake lumbered down the lawn to them. "Aw come on. I bet none of you has ever seen inside a real hearse before, have you? Come on. I'll let you sit in it."

The boy who had spoken shrugged his shoulders, "It's creepy, man."

Jake's mouth dropped in surprise. "*Creepy*? Aw, no man. There's not a body in it right now. Come on!"

The boy hopped off his bike. The others followed and they walked behind Jake to the hearse. I watched my cousin, the pied piper of hearses, lead the boys on a grand tour of the Pink Lady. Nervously I looked up and down the street then noticed Phyllis peeping out of her window blinds. When she saw me looking, she quickly snapped the blinds shut. Wait until she hears I'm moving in, I thought. I tilted my head back to gaze at the sky and groaned loudly, then I went inside in search of my brother.

CHAPTER 14

I flew through front door, yelling, "Neal, have you seen it? Can you *believe* it! A goddamn pink hearse! Didn't I tell you that if we let Jake get involved with Mama's funeral something was bound to happen. Jesus!"

Neal rose to greet me and gave me a wide-eyed look. "Laney Mae, we have company." I glanced past him and saw who it was and then everything seemed to stop. I felt a rush of emotion that caused me to bring my hand to my chest and hold my breath for a moment. I managed to blink back unexpected tears. My intense reaction was not for the man seated before me; it was instead, for the person he represented. "Oh." That was all I could say at first as I stared in happy wonder. Before my silence grew too awkward, I managed, "It's good to see you, Mr. Smith. I guess you heard–?"

"Yes, a neighbor called. Probably called everyone in this neighborhood by now. Told me there was a hearse in your driveway so I figured out the rest. I wanted to come and pay my respects. I'm very sorry about your mother's passing."

"Did the neighbor happen to mention the color of the hearse?" I asked, standing before him, forcing a grin and arching an eyebrow.

Edward Smith held his lips into a straight line to try to prevent himself from laughing. "Well, as a matter of fact, they did."

I gave Neal a sideways glance. He smiled and told our guest, "Our cousin leaves his unusual stamp on everything he does but . . . he means well."

The old man sat hunched over, leaning with obvious weariness on a wooden cane. As I moved toward him to sit on an armchair, he began to stand but I held my hand up to stop him. "Please. You don't need to get up."

He sat, and his face paled slightly. He clenched his teeth in pain. "Damn arthritis. It never lets up anymore."

"I'm sorry to hear that," I told him.

"Well, that's part of getting old." He sighed and pointed his cane toward the window in the direction of the hearse. "I guess I'm next."

Neal and I cast glances at each other. "Oh, don't say that Mr. Smith!" Neal told him, with an uneasy laugh.

"Well, it's true! I believe I'm the oldest living resident left in this neighborhood except for Clive Anderson. I do believe I'm the one who has lived here the longest." He frowned and stared at his cane. His face was heavily lined, his complexion pale, but his eyes were a soft hazel green with bright flecks of yellow that sparkled to reveal a lively disposition and youthful alertness that stubbornly defied the toll of age. He shifted those eyes toward me and said, "So Neal says you all are burying her back in West Virginia."

"Yes, in Second Chance."

He nodded. "Of course, that makes sense." He paused then looked at Neal with a slight smile. "I've only been there once." My brother nodded, gratitude on his face remembering when Edward Smith had, in the middle of a dark night in 1972, ferried him to the safety of Second Chance and away from the wrath of Art. To change the subject, the old man pointed a finger bent with arthritis toward the large window. "So that fellow is your cousin? He's driving her back in the pink hearse, huh? Never saw such a thing in my life." He chuckled and shook his head.

I laughed, "Well, as Neal said, with Jake you never know what to expect."

The old man shrugged his shoulders and said diplomatically, "Who said a hearse has to be black?"

Neal made a sound that was part laugh, part exasperation. "Jake doesn't try to break rules on purpose. He just doesn't understand them to begin with. He sees things his way."

Edward Smith nodded and said, "Every family has got someone like that; someone who marches to a different drum, as they say. Someone who looks at the world a little different than the rest of us." He paused and then added quickly, "Not that that's bad."

I managed a weak smile and we sat in an awkward silence. I felt Dandy nearby. *I know you wanna ask him about Greg. Well, go ahead. You'll be sorry if you don't.* I cleared my throat and said as nonchalantly as possible, "So, speaking of family, how is everyone in yours? How's Susan?" I paused. "And Greg? How's Greg?" There. I said his name. I had not said his name aloud to anyone for a very long time. Perhaps to Neal, perhaps during some conversation about a childhood memory revisited, or to lament his absence to Dandy but it had been quite a while. And yet his name, his face, the very memory of him had never, in the twenty-six years since I had last seen him, been far from my mind.

Edward Smith cleared his throat as though he were to begin a great oration. "Well, Susie and the kids are fine. Her oldest, Jeff, is a senior in college this year. He's at Virginia Tech. Her youngest, Emma, is a senior in high school. We'll have two graduations next spring. Susie and Bill are living down in Fredericksburg now. I see them every couple of weeks." He appeared to have concluded his family update. There followed a minute of complete silence as we regarded the old man with expectation. As the silence grew, I felt my adrenaline pumping in my body as though I had just run a mile. I willed Edward Smith to continue, to tell me what I longed to hear: news—even bad—anything, about Greg.

Neal broke the silence. "What about Greg? Where is he now?"

The old man turned his head slowly and regarded Neal. "You mean to tell me *you* don't hear from him?"

Neal shook his head.

"Well, I guess that makes me feel better, Neal. I thought *I* was the only one he didn't keep in touch with." He cleared his throat. "Far as I know, Greg is now in Philadelphia. He is working for a landscaping company up there. Some friend of a friend owns it. He doesn't say much about it, but I sense he likes it." He paused, shook his head and looked at the back of his hand resting on his cane. "You know, he left home so long ago. First, he went to Colorado. Of course, that didn't work out. Then it was on to Oregon and then on to Alaska. What was next? Oh, then New Mexico. Then . . . let me see. Maine. By God, he ought to work for National Geographic!" He attempted to laugh but it was not a happy sound and so he frowned.

I said, "We lost track of him—"

The old man's head jerked up quickly and he spoke sharply. "*You* lost track of him? He's my son and I lost track of him or rather, he lost track of me." He shoulders sagged. "Not because I *wanted* to, you know, lose track. He and I never got along too good. He blamed me—"

"No!" Neal and I said this together. Neal added, "He didn't, Mr. Smith. Really. I know he didn't."

The old man raised his eyebrow and his face flushed. He thumped his cane angrily on the floor. "Of course, he did. His mom took her life. He had to blame someone, so why not me?"

Neal put his arm around Edward Smith's shoulder. "That's simply *not* true. Do you want to know who he blamed? He blamed himself. He always said if he had just gone looking for her sooner that he would have found her in time." Neal paused then added, "I could never convince him otherwise. And I honestly think that is why he won't stay in one place or settle down. He has to keep running."

Tears welled in the old man's eyes and again none of us spoke for a moment then I asked, "Have you talked to him lately?"

"Actually, we email each other maybe once a month. That's not much but it's more than we ever spoke on the phone. It would seem that writing is easier than talking for my son and me. So, after I got myself a computer year before last, I got Susie's youngest to show me how to email. Can you believe it? An old codger like me doing email?" He laughed and thumped his cane on the floor again. "So, I got his email address and wrote to him. It took him a few days to respond. When he did, I was quite happy. Mostly he communicates with Susie. As a matter of fact, the last thing he's been saying lately to her is that he's coming home here for Thanksgiving. I cannot recall the last Thanksgiving we were together, but I believe Gerald Ford was president."

"That will be nice." I said and felt a fluttering in my stomach at the thought that Greg would be here, would be physically close. Would I see him then? Would he seek me out? Or would he come and go and never bother?

Neal stood. "I hate to, but I've got to go and pack. Mr. Smith, can you give me Greg's email address? I'd love to reconnect with him."

"Of course. Do you have a pen?"

"I'll grab a pen and paper," I said and jumped up. I went to the kitchen and hurried back and handed Mr. Smith the notepad and pen. He carefully printed the email address on the paper and handed it to Neal who put the information in his shirt pocket. Then,

Edward Smith rose slowly and with great effort. We watched as he stood hunched over for a moment in obvious pain. He slowly straightened and stood somewhat erect but his shoulders, which seemed to bear a great, invisible weight, remained slumped. He said, "Just as well. I should be going, too."

At that moment, the front door opened. Jake, followed by Christopher, blew in. "Oh, I could tell you lots of stories," Jake was telling Christopher.

Christopher ran over to me in a rush of excitement. "Mom! Guess what Jake told me?"

I ignored him and said, "Christopher, this is Mr. Edward Smith. He's a neighbor of Grandma's. He came to pay his respects."

Christopher glanced at the old man and said, "Nice to meet you." Then he turned back to me, bursting with excitement. "Mom! Guess what Jake told me? It's really cool. He said one time this dead guy, up at the funeral home just sat right up! Can you believe it?"

I looked at Jake, horrified. "Jake! What are you telling him? You'll frighten him—"

Jake waved me off. "Aw, now don't go getting upset. There's nothing scary about it, really. It's just a physical thing. Sometimes it happens."

Edward Smith spoke, "How can a dead man sit up? I assume he wasn't inside a closed coffin?"

Jake arched his eyebrows and laughed. He bent over and slapped his knee. "Oh, that's a good one!" He shook his head and playfully punched the old man on the shoulder lightly. Edward Smith swayed but grinned. Jake said, "I'd like to see that. Could you imagine? You'd hear this thump when the head hit the lid of the casket!" He laughed and went on, "I don't know for sure how it happened. All I know is one night I was alone with this dead guy. He was some old dude that died of a heart attack or something. Anyhow, I had my back turned and Chet—that's the funeral director, my boss—had left to go take a phone call. Anyway, we had the dead guy laid out on the table to start the . . ." he hesitated and looked at Christopher, and then mouthed to the adults, "embalming." He paused, arching his eyebrows. "Then, I heard this sound, you know, of someone moving, cause the table kind of creaked. I could feel every damn hair on the back of my neck rise up. I said, 'Chet? Is that you man? Cause I sure as hell hope it is.' Well, no one spoke so I turned around and damned if that man's body wasn't sitting straight up on the table. Like he had just set up in bed; like he was getting ready to go get his morning coffee. Whew! You should have heard me hollering! Chet raced back in and when he saw me and saw the dead guy sitting up, he just laughed. Oh man did he laugh! He knew it could happen and all. He said it's psychological or something."

I groaned, "Physiological, Jake. Phys-i-o-logical. Not psychological. That has to do with the mind."

Jake shrugged. "Well . . . I guess he had a *mind* to sit up!" He whooped and everyone laughed, except me. Jake continued, "Chet says it was something to do with rigor mortis setting in or whatever."

"I believe," Edward Smith said, thumping his cane on the floor yet again, "that's what's happening to me and before it does, I better get home." We laughed and called out our goodbyes. I followed him to the front door. He started out but turned back to me. "I'll email Greg when I get home and tell him about your mother."

I winced. Contact with Greg, even indirect contact, gave me pause. I said, "Tell him I. . . I mean tell him that *we* . . . we said hello."

He looked at me steadily. "I'll do that. I'll tell him *you* said hello." He winked.

As I watched Edward Smith step carefully outside to the landing, my mind returned again to the morning twenty-six years before when his son had last stood there. It was 1975, I was fifteen and Greg had come by to see me, unexpectedly when he should have been at work at his job as a bank teller. I had slept in since it was the first day after school was let out for summer. He arrived when he knew Mama and Art were at work to tell me he was going to Colorado. *For how long,* I had asked. *Forever,* he had replied, looking down to avoid my eyes. He was taking a job there and starting fresh. *Don't worry,* he had told me, his dad would keep sending messages back and forth from me to Neal up in Second Chance. *But you can't leave*, I had implored, *not after . . . not after . . . what had happened.* He looked puzzled then recalled the kiss between us that I took to mean undying love but to him, had meant nothing. Suddenly Art had pulled in the driveway. He had forgotten his wallet. *What is going on here*, he had demanded, me in my nightgown, Greg standing on the steps. *Nothing is going on here,* we assured him, but he would not listen. Greg, eager to get away, said a rushed goodbye and turned to run to his car parked on the street. Like slow motion I watched him run away, leaving me alone with Art who hissed that I was a slut and said that now he knew what I did when he and Mama were at work. He grabbed me by the shoulders and pushed me back into the house. Panic seized me when I heard Greg's car start and I fought as if for my life. I screamed and swung my arms and clawed at Art, desperate to get outside before Greg drove away. Art pulled me into a bear hug and laughed at my weak efforts to fight him. But I managed with both hands, to grab one of his hairy arms and I sunk my teeth into his flesh, and he howled in pain and released me, and I broke free and ran through the screen door, but then he grabbed a fistful of my hair and yanked me back and the pain stung so I yelped like a wounded animal. *You little bitch*, he growled. He yanked me backward, but I managed to ball up my fist and land a punch on his nose and he dropped his hold on my hair. I stared in disbelief at the blood oozing between his fingers. I bolted from door but had only gone down the front steps when I stopped. Greg's car was gone. I dropped to my knees in the grass, sobbing. Then, a shadow fell over me and from the corner of my eye, I saw Art's shoes, dirty and scuffed, standing beside me. I looked up to his bloody face and knew I was trapped. My prince had left me alone with the beast.

I watched as Edward Smith lumbered slowly down the front walk, his cane making a click-clack sound as he went. Unconsciously I raised my hand and ran it over the back of my head where Art had pulled my hair that day. Neal's voice startled me from my memories. Standing behind me he said, "Hey, wait. Did he *walk* over here? In this heat?" He stepped around me and opened the door. "Mr. Smith! Want a ride home?"

The old man turned slowly. "I could use the exercise but it's so damn humid. A ride sounds great."

"I'll be right there." Neal turned and spoke to me quickly. "I got to go. Try get some rest and I'll be back at nine o'clock in the morning and we'll hit the road."

"Behind a pink hearse." I grimaced.

"Aw, come on," he grinned. "It'll make the ride more interesting."

I rolled my eyes and decided to change the subject. "Are you going to email him?"

"Greg? Maybe. Probably not until we get back. I've got to pack."

"I think you're right about what you said, about Greg blaming himself and him needing to keep moving."

Neal nodded, "I think we're all running from something. Aren't we?"

I frowned, "No. I don't think so."

"Yeah, we are. We're all running from something in our past that haunts us. Mama was. I am. You are. And so was Greg. And he still is. It's a journey that has no end."

I started to disagree but instead said, "Go ahead and email him. Tonight. Tell him about Mama and . . . tell him . . . I said hello, that I'm moving in here and we want to see him when comes home."

My brother tilted his head to the side and smiled. "I'll email him, but we shouldn't get our hopes up. He's been running away for twenty-six years. Don't you think if he'd figured everything out, he'd have come back by now?"

"But he *is* coming back. Mr. Smith said so. For Thanksgiving. So maybe he has."

"I guess we'll see, little sister." He leaned in kissed my cheek, "See you in the morning. And be nice to Jake."

❦

THE HOUSE WAS TOO QUIET. JAKE AND CHRISTOPHER HAD GONE to pick up dinner from our favorite Chinese restaurant and I was suddenly aware that I was alone in the house for the first time since Mama passed. This realization and the lingering aura of death made me shiver as I hugged myself. The living room felt chilly. I stepped over to the thermostat and adjusted the temperature to make the air conditioning cut off. I turned and surveyed the room. I could almost hear an echo of the last two days: sobbing and murmured voices, the phone ringing, Mama's lifeless body being wheeled away, the music I played for Mama, the Mills Brother's "Daddy's Little Girl" song, Edward Smith's voice as he paid his respects and even the booming presence of Jake. Blocks of sun and shadows from the late afternoon spilled through the large window and draped across the living room in an eerie array of darkness and light. The shadows lay atop the empty hospital bed, its mattress flattened and bare, and fell across the unplugged concentrator that stood silent.

I brought my hands to my face and began to sob and with no one to hear me, I felt free to release my anguish loudly and so I wailed, overwhelmed by a loss that weighed on me heavily and, wracked with sobs, my knees buckled. I reached out my hand and held onto to the wall to steady myself as I slid down to the floor, the way

Mama had when she got the phone call that Rob had been killed in Vietnam. I came to rest on my knees, weeping, and I remained in this position for several minutes. I took great gulps of air and pulled my already stained t-shirt up to wipe my eyes and dripping nose. I stared at the hospital bed and wailed, "Oh Mama! Come back. Please come back! Why did you wait so long to talk to me? Why? Why? Why?" I lowered my head and held my face in my hands. A sudden anger enveloped me. "And by the way," I said aloud, "If your spirit is going to go around paying visits to people, why haven't you visited me? Huh? How come, Mama?" Dandy crouched beside me. *Now it ain't gonna do any good to yell at her now. You've got to find a way to move on.*

"No, Dandy! Don't make excuses for her. What did I ever do to make her punish me like this?"

It was at that moment that Mother growled. The dog had been subdued most of the day, alternating between sleeping beside the empty hospital bed and the front door. Now I watched as she raised her head, and a low growl came from her throat. I stared in amazement; the dog rarely growled or barked, not since she had all but lost her hearing. I watched as Mother struggled to rise on arthritic legs. She stood shakily in place and then stepped back, away from the hospital bed, tail down as if in fear. She growled again, ears back.

"Mother, what is it?" I said loudly. The dog growled again then suddenly, she seemed to sense something directly near the bed. Despite her limited vision and deafness, Mother was on high alert. *That dog is seeing something for sure,* Dandy told me. I watched as Mother cocked her head and then in an instant, all tension seemed to leave the dog and she relaxed. Mother's tail began to wag. And then, remarkably, Mother began to dance.

Mother's dance was a special trick Mama had taught the dog many years ago when she was a puppy. Mother would bop in a jumping motion round and round in front of Mama when she commanded the dog. "Dance, Mother! Dance for Faye!" The dog would jump up and begin her show. It was a special trick and had taken Mama many weeks and many treats to teach the dog but with age and arthritis, poor Mother had not danced for years.

Until now.

And what's more, Mother simply did not perform her dance for anyone except Mama. That was part of the trick. Only by the command of her mistress did the dog perform. But now, to my astonishment, the terrier danced her dance following over two years of retirement. *Well, would you look at that?!* Dandy and I stared in wonder as Mother danced.

"This isn't happening," I said. My body went cold. I swallowed hard and brought a hand to my mouth and my eyes darted nervously around the room. What was I looking for? Did I expect to see the hazy outline of my mother's ghost? Did I expect to hear Mama's voice telling her beloved dog to dance? Nervously, I rose from kneeling and approached the dog. Mother stopped dancing when she sensed me. The dog looked up at me and then sat down, panting from the exertion. I knelt down and took the dog's head into my hands and gently rubbed behind her ears. "What made you dance, Mother?" The dog licked my hand and stared back solemnly. *I think your mama's spirit is here and she told that dog to dance,* Dandy said.

"That's insane," I said. I continued to rub Mother's head and the dog closed her eyes. Whatever had so mesmerized the animal had ceased. I lifted the dog and held her closely. "It's okay," I said in a hushed voice more to myself than the dog. "You need to go outside? Huh? Let's go outside." I backed out of the room, glancing around nervously. I bumped into a dining chair and let out a yelp of alarm then shook my head. "I'm losing my mind, Mother," I told the animal, "I'm losing my mind."

I was pleasantly comforted by the heat. I had felt so chilly in the house and the late afternoon sun felt especially nice. I put Mother down and she slowly made her way out into the yard, sniffing here and there. I walked to the pond and looked down at the fish. They came to the surface to greet me and I smiled. Then I recalled the awful scene just two days ago when Mama had declared who was and wasn't worth remembering. I looked at the empty chair in which she had sat that night, her last night ever outside. Her angry voice was as clear in my head now and I almost expected to hear her speak again. I shivered yet again and turned around quickly, half expecting to see her standing behind me.

Uneasy, I fetched Mother and carried her back inside where the sounds of cabinets opening and closing in the kitchen and the clanking of dishes and flatware on the table told me Jake and Christopher were back with the food and I sighed in relief that I was no longer alone. I bent over to set Mother down and when I did, I caught sight of the Kennedy portrait. It was hanging dramatically tilted to the right, so much so that Kennedy's head was at an angle. It had hung perfectly straight on this particular wall in the TV room for decades, ever since Art had banished the JFK portrait from the living room when he and Mama married (Mama reluctantly agreeing to its relocation, yet another concession to her controlling new husband). In fact, I doubt the picture had been touched since 1969 except for a very occasional dusting of the glass. I looked around the room, feeling foolish, and then stared at JFK's eyes. I told myself Christopher must have accidentally bumped into the picture. I put Mother down and summoned him.

"What's up, Mom?" He entered the TV room, chewing food and holding a fork, Jake behind him.

I pointed to the tilted Kennedy portrait. "Did you guys accidentally knock the picture off center like that?"

Christopher looked at the portrait of Kennedy and then at me quizzically. "Why would I do that?"

"I'm not mad. Just tell me. Were you two horsing around and maybe bumped into it or something?"

Jake made a face. "Laney Mae, we were playing video games, but we didn't mess with 'ol JFK."

"Well, how did it get like that?" I pointed.

Jake laughed. "Maybe we had a little earthquake, and it shook him that way."

I gave Jake a look of disdain. I walked over and straightened the portrait.

Suddenly excited, Christopher said, "Mom! I know what happened. It's Grandma! She's sending you a sign. Something about JFK!"

I scoffed. "What? Don't start that again, Christopher! Somebody just brushed up against the picture and it slid a bit."

"Well, I didn't go near that picture," he asserted. "Neither did Jake."

"Ok, never mind. It's just a fluke, that's all," I said.

"Why did Grandma have that old picture anyway?" he asked, pointing the fork at Kennedy as he and Jake turned to return to the kitchen with me following.

Annoyed, I said, "It's a piece of history, Christopher. I've told you the story about how Grandma brought that home from the Pentagon the day President Kennedy was killed." I followed them into the kitchen and sat down at the table, suddenly feeling very tired.

Jake sat across from me in front of a plate piled high with food. He grinned. "Hungry?" He chewed his food happily and noisily.

"Well, yeah, I am. Did you leave me *any?*"

"Of course! Help yourself!" He motioned to the containers on the counter, and I grabbed a plate.

Jake said, "Now Christopher, let me tell you about that picture of Kennedy. It meant a lot to Aunt Faye for sure, but it was really special to your mom." He leaned his face closer to Christopher's and said, "She used to talk to him all the time." He turned to me, grinning. "Didn't you Laney Mae?" He winked at me, chuckled then took another mouthful of food.

"You did, Mom? You talked to a dead man in a picture. That's kinda weird."

I glared at Jake. I looked at Christopher and hesitated. How to explain this without sounding crazy? "I was a little girl and yes, sometimes I talked to him . . . the picture—"

Jake interrupted. "Oh, you talked to him, and you talked to your imaginary daddy more than sometimes and beyond when you were little, Laney Mae. Faye and Neal would tell us. I think they were a little worried about you." He grinned and put another heaping fork of food in his mouth and chewed thoughtfully.

Christopher asked, "Imaginary daddy? What do you mean?"

Before I could reply Jake said, "Well, you see, Christopher, that JFK picture in there was sort of like... hmm. . . let's see . . ." He hesitated, thinking. He snapped his fingers. "He was sorta like your mom's friend. What they call an imaginary friend." He took a bite of egg roll and chewed earnestly as he considered this. "Yeah. He wasn't alive of course, but he seemed real to your mom. You know, President Kennedy getting shot and killed upset everybody in the whole world! We was never the same after that. Ain't that the truth, Laney Mae?"

"Yes, but I knew he wasn't my father and—"

Jake cut me off. "I know that and later, you made up a pretend daddy in your imagination. You missed your real daddy. Nothing wrong with having a pretend one."

Christopher looked sad. "I miss my dad. Sometimes I think about things I want to tell him or say to him."

"Oh Christopher," I said sadly. "I'm sorry he's not here for you more. We can call him anytime you want to talk—"

"No. But sometimes I pretend to tell him things I wouldn't really say. Is that all right?"

Jake said, "Aw heck yeah. It's good to talk! I talk to my dad sometimes and he's been dead for years. But your mom, here, well, you gotta understand that she didn't remember nothing about her real dad—she couldn't call him up on the phone! Wouldn't it be nice if we could call Heaven? Anyway, she was lonely and always wanted to know why she didn't have a daddy and what her daddy was like, and you know your grandma wouldn't talk about him, so I think that explains a lot."

I snorted and said, "Well, aren't you the child psychologist."

Jake said, "You shouldn't feel bad about having a pretend daddy or dead president and talking to 'em."

Christopher asked, "What did you talk to them about, Mom?"

Embarrassed, I hesitated then said, "I don't remember everything I talked about but usually it was when I felt afraid. Or when someone was mean to me. Or I didn't know what to do so I had to think out loud about it. Sometimes, I would share things that I was excited about . . . like if I did something good at school. Or maybe about a boy I had a crush on." I smiled bashfully at my son. "Sometimes I'd just talk to talk." I winked and said with a laugh, "JFK never answered, you know."

"Well, one time he sort of did answer," Jake said.

Christopher stopped chewing his food and his eyes got wide. He leaned across the table closer to Jake. "What do you mean, Kennedy's picture answered?"

My cousin looked at me sideways and grinned. "Well, one time your mom decided to have a séance. You know what that is?"

"Yeah. You try and bring spirits back from the dead."

"Right. Well, one time I was down here visiting—we were about your age—and it was around Halloween and your mom decided she wanted JFK to come here for real. So, we got a candle and a group of us kids sat around in a circle on the floor, right out there in front of that picture, with all the lights out. Remember Laney Mae?"

I nodded. "Yes, and I summoned the spirit of John F. Kennedy to come back. I said, '*Oh spirit of John F. Kennedy come back, come back!*' and all of a sudden there was this knocking sound and a moaning."

Christopher gasped. "What? Did his ghost come back?"

Jake and I laughed. "Well, we thought so," I said, "Until we realized it was your grandmother hiding around the other side of that wall back where the washer and dryer are, drinking her third beer and knocking on the wall and saying, 'Ooooo' to scare us."

Christopher laughed and rocked in his chair. "Grandma was something."

"Yes, she was," Jake said. He put his fork down, lowering his head.

We ate in silence and then Christopher went to the counter and brought fortune cookies to the table. He placed one in front of Jake, one in front of me and kept one for himself. "Okay, let's see what our fortunes say," he said. "I hope mine's good."

Jake ripped the cellophane off his cookie and crunched it in his hand. He tossed the crumbled cookie into his mouth and read his fortune while he crunched. "Be a generous friend and a fair enemy." He grinned. "I like that. I consider myself a very generous friend and I would say I'm a fair fighter." He nodded to Christopher. "Open yours next."

Grinning, Christopher opened his cookie and took out the fortune. He read the words aloud. "You display the wonderful traits of charm and courtesy." He paused. "Ah, that's just dumb! I want a better one than that. That's not a fortune. That's boring!"

"No, it's not, not at all," I told him. "You are charming and courteous. Those are good things to be, and you are, Christopher." My son blushed and I reached over and stroked his hair.

"Okay, you're next," Jake said to me.

I broke the cookie and put a small piece in my mouth. I held the fortune up and read it silently. "Well, this is a dumb one, too," I said and tossed the fortune on the table and stood. "Come on now, Jake, you said earlier that you need to take Pink Lady to the gas station and Christopher, let's load up the Suburban so we're ready to hit the road in the morning."

Christopher shook his head. "You gotta read it to us, like we read ours. Out loud."

"Yeah, Laney Mae, read it out loud," Jake said.

"No, it's silly. Let's go."

Christopher grabbed my fortune and read it aloud, "That which you wish to obtain, you already possess." He looked up at her quizzically. "What's that mean?"

"I don't know. It doesn't matter." But I did know and felt uneasy. First Mother dancing then the JFK portrait tilted. And now this. Was Mama's spirit sending me signals? It was absurd! I shook off such thoughts and began to clear the table. I carried our plates to the sink.

"Wait . . . a . . . minute," Christopher said. "I know what it means."

I turned to him, folding my arms across my chest. "Okay Mr. Fortune Cookie expert, what does it mean?"

"It's just like what Grandma's spirit said to me, remember? In my dream? She told me to tell you that you already have what you're looking for."

Jake's eyes grew large. "What in the world are you talking about? Aunt Faye's spirit told you what!?"

"Don't even get him started," I said irritably. "He was dreaming."

"Mom!" Christopher stomped his foot. "Just cause I was dreaming doesn't mean she didn't talk to me." He then turned to Jake, and, laying his hand on our cousin's beefy shoulder, proceeded to tell him all about his dream and the special messages Mama sent to Neal and to me. "So, we know Mom already has what's she's looking for, but we don't know what it is."

"And we never will," I said, crossly. "So, whatever it is that I'm looking for, I already have, according to Mama and the darn Chinese Fortune Cookie manufacturers! I think we leave it at that, okay?"

Jake grinned, "Well, whatever it is, you're bound to find it, since you already have it."

I glared at him, "Get in your damn pink hearse and go to the gas station."

CHAPTER 15

With its stately brick facade, Parker's Funeral Home was a landmark. Commanding in both presence and purpose, it stood on the same block since 1900 and had handled the funerals of some of the area's most prominent families and regular folks, too. While other funeral homes had sprung up, Parker's maintained a respected reputation as the dignified choice for one's dearly departed.

As I pulled the Suburban into Parker's parking lot the next morning at exactly nine-thirty, I was filled great apprehension. What would the staff of Parkers think of the Pink Lady? And what in the world would they think of the Pink Lady's driver? I watched with a growing knot in my stomach as Jake drove past my Suburban and Neal's Toyota Corolla parked next to me. I grimaced as Jake guided the Pink Lady to the covered receiving area at the back side of the building.

"Mom, are we all getting out?" Christopher asked. He was in the front seat next to me, while Mother was curled up on the back seat on an old comforter. She raised her head to look out the window, then repositioned herself and resumed dozing.

"No, you can stay here with Mother. It's really hot so, keep the AC on and I'll be right back."

"I think I should go with you."

"It's okay, really you don't need to . . . what about Mother?"

"I'll hold Mother. We're not going inside, right?"

I nodded. "Okay. You can come."

Neal joined us, and together we walked over to the covered driveway area and stood a few feet in front of The Pink Lady. Jake got out and waved to us and I heard Neal gasp, "What is he wearing?"

I stifled laughter, or tears (both were on stand-by) as we observed Jake in the same cut-off shorts as he had worn the day before but at least with a different t-shirt on. I tilted by head toward Neal and said in a low voice, "As a matter of fact, I asked him why he was not dressed more formally, and he told me that what he had on was fine for the 'transporting' and that he had dressed much worse than this to pick up other 'customers.'"

Neal struggled to remain composed. "Worse? Customers?"

I elbowed him gently in the ribs. "You're the one who hired him."

Looking straight ahead my brother said, "No, Mama hired him. You can thank her."

"Well, as long as he stays with the hearse and doesn't go inside–" I said just as Jake went to the double doors of the building. He was starting to go inside when I called out to him.

"Wait, Jake! Neal or I will go in–you wait out here."

"I got to go in, Laney Mae," he said. "I have to receive the casket. I got to handle the paperwork and all."

"I'll go in and have them come out here."

"No, I got to do it."

Neal said, "Why don't we wait out here, Jake? Let Laney Mae handle this."

As we debated this, we did not notice that a man had come out of the building. He paused a moment then cleared his throat to let his presence be known and said, "Excuse me." He was an older man with gray hair that he wore slicked back. He was dressed in a perfectly pressed dark gray suit, starched white shirt and navy necktie. Despite the heat, he showed not one spot of sweat on his brow or his upper lip. He looked from me to Neal then to Jake upon whom he now settled his gaze. His eyes widened as he scanned Jake from top to bottom. Next, he turned to look at the hearse. "And what, is that?" he asked, motioning.

Jake answered, "It's a hearse, of course. That's the Pink Lady."

The man pursed his lips together and I could tell he was about to convulse into laughter which was most definitely not appropriate at Parkers. He brought his manicured hand up to his brow and rubbed his forehead then lowered his hand to cover his mouth.

Jake, oblivious, continued, "I didn't introduce myself. I'm Jake Hall. I'm here from Final Rest Mortuary in Second Chance, West Virginia, to pick up the body of Faye Martin; their mother," he pointed to me and Neal, "and his grandma," he waved his hand at Christopher who held Mother on her leash, "and *my* aunt, and return her to her home to be buried there." He held out a manila envelope for the man.

The Parker's man composed himself. "How do you do," he began. "I'm Bill Logan, I'm a funeral director here." He shook Jake's hand then turned to Neal, offering his hand as well. I held mine out and he smiled and gave it a gentle squeeze, "Faye Martin your mother?"

We nodded.

"We at Parkers are very sorry for your loss."

"Thank you," Neal and I said together.

"I have to say . . . " Bill Logan began, motioning to the pink hearse, offering us a smile showing teeth so white and polished that I determined must be dentures, "That never in my thirty years of working in this business have I ever seen—"

"Such a beautiful vehicle?" Jake interrupted. "Let me tell you all about it." He told the man about pink clouds and transporting souls and why hearses did not have to be black. The funeral director's eyes grew wide as he listened and, to my relief, he managed to maintain a polite air, showing Jake both patience and kindness. At one point, he closed his eyes and rubbed his forehead, bringing his hand down to cover his mouth, I was certain, to again stifle a laugh. Finally, Paul Logan could take no more. "This is all very interesting, but we really should proceed," he told Jake firmly.

Paul Logan went to the double glass doors, opened one and used his foot to set the doorstop, then he turned his attention to the other door. There, inside the entryway, was Mama's casket. I felt the now familiar sense of loss and tears stung my eyes. Jake stepped over and wrapped his arm around my shoulder.

"It don't get any easier, does it?" he asked.

Christopher stepped beside me, took my hand gently and smiled up at me. I looked at Neal who gave me a sad shrug of his shoulders, his hands shoved into the pockets of his shorts. We watched the attendants of Parker's Funeral Home wheel Mama's casket briskly through the doors and around to the back of the pink hearse. We moved around to the side of the vehicle and solemnly watched as the four men lifted the casket in unison and slid it inside with military-like precision. Without a word, they stepped away, pushing the wheeled carrier back inside the building. Paul Logan stepped forward and handed Neal an envelope. "Here is the paperwork and invoice," he said. "My sympathies for your loss." He looked once again—as though to confirm he had not imagined all this—at Jake then at the hearse. "Safe travels," he said as he swiftly kicked the doorstops up and went back into the cool darkness of the funeral home. The doors closed with a soft whoosh.

Jake spoke, "Okay you all. It's time to hit the road." He looked at his watch.

"Yes. It's quarter to ten," I replied. "I figure we'll make a stop for lunch and get gas then maybe one other stop to stretch our legs and let Mother do her business. Then, going at a reasonable speed and as long as there's no traffic, we should be in Chance by two. Sound right?"

Jake and Neal nodded.

"Now Jake," I continued. "When you pull out of here, just head straight up the parkway, past National Airport until you see Spout Run and then the 1-66 West sign. Got it?"

Jake rolled his eyes, "Laney Mae, I know the way home."

"I know, but I don't want to go the Beltway. I want to go the way Mama always drove us."

"Don't worry. I've got this. I know exactly what Faye wanted." He grinned and added, "Just be sure to follow me! If I have any trouble, it'll be good to know you two are riding right behind me."

I raised an eyebrow, "Trouble? What kind of trouble, Jake?"

"Well, you never know," he replied. "I've had a few issues with the Pink Lady here, but I have had her checked all the way, including last night but . . . it's just so darn *hot*." He pulled a bandana from his back pocket and wiped sweat from his forehead.

"What do you mean, Jake?" Neal asked.

"Well, you know, we don't want her to overheat. We got the mountains to get up and down and I got to keep the AC on, you know. I'm carrying a lot of weight." He motioned at the casket with his thumb.

"Are you telling me this hearse might break down, Jake?" I tried to keep my voice from sounding shrill.

"Anything can break down, Laney Mae."

I clenched my hands into fists and forced myself to take a slow, deep breath. Through clenched teeth I said, "This Pink Lady of yours better get us all the way home. You hear me?"

Jake shifted his eyes down at his boots and when he looked up tears were in his eyes. "Laney Mae, nothing is more important to me right now than to get Aunt Faye home. Nothing! Don't you go worrying. The Pink Lady and I will get her home. I promise."

Christopher poked me on the arm. "You made him cry again," he said.

"We'll all be crying sitting along the side of the road when this thing breaks down," I snapped.

Neal said, "Well, she's running fine now. We have faith in you, Jake... and in the Pink Lady. We'll make it."

"You better believe we'll make it!" Jake's exuberance returned and he looked at me hopefully.

"Ok. Fine!" I said, "Let's get this show on the road. And I do mean *show*!"

Jake grinned and stepped toward the hearse. "Okay Aunt Faye," he said, tapping the back window outside as if Mama could hear him in her casket. "Let's go home." He got into the hearse and turned the key. The engine sputtered but came to life.

"See Mom?" Christopher said, again taking my hand. "Everything will be just fine."

Neal, Christopher with the dog, and I walked back to our cars as Jake drove past in the parking lot. Suddenly he slammed the breaks and stopped. The driver's door flew open, and he jumped out of the door waving flags of some sort.

"Laney Mae, Neal, wait!" he jogged over to us. "I forgot to give you this to put on your cars." He held out a window flag with FUNERAL imprinted upon it.

I drew back. "No, I don't need that, Jake."

"Sure, you do. We're an official convoy. You just stick it in your window, and it lets people know that you are part of the procession."

"We're hardly a convoy, Jake," I scoffed.

"But still, Laney Mae, we need it, so people don't cut us off and get in between us and to be sure they show us respect on the road."

I looked at the bright pink hearse and snickered, "Respect? Get between us? I don't think anyone is going to–"

Before I could finish, Neal grabbed the flags. "We'll use 'em, Jake. Don't worry." He grinned with wickedness at me, obviously delighting in every part of this expedition. "Jake's right," he said, "we don't want anyone getting in our way, now do we?"

Christopher grabbed a flag from Neal. "I wanna put it in my window," he said merrily as he ran to the Suburban, "Let's go, Mom!"

I bowed my head then looked up at my cousin. "You win again. Now let's get going."

I started the Suburban and motioned for Neal to go first behind the Pink Lady as I eased in line behind his Toyota. Jake rolled his window down and stuck his arm out. He waved happily and then pointed his index finger to the sky as if to say "onward." He drove the hearse in all its bright pink glory, observed, no doubt, by the entire staff of Parker's Funeral Home from the building's windows, out the driveway an onto the street. I adjusted my sunglasses, sighed and, with the morning sun shining brightly above us, our small caravan began its drive westward toward Second Chance.

WE HAD NOT GONE A BLOCK BEFORE PEOPLE ON THE SIDEWALK began to stop and point and stare at the pink hearse. I tried to sink down in my seat and still see above the dashboard enough to drive. I groaned when we came to a stoplight. People walking in the cross-walk did double-takes, gawked and laughed.

"Mom, how come they're laughing?"

I looked over at my son, "Really, Christopher? You don't under-stand why they're laughing? That is a *pink* hearse? Come on!"

"Well, I like it."

I rolled my eyes thinking what an unbearably long drive this was going to be, at least until we got moving on the highway. Then I had a thought. I reached down into my tote bag on the floor and pulled out some CDs. I had planned to listen to Beatles music on the ride up to share their music with Christopher and what better time than when we were trapped in the Suburban for a few hours? I had already mentioned this to him and told him we'd make game of it as I professed to know every single word to every single Beatles' song ever recorded. If I messed up, he won a point, if I didn't I won. We'd figure out the prize later. I pulled out a CD and waved it at him. "Are you ready to play the game with the Beatles' music? I swear, Christopher, I know every word to every Beatles song. I really do!"

Christopher shook his head and squirmed in his seat. "Mom I really would rather listen to my tunes right now, okay?" He reached into his backpack and pulled out his Sony Walkman and prepared to put the headphones on.

I frowned, "But we agreed; we'd listen to Beatle music on the way, you'd get to click through the songs to test me to prove I know the words and we'd make a game of it."

"I just don't feel like it right now." He put his headphones on and stared out his window.

I was crestfallen and felt I would cry which made me feel completely ridiculous, but the song game was something I had looked forward and I added to my list of disappointments. I looked in my rear-view mirror to see Dandy. He tilted his head, and his face was sad. "Okay with you if I play the Beatles?" I asked aloud. Dandy smiled. *Whatever you want.*

Christopher noticed and pulled his headphones off. "What did you say, Mom?"

"Nothing. Just talking to myself. Who else do I have to talk to?"

He put his hand on my arm. "Mom, I'm sorry. Don't be sad about the song game. I promise we'll listen to the Beatles and do the game on the drive home. Okay?"

I pouted but shrugged in agreement. He jabbed my arm. "The light's green."

We drove slowly and soon we were past the stoplights and able to accelerate on the GW Parkway. Christopher pulled off his headphones and exclaimed, "Look, Mom! There's the Pentagon. That's where Grandma worked!"

I smiled, proud he recognized the building. I told him, "Mama was proud to work there. Did you know it's the world's largest office building?"

"No way! Is that really true?"

"It sure is. It's quite a place."

"How long did she work there?"

"She worked there from 1962 until I was in college or so."

"That's a long time," he said. "And that is the Washington Monument!" He pointed out his window across the Potomac.

"Right again," I told him, smiling, happy to be engaging with him. "Do you know the name of that bridge up ahead?" I tilted my head to the right.

"Not sure."

"That's the Memorial Bridge."

"Oh yeah! And that's the Lincoln Memorial. The bridge leads right over to it."

"Yep. I think you know just about all the landmarks but of course you've been on this trip a few times and–"

Christopher cut me off. "Mom! Why is Jake going that way?"

I watched as the pink hearse veered to the left exit off the parkway instead of proceeding straight. "What in the world is he doing?" I said as I leaned over the steering wheel, gripping it tightly, glad traffic was moving slowly so I had time to switch lanes. I watched Neal's car veer over, too. I sped up to be closer to Neal's bumper. I tapped my horn lightly once and then twice. Jake rolled his window down and he stuck his arm out, his index finger pointing straight, gesturing us to follow him.

"Good God! Maybe something's wrong with the hearse." I followed Jake and Neal around the traffic circle at the Memorial Bridge and saw he was headed for Arlington National Cemetery.

"Hey, I thought we were taking Grandma to Second Chance to be buried. Not here," Christopher said.

"Christopher, we *are* taking her to Second Chance. I do not, for the life of me, know what Jake is doing leading us here."

Jake turned left and drove through the tall golden gates at the entrance of the cemetery with Neal and I following. He eased the hearse over to the curb just inside the gate and parked as did we. I opened the door and bolted out of the Suburban and ran toward the hearse. Neal followed me, looking equally confused. I glanced nervously around expecting military personnel to come running and escort us and the ridiculous pink hearse off the hallowed grounds. I walked quickly over to Jake's window as he rolled it down.

"What are you doing Jake? Why are we here?"

"Is something wrong with the hearse?" Neal asked.

Jake got out of hearse. "Now listen you two, it's all right. I thought it would be special for Faye to swing by here on her way to being laid to rest so she could see the Kennedys' and Rob's graves one last time."

I was incredulous. "See?! Are you crazy? What do you mean,

Mama's going to *see* their graves? Is she gonna open up the casket, jump on out, walk up and lay flowers on their graves? Really Jake?"

He rolled his eyes and laughed, "Now you know I mean figuratively speaking, Laney Mae. It's symbolic. And look here," he turned and leaned back into the hearse. He pulled out a piece of paper. "I got the special pass. You know, because Rob's buried here and all. We can drive right on up, pay respects, and be on our way."

"This is insane," I said.

"But important," Jake replied.

Neal watched the encounter, his head shifting at me then Jake, as if it were a competitive tennis match. I looked at him with wide eyes, expecting his help in talking our cousin out of this ridiculous side trip. He said, "Jake, we probably ought to just get on up to Second Chance."

"I'm sorry Neal," our cousin replied shaking his head. "But I promised Aunt Faye I'd do this."

"You did what?" I was flabbergasted. "You promised Mama you'd do this? When?"

Jake smiled sheepishly, recognizing that he should have already mentioned this unusual request. "It was a couple weeks ago. When she was on the phone to Mom. Near the end. She asked me to swing by here on the way back to Chance."

"I don't believe you. She never said anything about this to me."

Jake shrugged. "Well, she did. Look, it'll only take a couple minutes. We're already here."

Neal, fighting a grin, attempted to be serious. "Well, if that's what Mama wanted, guess we better do it and get it over with."

I glared at my brother and looked with disdain at my cousin. I was past the point of battles. Dandy appeared. *Now take in a deep breath. May as well go along if it's what your mama wanted.* I bowed my head and inhaled slowly. I looked up and said, "Okay, Jake. If this is what Mama wanted, let's get it over with."

Jake grabbed me and pulled me into a bear hug, lifting me off the ground. "Laney Mae, you are making your mama's spirit happy!"

Christopher had gotten out and joined us. "Why are we stopping here, Mom?"

"Jake says before she died, Grandma asked him to drive her through the cemetery on the way back to Chance." I let that hang in the air. When my son appeared neither confused nor surprised, I continued, "Don't you think that's a little strange?"

Christopher shrugged and looked at Neal who also shrugged.

I scoffed, "Well, then let's get going. Let's drive this ridiculous pink hearse through Arlington National Cemetery, hope the guards don't apprehend us, pay our respects to JFK and RFK and Uncle Rob and be on our merry way."

"Uncle Rob?" Christopher said. "Oh yeah. Grandma told me about him. He died in Vietnam, right?"

"That's right," Neal said.

Christopher nodded and said, "We named one of the pond fish after him." He squinted and held his hand above his eyes as he looked up at Neal and me. "But I've never seen his grave before like I have the others up in West Virginia."

"Of course, you have," I replied. "I'm sure I've brought you here. I remember because you were in your stroller, and it was so hot and–"

But Christopher shook his head. "But I don't remember that at all, Mom. I was a baby! I've been up to the other graves in Second Chance with you and Grandma. But I don't remember this." I thought for a moment and realized he was right; I had not been to Arlington since he was a toddler. Mama had visited Rob's grave on her own, but not me or Neal. Phil and I had always been away around Memorial Day when she visited, vacationing at his parent's lake house. I said softly, "I can't believe I haven't brought you here since then." Dandy said, *Well then, it's a good thing we're here, isn't it? Things happen for a reason.*

"See?" Jake said. "It's a good thing we came here." He turned and got back into the hearse. "Follow me. We'll visit Rob first. I know exactly where he is."

Jake drove a down a hill and led us around a few winding turns to the place where Rob was buried. He eased the hearse over and parked beneath a tall tree that towered above Rob's grave. His was the last headstone at the end of row of graves nearest the tree. When I was a child and we visited his grave, this had always seemed special to me. It was as if Rob not only deserved but was somehow granted, an extraordinary place among the rows and rows of headstones beneath that protective tree. I had managed to convince myself that my uncle was special when all around me the endless white headstones relayed a different truth: here there was no one more special than the other; death was the great equalizer.

We approached his headstone in silence, Christopher leading Mother on the leash. I stopped in front of the grave and looked up through the tree branches and suddenly felt lightheaded as I watched the tree limbs sway slightly in a welcome breeze. How long had it been since I was here, I wondered. I stared at my uncle's headstone. *It's nice you named your son after him*, Dandy said solemnly.

ROBERT CHRISTOPHER HARTMAN
U.S. ARMY
VIETNAM
FEBRUARY 25 1936
JUNE 4 1967

"Wasn't I named after him?" Christopher asked. "He was Christopher, too?"

I felt as if I was punched hard in my stomach, and I swayed with the realization that I had allowed myself to forget my uncle. That I had permitted so much time go by without coming here. I raised both hands to my mouth and a lump formed in my throat. I stepped forward but stumbled on a tree root and nearly fell so I dropped to my knees. I leaned over and wrapped my arms around Rob's headstone. It felt cool against my face. I began a rambling apology to him as I wept, telling him how sorry I was that I had not visited, that I had not brought Christopher since he was a baby and I begged him to forgive me. Neal knelt down next to me and put his arm around me. "It's okay, it's okay," he whispered.

Guilt-ridden, I turned on my brother, pulling away from him. "But it *isn't* okay, Neal," I wailed. "I should have come here! He died for our country and I got so busy somehow that I couldn't find the time to come pay my respects to him. I used to! I used to come here twice a year. Greg drove me after you were gone then I'd drive myself. I would put a rose on Rob's grave and one on JFK's and one on RFK's. I should have brought Christopher here before now. He's ten now! So many years have passed, and I haven't visited Rob. I'm so ashamed." Dandy knelt beside me and said gently, *Now, there's nothing you can do to change that. But don't be so hard on yourself. It's not like you forgot him. He was still in your heart.*

"It's okay honey. You didn't really forget him," Jake said. He reached inside the pocket of his shorts and pulled out a handful of tissues for me. "Crying is good for the soul. And you know what? Uncle Rob is watching down over us all. He knows we love him."

I focused on Rob's headstone then looked up and out over the many headstones in our view. I was overcome with sadness. "Look at them," I said as I pointed. "Look at all the graves. They all died. We can't ever forget them." Christopher stepped over and knelt beside me. He gently took my hand. "Mom, I'm here now. And we'll come back. We'll come back and visit Uncle Rob again. I'm proud to be named after him. Don't cry, Mom. He's not mad at you."

I pulled Christopher into my arms. After a moment, we stood, and I blew my nose. I stared at Rob's headstone and said, "I wish I had something to leave, like flowers." I cast a look at Jake. "Of course, I didn't *know* we were coming here." Neal chuckled and winked at me and the mood lightened somewhat. I was about to speak when we heard the distinct sound of guns firing. Somewhere nearby, out of our view, over one of the rolling hills of white head-stones, someone else was being laid to rest. In crisp, quick succession, the shots echoed against the stark silence of the cemetery grounds.

"What's that?" Christopher asked, concerned. "Guns?"

"That's a 21-gun salute," Jake said. "That's the highest honor our nation gives someone when they die. Someone who served." He put his finger to his lips. "Next, they are gonna play Taps. Listen."

Christopher asked, "Taps?"

As if on cue, a mournful trumpet could be heard in its singular tribute. Christopher froze at the hauntingly beautiful sound and I watched as it transfixed my son. When the last note finished, he looked up at me, his face wet with tears. "I thought I was done crying," he said. "I thought I had cried all I could when Grandma was dying, and I was so sad."

"There's always more tears," Jake said softly. "I believe the heart pumps 'em out to keep from breaking."

I sighed, "I know we really need to get going but I don't want to leave him . . . now. Now that we're here. He's alone without us." My voice cracked.

"I know what we can do," Christopher said. He dug into the pocket of his shorts. He pulled out a small, plastic action figure. "Let's leave this guy for him." I started to object. I knew the char-acter was a superhero in one of the cartoons Christopher watched endlessly on TV. Dandy said, *Well I think that's perfect. Rob was sort of an action figure himself.* I smiled and said, "Sure. Leave it, Christopher.

Rob was sort of an action figure himself." I smiled at Dandy. Christopher stepped over Rob's grave and carefully set the figurine atop the headstone. He looked back at me and smiled. I stepped over and touched my fingertips to my lips, planted a kiss on them and then leaned over and touched Rob's name etched in the marble. "Thank you, Uncle Rob," I whispered. "We love you. You're our hero."

CHAPTER 16

We drove for about an hour with no further events or detours and, fortunately, with little traffic. As we approached the West Virginia border, I reached over and tapped Christopher's shoulder, "We're almost in Wild and Wonderful," I said.

He took off his headphones. "What, Mom?"

"The state border. We're almost in West Virginia."

He smiled and sat up in his seat. "How many times you think you've crossed this border?"

"I wish I had a dollar for all the times. We spent so much time up here. Holidays. Summers. Did I ever tell you that your grandma even brought us up here once when she thought the world was going to blow up during the Cuban Missile Crisis when Kennedy was President?"

"What happened?"

"Well, the Russians put nuclear missiles in Cuba. You know where that is, right? Off the coast of Florida?"

He shrugged.

"Well, JFK told the Russians to get the missiles out or *else* and for a few days everyone thought there'd be war." I looked over at him and said, "Nuclear war. That would have been really bad."

His eyes widened.

"So anyway, your grandma drove us to Second Chance late one night. It was the day before JFK gave a big speech on TV about it and everyone thought there might really be a war and the end of the world. Mama took us to Aunt Claudia's, got a couple hours of sleep and then drove all the way back to the Pentagon the next day to work. She was sure us kids would be safer in the mountains."

"And were you? Safer?"

"Yes, we were." I stared ahead at the back of the Pink Lady as we drove. A thought made me laugh. "Uncle Frank always joked that we would have been better off dying in a nuclear war in D.C. than living in Second Chance since the town was all but dead since the coals mines had gone." I chuckled.

"Well, I'm glad you didn't die. I would never have been born!"

"You and me both, kiddo!"

"How long 'til you could go back? You know, 'til Grandma knew it was safe?"

"Well, I was so young. The whole crisis was over in a few days so probably not long. I don't even remember. Neal and Grandma told me the story."

"Well, I'm glad you were safe. I'm glad Grandma had somewhere to take you to get away from something bad." He put his head-phones back on, hit play on his Sony and looked out of the window.

❧

THE RIVER MOUNT DINER APPEARED BEFORE US LIKE AN OLD friend. "There it is, Mom!" Christopher said excitedly. As though it could be missed. It was situated on a slight bend on the road leading out of town. It beckoned to everyone passing through River Mount (and most people these days were doing just that) as a friendly last chance for a brief rest and a stretch of the legs before the next round of mountains were to be tackled on the way to Second Chance which lay over thirty miles beyond with nothing except a few farms in between. The diner had always been a welcome respite for Neal and me when we were kids and Mama often used promises of the diner's famous French fries or locally renowned frozen custard (or both) as a lure to keep us on our best behavior on the car rides back home.

I pulled the Suburban into the parking lot behind Neal and watched as Jake slowly guided the Pink Lady to a stop. I was glad to see only two other cars and hoped we make this a quick break and hit the road again without a lot of people gawking at the hearse.

"We need to be quick," I told Christopher as I opened the door. The heat hit me with a force. Neal had walked over to my door. I told him we should take turns going inside and he and Christopher should go first, use the bathroom and order while I waited with Mother and Jake. I walked Mother over to a grassy area and let her pee then poured her some water in a small dish. I walked over to the Pink Lady where I found Jake sitting inside the hearse with the windows rolled up, his hands gripping the steering wheel tightly, staring straight ahead. Something about the engine didn't sound right to me; it sounded like an animal whimpering.

"Jake," I said, rapping on the window, speaking louder so as to be heard through the glass. "What are you doing? Come on out and stretch your legs or go in and get some food and use the bathroom."

He slowly turned his head and looked up at me with a grin that looked forced. He shook his head, cracked the window, and said, "I'll just hang out here with the Lady." He quickly rolled the window back up. Exasperated, I opened the hearse door. "Jake, come on. Stop being silly. You must have to go to the bathroom. Aren't you hungry? Take a break. I'll stand guard of the Pink Lady." Suddenly I realized my cousin was sweating despite the air conditioning blasting and this fact caused me to lean further into to the car. Wet lines of sweat ran down his pink face. Inside the hearse it was warm. Sickly warm. Nauseatingly humid. "Jake! Christ! It's hardly cool in here at all! What is going on?"

He leapt from the car, forcing me back. He closed the door and grabbed me by the shoulders and said, "Now Laney Mae, calm down. I got to tell you something but don't get upset." He paused then said with great seriousness, "The Pink Lady is in crisis."

I stared at him and moved my mouth, but no sound came out.

Jake continued, "It's important that we keep her engine running and get back on the road as soon as we can. Or . . . I guess I could shut her off and let her cool down but then I'd be scared about Faye getting all hot and then the possibility Pink Lady wouldn't start up again, you know?" His eyes looked wild. He gripped me by the shoulders then said, "I think, under the circumstances, that I ought stay right here with her and not shut her off."

I swallowed hard, trying to process what he was telling me. I said, "Jake, listen to me: I am going to *kill* you, you hear me? If that hearse breaks down before we get to Chance? I'm going to kill you and throw you in back with Mama. Do you understand?" Dandy stood beside Jake. He admonished me. *Now you don't mean that, Laney Mae. Don't say such things. It's not at all helpful.*

Jake grimaced and nodded slowly as a trail of sweat crossed down his face. "In the casket or next to it?" He forced a laugh. I glared at him. "It'll be okay Laney Mae," he said. "Let's just not be here too long, okay?"

Just then Neal and Christopher came out of the diner, happily oblivious to the Pink Lady's plight, along with Hazel and Dottie Thomas, mother and daughter, the owners of the diner. Though Hazel was in her early eighties, she still worked at the diner most days. Her daughter, Dottie, in her fifties, did as well. They were fixtures in the small town. They were happy, upbeat women who seemed like family to everyone. "Laney Mae!" Hazel called out, wiping her hands on her apron as she shuffled slowly toward the hearse followed by Dottie. "Is that your mama in there? I'm so sorry about her passing. I swear it seems like yesterday when she was here. She was too young to go!" They came to stand by the hearse asking questions about how Mama had died and wanting to know about the service and wondering why the hearse was pink while I patiently tried to answer their questions all the time watching the hearse and expecting it to blow up at any minute.

"Ladies, sorry but we really can't stay long. I got to use the restroom then we got to hit the road."

"What?" Dottie said. "You just got here! You need to have some custard on a day as hot as this. Stick around!"

I touched the woman's arm. "Dottie, I wish we could. I really, really do. But see this hearse here?" I motioned to the Pink Lady. The women glanced at the hearse and nodded. Dottie laughed and said, "How could we not?"

I managed to smile. "Ha! That's right, Dottie. Anyway, see, it's really *hot*. And the hearse is getting too hot and, well, if we don't get going soon, who knows what will happen!"

Hazel and Dottie gawked at the hearse. "Well, at least let us pack you something to take," Hazel said. "But it won't be ice cream!" She cackled and her daughter joined her. "It can be, but then it would be a milkshake in this heat!" Dottie laughed. I groaned and walked quickly to where Neal and Christopher sat at a picnic table. I passed Neal Mother's leash as I told him to eat quickly, that we had to go and then and ran to use the bathroom. When I came back, Jake was swallowing the remains of a chili dog and chugging a soda Neal brought him while the Pink Lady idled. Christopher was done eating and he was standing with Hazel and Dottie as they cooed at

Mother who could not hear a single word of endearment from them. Neal had gotten me a sandwich and soda and I ate quickly. I shooed everyone to our respective vehicles, and we said our farewells, promising to stay longer next time. Hazel and Dottie told us they hoped to attend the funeral Saturday, but it was usually their busiest day, and they'd have to see. As we waved goodbye, I held my breath as I watched Jake put the hearse into gear and sighed in relief when the Pink Lady moved forward and returned to the road. Dandy leaned over from the backseat and said, *Now, you see? It's all gonna be fine. Just you watch.*

☙❦

WE HAD DRIVEN ABOUT FIFTEEN MINUTES AND TRAVELLED UP AND down the first mountain when I saw the steam coming out from beneath the hearse's hood. The inevitability of this helped prevent me from screaming. Instead, it was Christopher who screamed, "Mom! Look! Oh my God! There's smoke coming out of the hearse! Is it on fire?" He leaned forward, seatbelt straining, wide-eyed as he stared out the windshield. "Mom!" he cried out, turning to me, "What are we going to do?"

An unexpected calmness filled me. I glanced back at Dandy and mumbled that I knew something would go wrong and now here it was. He shook his head sadly. *Now just remember, Jake means well. Don't be too awful mad at him.*

I kept my eyes fixed straight ahead and watched as Jake pulled the hearse off the road, followed by Neal in his Toyota wondering what my brother thought of the plan to involve our cousin now. I stopped the Suburban behind Neal's car on the shoulder of the road and sat gripping the steering wheel, shaking my head. I watched as Jake leapt from the hearse, ran to the front, raised the hood and disappeared from sight. Suddenly, I saw a fountain of liquid shoot straight up along with billows of steam. It reminded me of what Yellowstone's Old Faithful looked like in a TV special about the national parks that Christopher and I had watched. Almost simultaneously I saw Jake bolt away from the hearse and heard him scream as Neal ran toward him.

I opened my door to get out as did Christopher. "Hold it right there, mister," I barked as I grabbed his arm. "You stay far away from that hearse. For all we know, the whole thing will blow!"

His eyes widened. "I will. I just want to see if I can help." Before I could stop him, he hopped out and ran toward the hearse, but stopped several feet away when Neal put his hand up for him to stay back. Jake had pulled away from Neal to return to work under the raised hood. I jumped out of the Suburban and slowly walked to where Neal and Christopher stood, dread filling me with every step.

"Can you believe this?" I said to my brother as I approached. "What's he doing? He can't fix it, can he?"

"I don't know. He's trying to, which I don't think is possible. I wish we had a cell phone! I've been meaning to get one and I haven't yet. Damn it!"

My voice dripped with sarcasm, "Yeah, me too, but I'll be sure to go get one right after I get back from this delightful trip." As Jake puttered behind the hood, I scanned the surrounding roadway. There were no buildings in sight, just empty land that went on for miles and an old billboard with a jolly invitation to rent its space (like anyone would) and, in the distance, a barn that looked to have been constructed a century earlier. "Wouldn't be able to get service here anyway I assume," I said. We stood by as Jake piddled under the hood and we could hear him talking to the hearse. "Now, come on Pink Lady," he muttered. "You had plenty of coolant. I figure you got a leak somewhere. I just got to find out where."

Neal and I frowned at each other and stepped over to Jake. I waited, arms folded, until he noticed us. He looked over then closed his eyes and hung his head, dejected. He shook his head slowly, side to side. He held up a hand to stop me from saying anything. That's when I noticed burn marks on his hands, arms and face and realized that he had been injured by the hot steam. At that moment, rather than anger, I felt an unexpected surge of love. He had done his best, I realized. He had almost gotten us there. With unexpected tears filling my eyes, I embraced him, fully and with no reservation.

"Jake, Jake, Jake," I said in his ear. "You tried! I know you tried. But it's too late. The Pink Lady isn't going to make it." I stepped back and raised my hands to his face. I gently touched his cheeks. "Oh Jake! You got burned! I'm sorry." I held up his arm to look more closely.

"Oh man, Jake," Neal said as he too examined our cousin. "You're hurt."

Jake said, "I'm not worried about a couple of little burns." He arched his eyebrows playfully. "Hey! I thought you was going to kill me, Laney Mae. Remember? You said you'd kill me and throw me in the back with Faye if Pink Lady broke down."

"Well, we say things we don't mean sometimes. We're so close to home. All we need is . . ."

"Coolant!" Jake jumped to attention. "I am telling you, if I just throw in a bit more coolant and don't run the AC, I think we can get the Pink Lady and Aunt Faye home. We only got about another twenty-five minutes and we'll be in Chance."

"No. It's over Jake," Neal said. "We'll take my car back to River Mount and get help." Neal walked to the hearse and we watched as he opened the passenger side door and then walked around and opened the rear door. I followed and stood beside my brother as we stared at Mama's casket. Then I walked around to the driver's side and opened that door. "Got to keep the inside of the car as cool as we can," Neal said. "Until we get help."

The four of us stood together staring at the sizzling hearse. Neal asked, "Jake, you know the undertaker in River Mount?"

"Nah, Chet probably does."

My brother scoffed. "Well, guess what? You get to meet him today! And after we introduce ourselves, we're gonna ask nicely if we can borrow his hearse. Got it?" My normally low-key brother had reached his limit. "Let's go!"

Dejected, Jake gave me a sad look. "Now I've even made Neal mad. I'm really sorry. But we'll be back in no time. You all want to come?" he asked, turning to me and Christopher.

I scoffed in disbelief. "Are you serious? We can't leave Mama's casket sitting along the side of the road in an abandoned pink hearse!"

Jake said, "I don't think anyone would take her. I mean, do you know how heavy–"

"We'll wait here," I said sternly. "Go!"

Jake nodded and walked quickly to join Neal. Christopher and I watched as they drove away.

"Mom, it's so hot," he whined. "How long will it take them?"

"I hope not long," I said, nervously eyeing the hearse. "Come on, let's get in the Suburban. We'll cool off some then keep the engine off for a while. We don't want *our* car to overheat!"

I started the engine, and it took a moment, but the AC finally began to cool the vehicle. "Put your seatbelt on. I'm going drive a little up and down the road and pull up in front of the hearse so when the replacement hearse comes it can back right up to the Pink Lady." I put the vehicle in gear, looked out onto the empty road, and slowly drove a short distance. I made a wide, sweeping U-turn and headed back toward the hearse. I drove just past it, made another U-turn then pulled off the road and onto the grass and parked in front of the hearse.

"How much does the casket weigh?" Christopher asked. As we

waited, we talked about caskets and burials and headstones and car engines and mountain roads and Jake's burns and bad luck. All the while, I would start the engine for short periods to turn on the AC and give us relief as I kept an uneasy eye on the Pink Lady, grimacing as I watched the bright sun reflect off the hearse and tried to block thoughts about my mother's body within, getting warmer and warmer.

It was Christopher who saw the pickup truck coming toward us. "Someone's here," he said, pointing out the rear window. "Is it Jake and Neal? Are they gonna put Grandma's hearse in that pickup truck?" That awful idea caused me to leap out as the older, classic Ford pickup truck with faded red paint, passed slowly by the Pink Lady. I could see a man behind the wheel, his jaw dropped in disbelief, staring at the broken-down pink hearse. He gave me a quick wave, then pulled in front of the Suburban. Christopher and I walked to his truck.

"Are you here to help us?" Christopher said brightly as he ran over to the man as he stepped from the truck. "Our cousin's hearse broke down and we need help!"

"I guess you do at that," he replied. He scanned the scene and his eyes landed on me. He stepped over with his hand extended. "Hello. Name's Matt. What can I do to help?"

I stared at him and my apprehension evaporated. He was boyishly handsome, tall with light brown hair hidden beneath a baseball cap. I stared into his brown eyes. They were flecked with gold and I allowed my gaze to linger on their warmth. I quickly estimated that we were about the same age. Something about him seemed oddly familiar. Had we met before? Was he from River Mount or Second Chance? I held out my hand and he took gentle hold of it and I felt an instant connection to this stranger. There was a calm assurance about him that I detected and sorely needed at this moment.

"Yes. Hi, Matt. I'm Laney Mae Martin. Thank you so much for stopping. It's sort of a crazy story but my cousin's hearse broke down and he and my brother drove back to River Mount to see if the funeral home there can help. We kind of need another hearse." I chuckled.

He smiled warmly and looked from me to Christopher and said, "I'd say you're not having a very good day." We laughed. He added, "Do I want to know why that hearse is pink?" He grinned.

I could not help but smile. "Long story."

"Well, I've got some cold bottled water in a cooler. Would you like some?"

"Love some."

He stayed with us, promising to make sure Jake and Neal got back okay. We traded small talk. He worked for the highway department and was on his way to visit family. I told him about Mama, the cancer, our family and about Jake and white and pink clouds and why, after all, hearses did not need to be black.

At last, we heard a car horn and turned to see a glorious black hearse approaching. I let out a yelp of joy and Christopher and I waved excitedly. We moved closer to the Pink Lady as Jake jumped out of Neal's Toyota and ran up to the black hearse. He said something to the driver who made a U-turn and drove just past Mama's hearse to ease the rear end of his hearse toward the back of the Pink Lady, leaving a few feet between the vehicles in which to move the casket.

I ran over to the hearse driver and took his hand as he stepped out of his vehicle. "Oh," I gushed. "Thank you! Thank you so much! I am so grateful to you for bringing this hearse."

"Happy to help a fellow undertaker in distress," he said, smiling and giving Jake a wink. "Couldn't leave you all out here in this heat, now, could we?"

Jake said, "George Wilson, this is my cousin, Laney Mae Martin.

Laney Mae, this is George. He's the director at the River Mount Funeral Home." I nodded and patted George on his arm. He was dressed in a short-sleeve shirt with a tie—a tie! He had on respectable black slacks (I was certain the suit jacket was neatly folded inside the hearse) and wore polished black shoes. He was organized and self-assured and I liked him immediately.

I introduced them to Matt, and we all stood in a small circle between the two hearses, Jake talking nonstop, and my impatience began to grow. I felt sweat dripping on my forehead and chewed my lip to prevent myself from screaming at my cousin. I looked at Neal, my eyes wide with aggravation. "*We have to go,*" I mouthed. He nodded and turned to Jake. "We have to get going, Jake. It's been a while out here in this heat. Time to hit the road."

"Say no more!" Jake replied. To George he said, "Let's do this." The two men walked together to the rear of the black hearse, and we watched as George efficiently pulled out the folded stretcher—what Jake had told me was called a church truck—unfold it and get it set up. As they did this, I allowed myself a savored sigh of relief. We are almost home, I told myself; this awful day is almost over.

"Mom," Christopher's voice interrupted my thoughts. "Where's Mother?"

Everyone stopped. Eyes wide, I looked at him. A queasy feeling of dread flooded my body. I swallowed hard. "She's . . . over . . . in the . . . Suburban. Isn't she?"

He shook his head, his face pale. "I don't think so. I don't remember seeing her in there." He ran to the Suburban. I watched him scamper into the vehicle, calling the dog, knowing that the animal could barely hear and that his calling her name was futile. My stomach dropped when he came out of the car. "She's not in here, Mom."

"Aw Jesus," I groaned loudly. "Jesus!" I wailed. Everyone stared at me. I waved my arms at them, a message to convey the need for action and movement. "Mother is missing!"

Matt looked confused. "I thought your mother was *dead* . . . she's in the hearse?" He pointed to the casket.

"No!" I shook my head. "Mother *the dog*! My mother's dog is named Mother."

Matt's eyes grew wide, "Oh... Okay."

"I can't explain. She's a Welsh Terrier. She's deaf. We have to find her."

"It's okay," Matt said, "I'm here to help."

Jake, Christopher, Neal and Matt began dashing about the road and along the shoulder looking for the dog. Calls of "Mother" filled the hollow. They ran about in circles, nearly running into each other, as they sought to find our elusive terrier. They got down on their knees and looked beneath the Suburban, beneath the two hearses and beneath Matt's truck. They shook nearby bushes and ran up and down the road calling the dog's name. Me? I stood frozen and silent in my devastation. I bowed my head and bent over at my waist. I thought I might vomit. My legs felt thick and heavy with helplessness and despite my brain screaming at me to dash about and try to help find the dog, I could not move. I rose and again watched the chaotic search continue. I turned slowly in a complete circle but saw no trace of Mother in any direction. "Oh Dandy . . . what are we gonna do?" I muttered this over and over. *Maybe she went over across the road there* he said pointing. I looked there and wondered if Mother might have wandered in that direction and gone into a small patch of trees I saw, seeking shade. *Maybe she's asleep over there and we can't see her,* Dandy offered. My feet wouldn't move. We were running out of time. We had to get going. Mama's body had to get out of this heat. I clenched my fists and tears ran. Things like this just keep happening, I thought, ruefully. I have screwed this up, I chastised myself, just like I had screwed up my life and my marriage. *I couldn't even keep track of an old dog! How was I going to handle life all by myself and raise a young man alone?*

"Mom!" Christopher came to me, his face red from running, tears on his cheeks. "We have to find her! We can't leave her out here all alone! Come on, Mom and help us look for her! Why are you just standing there not doing anything?" He pulled on my arm and forcibly led me toward the Suburban. "When did we see her last?" he asked, taking on the role of the adult. "Let's retrace our steps."

I stopped and jerked my arm free from his grasp. I wanted to run. I took in a deep breath, leaned my head back and looked at the sky, the brightness of the sun stinging my eyes. Then, I let out a loud cry filled with all my despair and every ounce of my anger. My wail was piercingly loud, and its intensity made my throat hurt and my lungs feel strained. Quickly spent, I stopped and gulped great amounts of air as Christopher, Jake, Neal and Matt came toward me and formed a half-circle around me. I dropped to my knees. I began to pray, but not to God. Instead, I prayed to my mother. "Mama, you have got to help us," I cried. "I know you know where Mother is! Help us, Mama. Help us find her! Please!" My knees ached with each prick of the gravel in my skin but to me it was a pain I deserved, my penance. I raised my arms up to the sky and swayed back and forth. I looked up at Jake, Christopher and Neal whose faces reflected both my anguish and despair. I turned to look at Matt, this stranger, our pickup truck driver savior, and stared into his eyes fully expecting him to turn away, run to his truck and speed away from this insanity. But he held my gaze and something in his eyes calmed me. Now embarrassed, I sighed deeply. Dandy looked down at me too. *Honey, you have got to pull yourself together.* I opened my mouth to speak and was about to say that we had to leave, that Mother was old anyway, that it was all my fault, and I was sorry, but that we had to get going to get Mama's body home, when the clear, steady voice of George Wilson announced, "I found your dog."

A hush fell. We looked in the direction of the undertaker. He pointed to inside the Pink Lady. "She's in here. Come over and see for yourself."

With Matt's help, I rose unsteadily from my knees and joined the others as they ran over to George who stood behind the Pink Lady, pointing to the inside of the hearse. And there, somewhat hidden beside Mama's casket, lay Mother. She was curled into a ball, her furry body as close to the casket as she could get. No one said anything for a moment. We each stared silently at the dog. Mother seemed to sense us and waking from a dream, raised her head and peered out at us with sleepy eyes. She seemed surprised to have been discovered and cocked her head.

"Oh Mother!" Christopher cried. He crawled into the hearse. With some struggle in the narrow space, he gathered the dog into his arms. "How did you get in there, huh? How'd you get in there, girl? You hardly ever jump up at home anymore." I wondered the same thing. I reached for the dog, but Christopher pulled away from me with an indignant look. "No! You were going to leave her. You don't get to pet her now. I'm holding her all the way until we get to Chance." He buried his face in the dog's neck as he struggled to hold the animal. Matt stepped over to him. "So, this is Mother, huh? Can I hold her? Help carry her?" Christopher regarded him for a moment then allowed him to take the dog into his arms. Matt cast a quick glance at me and said, "I've never met a dog named Mother." He carefully sat the dog on the ground and Christopher clipped its leash on.

"And you've never seen a pink hearse either," I said, and we laughed. It felt good to laugh.

"Today's one for the books."

Jake's voice boomed, "Well, all's well that ends well!" He turned to the undertaker. "George! We owe you a lot my friend. You done saved the day—again!"

George smiled and nodded. "Best we get moving now," he said solemnly.

We watched as George wheeled the carrier over to the Pink Lady. Next, George and Jake, with Matt's and Neal's help, lifted the casket from the Pink Lady onto the stretcher, wheeled it the short distance to the other vehicle and slid it into the new hearse. The sound of the black hearse door closing comforted me. This latest ordeal was over and done and the solid slam of the rear door was the period at the end of a long, unruly sentence in time. George turned to face us. "I'll get her safely to Second Chance from here, don't you worry," he told us. "I'll get turned-around and ready to go while you all get in your cars to follow."

"I'm right with you, George," Jake said. "Just let me lock up the Pink Lady." He jogged over to the hearse, gathered his bag and a few items then quickly locked and closed the doors.

George waited a moment and stepped over to Jake. He laid a hand on his shoulder. "Jake, I think I'll take it from here. You ought to stay with your family, don't you think?"

I rolled my eyes. "He can ride with you, George," I told him. "I'll be just fine."

"No," Jake stepped toward me. "George is right. You are all upset and shouldn't be driving. I'll drive your Suburban from here."

I cackled, "The hell you will! I hope I never see you behind the wheel of a car again!" I turned to Neal. "Let him drive your car or ride with you."

Before Neal could answer Jake said, "No Laney Mae, I'm riding with you, my little buddy and 'ole Mother. You can drive."

"Oh, can I? Well, thank you, Jake. Then let's go!" I started to leave, then remembered Matt. I spun around. He stood with his hands in the pockets of his jeans. He smiled. I walked over to where he stood by the Pink Lady. "Sorry, Matt. I didn't want to leave without saying thank you. It's just been . . . insane, you know?"

He raised his eyebrows. "Uh, well, no I really don't know what you've been through," he replied. "But yeah, this is pretty crazy." He grinned.

I held out my hand. "I can't thank you enough for all you did. You were so nice to stop, to give us the water, help look for Mother, move Mama's casket. Everything."

Neal stepped over and shook hands with Matt as did Jake and Christopher. "I'm sure glad you stopped," Christopher told him. "Thank you."

"Don't worry about it," he said. "Made my boring day, interesting." He smiled. "Maybe we'll cross paths again. My aunt and uncle live not far from Chance. I pass through every now and again. Was on my way there now to visit, matter of fact when I . . . found you."

"Damsel in distress," I said, and we laughed. He opened the driver door to the Suburban for me and I climbed inside. I watched as he jogged over to his truck and hopped in, thinking about the many ways chance encounters can change our lives, if only for a moment.

"Well, goodbye and good luck!" he called as he pulled his baseball cap off, tipped it toward me and put it back on his head. We watched as he drove away.

I started the engine and we all groaned when hot air hit us from the vents. I turned off the AC and rolled the windows down. "Are we all accounted for?" I felt tired yet giddy with relief that this ordeal was behind us. I reached over and patted Christopher's head and mussed his hair then I swiveled around to look at Jake in the back seat with Mother beside him. Dandy grinning.

"Well, Jake," I said, "you did your best. Let's get home."

"Home sweet home!" he said.

I pulled out onto the road and eased into place behind Neal's car behind the George's hearse. As the Pink Lady faded from view, Jake sighed. "Chet is not gonna be happy, I'll tell you that."

I grunted, "You think?"

"Hope he's got the white hearse fixed." He chewed on his thumb nail. "Well, what can I do about it now? We'll just have the Pink Lady towed back and fix the leak and she'll be good as new." With that happy thought, he leaned forward and handed Christopher a CD. "Pop that in and crank it," he said, grinning.

"No–let's have some peace and quiet," I pleaded.

Christopher ignored me and slid the CD in. Soon the familiar opening of John Denver's "*Take Me Home Country Roads*" began to play and Jake raised his voice in song.

"Jake, no. I'm not in the mood . . . stop!" I yelled over his singing, but Christopher joined him and soon even I could not help myself and Dandy joined in, grinning happily at me as I glanced back in the rear-view mirror. We sang loudly and we knew all the words. We had always sung this song on the trip back to Chance. It was our anthem. Singing it now somehow felt right, more than right; it was a proclamation that we were indeed home. My cousin's voice was filled with such gusto that I smiled fondly at him in the rearview mirror. I had forgotten what a splendid voice he had and, as I looked at him now, I wondered if he still played guitar with the band he had formed in high school. The band had been his dream, I recalled, and now he worked at a funeral home driving a pink hearse and yet, he loved that, too. I grinned as I could easily imagine him singing old rock songs to the dead under his care at the Final Rest Mortuary. Yes, I could see that.

I glanced over at my son and was happy to see him singing, a genuine smile on his face. I sang louder and allowed myself to be swept up in the sentiment of the lyrics that stoked pride inside me for these mountains and the people who lived here. Nearing Second Chance felt like a pair of gentle arms, gently enfolding us like the embrace of an old friend. Singing seemed to make all the bad things that had happened to us on this day, and in all the previous days, fade away. It had the effect of making us feel, at least for a moment, as if we were driving toward a happy occasion, like a wedding, not a funeral. It was joyful and silly. And necessary.

At just after three p.m., our little caravan arrived in the town of Second Chance. Neal and I drove behind George's hearse as it slowly pulled into the driveway of The Final Rest Mortuary. I turned to Jake, "This is your stop, Jake. I'm not going in. You take it from here. I'll see you back at your mom's, okay?"

He nodded, collected his things and got out of the Suburban. "What a day, huh?" He chuckled and slammed the door. He leaned in the driver's window. "And don't you worry none about Faye's . . . condition. Chet's a miracle worker when it comes to restoration." He winked at me as he turned away. I tried not to imagine Mama's body inside the casket as I watched him run up to George. Suddenly I was overcome with a heavy weariness. I put my head down on the steering wheel. Christopher leaned over and put his hand on her shoulder. "Mom, you okay?"

I turned to look at him. "I'm just tired. But I'm okay now. Now that we're here. Now that we're in Chance."

I followed Neal as we drove a short distance and up the steep incline to the rugged and hilly area of the Hartman family homes. The Suburban seemed as fatigued as the rest of us as it climbed the steep hill until at last, I pulled into the driveway of Claudia's home, put on the brake and turned off the engine. We sat in silence for a moment and then Claudia appeared, stepping out on to the front porch. We watched as she wiped her hands on her apron and took the end of it up to her face and dab her eyes. The sight of us seemed to overwhelm her. She shook her head silently side-to-side, then put her hand up to her mouth in an attempt to remain composed. With her other hand, she nervously bunched up the apron.

With an energy I did not know I possessed, I leapt from the Suburban. I ran across the yard and up the steps. I tripped at the last step, caught myself and rose back up. I stood steps away from my aunt. I waited. Claudia opened her arms widely and I lunged, falling into her embrace.

CHAPTER 17

I heard singing and knew it was morning, but felt so tired I could not open my eyes and so I allowed myself to be pulled back down to the threshold of blissful sleep. But the singing was coming closer and getting louder. I recognized the song, and the singer and smiled, my face squished into the pillow as I lay on my side beneath the bedspread. I opened one eye, then her other.

Claudia appeared in the bedroom doorway holding a tray, singing a familiar song:

*"WHEN THE RED-RED ROBIN COMES BOB, BOB, BOBBIN' ALONG, ALONG
THERE'LL BE NO MORE SOBBING
WHEN HE STARTS THROBBING HIS OLD SWEET SONG"*

She sat down on the end of the bed, balancing the tray on her lap as she continued to sing:

*"WAKE UP, WAKE UP, YOU SLEEPYHEAD,
GET UP, GET UP, GET OUT OF BED*

Cheer up, cheer up, the sun is red,
live, love, laugh and be happy"

I pushed myself up and grinned, "Well, that's quite a wake-up service."

Claudia cackled, "Oh! Do you remember that song?"

"Of course."

She passed the tray to me and said, "Well, you should remember because we always sang it around here a lot, didn't we?"

"I used to sing it to Christopher sometimes, too. When he was really little."

"Well, that's special because your daddy used to sing it to you, too." She winked at me.

I frowned and my happy mood evaporated. "Well, I only know that because *you* told me. My own mother never told me anything about him, even when—" I caught myself.

"Even when what?" Claudia leaned closer.

I reached for the mug of coffee on the tray and sipped. "Even when she had the chance."

"Well, that was Faye," Claudia said matter-of-factly.

I grunted and took another sip.

"Did you think she was gonna break down and talk to you about your daddy before she died?"

"I hoped she would."

"Well, I'm sorry but Laney Mae, I can't say I'm surprised. For crying out loud, she never did forgive him. You know that."

"Yeah, but I do think at the end she wanted me to know something. She tried to . . ."

"Tried to what?"

I shook my head. *Why tell Claudia this now? It wouldn't change anything.* "Never mind. I'm just grateful for what I do know about him. And you're one of the only people who ever told me anything."

"I did what I could. I know it was hard for you."

"You know what I just realized: I'm an orphan now."

Claudia clucked. "Oh, for crying out loud! *Of course* you are an orphan. So am I. If things go according to plan, we all end up orphans Laney Mae. Christopher will too." She rose from the bed and put her hands on her hips. She was short and heavyset but had an energy that defied her physical condition. She had been athletic and slender in her youth. She still had a head of thick golden hair that she colored at home, which was about the only thing she did for herself; Claudia was put on this world to serve. Her eyes were always watchful, and everyone knew she rarely missed anything; you couldn't pull the wool over her blue eyes. Standing before me, I knew she was about to unleash a precise report of the current state of things as regards to the Hartman family and my mother's funeral. In another life (as a man no doubt, given gender role limitations) I could envision Claudia as a military commander rallying the troops, crossing the Delaware, charging up San Juan Hill or storming Normandy. Her verbal torrents came fast and with purpose; it was best to not even try to interrupt her. Her proclamations usually began with "Oh!" or "Now listen here!" as this one did.

"Now listen here, Little Orphan Laney. Ha! You rest as long as you want. Frank's downstairs asleep on the couch. Of course! Christopher is with Harrie wandering around somewhere already asking for another breakfast and Jake called from the funeral home and everything is coming along. He's heading back to get the hearse this morning with a tow truck. Oh! What if it it's not there? What if someone took it? Who would want a pink hearse? Ha! I still can't believe that happened! Oh! Neal's already up and had breakfast, and I sent him out on some errands. And Hilda woke up early and is probably back asleep already sitting there in her wheelchair, but she understands what's going on. I mean yes, she's eighty-years old and yes, she's had a stroke and all, but her mind still works. She knows

Faye died. Oh, my lands, how she cried. She can't speak in words anymore but when I told her, she wailed and wailed. So sad. Oh! And haven't seen Margaret or Ruth yet today but they'll be on over soon. Ruth is the laziest woman I ever met! She better step-up and help us today!"

I sighed looking for a way to interrupt. "I'm sure she'll be fine. Don't give her a hard time."

Claudia's eyes grew wide. "A hard time? Oh no! Let's not give *poor* Ruth a hard time! Oh alright. I'll stop with my ranting! But one more thing: none of us knows if Donnie is coming. Do you think he would honor us with a phone call and let us know? Of course not! His own mother hasn't seen him in at least three years. Poor Hilda! And she can't even say anything about it! He better show-up! We could sure use his help hauling his mother around in that wheel-chair! Then there's Ruth's two. I doubt very much either of them is coming up here to this mountain to pay their respects to their Aunt Faye. I can't remember the last time I saw them. But Margaret's two girls will be here with their kids. I expect they'll arrive early in the afternoon. Christopher can play with them. But Harrie and him are having fun together. She's so childlike, you know and just loves him. So, the bottom line is, I'm not sure how many to expect for food but I sent Neal out to get us some lunch meat and cheese and bread and chips and cookies and plenty of beer and soda and stuff, so we're set there."

I spoke quickly before she could start again. "Claudia, it's okay, really. Who cares if Donnie or any of the other cousins show up? If they come, great. If not, don't worry about it. What good are they now? Why is it that we only expect people to show up *after* someone dies? What good is there in that? Once someone's dead?" Claudia bowed her head and her shoulders slumped, but I paid little atten-tion as I continued my own rant, "I just feel bad for Hilda and Ruth. This is when they need their kids. While they are alive! You know?

So, don't worry about them. Just focus on those of us who are here. Okay?"

Claudia stared at the floor in silence. I was puzzled by her sudden reserve and when she looked up, she had tears in her eyes. She tilted her head to the side and bit down on her lip. She started to speak but hesitated which was totally uncharacteristic. Finally, she said, "Laney Mae, I want you to know that I'm really sorry I didn't make it down to Virginia to see Faye before . . . you know. . . before she died. While she was sick with the cancer. I should have been there to help you and Neal. I should have made Jake drive me down. All of us. Me, Margaret, Harrie, Frank, and Ruth—well, maybe not all of us; someone would have had to stay here to care for Hilda. But we should have come down. I just . . . I just couldn't. I didn't want to see her like—"

Anger began to simmer in my chest. I shifted by eyes to where Dandy stood in the corner. *Now don't be hard on her. She's got a lot to handle up here. Forgive her.* I held up my hand to Claudia. "It's all right, Claudia. I appreciate you saying that."

Claudia dabbed her eyes with her apron. "I just wanted you to know that."

"Don't worry about it. Really. I forgive you." Dandy winked at me.

"Oh, thank you sweetheart. And Laney Mae, I know how hard this has been on you and I want to promise you that this sad time will pass. You'll be walking through fields of flowers again, sweetheart. Just like the song. I promise."

"Oh Claudia," I said and now my voice broke and I was the one to fight back sudden tears. "There are no fields of flowers for me. There never were. My life has been mostly walking around with a big 'ole hole in my heart because a big part of me was missing and I can't seem to figure out who I am or what I should be."

"Oh honey, you're our Laney Mae! That's who you are and all you need to be. And you not having your daddy or Faye marrying that awful Art person or your husband leaving you for that other woman, well, you can't change that. None of us can change the things that happen *to* us. But, I do believe you can now start fresh. You got your whole life ahead of you."

This made my stomach knot. No, I thought, my life is behind me. I have nothing left. Only Christopher and he will leave me one day, too.

Claudia clapped her hands together, another trademark of hers she used to move things along or change the subject. She grinned and said, "Come on now! Enough tears! We can cry later, can't we? Eat your breakfast, you got a long day ahead. Oh! Bring that tray down when you come." She left the room humming.

I used the bedsheet to dry my eyes. I nibbled on the toast and sipped coffee. I glanced around the shabby bedroom with its peeling wallpaper of little pink and red flowers and mixed-matched furniture. A picture of Jesus, a photograph of JFK from an old LIFE Magazine, a framed print of Franklin Roosevelt and an oval mirror above the dresser adorned the walls of the room. Jesus, JFK, FDR, the mirror, and the wallpaper were a testament to a long-gone era from whenever someone had hung them there. I felt more a part of their world than my own.

※

A LITTLE LATER, I MADE MY WAY DOWNSTAIRS. I ENTERED THE living room and noticed the faint but distinct smell of coal that lingered in the air, especially near the large stone fireplace which had been built nearly a century before by my great-grandfather. The smell of coal was a constant, despite the lack of active mining in the town and despite the fact that no coal burned in the fireplace on this late summer day. It was embedded in the home's wooden structure, in the fabric on the furniture and the curtains, on the floor coverings and in the seemingly constant thin layer of soot that coated everything. From the odd assortment of knick-knacks displayed on the mantel to the lamps and ashtrays on the tabletops.

Scanning the room, I considered that if the stone fireplace represented strength and balance, the rest of the room represented disorder and the random accumulation of things. Things that were needed to survive on a mountain where life was hard and money scarce. Placed here and there about the room, with no sense of order, was a mixed-matched assortment of cushioned and wooden chairs, and side tables. Their collective randomness was much like our family: many stayed put for years while others kept moving about.

I found Harrie and Christopher on the floor eating cereal and watching cartoons on an old television situated in a corner of the room. Mother the dog sat in front of them keeping what was left of her eyesight on each spoonful they took, hoping some would drop. Next to them was Aunt Hilda in her wheelchair. Claudia had positioned her in front of the TV where she sat slumped to the side, staring wide-eyed at the cartoons. I knelt beside her.

"Hi Hilda," I gently rubbed her arm. She shifted her gaze toward me, and her eyes lit up in recognition as she reached, with her good arm, to touch my face. She moaned in happiness. Tears filled her eyes as she stroked my face and then reached down to grasp my hand. Her mouth worked as she tried vainly to speak, reminding of Mama's last attempt to speak to me. "I know, Hilda. I'm sad Mama died. I know you are, too," I told her gently. I rose and kissed her cheek. Hilda rocked her head up and down in acknowledgment as her tears ran. I pulled a tissue from the pocket of my shorts and dabbed away her tears. "It's okay," I told her.

I stepped over to where Christopher and Harrie sat on the floor, cross-legged. "Well, good morning," I said, patting the top of Christopher's head.

"Hey, Mom."

"Did you sleep good? I didn't hear you get up."

"Yeah, really good but Harrie and I got up early and we've been out exploring, and this is really our second breakfast."

Harrie said, "That's right. But we had eggs for our first breakfast. Claudia made 'em." She grinned, crunching the cereal loudly. I smiled at her. Even at sixty-three years of age, Harrie retained a childlike manner and cheery disposition. Looking down at her now, I noticed wrinkles around her eyes and that her hair, kept short for easy maintenance, was streaked with gray. Like the rest of Mama's siblings, Harrie was getting older and yet she thrived with an energy that defied both her age and condition.

"All right then," I said. "Two breakfasts are better than one. Has Mother been fed and taken out?"

"Yep," Christopher replied. "She did her business."

At that moment Margaret, Ruth and Claudia, chattering loudly, came into the room from the kitchen. My aunt Margaret spotted me and squealed, "Well, look who decided to get up!" She grinned and spread her arms wide and strode over to me and wrapped me in a tight embrace. "How are you doing, sweetheart? I know this is hard for you." She smelled of powder and hairspray. She stepped back, still grasping my arms tightly. "Honey," she said, frowning deeply, "you look tired."

"Well, I slept well." I gently extracted myself from her arms.

Ruth spoke, "So, is everything ready for the viewing? After what happened?"

I turned to regard her. Ruth's expression was dour. I could not recall the last time I had seen my aunt smile, or if I had ever seen her smile. Ruth had been the closest in age to Harrie and it had fallen mostly to her to keep an eye on her special sister. My theory had always been that the toll of that responsibility and repressed bitterness over the task, plus what was probably just her natural personality, made her generally grumpy. Estranged from her own two adult children, forlorn and judgmental, Ruth kept mostly to herself and that was fine with everyone.

"As ready as it can be, I guess."

Ruth frowned more deeply, "I hope you do more than guess! I don't know that I'd trust Jake and that boss of his to get this right."

"Ruth!" Claudia snapped. "You just stop that right now! Why are you saying that? Don't you talk about my boy like that! Why do you always like to cause trouble?" Claudia turned to me, "Don't listen to her, Laney Mae."

I rolled my eyes and suddenly felt an overwhelming urge to scream. I gritted my teeth and with effort, forced the tone of my voice to remain polite. "I'm sure everything will be fine."

The three women continued their sniping and so I walked over to the old lumpy sofa where Frank lay snoring, his face smooshed into a pillow. My frown deepened as my eyes scanned my uncle's thin body, rolled on its side, facing away from the room. Which was appropriate, I thought, for a man who in actual life had turned his back on the world. His right hand shaking erratically, and an empty bottle of gin caught my eye. At some point during his binge, he had tried to tuck it beneath a cushion. It was ridiculous. *Did he really think no one knew he was drinking?* He'd been on the sofa since we arrived, exhausted from our car ride, yesterday. He had not even stirred to greet us. Claudia had made apologies and told me to let him be. I'd been too tired to care about it then, but now I felt anger.

"Hey, Frank," I barked, standing over him as I nudged his shoulder roughly with my knee. "Time to get up!"

Frank grunted and rolled onto his back. He rubbed his eyes and squinted up at me, "What?"

"You've been on that sofa since we got here last night," I said angrily.

"Hell, Laney Mae, I've been on this sofa since before you was born." He grinned, showing stained teeth badly in need of brushing.

"And I see that bottle of gin."

He looked down at the bottle and back up at me. "Aww come on honey, I'm just drowning my sorrows. You know, over your mama." His voice was hoarse from lack of use.

"Oh Frank," I replied sarcastically, bringing my hands up to my heart in a prayer-like pose. "I'm *so* touched." I bent over him, ignoring his body odor, and put my face up to his. "Sit up! Now!"

He scowled but something in both my tone and eyes made him oblige. With some effort he swung his thin, seventy-two-year-old legs to the floor and pushed himself up. He leaned against the back of the sofa and brought his hands up to cover his unshaven face. He kept them there as if to hide from me. His shirt was filthy and torn, his hair a greasy mess and the fly of his pants gaped open. To top this off, he burped. He dropped his hands to his lap, "I was getting up. You just beat me to it."

"You best get up and pull yourself together, for the next twenty-four hours. Can you do that? Can you?" My harshness surprised even me. Dandy shook his head. *Now why you going and talking to him like that? He's in pain.*

"No, I'm the one in pain," I replied out loud.

Frank looked alarmed and confused. "What? You hurt Laney Mae?"

Claudia heard this and stepped over to us. "Frank! I told you to get up and get moving," she scolded. Turning to me she said, "Honey, you don't worry about this old goat. I'll make sure he is up, showered and dressed and presentable by the viewing this evening. I promise."

From across the room Ruth said, "Him? Presentable? Ha!"

I looked from Claudia to Frank and back to Claudia. "I think," I said through gritted teeth, "I need to go for a walk."

Claudia said, "A walk? Where?"

"Just a walk," I answered.

"But what for?" Ruth asked.

I looked over at her, "To clear my head. Okay?"

"Well, that don't make no sense," said Margaret. "You just walking around. Why?"

"Let her go," Frank snapped. He looked up at me with sad eyes, but they did nothing to soothe my frustration.

"Tell you what," Claudia said, squeezing her body between me and Frank. "I got a couple bills need mailing. Will you mail them for me Laney Mae? Down at the post office? That way you can get your walk and get something done at the same time."

"Sure," I snapped. "Give me the envelopes."

Claudia scampered off to the kitchen and rushed back and I grabbed the envelopes from her and stomped across the room, whipped open the door and stepped outside, slamming the door with such force that the windows rattled. I winced and imagined the shocked expressions of everyone in the house. Scowling, I made my way down the porch steps into the yard but stopped at the sight in front of me. My scowl melted away. I felt my shoulders relax. I breathed deeply and exhaled slowly, and soon my anger began to dissipate. The mountains always had a calming effect on me. I slowly turned around in a complete circle, taking in the glorious beauty. As a child, this very view from my grandparent's house, situated as it was upon the side of a mountain, had always made me feel on top of the world. Having such a grand perspective had always been reassuring and this moment was no different. Before me now, I noticed that the treetops were just beginning to show a slight change of color and I felt the corners of my mouth unexpectedly tugging upward into a smile. As a young girl, the vastness of the mountains sometimes had the effect of making me feel very small. At the same time, they made me feel very safe and well protected. Feeling safe now was worth the price of feeling small for the fortress the mountains created gave me at least a temporary shelter from the reality that lay on the other side of them: life without my mother, the hopelessness of ever knowing about my father, the divorce from Phil, the pain and uncertainty in my life—none of that mattered to me at this moment.

From here the vantage was high enough to see the rooftops of nearly every one of the fifty or so homes in Second Chance, with many now abandoned. I would often imagine my grandfather, covered with black dust, his body wracked with pain from years of the backbreaking labor, walking slowly up the mountain after his shift to his home. Having spent long hours in the bleak darkness beneath the earth, I was certain that the view from his front yard must have washed over him like baptismal water. Here, high on the mountain, he could breathe in the fresh air. Here, he could stand proudly and enjoy the fruit of his hard labor. Here, he had a wide open, straight view of the sky and the treetops. He could look down upon the houses and other buildings, the town's main street, its city hall, the post office, the train depot and the railroad tracks. Beyond that he could watch, over time, as the transportation system developed from a dirt and gravel road when he was a young boy into a two-lane asphalt roadway by the time he passed away in the 1950s. Past that, he could see where the edge of a steep hill rolled down to meet the river, a waterway so forbidding and muddied from a combination of natural elements and decades of mining activity, that no one dared swim there.

Looking at the river, I realized I didn't know its name. This made me frown, and I understood with some sadness that although these mountains were home to three generations of my family, I was just a visitor here. I could not claim this as my kingdom. I turned back to face the house and tried to imagine how it might have looked when it was first built in the late 1800s. Freshly painted, window glass shiny and the siding free of the coal dust that would come to perpetually coat its exterior. I sighed at how sad it looked; dirty with cracked siding and trim, soot-covered windows and a roof that was in need of replacing. The porch seemed to frown back at me as several of its floorboards were warped and one of the railings had detached from the house as though kicked off. Despite its dilapidated condition, it was an otherwise solid structure and Mama had always told us that it, and the other three homes Pop had constructed, had been considered among the nicest homes in town.

I walked across the grass of the open yard and stared at the fourth house on the property. It stood on the far corner of the large plot. It had always been intended for my uncle Luke. Pop had constructed it with careful detail and provided a dignified distance from the other homes for his older son, his future bride and anticipated children. But none of that had worked out and Luke left West Virginia for Florida. "Luke's house," as it had always been called, sat uninhabited for periods of time, as it did now. Hilda had lived there before her stroke and Ruth, Frank and other Hartman siblings and some assorted cousins had rotated from Luke's house to the other three over the years, but I doubted anyone ever went inside it anymore.

I stood with my hands on my hips considering all this when I had a sudden, inexplicable impulse to go inside. *When was the last time you were in there?* Dandy asked me as he peered at the house.

"I don't remember ever being in that house," I replied aloud as I began to walk toward it but stopped, looked at my watch, and realized I ought to go mail the letters for Claudia so I could get back in time to help Neal unload the groceries. I shook my head, turned, and began the walk down to town.

Main Street was quiet. Only a few cars drove by me as I walked and the drivers slowed to look at me closely. One or two waved, so I waved back. Soon I came upon the crumbled remains of a building. I had no memory of what it had been. A store maybe? Now just the front remained, literally only the front wall, the inside a crumbled mess of bricks, drywall and trash. *How long had it been since I had walked around the town?* I sighed with a mixture of sadness over the demise of the town and guilt that I had not bothered to appreciate what it once was. I shook my head and continued on, passing building after empty building as my depression grew. I arrived at the post office and dropped the letters into the mailbox. I turned and began the walk back. My legs struggled as I started the climb up the mountain. The road grew steeper. *I am out of shape on top of everything else*, I thought. I had to pause and take a deep breath, wishing I had brought a water bottle. It was hotter here than I expected. I pushed on and was finally just a block away from Hartman Hill when a car horn blared behind me that caused me to jump in alarm and yelp. I whipped around, ready to rage at whoever had the audacity to blow their horn at me, until I saw who it was.

"Uh, excuse me," Neal called out from his car window, grinning. "Can you help me? I'm lost."

"Neal!" I cried happily. For some reason, the sight of his old Toyota struggling up the hill and him smiling and leaning out the window, filled me with unexpected gladness.

He grinned. His eyes were mellow and slightly red.

I leaned in the window. I caught a familiar whiff. "You high? Never mind. You are. You went grocery shopping high?"

He laid his head back on the headrest and giggled like a five-year-old. He draped his long arms over the steering wheel and leaned forward, shaking his head side-to-side. Unstoppable laughter took hold of him, his eyes streaming with tears. He caught his breath and managed, "No, did the shopping first. Then I got high." He wiped his face and feigned seriousness. "I am, after all, the responsible one." He motioned at the bags of groceries in his back seat. "And what if I am high? How the hell could I deal with all this otherwise?" He grinned; his eyebrows arched playfully.

"Well, I'm dealing with it, brother." I punched his arm playfully.

"Well, little sister, I got an extra joint with your name on it."

We grinned as we regarded each other. I asked, "Remember the last time we were here?"

Neal's silliness faded at the memory of bringing Mama back home for what ended up being the last time. He cleared his throat and said, "You know, if Mama had known then that she had cancer and was dying, she could have just stayed up here." He frowned and then, trying to lighten the moment, said, "Would have saved us a trip. With a pink hearse." He cackled.

"She would have rather died," I said, and we both laughed.

"That she would," Neal said.

"That she did."

This caused the melancholy hovering above us to land again. "Hey," I said to lighten the moment, "I'll race you to the house. Loser has to deal with Ruth the rest of the day!"

I turned and tried to sprint up what was the steepest part of the hill. My legs felt like heavy tree stumps. I was laughing so hard–a good old bellyaching laugh–that tears ran and caused my vision to blur. My flip-flops caused me to stumble, and I nearly fell. Neal inched the car up slowly beside me, then passed me, then slowed to let me get ahead as he cackled, leaning out the window, his hand banging on the door, spurring me on.

In the end, we tied.

CHAPTER 18

The Final Rest Mortuary could, to those unfamiliar, appear to not be a funeral home at all. It was a large and rather cheery house with white clapboard siding and dark green shutters. It stood appropriately separated from the rest of town at the very end of Main Street. It had a neatly kept lawn, trimmed hedges and pretty seasonal flowers in pots situated in a welcoming manner along the walkway to the entrance. On holidays, the house was adorned appropriately: greenery and twinkling lights at Christmas, American flags and banners on the 4th of July and even carved pumpkins, scarecrows and ghosts twirling from branches of the trees in front on Halloween. In fact, many would have agreed it was the nicest maintained house in town.

Business was, after all, steady.

Inside the main door a tastefully decorated, dark and subdued lobby greeted visitors with comfortable sofas and chairs situated along the walls. On either side of the lobby were two nearly identical viewing rooms and into both, glorious natural light fell from large bay windows, defying the notion that death meant darkness.

Beyond the lobby was the funeral home main office and across the hall from that, a large kitchen. The kitchen was complete with modern appliances, including a dishwasher which was rare in Chance. It also contained one long table used mostly for buffets and dozens of assorted folding chairs were stacked along the wall ready to be called into service. Here, family and friends were welcome to bring and store any variety of casseroles, side dishes and desserts for mourners following the funeral service. And although there were churches within a five-mile radius perfectly able to put on a good funeral, many people over the years preferred Final Rest as the site for their final viewing and celebration of life. It was just so family-friendly.

To my relief, Jake was dressed in a neat black suit with a white shirt and gray tie. He stood waiting for us on the front porch of Final Rest. Neal drove the Suburban carrying me, Christopher, Harrie, Margaret, Ruth and Frank. My cousin Tim, who was Jake's younger brother and whose job as a long-haul truck driver made his schedule unpredictable, had surprised us and thrilled Claudia when he showed up to attend the viewing and funeral. As quiet as his brother was loud, Tim had kindly volunteered to be in charge of getting Hilda to and from the viewing since, as predicted, Donnie did not appear. Claudia accompanied them. When our cars pulled up, Jake dashed down the porch steps and motioned for us to park near the entrance since we were family and to make it easier for Hilda's wheelchair. I was glad to see Final Rest had a ramp leading to the entrance.

"Everything is just right," Jake said as we got out of the Suburban. "Faye looks really, really good and very peaceful. Like she's sleeping." He positioned himself between Neal and me and said, "Come on you two, I'll take you up to see her."

Inside the lobby, Chet Anderson, the funeral director, came over, embraced me and shook Neal's hand. "I'm very sorry for your loss.

Faye was a unique lady. Thank you for allowing us to take care of your mother."

I moved into the room noting its brightness, the shiny hardwood floors, tastefully subdued area rugs, neatly arranged with comfortable seating and the slight but pleasant aroma of flowers. I was happy to see about a dozen people had already arrived, but only a few of them were familiar to me. The guests momentarily stopped what they were doing when our family appeared at the entrance to the room. A few smiled and nodded, and I was grateful for their presence. I looked past them to the casket. I could see the familiar profile of my mother, her prized hair freshly coiffed. It seemed like a decade since I had seen her, and a lump suddenly formed in my throat. Looking around to distract myself from crying, I noticed the stand with the guestbook on it and walked over to have a look. But I really went over to postpone, for a moment, viewing Mama. I glanced down at the names and saw Jake's lavish signature by which he had placed a silly happy face. I rolled my eyes. I turned and nearly bumped into Christopher who looked uneasy. He took hold of my hand. I clutched it and with my other, took Neal's. We began to walk behind Jake toward the casket. "You okay?" Neal whispered. I was about to reply when Christopher suddenly stopped. He pulled free of my grasp.

"I don't want to want to go up there."

We stared at him.

Jake leaned over and said, "Aw, come on Christopher. You wanna see your grandma, don't you? She looks really nice."

Christopher shook his head. "I saw her dead already. It's not her anymore. I don't want to look." He took a step back, spun around and left us standing there. I watched as he walked over to a loveseat and sat next to Frank.

Jake started to follow him but I grabbed his arm and said, "It's alright. Let him go. He needs to deal with this in his own way."

"I understand," Jake said sadly. "You all ready? Let's go on up."

He led us to the casket and, gripping Neal's hand, I looked down. Mama did look like she was sleeping. The blue suit was perfect. Her hands we posed with a bible. I felt relieved. Timidly, I reached out and held my hand above her head then gently touched her face. Pulling my hand back, I took Neal's hand and said, "She looks good."

"Yeah, she does," he replied.

Jake leaned in between us and whispered, "See! I told you all that Chet was the best. Hair, makeup, all kinds of restoration work—you name it!"

"Yes, Jake," I replied. "He did a nice job." I twisted my head over my shoulder and lowered my voice to say, "Considering her body sat in a hot hearse along the road for what was it? About an hour?"

Dandy whispered *Now come on. Jake meant well. Don't you forget that. You got to let up on him. All's well that ends well.*

Jake grinned and shook his head. "All's well that ends well, Laney Mae."

I was about to say, "Lucky for you" when Neal, who had been gazing out at the guests in the room gasped and said, "I don't believe it!" I looked up at him quizzically. I saw him staring across the room and turned, my eyes followed his sightline and just as he said, "Look who's here," I saw him: Greg Smith. The activity around me seemed to stop, all the low murmuring voices, to quiet. At that moment, Greg seemed to sense me too, and his eyes landed right on me; those blue eyes I had stared into so many times when I was younger, the eyes that now had crowfeet lines around them, the eyes a part of a face that now included a neatly kept beard and mustache streaked with gray, an odd but, becoming addition. Greg's face broke into the most splendid grin, the dark beard making his teeth look brilliantly white, and he began to walk toward us. I felt my knees shaking and my body suddenly felt very warm. *He was here! He was really here!* I went from subdued sadness to euphoria in seconds.

"I *cannot* believe it!" Neal cried out, unable to contain his emotions. He grabbed his old friend and pulled him into an embrace. They stood holding each other, my brother's eyes closed tightly in a vain effort to stop tears that began to run down his face. My own eyes filled as I tried to collect myself, dizzy with the unanticipated joy Greg's presence brought. I forgot where I was, forgot I was standing near my mother's casket, forgot about the ordeal of her death, my unfulfilled hopes, the pink hearse, my sad son and my own despair.

None of it mattered now because of Greg.

Neal released Greg and stepped back. Greg turned to face me. I noted there were no tears on his face to match my brother's. His eyes were happy and his splendid grin even more so up close. "Hey," he said softly.

"Hey," I replied. He seemed taller. Was that possible? In one quick motion I stepped forward and threw myself into his arms and we embraced. I wrapped my arms around him and felt enveloped in a physical warmth that was so comforting and so calming that I clutched him even closer, held him even tighter; hoping to linger there and not wanting to let him go.

Greg stepped away first, but he kept his hands placed lightly on my shoulders for a moment then shoved his hands into the pockets of his suit slacks. I thought he seemed slightly unnerved by my tears and Neal's as well. "It's been a long time. I am so sorry about your mom." He turned back to Neal. "I got your email and then my dad emailed me, so I just hopped in my car. I wanted to be here for you."

"I can't believe you're really here," I said. I needed to touch him again and so I gently put my hand on his arm as though to reassure myself this was no dream.

He nodded and reached over and gently wiped a tear off my face, "How could I not?"

Christopher came over to us, careful to keep our bodies between him and Mama's casket. He pulled on my arm to lead me a few feet away from it and I followed him reluctantly; I wanted to stay close to Greg. He clutched my hand and pulled me down so that he could whisper in my ear. "Who's that man?"

I smiled and used this as a reason to turn back to Greg and motion for him to step over. He did and smiled warmly. I said, "Christopher, this is our friend Greg from a long time ago. Isn't it nice? He's driven all the way from Pennsylvania to be here to honor Grandma."

Christopher looked up at Greg warily. "Hullo," he mumbled.

"Greg, this is my son Christopher. He's ten."

Greg leaned down and smiled. "I've known your mom since I was even younger than you and I am so glad I knew your grandma, too. I used to hang out at their house all the time when we were kids."

Christopher said, "You and my uncle Neal were friends."

Greg nodded. "That's right. I grew up right around the block from your grandmother's house. And I came up here, too, for visits once or twice, in the summertime."

Christopher nodded, "We met your dad the other day. The old man. He came to our house. He walks with a cane because his back hurts so bad."

Greg's smile fell. He swallowed hard and looked down at his shoes. Hoping to put him at ease I said, "Your father was very nice to visit and pay his respects. He's doing fine. Very sharp."

Greg managed a smile but something in the air had shifted.

Harrie, who had been standing nearby stepped closer. "I remember you too," she told Greg, poking him in the arm with her finger. "We played Beatles records together and danced. And you and Neal put fireworks under Frank one time."

This made Greg laugh. "Hey, that's right, Harrie," he said. "Neal and I put some firecrackers near your uncle's hammock one time. We laughed so hard."

"I don't remember that!" I said but I smiled at the thought of Frank flipping out of the hammock in surprise, yet another rude awakening to life that went on all around him.

Greg said, "We were the wild youth of the 60's. What can I say?"

"You are not sixty, are you?" Harrie asked. "I'm sixty-three."

"No, he means back in the 1960s Harrie," I replied. "Back when we were kids." I paused then said, "Gosh Harrie, that's really something that you remember Greg after so many years."

"I don't forget," Harrie said with unusual seriousness.

Greg smiled at her, "I remember too, Harrie."

Wanting to shift the conversation, I grinned, stepped closer to him and laced my arm through his. "I can't believe you're here. You don't know how much it means to me . . . *to us* . . . that you're here."

He nodded and said, "You all were family to me. I had to come."

AFTER THE VIEWING WE RETURNED TO HARTMAN HILL FOR A relaxed gathering with family, some neighbors and old friends. It was refreshingly cool outside, a full moon shone down upon us and a not unwelcome festivity engulfed us. I had stayed as close to Greg as I could at the funeral home, following him around like a lost puppy, my eyes keeping watch on his whereabouts. His presence helped me coast through the viewing I had been dreading with its combination of small talk and awkward silences. When people came up to speak to me, I would pretend to listen while I kept my eyes fixed on him as he made his way around the room or sat on one of the loveseats catching up with Neal. I feared that if I allowed him out of my sight, he would vanish, and decades would pass before I'd see him again. At one point Gladys and her daughter Francine were speaking with me but I was distracted because I lost sight of Greg who, it had turned out, had just gone to the restroom. Gladys, who had some knowledge of my long crush on Greg, had raised her eyebrow as she watched my behavior and had shaken her head. "I know you haven't seen your friend in a long time, Laney Mae, but there are other people here you need to pay attention to." I had apologized and forced myself to focus on her and Francine who I also had not seen in years. But Francine was as guilty as I was for her attention was also elsewhere. I noticed her dreamy eyes following someone around the room too: my brother. This caused me to smile, and I shifted my attention fully to her and wondered if we shared the same eagerness about the possibilities presented to us, this chance to start over. Could we, after all these years, reclaim what had been lost by circumstances out of our control?

Claudia, the perpetual hostess, was in her element as she ran back and forth making sure everyone was properly welcomed and thanked and had food and drinks, pausing periodically to wipe her face with her apron. She had shooed everyone outside to the patio situated on part of the large yard area between the main houses and across from Luke's abandoned home. She had plugged in some string lights with a few candles burning and she brought the radio outside to add music to set a relaxed mood. Sandwiches, potato chips and beer—lots of beer—was carried out and everyone began to drink and relax. I sat on the back steps of the main house and stared at Greg as I took another sip of my second beer. He and Neal sat in old lawn chairs across the patio from me. I watched as they talked and sipped their beers, several discarded bottles strewn around the ground beneath their chairs provided proof that they were well ahead of most of us on the quest to forget why we were really here. I felt the warm buzz as the two consumed beers hit me, making me light-headed and giddy. I stared at Greg, not at all shyly, and resisted the temptation to bolt over to where he sat. I imagined grabbing him by both arms, pulling him up from the chair and leading him off into the woods, away from all the people, to discover if we could in fact, pick up where I believed we had left off so many years ago. I noticed Francine seated next to Gladys at the table on the patio, also sipping a beer, and also keeping her eye on Neal. We formed an unspoken alliance, the two of us, in the unexpected opportunity death had delivered.

Christopher and his younger cousins, Francine's girls Jasmine and Rose, along with Harrie ran about the yard playing tag. I smiled at them, relieved to see my son carefree and relaxed; his sense of belonging replenished here on the mountain. I finished my beer and stood, grabbed another from the ice chest, and made my way down to the yard. I motioned for Jake to come over. I complemented him on the viewing, how well Mama looked and thanked him for all he had done. Then I asked, "Hey, you got your guitar? I see some of your band buddies are here. Do they have their instruments? Why don't you play us some music? Claudia's radio just ain't cutting it. Get our minds off of things?"

My cousin beamed and bowed with flourish. "Your wish is my command." He trotted off to assemble his musicians and soon he had his guitar and three of his band mates standing with him, instruments ready, just off the patio, the string lights twinkling like an unnamed constellation of stars above them. He called out to everyone, thanking them, and inviting all to enjoy some music and dance. Next the opening strains of Neil Young's "Harvest Moon" enveloped us and my body tingled when I recognized the song. It was the perfect choice, what with the moon, vivid and magnificent in its solitude, hanging directly above us. I tilted my head back and stared at its face. I was suddenly struck by the thought that the moon was something I still shared with my father. It was the same moon that he had surely stared at, dreamed over, danced beneath and ultimately, taken his last breath below as it shone, silently hovering in the dark cold sky, that awful night. It's the same old moon, I thought, shining like it always had, steady and constant, a witness to sadness but also to joy. My father was gone. My mother was gone. But, I thought, the moon was still here, and it would still be here after I was gone, too. My eyes sought my son and as I watched him laughing and running about, my heart swelled at the thought that if I never did anything else right in this world, anything worth anyone's recognition or acknowledgement, at least I had given it him and he would carry on without me just as I had to carry on without my parents.

Jake's voice rose gently and when he sang about still being in love, I sat my beer down and stared at Greg longingly. *You ought to go ask him to dance*, Dandy said. *On such a beautiful night, who could say no to a dance?* Emboldened, I walked over to Greg. I stood before him as he sat in the lawn chair, a fresh bottle of beer at his lips. He grinned up at me and I held out my hand and said, "Dance?" He smiled, sat his beer down and took my hand. I led him out onto the patio where a few others were dancing and swaying, including, I noticed, Harrie and Christopher, imitating the other couples as they giggled. Greg and I began dancing slowly.

"I haven't danced in a long time," he said.

"Me either." I added, "Well, not since the divorce."

"Neal told me. I'm sorry. That must have been hard on you and Christopher."

"Yes, it's been hard." Suddenly shy, I looked down at the ground to my feet and focused on the wonder of just feeling his hand on my shoulder and his other, upon my waist. I closed my eyes. Was it the beer, the music, the moon? I felt lighter than air and happier than I could remember feeling in a very long time. I glanced up at him, hoping the extra effort I had made with my makeup made me look pretty to him, and younger, too. A flash of me looking at him shyly from beneath a lock of my hair decades earlier while we danced alone in the dark, a few weeks before he would leave for Colorado in his basement to the song, "Baby, Baby I'm Falling in Love," went through my mind. I recalled how he had, laughingly twirled me around and when I stopped, we had stared at each other. He had paused, looking at me intently and then smiled and nodded slightly as if to confirm that his intention was acceptable. My smile granted him permission and he had bent over and kissed me, a warm, full and long kiss that aroused in me a feeling of longing I had never known.

Until now.

Jake continued the song, and more people began to dance when suddenly, during the instrumental, the unexpected, sweet twang of a harmonica filled the air. I gasped and spun around to find the source of the sound. What I saw made me cry out and bring my hands up to my mouth in wonder. *It was Frank!* My melancholy uncle, the perpetually despondent brother of my mother, the lonesome surviving Hartman brother who drank to drown his loss and guilt, now held a harmonica hidden in his hands, soulfully playing, swaying as he did, his foot keeping time. He winked at me.

"I don't believe it!" Claudia cried from where she stood near the kitchen door, holding a tray of food. "Frank! Frank is playing again. Oh Frank! How wonderful!"

Each member of the Hartman family stopped what they were doing and watched Frank in amazement as he played, some in tears. Jake was one of those. When the vocals resumed, his voice was a little shaky but joyful. I smiled at my uncle, so moved that I could not stop staring. In between playing he grinned and motioned for me to continue dancing which I did, taking Greg's hand but watching Frank and savoring each precious note he played.

To Greg I said, "He hasn't played the harmonica since . . . I can't even remember! He's been so sad and such a lost soul for so long. This makes me so happy." Greg smiled but then stopped dancing and returned to get his bottle of beer from the patio table. I watched as he held it up in a toast to Frank and then tilted his head back and drained it and put it back on the patio table and took another bottle from the cooler.

At that moment, Christopher, full of excitement, rushed over to me. "Mom! Uncle Frank is playing the harmonica like I asked him!"

"You asked him?"

"Yeah. When we were talking back at the funeral home. I told him I was going to learn an instrument this year and asked him if he played anything and he told me he used to play the harmonica. I asked him to play it and he told me no, that he hadn't played it in a long time and couldn't anymore. But I told him, of course you can! And I told him I wanted to hear him play and for him to teach me sometime."

Smiling I stroked his cheek. "Well, I'm glad you asked him because he hasn't played it in a long time. "

Christopher said, "I know. He told me that he used to play but something happened, and he got really sad so he stopped playing it but I told him that I got sad sometimes, too but music always makes me feel better. You know?"

"I sure do." I stroked his cheek, full of love for my son.

"I'm gonna go dance!" He ran off and I watched, smiling.

Greg had returned and had listened to this exchange. "He's a great kid. I wish I had his spirit. His hope."

I turned back to him, "Don't we all?"

"Maybe I would if . . . well . . . if I had had a mom like you all my life." He smiled sweetly.

"Oh Greg . . ."

Jake and his ensemble started a new song and Greg shook off his sadness and took my hand. "Say, do you remember the last time we danced?" He leaned on me and seemed off-balance. I looked into his eyes and noticed they looked glassy; my Romeo was getting drunk.

"I do. I was just thinking about that a minute ago. It was before you told me you were leaving for Colorado."

He frowned. "I know you were mad at me for leaving."

"I wasn't mad. I was sad. With you and Neal gone, I was all alone."

"I'm sorry."

"I know."

We moved slowly to the music and then, out of nowhere, Greg began to sing, "Baby, Baby I'm Falling in Love" into my ear. He laughed and then pulled me closer. "I bet you didn't think I remembered that song." Suddenly serious, he whispered, "Should we pick up where we left off?" I knew he did not mean dancing.

His question caught me off guard and I stopped dancing, letting my hands drop from around his neck. Shyly, I looked down at the ground then stared into his eyes. With every ounce of my being, I wanted to pick up where we had left off, but doubt nagged me. *He's had too much to drink, Laney Mae.* Dandy told me, shaking his head. *Don't rush this. You're gonna get your heart broke all over again.* But I tuned Dandy out. I didn't care. I wanted this. I needed this. He was worth the risk.

Composed and feeling certain, I nodded. Blushing, I quickly glanced around to see if anyone was watching us, but it appeared no one was. I saw Neal and Francine sitting close together, chatting and laughing, paying no attention to us, lost in their own world of reconnection.

Greg whispered, "Then come to me. I'm in the back house. Your aunt Claudia put me in the room with the wallpaper that has the little birds and bees on it." He laughed and looked intently into my eyes. I felt my insides melting. "Will you come find me?" he whispered into my ear. I could smell the beer, heavy and stale, on his breath and uncertainty gnawed at me.

I stared into his eyes, hesitating, knowing that this was not likely to have a happy ending but decided to live in the moment as Death had taught me to do.

"I'll get Christopher to bed," I told him. "Then, I'll come find you."

⊗⚮⊗

I FELL ASLEEP SNUGGLED NEXT TO HIM BUT WOKE WITH A START IN the middle of the night, forgetting for a moment where I was. Greg lay sleeping, snoring lightly, one arm beneath me, his other dangling off the side of the bed. My mind raced to recall the events that had brought us here, the fumbling around in the dark like teenagers, the whispering, the giggles, the lustful kisses. I sighed contentedly, staring adoringly at his outline, lightly using my finger to touch his lips. I rose and quietly gathered my clothes and put them on, reaching blindly around the floor for my sandals, only the faint glow of a nightlight in a wall socket helping me see. I peered at the clock next to the bed and saw that it was just after three a.m. I needed to get into my own bed where Christopher was sleeping. I suddenly worried that he may have awoken and looked for me and guilt flooded me. I tiptoed around the bed heading toward the door but before I left, I had to stop. I looked down at Greg as he slept, listening to his breathing as I had Mama's on her last night. Filled with gladness, I knelt to my knees as though in church and leaned over to kiss his lips ever so gently, not intending to waken him, but his eyes fluttered opened. He seemed disoriented. "Hey," I said softly. "I didn't mean to wake you. Go back to sleep. I've got to get back to my room. I didn't mean to fall asleep here."

He sat up quickly and scooted back to lean against the headboard, the bed creaking under his movement. He did not speak and seemed to be collecting himself, trying to recall what had happened. He held his head in his hands and I smiled knowing a hangover was brewing for him. I rose from kneeling and sat on the edge of the bed. I took his hand. "I'm so happy," I whispered. "I never thought I'd see you again, let alone . . . be with you."

He let out a forced laugh and said, "I know."

"I've waited so long for you to come back."

He squeezed my hand tightly. Haltingly he said, "Laney Mae, I . . . I didn't mean for this . . . this shouldn't have happened. I drank too much, got carried away and I shouldn't have . . . especially now . . . the night before your mom's funeral. It was wrong. I'm sorry."

Though his sober summary had not been totally unexpected, I still felt as though I'd been slapped. I stood in a rush, dropping his hand. "Wrong? Please don't say this was wrong. And *we* let this happen, Greg. Not just you. *We* did. I wanted it to happen."

"Okay. . . I . . just . . . don't want you to think that—"

"Think what? Think that you *love* me?"

"Of course I love you." He looked up at me, but I could barely see his eyes in the dim light. He continued, "I love you but that's not the same as being *in* love."

I thought I was prepared for this, for him to love me and leave me but I began to cry. He swung his legs off the bed and stood. He took me into his arms, but awkwardly, attempting to hold me but keep some space between our bodies as though we were eighth-graders at our first dance with our chaperone hovering nearby. He murmured how sorry he was that he lost his head, that the last thing he wanted was to cause me pain.

This angered me. "Well, you know what? You did that a long time ago," I said ruefully, stepping out of his embrace. I wiped the tears off my face. We stood silently, I think both uncertain of what to say next and how to end this. I took in a deep breath to calm myself and said, "Look, what happened, happened. I'm not sorry it did. And you're right, we both had too much to drink. But I don't regret it."

I waited for him to say something, to tell me he did not regret it either, that everything was alright, to tenderly pull me into his arms, to lead me back into the bed, to lay me down upon the sheets and blankets that had been warm with passion just a short time ago but that were now cold, unmade and used up.

The way I felt.

"I'm sorry," was all he said.

I scoffed and turned away, opened the door and walked into the hall, quietly pulling the door behind me when I really wanted to slam it hard. Weary and suddenly so tired I thought I might collapse, I leaned against the door for a moment in an unsuccessful attempt to compose myself, then moved swiftly down the stairs and went outside, tears streaming. Dandy appeared to me. *Now, you knew what you was getting into. Best not take this too seriously.* "Oh yeah. Let's not take this too seriously." I began to cry again. "I feel so used," I said aloud.

Aww no honey, not when there's love. You weren't used. He loves you. Maybe not in the way you wish, but he does love you.

I sobbed and whispered aloud, "No one ever loves me like I wish they would. No one."

Now that ain't true at all. Lots of us love you. Don't take that love for granted. Ever. You hear?

I shook my head. Sulking, I looked up at the moon. It looked different to me now. It seemed pale and washed-out and the magic I thought I had witnessed earlier was gone. It was just a big round object in a cloudless sky. It was plain, cold and indifferent to me even as it observed my pain and watched me scurry back to where I belonged, my heart splintered in so many pieces I feared it would never be whole again.

CHAPTER 19

I dreamed and in my dream my mother–dressed in the blue suit selected for her burial–floated toward me with her arms open wide. I fell into her embrace. I leaned back and took hold of Mama's face with my hands and said, "I miss you, Mama." She smiled, she looked radiant, healthy and young. There was such warmth, such a sense of love that, as I dreamed, I began to weep. I again embraced her tightly but suddenly, she was gone, and my arms were empty, and I cried out. Now awake, I felt the wetness of tears rolling down my cheeks and I brought my hands up to my face. My heart raced in my chest as if I had run up a hill. *Could I have such a physical reaction over just a dream? No, it was impossible,* I thought. Mama's spirit had come to me, just like Christopher had claimed she had in his dream. Now I was sure and with this certainty, a comforting sense of peace filled me. Mama was not gone after all, I thought, not really. She was there. Somewhere. And if my mother was there, surely my father was as well.

I remained very still and tried to remember if she had spoken to me in the dream. I had read once that if you don't move your head at all when you first awaken, your brain can more easily replay the content of your dreams for you. Once you moved your head, however, the remnants of your dreams scatter like the gray dust in an Etch A Sketch. Keeping still, I closed my eyes but nothing came to me.

And then I remember Greg and what happened.

I sighed and sat up slowly to not disturb Christopher. I looked down at his head peeping out from beneath the blanket as he lay on his side, blissfully lost in dreams. He had stirred and mumbled to me when I returned from Greg's room but had gone right back to sleep while I tossed and turned until I finally took half a Xanax and drifted to sleep.

Overtired, my head aching from a hangover, I eased myself to the edge of the bed and stood slowly. I pulled the curtain away from the window behind the bed and frowned at the dreary, overcast morning. I had not given the weather forecast much thought but accepted that rain and a gloomy sky were certainly appropriate for a funeral.

I tiptoed toward the door to head downstairs for coffee, but Christopher's sleepy voice stopped me. "Mom," he said hoarsely, "What time is it?"

"It's early. You can sleep a little longer if you want."

He rose up on his elbow. "Today's when we bury Grandma, right?"

"Yes."

"At the cemetery, right?"

"Yes, that's right."

"Will everyone be there?"

"Probably most will just come to the funeral and a few of us will go to the cemetery. Then we'll go back for a reception."

He nodded. "But Mom, isn't Dad coming?"

His question surprised me, and I hesitated. "No. He's not coming. Why did you think that he was coming Christopher?"

He frowned and shrugged. He scratched his head absentmindedly, "I don't know. I just thought he would be here. Shouldn't he? Didn't he love Grandma?"

I stared at him and thought about all the different levels of love people had for each other. These were unequal and ever-changing. Had Phil loved Mama? He had not. Had he loved me? He said he did once. Did he love our son? I knew he did, but Christopher was stuck now on another level, and his father's love was like an elevator that rarely went to the basement where his son resided, waiting for him. Like a punch in my gut, it hit me that my son would grow up without a father in his life just as I had. Was it worse to have a father who was dead or worse to have a father who had rejected you and was very much alive? If alive, wasn't there always the hope of reconciliation and healing? If dead, could one at least hold fate accountable over the failings of the one who had given us life?

"It's not about whether he loved her or not," I said gently, "he's really not part of this family anymore, Grandma's family. You know?"

He slumped back onto the pillow and frowned. "I don't understand you grown-ups," he said. "Why does everyone hurt each other all the time?"

"I don't know honey," I said, crossing the floor and leaning over to kiss his forehead. "Look, you're tired. We all are. It's early still. Why don't you close your eyes and rest a bit more? It's going to be a long day." He nodded and let me tuck the blankets under his chin "I'm going to get coffee and see what's going on. I'll be back up in a little while."

I tiptoed downstairs in shorts and t-shirt with bare feet where I found Claudia alone in the kitchen seated at the table, her hands wrapped around a mug of coffee, a cigarette burning beside it in an old ashtray. She wore curlers and a too-tight bathrobe with black and white polka dots. Mother lay on the floor next to her. The room was gloomy with only the stove hood's dim light and the meager rays of daylight from the window above the kitchen sink.

"Hey there, Laney Mae," Claudia said softly, her voice raspy. "How'd you sleep honey?"

I saw Greg's face in my mind. "I slept okay. I need coffee."

"Just made a full pot. Help yourself." She coughed the raised the mug to her lips. "You're up early."

"I just woke up. Christopher woke up too, but I made him go back to sleep."

Claudia nodded, "I'll get breakfast going in a while."

I poured coffee and sat beside her. Without a word, I reached over to the ashtray and put the cigarette out. Claudia raised an eyebrow and smirked at me. She chose to change the subject, "I think this rain is gonna clear off."

"Whatever. As long as it's not pouring. It's kind of nice it isn't so hot."

"You all still heading back home on Monday?"

I nodded as I sipped the coffee. "I was thinking about tomorrow, actually. I have to get Christopher back to school. Back to normal."

Claudia's face dropped, "Oh, I wish you'd stay until Monday as you planned."

I shrugged. I hated to disappoint her. "We'll see."

"Well, look at these sleeping beauties," Frank said as he walked into the kitchen. He was dressed in clean clothes and his face was shaven. He grinned, poured a cup of coffee and joined us at the table. I brightened and smiled at him, recalling the magical moment when he played the harmonica the night before.

"That was nice last night," I told him.

He shook his head and stared humbly into his coffee cup. "I don't know what you're talking about. Ain't nothing nice about me."

"You know what I mean; hearing you play," I said.

Claudia nudged him. "It was nice Frank. It was so good to hear you playing the harmonica again. I can't tell you."

"Then don't," he said but he winked at his sister.

I looked from Claudia to Frank. "Have either of you decided who will do the eulogy today?"

Frank's eyes grew wide. He looked at Claudia and arched his eyebrows. He turned to me and said, "I played the harmonica Laney Mae. That don't mean I'm ready to deliver the Gettysburg Address."

"Don't look at me," Claudia said, pursing her lips together. "I told you I'd think about it and I did. I don't know how to think up something like a eulogy."

"I can do it."

We all turned to see Gladys standing in the doorway.

"Well, good morning," I beamed. "Why are you here so early?"

She frowned, "I am *always* early."

"Did I hear you say that you'll do the eulogy?" I asked, smiling.

Gladys tilted her head to the side. She looked first to Claudia then to Frank, the hint of a smile on her face. "Why not? I knew her since we were kids. I'll figure out something."

"I think this is a perfect solution," I said. "Who says it has to be family? It can be friends."

Gladys sat down at the table. "Yes, who says? And it ought to be me. I mean, did Faye have any other friends?"

Frank found this so funny that he spat out the coffee in his mouth and soon we were all laughing.

"Well, as a matter of fact," he leaned over the table and spoke to Gladys. "Based on what I seen happening last night, I think you'll be family soon enough." He grinned at her.

Gladys grinned back. "Yes. As a matter of fact, I have not seen my daughter all night. Jasmine and Rose are still sleeping but are going to wonder where their mom is when they get up soon."

"What do you mean?" I asked. "Where is Francine?"

They all looked at me knowingly and then I realized she was with my brother and had been all night. I hoped their evening turned out more happily than mine. My eyes tried to read their faces as I wondered if any of them knew I had been with Greg.

"I saw them head up to the back house not long after you took Christopher to bed, Laney Mae," Frank offered. "They was looking pretty romantic." He chuckled.

Gladys rose. "Well, my romantic daughter needs to get up soon and get her daughters and herself ready for the funeral." Something caught her attention out the kitchen window. "Well, there's one half of the equation," she said as she stepped around the table to look outside.

I stood and moved to stand beside her. I looked out the window and saw Greg, duffle bag in hand, opening his trunk. Behind him stood Neal and, out of direct view, I could see Francine, leaning against the house with her arms folded across her body. My eyes darted from Neal to Greg and as I watched, I quickly understood: Greg was leaving. Neal was trying to convince him to stay.

"I don't believe it!" I cried out. I turned to Gladys, Claudia and Frank, incredulous. "Greg is leaving! He's leaving!" I spun around to the widow and pointed. "See? What he's really doing is, he's *sneaking* off. He wants to get away and not look back. He's leaving me just when I need him the most. On the day I'm burying my mother!" I ran my hand over the back of my head again recalling the pain from Art pulling me by the hair that day so long ago, the last time Greg had left me. "Can you believe he would do this to me? To us?"

Claudia rose. She lumbered over to stand beside me. "Honey, you don't know he's leaving. He might just be packing up his car to be ready–"

"No! He's leaving." I began to cry.

"Why are you so upset? Let him go," Gladys said, reaching to take my shoulders firmly. "He showed up. He paid his respects. And for crying out loud, why do want someone to stay somewhere he doesn't want to be?"

"I don't care if he leaves," I snapped. "He's just going to look me in the eye before he does this time!" I strode to the back door where I paused and watched what I could tell were the futile efforts of my brother to coax Greg into staying. I heard Neal say, "Come on man, it's just another couple of hours . . ."

At this, I threw open the screen door with such force that it hit the side of the house with a bang. Startled, Greg, Neal and Francine turned toward me. I heard Greg mutter, "Oh shit."

I began striding toward him filled with anger that burned hot in my chest, but because I was barefoot, I was forced to tread slowly on the rough gravel in the driveway and I cringed with each painful step. As I advanced, I kept my eyes fixed on him and in my fury, told myself that this would be the last time I would ever see his face, the last time he would ever hurt me. I stepped gingerly, wincing as a sharp rock gouged my left heel. I stopped for a moment, never taking my eyes from his. I wanted to remember his eyes, remember the way his hair fell across his forehead, the vertical lines that had sprouted between his brows and the crowfeet around eyes, the beard with its flecks of grey, his lips beneath it, lips I would never kiss again.

And yet, with each painful step, as the gravel ground into my feet making me wince, I recalled images from our youth: how kind he had always been, how protective he was of me, how he could always make me laugh, how he would grin shyly whenever he caught me staring at him with lovesick eyes, how he punched the mean bully in the neighborhood for picking on me, how he drove me to Arlington Cemetery to visit and lay roses on the graves of JFK, RFK and Uncle Rob twice a year until he went away, how his was my first real kiss, and how he tried always, to be both a brother and guardian when Neal had to run away. Dandy walked slowly beside me. He said, *Now I know you're mad and hurt too, but you need to remember that he was a friend to you. No matter what, don't you ever forget, he cared about you and was your friend. And that counts for something. Think about him, what he's been through. He's sad too. You're not the only one who's lost someone.*

I stopped as Dandy, my dear imaginary conscience, forced me to consider this truth. I moved forward again, each painful step now seemed like a penance I had to pay, a punishment I deserved for not understanding Greg's pain. With each step closer to him, I realized that Dandy was right; in all the years we had known each other, I had neglected to pay attention to the constant shadow of sadness that always trailed Greg. I had allowed myself to believe him when he tried to pretend he was alright, too self-absorbed in my own troubles and unhappiness to pay attention to his. How could I have ignored his despair? Looking at him now, I could clearly see that it covered him like a shirt, tightly, buttoned clear up to his neck. I could see that he relived his mother's death every day of his life. Dandy said, *You found the courage to ask your mama to forgive you for not understanding her pain before she died. Can't you forgive for Greg? It'll free you, and I bet, free him of some of the guilt and regret he had over what happened between the two of you.*

I reached Greg whose face showed apprehension and dread and he seemed to brace himself for my wrath. Instead, I took his hand gently and smiled. "It's okay," I told him. "I understand. Go if you have to. I'm not mad." I stepped closer and wrapped my arms around his waist and buried my face into his shirt. Wordlessly, he pulled me to him. I breathed deeply and noticed his scent, noticed how his body felt as I pressed it close to mine, made a note of how his arms felt wrapped around me and the warmth of love in which I was enveloped. He was not in love with me, but he loved me. It was that simple. I dropped my arms and stepped back, smiling through tears. "I'm sorry I never tried to understand you and why you stayed away. You had your reasons. I know that now. That was selfish of me. Forgive me, Greg."

He shook his head, "I'm the one who was selfish. I should have kept in touch."

"No, you weren't. You were just trying to cope as best you could." I wiped my tears and forced a smile and said, "Thank you for coming, Greg. I can't tell you how much it meant to us. And that's what really matters. That you were here. Now."

He stared intently, as if seeing me for the first time. He exhaled a breath he had been holding. "Thank you for saying that. I'm glad I was here. I needed to be." He turned to Neal. They embraced.

Neal said, "Come home sometime. Your dad really misses you. He needs to see you. You need to talk to him. He thinks you blame him for—"

Greg's face suddenly contorted with pain. "No, I don't blame *him*. It was *my* fault. I should have found her sooner. If I had . . . No . . . it wasn't his fault. It was mine." He hit himself hard in the chest. "He knows that."

"No, he doesn't," Neal told him. "You need to let him know that. Before it's too late."

Greg's eye grew wide. "I'll go see him," he said softly, nodding. He turned to me and tilted his head to the side, tears in his eyes. "It's about time, huh? That I go home."

"Yes. You father needs you. If I've learned anything in dealing with Mama's death, it's this: don't leave things unsaid." Dandy grinned. *That's right good advice.*

Greg nodded solemnly then looked up to the sky and sighed. He got into his car and rolled down the window. He started the engine. He extended his hand to me and I clutched it tightly for a brief moment then let go as he began to slowly drive away. Neal, Francine and I waved to him and watched as he drove down the mountain until his car was out of sight.

NEAL, CHRISTOPHER AND I STOOD IN THE ENTRYWAY OF THE Final Restaurant Mortuary while we waited for Jake to give us the sign to enter the room for the service. I could see a couple dozen or so people seated on folding chairs arranged so that there was a middle aisle. I was disappointed that there were not more people present including, of course, Greg who was probably close to Pennsylvania by now. Still, I smiled, glad that we had parted in peace.

Jake, dressed in the same black suit he had worn the evening before, stood at the front of the room with Chet and the Minister from the nearby Methodist Church near the open casket. He spotted us, motioned for us to enter and then turned away. He bent over a floral arrangement behind which he had hidden a CD player and suddenly the Royal Philharmonic Orchestra's chorus followed by the deep, rich voice of Elvis Presley enveloped the room with "How Great Thou Art." It had been one of Mama's favorite songs. In fact, the playing of this song was one of the only references relating to her final wishes that she had ever been clear about, and it was long before the cancer diagnosis.

We moved slowly up the aisle between the rows of folding chairs. Attendees rose from their seats. I clutched Neal and Christopher's hands as I glanced at the faces staring back at me. A beautiful arrangement of flowers of red, pink and white roses and fluffy white and blue hydrangea blossoms set on top of the middle of the coffin; and I wondered who had sent them. Again, I looked at Mama's face but with the grim knowledge that soon, at the end of the service, our family would be invited to lower the lid of the casket, forever enclosing Mama's body into complete darkness. I squeezed Neal's hand harder. He squeezed my hand back. "Almost over," he whispered.

Chet came over and guided us to seats in the front row of

folding chairs. Just then, Harrie, dressed in a black skirt and white blouse with a floral headband atop her gray hair, ran to me. She wrapped her arms around me and squeezed me tightly. "I'm so sad," Harrie said loudly. "I miss Faye."

"I know, Harrie, me too."

Claudia stepped over and gently took Harrie by the arm. "Come on now, Harrie," she told her, "The service is gonna start. We got to sit and be quiet." Harrie reluctantly followed Claudia and sat down so hard on her chair that the force of her landing caused it to scoot slightly toward the row of people now standing behind them. Harrie bent over and covered her face with her hands, sobbing. Claudia gently patted her back, cooing gently in comfort.

I guided Christopher forward to his chair and held his hand as we stood with Neal beside us. Further down the row next to Harrie and Claudia were Margaret, Frank and Ruth who stood next to Hilda in her wheelchair at the end. Behind them, assorted neighbors and friends smiled sadly and nodded when I turned to acknowledge them. I leaned forward a bit to glance to my right to the front row opposite the aisle and saw Gladys, Francine with Jasmine and Rose who were already squirming as they pulled on Francine's arm impatiently and fussed at each other.

I leaned to whisper in Neal's ear, "I see a few people I don't know."

He shrugged at me and arched his eyebrows playfully. "Mama must have had more friends than we knew about," he whispered back with a wink.

When the song ended, the minister stepped to the lectern and told everyone they could be seated. I realized with some guilt that I could not recall his name even though I had met him the day before. After a brief prayer, he began speaking about life and death and purpose and loss and sorrow and the glory of Heaven, but I found it difficult to focus on his words. Instead, I again stared at Mama's body with its terrible and unnatural stillness. I found comfort in the gentle, monotonous voice of the Minister and allowed my eyes to slowly close until there was a sudden sound of movement and I felt the air about me change, felt Christopher shift in his seat and Neal nudge me. I opened my eyes to see that Gladys, true to her word, stood before us to begin her eulogy.

"Now, I know I'm supposed to say things about my dear friend Faye," Gladys began. Dressed in a navy-blue dress that complimented her silver hair pulled back tightly into a bun, she clasped her hands in a prayer-like manner and let them rest on the round of her stomach. "But truth be told, I have struggled with what to say." She looked out at the faces in front of her then rested her eyes on first Neal and then me. She said, "I can't believe Faye is gone." She allowed this to hang in the air a moment. "Let me start again. I can't believe she is gone because . . . you know what? She isn't!" There was a murmur in the room, and someone said, "Amen." Gladys stood taller. "That's right! I believe no one really is ever gone. Not if they loved us. Not if we loved them. That doesn't die. That doesn't go away. No matter what happens to our bodies. Ashes to ashes. Dust to dust."

The minister nodded and smiled, and quiet murmurs of agreement spread through the room.

Gladys continued, "So instead of writing up a eulogy, I thought of another way to pay her tribute and I think she would have liked it." She looked over to Jake who nodded. He walked behind Mama's casket, bent over and rose with his guitar and swung the strap over his body. He stood near Gladys and began to strum out a song. Then the low, melancholy voice of Gladys Johnson began to sing the opening lines of "Will the Circle Be Unbroken."

I smiled at Gladys and was pleased with the musical tribute and this particular song. Then the chorus began and some in the room rose from their seats to join in, but I remained seated and looked at

Neal to see his reaction. He turned and smiled, putting his arm around me, and pulled me toward him in a hug as he sang along. I stared at him quizzically, wondering what had gotten into my brother, singing gospel music.

Jake strummed the song, smiling but I noticed, with tears running down his cheeks. Just then, I sensed movement and saw Frank rise from his chair and step to the front of the room to stand by Gladys. To my astonishment, my uncle sang the next verse. I stared in disbelief and marveled at his conversion from hermit crab to crooner in just a few days. More people in the room rose and began to sing the chorus and, as he had done the night before, Frank played his harmonica while Jake continued on the guitar. I felt giddy and I also felt something else. What was it? It was joy. Pure, unexpected joy on this most mournful day.

Neal stood and winked at me. He stepped to the front to join Gladys, Frank and Jake, and to my shock, turned around and sang the next verse, his voice loud and strong. Christopher jumped up from his chair and pulled on my arm as the voices around us rose singing the chorus. "Sing, Mom!" he exclaimed. I stood, put my arm on his shoulder and grinned as I watched Jake and Frank play together with my brother and Gladys beside them. As I watched them play, I turned to see Claudia ambling up toward the group. I watched as my aunt turned around to face the room and look nervously about at all the faces as she waited for her moment to sing. Her eyes found me. "I love you," Claudia mouthed. I blew her a kiss. Tears spilled onto my cheeks, but these were tears of elation, not sorrow. This time I joined the chorus, singing loudly. Filled with emotion I thought how appropriate the song was and suddenly it made perfect sense to believe that life and death are an endless circle and that it is up to us, who remain, to not let it be broken. Dandy stood beside me, grinning, and singing. *Well, ain't this just the perfect song? Just the perfect song!*

When the last note was sung, the room went silent. Someone applauded and soon the whole room erupted into clapping and cheers, everyone on their feet. Jake bowed to the crowd playfully. He removed his guitar and placed it back behind the casket. Gladys, Frank, Neal and Claudia returned to their seats. The minister stepped to the lectern, smiling. "What a joyful tribute, thank you all for that." He bowed his head and when he looked back up, his face had become solemn. "And now, we invite the immediate family to say their final goodbye."

So this was the end. Neal cast me a sad look and took my hand as I reached for Christopher's. We began to move toward the casket, but Christopher shook his head and pulled on my hand. "I don't wanna do that," he told me. I nodded and told him it was okay. Neal and I walked to the casket followed by Claudia, Frank, Harrie, Margaret and Ruth. Tim pushed Hilda who was moaning in her wheelchair. We watched as Chet removed the floral arrangement, handing it to Jake. Next, he began to fold the satin lining inside the casket, carefully making his way around to the top of the coffin. He finished preparing the lid to be closed then turned to us and said simply, "It's time."

I stepped closer to the casket. "Goodbye Mama," I said softly. I lightly touched her face. Neal moved closer and reached past me to place an envelope atop Mama's chest near the Bible. "It's a poem I wrote her a long time ago," he said softly. "It was Mother's Day. Seemed like I should send her off with it." Next, Claudia sobbed as she reached in and touched her sister's face and then leaned in to kiss her sister's cheek. "I'll miss you, Faye. 'Till we meet again." Harrie pushed her way past Claudia. She leaned over Mama and said loudly, "I love you, Faye. You was good to me. I will always remember." This made Frank choke up. Standing on the other side of Neal he said, "Goodbye, sis. I'll see you soon enough." Ruth, who had been standing behind the group, now pushed past Claudia and

Harrie to say goodbye to her sister. I was surprised to see tears on her face. "I sure am gonna miss you, Faye," Ruth sobbed. "You was the only one that ever gave a damn about me!" Margaret gasped and frowned at her sister and jabbed her in her ribs with her elbow. "What kind of a thing is that to say? How dare you say that? You know we *all* care about you! You are so ungrateful!" Ruth sneered at Margaret. "No, she was the only one! The rest of you just pushed me aside. You never cared about me!" This caused several comments of indignation and irritation and voices began to rise among my aunts. Frank rolled his eyes skyward, and I cringed, shaking my head at Neal.

"That's quite enough!" the minister's voice cut into the clamor, "Really, ladies! Dear God! Kindly say your goodbyes and close the casket. It's time go to the cemetery." Like scolded children, we all bowed our heads and then, in unison, we reached together to prepare to close the casket. With Chet and Jake helping and us all weeping, we slowly lowered the lid until it closed with a click.

We returned to our chairs and watched as Chet and Jake walked around the casket, ensuring all was as it should be. Next, Chet motioned to the volunteer pallbearers to come forward. The men positioned themselves around the casket and then lifted the coffin onto the wheel truck. They stepped back slightly as Jake, carrying a folded United States flag, stepped up and, with Chet's help, unfolded it and with great care, then began smoothing it out atop the casket.

I shook my head and nudged Neal. I whispered to him, "That's not right. Why is he putting a flag on her casket? That's only for the military."

"Let him do it," Neal whispered. "It was his idea. I told him it was okay. She was a public servant. She served her country. That flag meant a lot to her."

I watched as Jake gently ran his hands over the draped flag. He walked all the way around the coffin to ensure it hung evenly on all sides. Satisfied, he turned and found my eyes. Dandy said, *Now, don't you worry. Jake means well and as far as I'm concerned, your mama deserves the American flag draped upon her casket.* I smiled at Jake and thought to myself, yes, Faye Rose Hartman Martin, civil servant and devout Patriot, who flew the flag daily, who stood for the National Anthem even watching TV at home, who could recite the preamble to the Constitution, most of the Declaration of Independence and JFK's entire inaugural address by heart, would have been proud to have the American flag on her coffin, covering her protectively like a blanket, as she was taken to her grave.

CHAPTER 20

The rain had stopped but the sun remained hidden behind clouds making the cemetery appropriately dreary. Only a small group of friends and neighbors joined us at the gravesite. As car doors slammed and people made their way to stand beside the grave, Christopher pulled on my arm urgently. "I don't like this part. Can't I go wait in the car?" he pleaded. I glanced around to see who was there and saw my aunts and Frank chatting with friends near the cars. I watched as my cousin Tim and one of the volunteer pallbearers lift Hilda into her wheelchair and struggled to push her toward the gravesite on the soggy ground. Gladys, who had donned a large-brimmed black hat, led her grandchildren toward the grave holding their hands, followed by Francine and a few other people I did not recognize. I looked down at my son and was about to tell him that he must stay, that it was the proper thing to do, that it was almost over but I reconsidered. *Why put him through this?* I said, "If that's what you want to do, yes, go wait in the car."

His face lit up. His voice was filled with relief. "Really?"

I nodded.

"Thanks, Mom. I'm sorry I just don't wanna—"

"Don't worry about it. Go on."

I stepped to the grave and stared into the rectangle of earth that would be my mother's resting place and breathed in the smell of freshly uncovered, damp dirt. I swayed a bit and shifted my feet on the soggy ground. Francine walked over to me and hugged me. "You okay? I thought the service was really nice."

"Thanks to your mom," I told her. "I loved that they sang the song as a eulogy. I know Mama would have liked it." I added, "It's good to reconnect with you."

She smiled somewhat bashfully. "It's been too long," she said. "I missed you all."

"Anyone you missed in particular?" I chuckled and she laughed.

"Maybe," she said demurely. She turned and looked for Neal and I watched her face when she saw him. I felt a pang then, wishing for Greg, wishing someone would look at me the way Francine looked at my brother.

Claudia came over to us, followed by Harrie. "Are you doing okay, honey?" she asked me. "I hope you are. This is hard but Faye would have loved this send-off, I think."

"She would have. Thank you, all of you, for the song. It was beautiful."

Claudia blushed. "I'm just tickled we got Frank and Neal up there. Oh! Can you believe it! How I wish Faye had been here to see it!"

"I think she was watching," I said.

Claudia beamed and nodded. Something caught her attention and she spun around. Harrie was standing too close to the edge of the grave. "Harrie! You're too close to the edge. Come stand with me," she told her. Harrie came over and loudly asked, "Are they gonna put Faye in the ground? Is she gonna be here now?"

"Yes, this is where she'll be buried," I told her.

Harrie said, "So she will be dead and buried?"

Claudia took her hand. "Yes, honey. Dead and buried. That's what we do. We bury people in the ground when they're dead."

Harrie considered this but frowned, "Are they gonna bury her now?"

"Well, in a few minutes," Claudia replied with the hint of impatience. "Why are you asking so many questions?"

"Harrie, come stand by me," I coaxed. "The minister is going to say a few words, then we'll go on back and have food and drinks. And once we leave, the men who work here will bury Mama. Ok?" I took her hand gently and pulled her over to stand beside me.

The minister began to speak, thanking everyone for taking the journey to Mama's resting place. My mind wandered and I did not really listen and soon he was finished. I watched as he nodded toward Jake who stepped up to stand beside him. "And now, we have something really special to honor Faye as we lay her to rest," he announced. He made a motion to someone in the crowd, and I turned to see a teenaged boy dressed in a Boy Scout uniform, step forward to stand near Mama's casket. It was then that I noticed the bugle. Taps. Jake had arranged for the boy to play Taps.

"What's he gonna do?" Harrie asked loudly. "Is he gonna play that horn?"

Heads turned toward us, and I heard some muffled laughter. I leaned close to her and whispered, "Yes, Harrie. It's a special song played at the end of the day or when someone is buried. I bet you've heard it before."

"What's it called?"

"Taps."

"I know that song," Harrie announced, grinning widely. "I know all the words, too. Faye taught me."

Claudia leaned around me and said, "Harrie honey, I know you know the words but for now, we got to let the boy play his bugle and be really quiet. Okay?"

Harried nodded. "Okay Claudia. I'll be really quiet." She put her index finger to her lips and made a loud "Shh" sounds.

"Good honey. That's good."

Jake said, "This here is Brian McNair. He's with our local Boy Scout troop and I want to thank him for doing this." He turned to the boy. "Anytime you're ready."

The Scout, quite lean and very tall for his twelve years, raised his bugle, straightened himself, squared his shoulders then, inhaled deeply and began to play. The mournful notes floated through the air and swept over us in a virtual blanket quilted together of all things sorrowful. I felt the hairs on my neck rise. As it had in Arlington, the song triggered deep emotion with each heart-wrenching note. I closed my eyes. I did not want to cry, and I tried to steel myself but in doing so, I gripped Harrie's hand far too tightly.

"OUCH! Laney Mae you are hurting my hand," Harried cried out. I dropped her hand. The minister gave her a most unpleasant look and I cringed. The boy hit a note off key but recovered quickly with a dignity beyond his years and with that, big wet, warm tears filled my eyes and flowed down my face. They fell to the grass as I wrapped my arms around myself. Sniffling, I reached into my suit jacket pocket hoping to find some tissues and instead, I pulled out something else: the photograph I had put there that day back in the apartment when I had packed for this trip. I stared at it now, letting the familiar image of JFK holding me, distract me from the end of Taps.

Harrie leaned over closely to me. "What you got there, Laney Mae?" she asked, loudly. The minister's eyes grew wide with irritation.

"It's that photo," I whispered. I held it up. "It's the one with JFK. I forgot that I put it in my pocket a few days ago."

Harried stepped closer and leaned over to peer at it. She said loudly, "I remember that picture! That picture is special to you."

"Shh. Yes, it is. And it was special to Mama."

"And special to your daddy, too."

I nodded. "Yes, I guess it was." I shrugged as I reached into my other pocket but found no tissues there either.

"Yes," Harrie said. And then she took her index finger and placed it on an exact spot in the photo. A most particular spot on a man's face in the crowd. A spot I had never once before focused on nor had any reason to and said loudly, "Gil was there that day, too. He was right *there*." Grinning, she tapped the photo once more and held her finger on the spot.

My eyes widened, "What are you saying, Harrie?"

"Your daddy. He's right there in the picture." She tapped the photo once more. "See?"

Slowly, almost afraid to do so, fearing that the man's face would somehow be gone, I shifted my eyes to where Harrie's finger pointed in the photograph. And there, above my aunt's chubby finger with its overly chewed nail, was the face of a man, a face that had always just been in the background with other the faces. I gasped.

"It's your daddy. See? But I couldn't tell you before because Faye—"

"What?" I shrieked and everyone turned to stare at me.

The minister had resumed speaking and now stopped. "Excuse me? Can we please have silence now? We're almost at the end of the service. Let's show some respect. Please!"

Ignoring his admonishment, I pulled the photo up to my face. The man Harrie had pointed to stood in the background to JFK's left, about six people deep away from the candidate. The man Harrie was telling me was my father was smiling at Kennedy. Like everyone in the photo, he stood shoulder-to-shoulder, jammed in with people all around him pushing in to shake JFK's hand. I now noticed the other faces, faces I had never given a thought until now. Were any familiar to me? There. That smiling woman in a hat with sunglasses. Who was she? The teenage boy with glasses gawking at JFK, his round face peeking over a policeman's shoulder. Was he someone our family knew? And close to him, a woman, her head covered in a scarf tied beneath her chin, stretching her arm over a little girl's shoulder, reaching as far as she could to try to touch Kennedy. So many faces! I scanned them in a split second then my eyes returned again to the man Harrie had pointed to. He was just another face in the crowd and yet . . . and yet. . . the was something familiar. Was it his full head of wavy, dark hair? Was it the friendly expression on his handsome face, with its square jaw? Or was it his eyes? Yes, there was something about his eyes. They were familiar . . . they were recognizable because . . . because . . . I realized with a jolt: his eyes were like Neal's! The shape of his face, his broad fore-head, his nose, his mouth! As clearly as I could see the back of my hand, the resemblance was undeniable. As though struck by a bolt of electricity, my body jolted with a rush of surreal recognition. The man was staring in awe at John F. Kennedy, the future president of the United States, as he held me, his baby daughter. Gil Martin's daughter.

Trembling, I screamed, "Harrie!" I grabbed my aunt's fleshy arm. "This is my daddy? That's his face! I've had this picture of my daddy all along?"

The minister slammed the bible closed. "Alright, that's *it*! I am going to stop until we have respectful silence."

Harrie giggled loudly and clapped her hands together in joy. "Yes! Laney Mae. That's Gil! Luke said I couldn't tell you about him until Faye was dead and buried. Now, I can tell you."

In a flash I remembered Mama's words the night she died, "*I should have told you. . . You have . . . the picture . . . Go see . . .* " The fortune cookie, "*That which you seek, you already possess.*" I recalled the odd way the portrait of JFK had tilted the morning after Mama died. Was this insanity?

"What in the world is all this disruption?" Ruth yelled, standing near Hilda's wheelchair several people away from me.

I held up the photo and cried out, "It's my daddy! He's in this picture! Oh, come see!"

Claudia, Neal, Jake, Gladys, Frank, and Margaret gathered excitedly around me with Harrie standing by proudly. They all clamored to know what in the world had gotten into me. I began to weep in joy that bordered on hysteria. "Look! Look!" I grabbed Neal's arm and shoved the photo at him. "He's right there Neal! Isn't it wonderful!" Neal stared in wonder and shook his head, speechless.

Claudia took the photo next, and her mouth dropped. "Oh! It is Gil! My goodness! I had no idea, and I *took* the darn picture!" She shook her head, "Oh! I cannot believe this."

Ruth elbowed her way in and snatched my prized photo from Claudia. She peered at the face and nodded as though a judge viewing evidence during a trial. "Of course, that's Gil! And I bet Faye knew his face was in this picture all the time too and didn't tell you! That's a damn shame!" She huffed with anger then swung around to Harrie, her voice harsh. "Harrie! Why didn't *you* tell Laney Mae this before? You knew this all along and you didn't tell her?! You knew how much she wanted to see a picture of her daddy! You knew Faye threw all his photos away! Why didn't you show her this before? That's just awful!"

Harrie's face fell, and her lips to trembled. Her eyes filled. "Luke told me not to." She bowed her head and her face reddened with embarrassment.

Margaret pulled Ruth's arm. "Now you stop that! You hear me. That's just mean. Don't you yell at Harrie!"

Frank thrust himself into the mix. Raising his voice above theirs he said, "Can't you all stop bickering for even a minute? Ruth you are always looking for trouble!"

"Frank Hartman you of all people have no right to speak to me like that. You *always* take the other side against me, no matter what!"

"It's alright, Ruth!" I said, my voice rising. "I know now! It's alright, really. I'm so happy." But she and Margaret and Claudia and Frank ignored me and continued to quarrel while I stood surrounded by other relatives and friends marveling at the wonderful discovery, holding the photo protectively for others to see.

The minister's voice rose angrily above the noise. "Ladies and gentlemen, I do not, for the life of me, know what is going on here but, for the last time, I ask you to compose yourselves!" His nostrils flared and his face was flush with anger. When the bickering still didn't cease, he stomped over to the Boy Scout and grabbed the bugle, raised it to his lips and blew, his cheeks puffing out, his eyes bulging. The noise resembled not a musical instrument but a mule braying. Everyone stopped bickering and turned to face him. My aunts and uncle stepped away from each other, heads bowed. The minister handed the bugle back to the shocked Boy Scout who made a face and wiped the mouthpiece off on his shorts.

Christopher had been watching all this activity from the car and could tell something was up. He rushed over, alarmed to see me laughing and crying. I told him what I had and hugged him. "Look! Here's a picture of your grandfather, my dad, Gil Martin!" He took the photo from me, marveling at it then his face broke into a wide grin. He looked from the image to me and then to Neal. "You look like him, Uncle Neal," he said. To me he said, "And Harrie was the one who showed you?"

I nodded happily, beaming.

I turned to find her, but Harrie was no longer standing beside me. Concerned, I called out, "Where's Harrie?"

A flash of fear crossed Claudia's face. "Oh dear God! She's run off!" Claudia clutched her heart. Turning to Ruth she screamed, "This is all your fault! You shouldn't have yelled at her!"

Ruth railed and the bickering began again. My eyes quickly scanned the rows of headstones and then up past them where there was nothing but trees and beyond that, the mountain top. Had she gone there? I looked back to the road where our cars were parked. She must have gone home, I thought. Frank came to stand beside me. "Don't worry, we'll find her. She's not lost. She's run off before. She knows these hills and mountains better than any of us." He put his arm around me. "She'll come home. She always comes home."

CHAPTER 21

We searched for Harrie to no avail and soon decided to call for help but the Sheriff, Len Conti, was as perplexed as we were. "So far, we don't see any sign of her. Nothing. We've been searching since earlier and we went all over the cemetery and outward in all directions. There's been no sign of her, but we'll keep looking." He tilted his head back and looked at the blue, cloudless sky. "At least we got good weather to look for her."

"But can't we do more? How about helicopters?" I asked.

Conti looked at me with disdain, "Helicopters? Do you know what that involves?"

"It's just a thought," I replied. I felt like a scolded child. I lowered my head. I pulled the photo with my father's face out of my pocket and stared at it again, still in disbelief. It gave me a jolt of hope.

"Look," Conti said, his tone a little softer, "I know all of you are worried and here's the thing: you all have told me you think she's upset and thinks she did something bad. Well, I'll tell you what I think: in my opinion, she'd hiding somewhere. It's as simple as that."

"But where, Len?" Gladys asked. "If you think she's hiding, how about instead of the woods, why don't you all check out some of those empty buildings down in town?" She waved her hand in the direction of Main Street. "Did you all even look there?"

Conti's mouth dropped open and he shook his head. "Hell, Gladys! We only got started a couple of hours ago. I told you we were working from the cemetery out. That's where she was last seen. How many people do you think I have? We can only cover so much ground-"

"We know that Len," Frank interrupted. "All we're saying is you ought to-"

"And I'm saying if you all want to go look in those empty buildings, go ahead, but don't suggest that we aren't doing enough because let me assure you, we are . . ."

I turned away, despair growing inside me. I tuned out their bickering voices and tilted my head back to look at the sky. "Help us find her," I whispered as I had when Mother was lost along the road. "Please help us." Sighing, I lowered my head and caught sight of Mother herself, curled into a ball, sleeping on the front porch of Luke's old house. *Wonder what Mother's doing over there?* I looked and expected to see Dandy but instead I saw my father's face, my *real* father. I smiled. His image was no longer a mystery or a creation of my imagination. I closed my eyes and saw him clearly. I reached inside my suit pocket and clutched the old snapshot, happiness spreading through my body. *I think she's in there. Go see,* his voice told me.

Without a word, I began to walk purposefully toward the dog and the abandoned house and with each step, I felt a growing sense of certainty that Harrie was indeed inside. But suddenly I felt something else, something most unexpected: my imaginary father was slipping away. He was no longer beside me. He was no longer accompanying me on my journey. Instead, he was staying put, in my past. I stopped and spun around, and he was gone. For a split second I felt a rush of sadness, but that was instantly replaced by a powerful sensation of love and the realization that I didn't need an imaginary father anymore. I could let him go. I said a silent thanks to my beloved Dandy and all the other imaginary faces of imaginary fathers I had carried with me most of my life.

I continued to walk toward the house. As I neared the porch, I paused. The dog lay still, lost in slumber. I scanned the front of the house and waited, half expecting to see the front door open suddenly or to see a flash of a person inside ducking from a window.

"Mom? What are you doing?" Christopher called to me from the driveway.

I turned around and waved at him then pointed to Mother to indicate I was just getting the dog. I tip-toed up the steps and waited but the dog did not move. A coldness ran through me at the awful thought that Mother may have roamed over to the abandoned house to find a quiet place to die. *Wouldn't that be just my luck*, I thought. I knelt and hesitantly reached over to stroke her back and felt a wave of relief when my hand touched her. At my touch, Mother jerked awake and struggled to stand. I helped her to her feet. Kneeling, I peered into her eyes. "She's in there, isn't she Mother?" The dog shook her body with indifference. I lifted her and carried her down the porch steps and gently lowered her to the ground. I motioned for Christopher who bounded over.

"Take Mother back to the main house. It's time to feed her."

Christopher took hold of the dog's collar and began to gently lead the dog away. He noticed I was not following. "Mom, what are you doing? Aren't you coming to help look for Harrie?"

I stepped over to where he stood and leaned in close to his face and said in a low voice, "Don't say anything, but I think I know where Harrie is."

He looked confused, then his eyes widened, and a smile spread across his face. "Mom! Is she hiding in this old house? Is that what you think?"

I raised a finger to my lips. "Shh. Don't say anything to them yet. If she's in there, the last thing we need is a bunch of people over here scaring her."

"Go in, Mom. I'll take Mother. I won't say anything." He gently lifted the dog into his arms. He buried his face into its neck as he so often did and said, "Good 'ole Mother. You found Harrie. Good girl." He turned and walked away, holding the old dog on his hip, spinning around once to give me a knowing grin.

I faced the house and recalled the strong pull I had felt just two days ago when I had set out to mail Claudia's bills. I felt it again, only stronger now. I walked up the steps and faced the front door. I hesitated, trying to decide whether to knock or just walk in. Whatever I did, I must not upset Harrie. I pressed my ear to the door but heard no sound from inside. I put my hand on the knob, turned and felt great relief that the door was unlocked. I pushed but the door stuck a bit, so I had to use my foot to force it open. The door grunted in protest but swung wide revealing a small living room—or what had once been a living room—that now appeared to serve only as a storage place for unwanted junk. I stepped into the dimly lit space and allowed my eyes adjust to the shadows. A still life of mismatched furniture scattered about greeted me. To my right, a wooden table with a badly scratched surface stood idly next to a chair missing an arm and beside that, another chair, worn and dirty, its upholstery moth-eaten and faded. Near that stood a dresser without any drawers and next to that, a stack of four interior doors lay with great resignation where they had been rudely abandoned, probably decades ago. Directly across from me was a very old woodstove, most likely original to the house, covered with a heavy layer of dust and soot. Nearby stood its stovepipe, unceremoniously removed and standing at attention like a soldier awaiting an order. I listened for any sound but heard nothing.

I stepped across the room toward the staircase and stopped when I heard the distinct sound of a door closing. It came from upstairs. Excitedly, I walked quickly to the stairway and began climbing, cringing when the fourth step creaked loudly. I froze. Exposed for sure, I figured I may as well let my presence be known. "Harrie? Are you in here?" Silence. "Harrie? It's me, Laney Mae. I know you're in here. Come on out. It's okay."

Again, I heard the sound of a door open and close. I jogged up the remaining stairs to the top and stood in a dark, narrow hallway. No natural light fell here because the doors to all four rooms on this level were closed. I started to walk toward the door at the far end of the hall when I again heard the sound of the door opening and closing and knew for sure it had come from the room near the top of the stairs. No need to even check the other rooms; I knew with certainty where Harrie was and could easily imagine my aunt hiding in the room's closet, opening the door to hear better, then quickly pulling it shut. I smiled with the knowledge that this search was at last over.

I placed my hand lightly on the knob and pushed opened the door. Nearly total darkness greeted me. The room had three windows, and all were covered with what looked like old towels or blankets, haphazardly nailed to the wall above them. I could see a variety of cast-off items including a step ladder, a couple of wooden chairs, an old crib and a highchair. In the dim light, I could just make out the shapes of what appeared to be a mattress lying flat on the floor with blankets and pillows. Assorted cardboard boxes filled the room and these were stacked and arranged in a way that made me think that someone had purposefully used them to design a fortress of sorts. I squinted, trying to see a clear path to the closet at the opposite side of the room where I knew Harrie hid. Instinctively, I ran my hand along the wall hoping to find a light switch and sure enough, ran my fingertips across one. I flipped it, not really expecting anything and was startled and let out a gasp when an overhead light popped on.

"Harrie?"

Across from me the closet door slowly opened a small crack. "Laney Mae?"

"Yes, it's me, Harrie. I'm here. I was so worried about you. Everyone is worried about you."

"Is it just you?"

"Yes. It's just me. I'm the only one who knows you're here. It's okay. You can come out. You don't have to hide."

But instead, Harrie pulled the closet door shut again with a firm slam.

"You don't need to hide, Harrie," I said gently. "Everything is fine. Come on out." I made my way to the door and tugged on the knob but Harrie held fast to her side. "Harrie!" my voice rose with exasperation. "Come on honey, please open the door."

Slowly, the door opened a crack. First, I saw the top of Harrie's head as she peeked around the door, then her forehead came into view and then her bushy eyebrows and next, her eyes, wide and red from crying, then her full face, tear-streaked. "Don't be mad at me."

"Oh Harrie! I'm not mad at you." I held my arms out and Harrie bolted from the closet and threw herself into them almost causing us both to tumble over backwards.

"Everyone is mad at me!" Harrie wailed.

"Oh Harrie, no! We are *not* mad! Do you know how happy you made me? Showing me that my daddy was in that picture?" I held her close and rocked her in my arms the way I sometimes did Christopher.

Harrie stopped crying. A wide grin transformed her face, making her look younger. "Very happy?"

"Oh yes! So very happy!"

"I'm glad Laney Mae!" She clapped her hands together joyfully. "I got lots of things to show you. Luke and me, we hid stuff here a long time ago. It's Gil's. It's what Faye threw away back when Gil died, and he made her so mad. But Luke and me, we got it out of the trash, and we saved it. Most of it. And now, it's okay. Faye is gone. She can't get mad. I can show you now! Luke told me I could show you if Faye said it was okay or if she died. Faye died so I can show you."

"I don't think I understand what you're telling me, Harrie."

Harrie smiled mischievously. "I will show you." With that, she took my hand and led me into the closet. I squinted into darkness but Harrie reached up and, with a grunt, pulled on a chain and the space filled with light.

"See?" Harrie said, waving her hand dramatically. "I told you." She stepped back so that I could move forward and stand in the center of the closet. I turned my head from left to right, taking in the scene. Unlike the clutter and disarray throughout the house, this closet space was neat, orderly and felt lived in. A faint odor that reminded me of old library books that hadn't been opened for years plus a whiff of mothballs filled my nostrils. There was another scent too, something vague that evoked a strong sense of familiarity. What was it? I stepped further into the closet and peered at the cardboard boxes before me, about a half dozen of them, stacked neatly against one wall. Then I noticed a wooden trunk, draped protectively with an old quilt, sitting at the back of the closet. To my right, neatly hung, was a small collection of men's shirts and pants plus two jackets: one a suit coat, one a windbreaker. A bright red and black checked flannel shirt caught my eye and I stared at it. Something about it was oddly familiar.

"Harrie, what is all this? Are you saying this was my dad's stuff? All this?"

"Yes! I told you. Luke and I saved it. We got it out of the trash pile back at your house in River Mount after Gil died in the car crash with that woman. Faye was gonna throw it all away, but we saved it."

I grabbed Harrie by the shoulders excitedly, "Harrie, are you serious?" Before she could reply, I asked, "Who else knows about this?"

"Nobody. Except Luke."

"Neal?"

Harrie again shook her head.

"Claudia? Frank?"

"No. I couldn't tell anyone."

"What about my mama? Did she know?"

Harried lowered her head. She shrugged her shoulders. "I think so," she said to the floor. Looking up she added, "One time, I saw her coming out of this house and she looked all upset. I think she found it. She saw me and walked over to me and just stared at me and she looked really mad, but she didn't say nothing."

"When was that?"

Harrie thoughtfully tapped her cheek with her index finger, trying to recall. "Back when she was married to that mean man named Art."

I could not understand why Mama had not let me and Neal know about this. I felt anger rising but refused to let it take hold of me. Curiosity and anticipation filled me, and I stood contemplating what wonderful, magical and mysterious things awaited me here. Tears welled in my eyes, and I whimpered with both excitement and fear. I tried to take a step but couldn't. I stood frozen in that closet doorway in that abandoned house on the side of an old mountain in West Virginia because I knew I was now suspended, hovering between the past and the present. Surrounded by belongings of a father I could not recall and yet who I could now feel all around me, I stared, wide-eyed at the cardboard boxes, the mysterious wooden trunk and the men's clothing. And I still could not move a bit, not even a single step. I was fearful that if I did, it would all disappear.

"Come on Laney Mae," Harrie said, taking my hand. "Don't you wanna see?"

"Oh, yes. I want to see."

I looked over at the clothing—my father's clothing—hanging so patiently, waiting, it seemed, for me to come find them. With two tentative steps, I stood inches from the lifeless garments and, as I had done just days before in Mama's closet, I wrapped my arms around them, pulled them up to my face and allowed myself to be enveloped within them. I breathed in deeply and was not disappointed by the musty smell. I let the clothes fall back and stared at them, transfixed. I looked again at the red and black checked flannel shirt. I stroked it gently and then pulled it off the hanger and brought to my face. Its fabric was itchy. I pulled the shirt on, gently rolling the sleeves up and hugged myself tightly.

"Gil wore that a lot outside," Harrie told me.

"There's something about it that's familiar. I don't know why."

Harrie nodded. She left the closet and returned with one of the old wooden chairs. She dragged it up to me. "Sit here. I will bring pictures and other things for you to see."

THERE WERE DOZENS OF MOSTLY BLACK AND WHITE SNAPSHOTS and a few more formal portrait photographs taken at a studio, still in their original studio covers. Harrie brought all these to me and laid them at my feet as if in holy offering. I eagerly pulled them out of the manila envelopes and assorted shoeboxes where they had remained in purgatory for decades. A few were dog-eared and curling at the corners, but most were in surprisingly good condition. The photographs were in no particular order but that was alright to me for each was a treasure. I focused on each photo so intently that soon my head ached. There were photos of him at various ages; one in a graduation cap and gown, one of him as a baby, sitting on a blanket outdoors, a wooden spoon in his chubby hand, his mouth smiling, frozen for that instant. "Gil, 1926" was written in cursive on the back. A series of school photos were mixed in. I found myself focused on one in which my father appeared to be about Christopher's age and delighted in the fact that I saw a definite resemblance.

Next was a batch of photos from before I was born, photos featuring Neal as a baby with the proud new parents. *Wait until Neal sees these*, I thought and remembered with a sudden jolt that everyone was still out searching for Harrie! *How long had I been sitting here in this closet?* I jumped up from the chair, aghast. "Oh Harrie! We've got to let everyone know you that we're here and that you're okay."

Harrie's mouth curled downward into a frown. She shook her head, "No. I like hiding."

"Harrie! You don't need to hide. Everyone's worried—"

Just then, we heard the front door open. Christopher, sounding upset, called from downstairs. "Mom! Where are you? You never came back out. Mom! Did you find Harrie?"

"Up here!"

He followed my voice and came to stand in the doorway, hands on his hips, face reddened. "Mom! You were supposed to come out. Did you find Harrie . . ." He stopped speaking when he caught sight of her and exclaimed, "Harrie! There you are!" He stepped over to his great aunt and embraced her. "Why are you hiding, Harrie? Everyone was looking for you all over the place."

"I was scared," Harrie told him. "Ruth was mad at me, she said I was bad."

"Everything is okay now," he told her. He turned to me. "Mom, it's hot up here. Why are you still in this old house? Why are you wearing that shirt?"

Before Harrie could reply, I grabbed a handful of photographs and held them out to him. "Christopher, I have something amazing to show you. The most wonderful thing! All this stuff in here? All this belonged to my dad—your grandfather! Harrie saved it all for me back when he died. She and my uncle Luke—you remember Luke, the oldest of Grandma's brothers? When my dad died, Mama threw all of his stuff out in the trash but Luke and Harrie got it and hid it here.

He looked confused, "I don't get it."

"You know how Grandma would never talk about him or tell me if there was a picture of him or anything? Harrie kept this here until now, and now that Grandma's gone, she thought it was okay to show me."

"Faye can't get mad now," Harrie said.

"So this was all his," I said. "His clothes, photos, all sorts of stuff. I've only started to go through it all. That's why I haven't come back out, I was so excited! See? This old shirt I'm wearing? It was his."

His face slowly transformed from confusion to comprehension. Smiling, he came to stand before me and reached up to gently touch the shirt that had been his grandfather's. He looked down at the photos in my hand. I held a random one up for him to see. "Look, this is one where he is with Neal, when Neal was a baby." In the black and white snapshot, a grinning Gil holds his infant son up while baby Neal's face is contorted unhappily in a wail one could almost hear. "And this one . . . this is of Grandma with my dad. I think it must have been when they got engaged. Look how young Grandma looks."

He stared at the photo. In it, she was holding the hand of the man who was his grandfather as she gazed up at him lovingly.

Christopher said. "Look at her face! You can tell she loved him."

"Yes. She did."

"Wait 'til Uncle Neal sees these," he said excitedly.

I gasped. "Neal! Yes! Go get Neal, Christopher and tell Claudia and Frank and Gladys. Tell them to tell the sheriff and everyone that Harrie is here and she's fine."

"No!" Harrie cried. "I don't want them to find me yet. I want to stay with you. There is more to show you."

I smiled. "Harrie, honey, don't worry. I want you to show me. I *need* you to show me."

Harrie hesitated, frowning. "Ok," she replied glumly. "You can let them find me."

I turned back to Christopher. "Tell Neal there is a special surprise and that he needs to come. Get Frank, too. And Claudia and Jake. Okay?" I paused then said, "But Christopher, don't tell them what the surprise is yet, okay?" I winked at him.

He nodded and gave me a thumbs-up and started to dash out of the room. He stopped suddenly, grabbing hold of the doorframe with each hand. He turned around slowly. "I was right you know," he said.

"What do you mean?"

"About Grandma. Remember? Me telling you about her coming to visit me in my dream after she died and what she told me. 'Tell your mom she already has what she's looking for.' But you didn't believe me."

We stared at each other. I struggled to say something but only stammered.

"It's okay, Mom," he said. "You had to find it for yourself."

WE CARRIED MANY OF THE BOXES FROM LUKE'S OLD HOUSE TO THE living room of the main house. Harrie had fretted over the removal of the boxes and assorted items like a mother bird watching its babies leave the nest. After the shock of the discovery had worn off and things had settled down somewhat, Claudia had whipped up dinner, beer bottles were opened and another of my father's old record albums, *Patsy Cline Showcase*, found in the old trunk, played on the stereo in the dining room.

Everyone reacted differently to Harrie's secret surprise. Neal had been stunned and rendered nearly speechless, his eyes glistening with tears as he viewed and touched our father's belongings. Claudia was a jittery mess of excitement. She could not stop talking and had run in and out of the kitchen as she cooked dinner, expressing an endless stream of shock along with profuse apologies to both me and Neal that she had not known about the hidden treasures for all these years. "I am beside myself! Oh! I'll never get over this! I should have known!"

Margaret had circled a few of the boxes and poked around in them, mumbling to herself about Harrie's ability to keep a secret for so many years while Hilda napped in her wheelchair, oblivious to the commotion. Frank had seemed mystified but in a state that could only be called elation over the discovery. He couldn't seem to stop grinning. "Luke was the smartest one among us," he said aloud, with pride. "He knew! He knew Faye would regret throwing all Gil's stuff out one day."

"I would disagree with him being the smartest one," Gladys said with a nod to Harrie. "Nope. I would say Harrie was the smartest of all and the most determined to keep all this safe and protected until now." We all turned to Harrie who blushed. "I knew I had to," she said with great seriousness. "It was important."

Ruth, chewing a wad of gum with intensity as she was known to do when high strung (which was most of the time), offered her editorial with a scowl. "Are you all forgetting that Faye must have known about all this? Harrie, you said you thought she knew you had it hid over there. And if she did, and she didn't tell you kids it was there? Shame on her! The least she could have done is let you all know about it. Laney Mae, especially you—always obsessing about your daddy—but no! She didn't tell you. Faye was so damn stubborn," she snapped.

Jake, who had already consumed three beers, was philosophical, "Aunt Ruth, you need to stop. We'll never understand why Aunt Faye did what she did. You need to celebrate this and stop fussing."

I paid little attention to all this chatter. I was so deeply immersed in all the photographs and my father's various belongings that most of the talk went in one ear and out the other. The cheeks of my face hurt due to the constant smile I wore as I pulled items from boxes. There was a mixed-matched assortment of the most basic and even mundane things, but even these caused delight for they held a magic because they had been *his*. There were his neckties, his wristwatch, a box of old coins he had collected, and his deck of playing cards. I delighted at Neal's discovery in a shoebox (that looked older than him) of a small stack of letters tied up with a ribbon that were all from our daddy to Mama, written as he traveled about the state selling insurance. *I could read his words!* In other boxes there was a variety of things that told the story of our father, things like a bowling trophy, a baseball card collection, a JFK for president button, a West Virginia Mountaineers pennant and old school textbooks. In one box I found some of his grade school papers and report cards spanning several years and a graduation cap. I was just opening his senior yearbook when Christopher leapt up off the floor where he had been exploring an official-looking metal box that had been inside the old trunk. He rushed over to me. "Mom! Did you know your dad was in the Navy?" He held up a photo of my father in uniform grinning at the camera on the deck of a ship, one hand on his hip, his sailor cap dangling from the other.

"Well, look at that!" I turned to Neal. "Did you know he was in the Navy?"

Neal shook his head. Claudia spoke, "I think I recall him or Faye talking about someone he knew while he was in the Navy or something like that. Didn't say much, though. I'm sorry I didn't pay more attention."

Harrie, who was sitting at the dinner table eating with Claudia said, "We saved all that from when he was in the Navy. He had pretty ribbons, too. They are there."

I looked at Frank and we walked over and knelt down next to Christopher. I reached in and pulled out a few more photos of my dad in uniform and then, when I lifted some papers from the box, there lay a band of four colorful ribbons, sewn together, adorned with medals. "Oh look," I said excitedly. Gently, I lifted them and held them up for Frank to see. "You were in the military, Frank. What are these for?"

Frank peered closely. "Those are his service medals." He tapped one of them with his index finger and I noticed his hand was shaking slightly. "I recognize this one," he said. He spoke in a low voice. "It's for service in . . . Korea."

"That's where you served, too, Frank," Claudia said and added softly, "And Kurt." She bowed her head.

Frank's face fell at the mention of his brother's name. He stiffened and cleared his throat in an effort to compose himself. "I had no idea Gil was in Korea. He never said anything about being there." His frown grew deeper. "Of course, I didn't talk about it either." His voice broke as he said this. His sudden sadness swept across the room and a tense silence fell. Hoping to distract him, I asked, "Frank, what are the other ones for?" He stared blankly at me with sad eyes, the wet trail of a tear on his cheek.

"Tell me," I coaxed. "Please? I want to know. What are the other medals are for?"

He stared at me forlornly. *This is too much for him*, I thought, guilt rising from the pit of my stomach. The boxes held reminders of other ghosts, too, I realized, and they did not all belong to me. I suddenly feared he would bolt from the house, go off by himself and drink, overcome by renewed sorrow. We would find him tomorrow, hungover, on the couch as before, his back to the world once again.

I held his eyes and silently willed him to be alright. I reached for his hand and squeezed it firmly. Frank took a deep breath then cleared his throat and focused his attention on the medals. He tapped another of them. "You see this one here? This one is from service in China. I guess Gil must have ended up there at some point when he was over near Korea. And this one here is for service in World War II. He must have signed up young." He managed to smile at me which warmed my heart. "That's brave but I bet his mama didn't like that." He winked at Christopher who grinned back. "This other one," he pointed to the last, "this would be his U.S. Navy service medal." He shut his eyes, lowering his chin to his chest.

Christopher reached back into the box and rustled around. His hand landed on a small box covered in dark blue fabric. He pulled it out and opened it. "Here's another! This is a pretty one. It's got George Washington on it. What's this one for?"

Everyone stopped what they were doing to look. Frank's mouth dropped open when Christopher handed him the box. "Well, look at that," Frank said. "That is a Purple Heart. This means Gil got wounded in action." He shook his head and said quietly, almost to himself, "I can't believe I never knew it."

"Well, Frank," Claudia said, rising from her chair and moving toward him. "You got one of them too."

Frank turned toward her with sudden anger. I watched as he

struggled up from kneeling on the floor. "Now why the hell did you go and say something about that, Claudia?" he growled.

Claudia shook her head and held her arms out to him, "But Frank, I'm proud of you."

"For Christ's sake!" Frank waved my father's Purple Heart box around and glared at his sister. "You know I didn't want everyone to know about that medal and think I thought I was some big deal when my poor brother didn't come home from there!"

"Oh no, Frank! Of course not," Claudia offered, wringing her apron tensely. "No one talked about it after Kurt died."

He frowned deeply and his voice rose as decades of angst finally surfaced. "Kurt got one of these, too, you know! Why should mine matter? By the way, so did Harold and so did Rob. And they *deserved* theirs! You hear me? They died!"

Ruth said, "You deserved yours, too, Frank. You surely did."

Frank scowled at her. "I did not! Hell, my injury wasn't any big deal. It was just a nick, really . . . compared to . . . what happened to my brothers." His face crumpled and he let out a mournful sob. He bowed his head, covering his face with one hand while the other clutched my father's Purple Heart. He began to sob.

I rose and watched helplessly as my uncle wept but could not think of what to say to comfort him. I was about to reach out to simply take his hand but at that moment he bolted forward–as I had feared–to leave the house. Neal reacted quickly and stood, blocking his path. He pulled Frank into a tight embrace. "It's alright, it's alright, it's alright," Neal murmured over and over until at last, Frank stopped resisting and allowed his nephew to hold him. He sobbed quietly on Neal's shoulder, his thin body shaking. Neal told him, "It *was* a big deal. Your service was a big deal, Frank." He stepped back slightly, keeping a firm hold on his uncle's shoulders. "And it's not your fault that Kurt died or that Harold died or that Uncle Rob died. We're glad you *didn't* die. We're glad you came home. That was your purpose, Frank. To come home and be here—for us. To help tell their story, hell, to finish their story. Because that's what we have to do, all of us, finish the story—or the next chapter, anyway—for the ones who can't finish it themselves."

I stepped over and wrapped my arms around Frank's back, reaching my hands around to clutch his chest near his heart. I sensed others coming toward us and I shifted to allow Christopher to push his way into the center of our bodies. Next, Claudia and Harrie came and wrapped their arms around us as well, Claudia weeping quietly and grinning at the same time. Gladys joined us along with Francine and even Ruth ambled over, not quite joining the embrace, but instead reaching out to gently pat Frank's arm. We stood like that, until Jake, overcome with emotion and the effects of another beer, rushed over bellowing "Group hug!" and nearly knocked us all over.

Unable to not, Frank laughed. He pulled a handkerchief from his back pocket and wiped his face and blew his nose. He handed me my father's Purple Heart box. He cleared his throat and, taking a moment to scan each of our faces he said, "Well, you know, the thing about a wound is, if we're lucky, eventually, it heals."

⚜

A LITTLE LATER THAT EVENING, NEAL STOOD IN FRONT OF ME AND dropped his packed duffle bag with a thud on the floor. "Well, I got to get going," he announced. I jumped up from the couch and said, "Oh Neal, no! Please stay. Go back home tomorrow when Christopher and I leave. We still have lots of stuff to go through. Jake, Harrie and Christopher just went over and are bringing the last boxes back."

"Laney Mae. I wish I could stay but I got to go. I've got to be at work at eight o'clock in the morning. It's late. I've got to hit the road."

"But just call your boss and . . ."

"And be told 'you're fired?' I don't think so," he grinned at me. "Look, we'll keep going through all this. You're bringing a lot of it home, right? And we can come back up anytime for the rest of it."

"I just wish you could stay."

"I know. Me, too." He held my eyes. "Can you believe it? I mean . . . really believe this? It's amazing. And I'm glad for you, you know? I could at least remember him."

"And now I can, too."

"And no one will ever take him away from you again."

"Us. No one will ever take him away from *us* again."

Gladys came over with Francine and a sleepy Jasmine and Rose. "We have to hit the road, too," she said. "Two little girls who can't stay awake." She held her arms wide for me and I fell into them and savored the warmth and comfort.

"Thank you, Gladys, for everything. I don't want so much time to pass between us seeing each other."

Casting a look at Francine and Neal she winked. "I don't think we need to worry about that." I smiled. She continued, "I'm so happy for you about all this. I'm a sucker for happy endings."

I grinned at her. "I think this might be a happy *beginning*."

At that moment, Jake, Christopher, and Harrie paraded into the house, their voices loud with excitement as they carried another assortment of our father's items over from Luke's. "Wait 'til you see what we found!" Jake's voice boomed. He struggled with a heavy box he hugged tightly to his chest. He slowly squatted down, his face turning red, and set the box on the floor. He grinned at everyone and playfully wiggled his eyebrows up and down. "Prepare to get excited!" He lifted the lid off and from within he pulled out a metal canister containing a movie reel. "Home movies!"

I squealed. "Jake! I never even thought about finding home movies!" I turned to Neal and Gladys. "Now you all have to stay, okay? Let's watch just one. It'll be just a few minutes. Please?" They agreed to stay.

We located the movie projector, but Claudia could not recall where the screen was and sent Frank and Jake off to search for it, which caused much accusatory grumbling among Claudia, Ruth and Margaret about people who didn't put things back in their proper place. Christopher could not stop examining the old movie reels and wondering aloud why they were not on VHS tape. Finally, everything was assembled and the movie reel, which, according to the label on the canister contained the Gil and Faye Martin family history from October 1961 to January 1962, was carefully loaded and the film fed through the projector. Images—in beautiful color but lacking any sound—of Halloween revelry began to play. The camera panned what must have been the living room in our River Mount home. Mama was dressed in a costume that seemed to resemble Minnie Mouse. Neal, about age 6, was decked out head-to-toe as a cowboy. He repeatedly drew toy pistols out of his hip holster and fired at the cameraman, in this case his father. A scene later, I appeared, held by Mama. I rubbed my eyes from the glare of the bright camera lights, obviously fussy and unhappy as Mama tried to get me to look in the camera and smile. Following Halloween, the next scene was outside on a sunny afternoon, trees dressed for fall, their leaves in various shades of red, yellow and orange. Young Neal was grinning as he rode what looked to be a shiny new red bicycle up and down the sidewalk. "I remember that bike," Neal said. "I must of rode that bike a hundred miles up and down the street in the first week I got it. I loved that bike."

As the camera followed Neal zooming by, the scene went out of focus for a brief moment and then our father came into view, standing atop the back of a tricycle with me on the seat, my legs too

THE ROAD TO SECOND CHANCE

short to reach the pedals and my feet hanging in the air. I would have been almost two and, as my father glided me along the sidewalk, I giggled with delight.

"Oh, look there, honey," Claudia said. "You and your daddy! Just look at that. My how he loved you. I'm just tickled you get to see this!"

I was unable to take my eyes from the screen. The film cut to the next scene which unfolded almost as if in slow motion. There I was in my father's arms as he danced about. His mouth moved in song. "Mom! He's wearing the shirt you have on!" Christopher said excitedly. I wrapped my arms around myself. As I watched the movie, I realized that the setting was right here in the Hartman home, the very room where we now sat. In the film, my father, in his red and black buffalo checked shirt, commanded the room, grinning and dancing with me in his arms. Family members laughed and their mouths moved as they sang along with him. The camera's jerky, quick pan around the room showed Grandmother Hartman, a much younger Claudia, her husband, Pete, little Jake, his baby brother Tim and an assortment of other Hartman family members, though I noticed, Frank was not among them. I saw a Christmas tree and holiday decorations in the background. This was his last Christmas, I thought. Our last Christmas as a whole family. In the next scene, Harrie, who would have been in her early twenties, rushed toward the camera and twirled happily as she danced near my father, hugging what appeared to be a large jar. Near her, Neal is laughing and jumping about the room, making comical faces at the camera.

"That's the moonbeam song!" Harrie cried out. "I remember that! That was Gil's favorite song."

"What's that?" I asked.

"Swinging On A Star," Claudia said. "The Bing Crosby song. Come on, you know it, don't you? About the donkey and pig and fish and all." She began singing the song and Harrie, Jake and a few others joined her, all singing loudly.

"Oh yes. I know that song." I smiled thinking about the album Uncle Rob had brought us so many years before.

The movie ended then, the strip of film flapping against the projector until Jake jumped up to switch it off and rewind the reel. Claudia turned the overhead light on, and Neal came to me and picked up his bag. "Now I really am leaving," he said. "I'm glad I stayed but I have go. We'll watch all the movies soon. I promise."

I rose and gave him a hug. "Be careful driving. Just give the phone a couple of rings when you get home to let us know you made it safe."

Harrie ambled over to us carrying a large jar. I stared at her, puzzled. I recalled seeing her in the home movie carrying what looked like this very jar.

"Harrie what in the world is that?"

Harrie grinned. "It's Gil's moonbeams," she said. "Moonbeams in a jar. Like the song. He put them in here a long time ago. I have kept it safe."

Neal cast a quick glance me, his eyebrows raised. "Harrie, you kept everything safe. And we are sure glad you did." He leaned down and kissed her forehead. Harrie beamed.

After hugs and farewells, Neal finally got out the door followed by Francine. They went outside alone, and Gladys and I smiled knowingly at each other. She was coaxing the girls, both quite sleepy now, to rise up from a large chair where they had been sitting telling them it was time to drive home. My aunts and Frank rose, yawned and stretched and began saying their good-nights. Christopher came to me, wrapped his arms around me and announced he was ready for bed. "Well, that's a first," I laughed. "You go on up, brush your teeth and I'll be up soon. We're heading home tomorrow."

Soon all had gone off to bed or departed, leaving just me and

Jake. He asked me if he should start to load up the Suburban. I told him to just wait until morning. "There are so many boxes. I'll have to take some now and more on my next trip."

"Speaking of boxes, I brought over a couple that had some official looking stuff inside. It's that one over there. See if you want to take it now."

I walked over to the box and, yawning, shifted through the contents. One item caught my eye. It was a yellowed newspaper. When I realized what it was, I gasped. "Look! This has a news story about the car accident." The paper was folded into a quarter page and the story was outlined in dark black ink. Someone—Mama?—had traced around the story with a pen with what looked like dark, angry repetition. I read the headline aloud.

"Local Man, Woman Killed in Crash"

I looked up at Jake who stared at me with wide eyes. I read it aloud, "Two local residents died late Saturday night following a collision with a coal truck. Gilbert Martin, age 36, of River Mount and Dorothy Gray, age unknown, of Glad—"

Jake interrupted, "Don't be sad, you're in Glad."

"What?"

"That's the town's slogan. 'Don't be sad, you're in Glad.'" He laughed.

I rolled my eyes and continued reading, ". . . died instantly following the head-on collision on West Virginia Route 309. Police said the coal truck driver, whose name is unknown, suffered a mild concussion, cuts and bruises. Police said freezing rain, ice and poor road conditions contributed to the tragic accident."

"It's tough to read that, isn't it?" Jake said.

"Yes but, like everything else we found, I'm glad to have it. I needed to know."

Jake rummaged through the box and spied another yellowed newspaper. He pulled it out. Like the other, this was folded and outlined in black ink. "Well, look here," he said, "It's her obituary." He held the paper out to me. I looked at him, confused. "The woman, the woman in the accident with your dad."

"Oh!" I gasped. I took the newspaper and stared at the face of the woman who had haunted us for decades. *This was her?* This woman who looked so . . . so kind and friendly and, well, ordinary. Plain, actually. I had always envisioned the other woman as cheap looking, with too much make-up and a porn star come-hither expression. But instead, I saw the face of a woman who slightly resembled a very nice teacher I'd had in elementary school, Miss Stone. Neat. Prim. Respectable. I stared at the obituary headline and said the name aloud, "Dorothy 'Boots' Gray." I looked up at Jake. "So, this is her? This is the other woman?"

"What's it say? Read it."

I cleared my throat and began to read, "Dorothy 'Boots' Gray of Glad, West Virginia, departed this world unexpectedly on January 27, 1962 at the age of twenty-seven. Born March 1, 1934, Dorothy Renee Gray was the daughter of Walter (deceased) and Shelby Gray. Dorothy attended Glad High School. After graduation, she attended St. Mary's School of Nursing in Huntington. She served as a nurse at Potomac Hospital for several years. She is pre-deceased by a brother, Walter Gray, Jr. She is survived by her mother, Shelby Gray (nee O'Neill), a brother, Paul and sister-in-law, Barbara (nee Peterson). She is also survived by a son from her marriage that ended in divorce. A Mass of Christian burial will be held on Friday, February 2, 1962 at St. Anthony's Church at 1:00 o'clock p.m. Burial will take place immediately following at the church cemetery."

Jake said, "She sounds like a nice person. I know your mama made her sound awful, but she doesn't sound like that at all. She was nurse."

"I know. Mama always made her sound like a floozie, a loose woman who hung out at bars and lured men like my dad. She hated her." I stared at the photo. "How could anyone who had a nickname like 'Boots' be bad?" I laughed softly. "Jake, does she look familiar? Does her family name sound familiar?"

"Heck Laney Mae, I was little too! I don't remember. We can ask Mom in the morning. Or Frank or Ruth or Hilda. Maybe even Harrie knows something."

"This may be a mystery we never solve."

Jake grew excited. "Hey! I know! Glad is only about a half hour away. Why don't we drive there tomorrow and try to find her family? This brother of hers? Paul Gray? Shouldn't be too hard since we have his full name. Unless . . . they are . . . you know, passed away themselves."

A sudden and overwhelming tiredness came over me and my head ached. I shook my head and said, "No Jake. I can't. I just can't go looking for this woman's family. Not now. Maybe on another trip, I'll try. But not now. I've got to get home tomorrow."

Jake smiled. "Well, when you're ready to go look for him, I'm ready to take you."

CHAPTER 22

I sat at the kitchen table in of my grandparents' house. Before me lay a single spool of light blue thread. In my hand, a threaded sewing needle. I focused on my work, holding the fabric taut with one hand and carefully guiding the needle with the other, I meticulously stitched so the thread would not show on the front. The colorful ribbons that had been awarded to my father looked brilliant against the pale blue fabric to which I so carefully attached. It occurred to me that I mustn't accidentally prick my finger lest I get even a drop of blood on Mama's burial suit. As I bent over and concentrated on my sewing, I sensed a presence coming toward me. I glanced up quickly then back down, averting my eyes from my mother's.

Mama asked, "Are you finished?"

With great reluctance, I raised my head. Mama appeared before me, a calm and peaceful aura surrounding her. "Not yet," I replied. "I think that I really ought to start over. It's not perfectly straight." I looked back down at the ribbons and dread filled me. I knew that once I finished sewing my father's ribbons onto Mama's blue burial suit, she would really, finally and most terribly, be dead.

Mama said gently but firmly, "Now, Laney Mae. You have got to finish. I have to get going."

I cried out. "No! No! I don't want you to go, no . . . no . . . no," I wailed. I allowed the suit, with the ribbons barely attached, and the threaded needle to drop from my hands. I leaned forward and grabbed my mother around her waist and clung to her. Mama embraced me but then seemed to float away from me, just out of my reach. "I have to go, Laney Mae. You have to finish and let me go." I shook my head and tried to say something, but Mama continued. "And you need to do one more thing." She hovered closer and stared into my eyes intently. "You need to go find him. Do it. Go find him."

I shook my head and sobbed and then I bolted upright in bed, sweat beading on my forehead, my body shaking. The dream had been so vivid. Mama's voice had been so clear. Dazed, I sat wide-eyed in the dimly-lit bedroom. I was breathing hard, as though I had run quickly up a flight of stairs. I glanced down at Christopher who lay sleeping undisturbed beside me. The faint light coming through the window told me it was probably dawn. I struggled to remember more details from the dream. I must go find him. *Who did Mama mean? Was this all nonsense?*

With a sudden jolt it dawned on me: the brother! The brother of Virginia "Boots" Gray. That's who Mama wanted me to find! The man from Glad. I felt the hairs on the back of my neck stand, and with every fiber in my body, I knew I had to go, to do as my mother told me, even if it was just a dream. I would go today.

I leapt from the bed, my feet thumping on the floor, and ran downstairs.

⚜

JAKE AGREED TO DRIVE. CHRISTOPHER WAS DELIGHTED TO AGAIN postpone the drive back to Virginia and welcomed another delay from returning to school. I sat beside Jake who drove the Suburban through the winding mountain roads, weaving across the yellow line to efficiently tackle the curves on the mostly empty two-lane road and accelerating on the small, hilly rises on the straightaway sections to ensure we all got a belly tickle. Each time this happened, Christopher, sitting in the back, let out a hearty laugh and begged Jake to stop but we knew he didn't really mean it.

I had never visited the town of Glad and with each mile I grew apprehensive. "How am I ever going to explain myself this man? This is crazy! I mean if he's even still living and even if he's willing to talk to me. Think about it: if some strange woman called and said, 'You don't know me, but my father and your sister died together almost forty years ago'—oh my gosh. I think I'd hang up the phone!"

"You got the strange woman part right," Jake teased, casting me a wink. "But you don't know how this man will respond. He might be really nice and willing to talk to you." He paused then asked, "Why'd you decide to do this? I mean, last night, there was no way you wanted to do this today let alone anytime soon."

"I just thought about it more, that's all." I had not mentioned my vivid dream about Mama to Jake.

"Well, I'm glad we're going to Glad," Jake said with a laugh. "Let me tell you all a little about it." It was a town, he said, that rose to become a source of lumber and paper. Situated on both a waterway and near the railroad, Glad had been home to a paper mill from which such a malodorous smell emanated that the town had earned yet another slogan.

"And what is the other slogan?" I asked.

"Well, on account of the paper mill and all . . . 'Smells so bad, we must be in Glad!" He roared laughing.

Christopher leaned forward. "How bad will it stink?"

"Won't stink at all," Jake replied.

"How come?" Christopher looked disappointed.

"The mill shut down about five years ago when the company got sold to a bigger mill in Ohio. That company decided they didn't need this one anymore. So there's nothing being made there now. Lots of folks lost their jobs."

"That's sad," I said.

"Oh yeah, well it kind of made the town slogan change again," Jake explained. "Now it's, 'If you are stuck in Glad it's okay to be sad.'" We did not laugh. Jake shrugged his shoulders, "That's what I hear anyway."

I said, "If the paper mill shut down and the town all but died, this man probably doesn't live here anymore. That is, if he's even still alive." I sighed and looked out the window. "He better be here. Why else would Mama tell me to come—"

"What?" Christopher leaned up over the seat to get close to my face.

"What are you talking about Laney Mae?" Jake asked.

Sighing, I reluctantly recounted my dream. "She may not have even meant this man. Maybe she meant—"

"Oh no! She meant this man for sure!" Christopher exclaimed, beaming. "Grandma came to you in your dreams just like she did mine!"

"Christopher, it was just a dream. I mean, it was on my mind. My subconscious made me dream that she said that to me."

Jake shook his head. "Nope. I think Christopher is right. Again. Aunt Faye told you to come here and find this man for a reason."

"Well, I guess we'll see, won't we?"

"Hey," Jake said, grinning. "I thought of a new slogan: Laney Mae is mad, but her answers are in Glad!"

"My answers? I didn't know I had any more questions!"

"Of course there are questions," Jake said. "What was your dad doing that night and how did he end up with that lady?"

I frowned and my stomach churned. "Maybe I don't want to know." My body went cold. *Maybe this is a bad idea,* I thought. I had finally discovered so many wonderful things about my father, and now I faced learning something about him that might be hard to hear.

"I know you, Laney Mae," Jake said. "It will drive you crazy if you don't find out what happened."

"What if . . . what if it's bad? What if he was . . . cheating on Mama that night like she always said? And maybe even before then?"

To my surprise, Christopher said, "Well, it happens. That's what my dad did."

I swung around to face him. I pursed my lips tightly and shook my head, feeling tears sting my eyes, cursing myself silently for mentioning something far too close to my own home. "Oh Christopher, I'm so sorry—"

He held up his hand. "It's okay, Mom," he said calmly. "He's still my dad."

۞

WE ROLLED INTO THE TOWN AND EASED TO A STOP AT WHAT appeared to be Glad's only traffic light. We did not see a single person or any other cars. The abandoned mill sat before us about a half mile further up the road and loomed, empty and silent. Its large metal exterior connected to a cement structure and what appeared to be the original portion of the mill. The metal portion, painted a pale yellow, offered no brightness to the surroundings, even on this sunny day. The facility's towering smokestack protruded rudely against the backdrop of the mountains like a middle finger. The parking lot lay empty and the train tracks beyond, solemn in their uselessness.

"Used to be lots and lots of smoke rising from that old stack," Jake said. "And whew! The smell!"

"How did the people who lived around here stand it if it stank so much?" Christopher asked.

"That smell was the source of their paycheck Chris," Jake replied. "They got used to it."

The light turned green, and Jake drove on. "I figure we'll go to the main street here and find a telephone booth and look up Mr. Paul Gray." I nodded but my stomach churned.

The main street was desolate. Most buildings appeared to be empty and stood despondently along each side of the road. An old boarded-up restaurant with an RC Cola sign reminded me of Second Chance and I felt a wave of sadness for towns that died and the people in them. "What's RC Cola?" Christopher asked. I told him it was just another soda like Coke or Pepsi. He wanted to try it. "I don't think they make it anymore," I told him, frowning as I leaned my forehead on the window.

"That place there," Jake said, "hasn't sold an RC Cola probably since I was your age, Christopher."

We drove on in silence. I shifted nervously in my seat. "I don't think he's here," I said, reaching over to lay a hand on Jake's arm. "Let's go back. Turn around."

"Are you kidding? No way! Now I know it looks depressing, Laney Mae, but we've come this far so I'm not turning around." Then he grew excited, "Look! A phone booth and people!" He pointed ahead. An elderly couple walked up the street, heading into what appeared to be a small drug store. He drove slowly and pulled over. "All we've got to do is look him up in the phone book and you call him." He jumped out of the Suburban. "Come on Laney Mae, time's a-wasting!"

I opened the door and let my feet drop to the ground. Reluctantly, I walked to the booth and watched as Jake grabbed the phone book. "Hell, it's got listings for all the local counties in here. We could have looked him up at any phone booth but that's okay. Here's Glad." He licked his thumb and forefinger and flipped to the "G's" then exclaimed, "Bingo!" He held the book, attached to the booth by a metal cable, as high as he could for us to see. "Paul Gray. Here he is. Call him!"

I stepped over and peered at the name and phone number. I dug through coins in my wallet and fished out thirty-five cents. "Okay, here goes." I dropped the coins. "Read the number to me Jake." I punched the numbers and waited. On the fourth ring a man's voice answered. I paused. "Umm, hello. Is this Paul Gray?"

"Yes. Who's calling?" His voice was pleasant.

"Well, Mr. Gray, um, you don't know me but . . . um . . . well, my name is Laney Mae Martin, and my family is from Second Chance . . . Well, actually my parents lived in River Mount . . . uh ..."

Jake rolled his hand in a fast loop to indicate I should get to the point.

"I'm sorry," Paul Gray spoke. "What's this about?"

"Well, you see my father, Gil Martin, he was killed in a car accident with your–"

He gasped, "Oh. Oh! You're Gil Martin's . . . I'm sorry. Did you say you were his daughter?"

My mouth dropped open. I didn't think he would make the connection so quickly. "Yes. I was very young when it happened, and I never understood exactly what happened and I just found out more about the accident and wanted to see if I could meet you since my dad died with your sister." I heard him draw in a breath and feared he was about to hang up, so I continued, speaking quickly. "I'm sorry to catch you off guard and all so, maybe I'll just write to you?" Part of me hoped he would agree to this and we could leave.

Jake shook his head fiercely and mouthed 'No!' to me. I put my finger to my lips to tell him to not speak.

Paul Gray recovered. "No. I mean, yes. Yes, I'll talk to you. Do you want to talk now? On the phone? I can do that."

"Well," I laughed nervously. "I'm . . . uh . . . actually here in Glad this morning. Could I visit you? Now?"

He was silent. "You're here? Now?" He sounded surprised.

"Yes. With my cousin Jake and my son, Christopher. He's ten. I've been up to bury my mom, Faye Martin, Gil's wife, his widow."

"Oh, I see. Sorry for your loss." He paused. "Well, I'm home. You have my address?"

"In the phone book? Yes."

"Okay, where are you now?"

"We're in town in front of the drug store."

"Okay then. We're just about two miles from there. Let me tell you how to find us."

"Okay, let me put my cousin Jake on. He knows the area better and is driving." I handed the phone to Jake.

෯

PAUL GRAY'S HOME WAS THE LEFT SIDE OF A DUPLEX ON A STREET OF homes that all looked mostly alike except for some variation in design, color and upkeep. The home was set high off the road surrounded by a stone retaining wall with steep cement stairs leading up from the street to yet another flight of stairs that led to the front steps, a physical reminder that the town was built among the mountains. It was a neatly kept home, painted a yellowish-gold with green shutters. An enclosed porch with metal windows—the kind you cranked open—concealed the front door. The home attached to it on the right was painted the identical yellow-gold color but was less well-kept with trash cans on its porch, a broken upstairs window, two missing shutters and a Confederate flag strung across the face of the retaining wall in front.

"I thought West Virginia fought for the Yankees," Christopher said, pointing. "How come those people have a rebel flag?"

"Maybe they came up here from the South and no one told them who won," Jake said, laughing as he parked.

With Jake leading the way, we climbed the steps and arrived at the door of the enclosed porch. Before we could knock, the door opened and there stood Paul Gray. He smiled and I instantly felt more relaxed.

"Hello and welcome," he said opening the door wider. He held out a hand to Jake who shook it so enthusiastically, the man was pulled forward and nearly lost his balance. Laughing, he stepped back inside and motioned for us to enter. The porch was small but cozy with a wicker loveseat and two matching chairs. Paul lowered himself onto one of the chairs and motioned for us to be seated.

"Thank you for letting us pop in on you like this, Mr. Gray," I said as I studied his face and tried to guess his age. He looked younger than expected. His face was smooth, his hair was thinning with streaks of gray running through the natural black. He appeared fresh shaven, and the distinct smell of aftershave hung in the air. He wore heavy horn-rimmed glasses behind which his brown eyes peered closely back at me.

"Call me Paul."

"Thank you, Paul," I said. "So, I know that your sister and my dad died together in the car crash that night. But I never knew much about her until I found her obituary in some old papers with my dad's stuff that I only just now located."

"I bet you are wondering what my sister was doing out with your daddy late on that night. Am I right?"

"Well, yes. I mean, Mama—my mother—always said he was cheating on her with . . . the woman who died in the accident and that . . ." I looked down at the floor, "they got what they deserved."

I looked back up at him, frowning. I shrugged. "I'm sorry but that's what she always said."

Jake chimed in, "Oh she said a lot worse than that! Whew! She was spitting mad about it. She wouldn't even say Gil's name or talk about him or anything after that accident. My mom–Faye's sister–always said it was a good thing the other woman died because Aunt Faye would have killed her if she hadn't." He grew serious, "No offense."

"Jake! You don't need to share all that!" I snapped.

Paul held up his hands. "I can assure you your father and Boots were *not* having an affair."

"Really?"

"Really. As a matter of fact, your father was trying to help Boots that night."

"Help her? How?"

Sitting back in his chair, Paul said, "I'll tell you, but it requires a little background." He sighed. His eyes scanned the floor as he collected his thoughts. "Well, the first thing you need to know is that Boots was married to a guy named Derrick. She'd met him when she was down at nursing school. He wooed her and he was good-looking, but I never liked him, he was slick, you know? Anyway, they got married and she finished school in Huntington. Then came back near here and Boots was working at the hospital, but he just couldn't hold a job anywhere. He drank too much, and he started getting really jealous anytime she was away from him. He thought other men were after her and that she was going to leave him. It got to be really hard for her to live with him. Back then, no one talked about abuse, but that's what it was. She left him a couple times and moved back in with Mom, or she'd stay here with me and my wife, Barb. You'll meet her when she gets back."

He cleared his throat and continued, "Anyway, Boots would say she was going to leave for good, but Derrick always managed to sweet talk her and convince her that he'd change, you know? She'd go back but it would just start over again. And then, she got pregnant. Well, I remember being really worried because that meant she really needed to stay married and was stuck, you know?

But then, for a while, Derrick seemed okay and even excited about the baby. But, not long after the baby was born, Derrick started drinking more and somewhere—God knows where or why—Derrick came up with the idea that the baby *wasn't* his! It was crazy! I'll never forget Boots showing up here one night when it was really raining, she had the baby, and she was crying, and she said she was so scared Derrick was going to kill her and the baby. He had slapped her that night and that was new. He had sometimes shoved her around but that time, he slapped and punched her and pulled her hair; but she got away, got the baby, got in the car, and drove here.

Well, I had had enough. I called the sheriff and they arrested him, and he got put away. Boots moved back in with Mom, started working at the hospital again, and Mom and Barb helped watch the baby and it seemed like finally Boots was going to get her life back together. She was waiting on a divorce. And then, Derrick got out of jail."

He sighed and shook his head, "First thing he did was start calling her. Begging her to give him another chance, begging her not to go through with the divorce. He'd call her at home, he'd call her at the hospital. Then, he started showing up. I had a confrontation with him, and I told him in no uncertain terms that she was not interested in being married to him, she wanted the divorce and for him to stay away; but he wouldn't listen. Finally, we got the sheriff involved again and that helped because Derrick took off. There was no sign of him for weeks, so we went on about our business."

Paul slumped in his chair. "And then came that night. That awful night."

"Did Derrick come back?" Jake asked.

Paul nodded, "Yes. He was following her around—stalking her—but we didn't know it. That night Boots and a bunch of her nurse friends went out because one of them was getting married. It was a bachelorette party. They almost didn't go because they were calling for bad weather and, God and I wished they hadn't. I only know what happened because Boots' friends told me later. They were at that Crystal's place dancing, having a couple of cocktails when guess who walks in? Derrick. Boots and one of her friends were coming out of the ladies' room and spotted him sitting at the bar glaring at her. She tried to avoid him and hoped he wouldn't bother her but that was wishful thinking. Add to it the fact that he was drinking, and you can imagine things got bad really quick."

"My dad was there, wasn't he?" I asked. "My brother told me that he'd been to Crystals."

He nodded, "Yes. Boots tried to leave, and Derrick blocked her way, got hold of her arm and no matter how she resisted and twisted to get loose, he held tight. He was saying things like, 'you're my wife' and, 'you're a slut being here in a bar' and, 'what kind of mother are you?'—those sorts of things. Everyone was standing back not knowing what to do. They were afraid of setting him off even more. The bartender told Derrick and Boots to leave—*them*! Like they were *both* causing trouble!

That's when your daddy got involved. He walked right up to Derrick and said, 'Get your hands off her. She doesn't want to go with you.' Well, you can imagine Derrick didn't like that, and he told your daddy to butt out and called him some pretty nasty names. All the while, Boots is crying and pleading for Derrick to let her go. One of Boots' friends tried to pull her away from Derrick but that made him madder. Next thing you know, he starts to head out the door dragging Boots with him and that's when your daddy let him have it! He hauled off and punched him so hard that he knocked Derrick down to the floor. Pow! I would have loved to see that!

Then, your daddy told Boots to run. But Boots didn't have a car because her friend had driven them but gone off to take another nurse friend home and hadn't gotten back to Crystal's yet. So, your daddy said, 'Ok, come on. I'll drive you home.' And they got out of there fast with Derrick getting up off the floor and chasing after them. Off they went on that icy mountain road: my sister with your daddy who was trying to help her get away."

He removed his glasses and covered his eyes with his hand. No one spoke. After a moment, Paul lowered his hand and looked at me. He slowly put his glasses back on and swallowed hard. "After all these years, I still can't get over it. Why they died. Why that coal truck wasn't reserved for Derrick." He leaned toward me and took my hand. "I want you to know that I tried to get in touch with your family. I wanted to thank them for Gil trying to help Boots. I called your mother a couple of times, but she wouldn't talk to me. We were all torn up about Boots of course, but after the funerals, when I learned more details, I did finally reach your daddy's parents and thanked them. They were just inconsolable about him dying. They didn't really want to know about Boots and our family. I didn't blame them. And I felt guilty for a long time like it was Boots' fault that your daddy died. But it wasn't her fault at all." He paused and shook his head sadly. "You could say it was Derrick's fault but . . . I've come to realize . . . it was just their time."

I rose and Paul stood, and I stepped over to him and we embraced. I looked up at him and said, "Thank you. I needed to know . . . I needed to know that he was . . . that he was . . . a good man." I choked up as I said this.

"Oh, he was a good man. Yes was! He gave his life for my sister. That's the way I look at it. Either way, though, I think Boots would have probably died that night or some other night at the hands of Derrick." Tears welled in his eyes. "I'm sorry your daddy had to die, too."

We stood in silence and then Paul said, "Well, I'm sure glad you found me but you all can't leave yet. Barb will be home any minute. She will want to hear all about this and to meet you. And be prepared: she *will* make you stay for lunch!"

⚜

BARB GRAY ARRIVED SHORTLY AFTER HER HUSBAND HAD FINISHED sharing the story. She scolded her husband for not inviting us into the house to begin with, "You made them sit out on the porch?" Then she served a delicious lunch of chicken salad, chips and iced tea with sliced strawberries and bananas with cookies for dessert. She sat spellbound and marveled as she listened to our story, especially when we shared the part about Harrie hiding all my father's things in the bedroom of the vacant house in Second Chance. "I'd say this is nothing short of a miracle," she exclaimed after lunch. "Fate brought you here, Laney Mae. It surely did."

We all pitched in to help clear the table and began, reluctantly, to prepare to leave. Paul and Barb Gray felt like old friends to me although we had known each other just three hours. I hoped to see them again. I knew Claudia and Barb would become friends. They were cut from the same practical and caring cloth.

"I wish I could have known Boots," Christopher said to Paul as they stood around the dining room table. "She sounded like a neat lady."

"She was indeed," he replied. "I miss my sister every day. Even after all these years."

"But wait!" Christopher exclaimed. "What happened to her baby? Did Derrick take him away after she died?"

Paul grinned, "Well, that's about the only happy thing that came out of all this. Derrick just left town after Boots died. We never saw him again. Barb and I got custody of the baby and we raised him as we would have our own son."

"That's right," Barb added. "We were not blessed with our own children, so we were very happy to adopt Boots' baby."

I asked, "Did he know? About his real mom? About his dad? Or did you decide it was best to not tell–"

"Oh Heaven's, yes!" Barb exclaimed. "He knew all about his mother, who she was, what all happened. We didn't tell him every detail about his father but . . . most of it." She seemed surprised at my question at first but then understood. "Oh dear," she said, reaching out to lay her hand on my shoulder. "I know you are only finding out about your daddy." Sympathy filled her voice. "But in this case, Boots was as much a part of that boy's life as we could make her. We could not let him forget her. In fact, I think that's why he got into the work he does. He works for the highway department. He doesn't want to see anyone killed on the road like his mother was."

Christopher pulled on Barb's arm. "Do you have pictures? Of Boots and her baby?"

Barb grinned. "We sure do. Just go in the living room there and look at the photo wall. There are all sorts of photos there. Go ahead, I'll follow you and show you."

Christopher ran to the other room with Barb following him.

Paul chuckled, "We don't see Matt as much as we would like now. He lives about forty-five minutes away. Like Barb said, he has a good job with the state department of transportation. He's a highway administrator but working on a civil engineering degree. He travels around the state a lot, so he doesn't get up here that often, but we did just seem him a few days ago." He abruptly stopped speaking. His eyes widened and a look of confusion settled on his face. He stared at me intently then said, "Wait a minute! Didn't you say something about a hearse breaking down on the road?"

I thought this was odd but nodded. I motioned toward Jake with my thumb. "His hearse. It broke down just past River Mount."

Paul's eyes grew wide, "Was it by any chance . . . pink?"

I was aghast, "How did you know?"

"Because our nephew visited the other day . . . would have been Thursday . . . and told us the funniest thing about people with a pink hearse broken down along the road . . ."

At that moment, Christopher flew back into the room holding a framed photograph. "Mom! It's the guy!"

I looked from Paul to my son and then to the photograph he was holding. "What guy?"

"The guy who helped us," Christopher exclaimed. "The man in the pick-up truck. Don't you remember?" He moved closer and held the framed photograph up to my face and my heart skipped a beat. I stared at the face in the photo then looked up at Paul and over to Barb. I pointed at the photograph and made sure Jake saw who it was. My cousin gasped. I opened my mouth to speak but no words came out so instead, I took the framed photo from Christopher and held it so my eyes looked directly into the eyes of the nice man in the pick-up truck. The man who had pulled over to help us after the Pink Lady had broken down. The man who had given us water when we were thirsty. The man who had run around the road trying to help find Mother when she went missing. The man who opened my door as I got back into the Suburban. The man who lifted his baseball cap off his head and waved as he drove off, like John Wayne in an old Western movie. The man whose mother had died with my father on an icy mountain road in 1962. The man who was the son of Virginia "Boots" Gray.

Without a word, Paul went to the phone. We watched as his hand shook while he dialed the old rotary phone. We heard him say, "Matt? Hey, how you doing?" He paused and then said, "Say, I need you to come up here to the house... Yes, now... No, we're alright. It's something else." He looked right at me and smiled, "Well, let's just say you'll understand when you get here, and you won't believe it."

❦

W<small>E TALKED AND TALKED THERE IN THE LIVING ROOM OF</small> P<small>AUL</small> and Barb Gray. Often, Matt and I found ourselves looking at each other silently, in awe of our circumstance and the very presence of each other. Later, Matt and I stepped outside into the small, neat yard on the side of Paul and Barb's duplex. Alone for the first time, Matt guided me over to a picnic table and hopped on the top and motioned for me to join him where we talked more about our lives, more about his mother and what I had recently learned about my father. We rose to go back inside and as we walked toward the door, I asked him where his mother was buried.

"Just outside town, in the church's cemetery."

"Can we go see? I'd like to pay my respects."

He looked at me intently. "Do you really want to go?"

"Yes, I do."

"You mean *now*?"

"Yes."

He smiled, "Okay, I'll take you."

We went back inside and let everyone know we were going to the cemetery to see Boots' grave. "Cut yourself some flowers," Barb told me, and I returned outside and snipped an arrangement of hydrangeas from the yard. Barb put the stems into a plastic bag with water and looped a rubber band around to hold them in place. She gently wrapped them in plain white paper towels. "There you go," she told me. "Hydrangeas were her favorite."

Christopher insisted on joining us while Jake stayed behind with Barb and Paul, having a second helping of the chicken salad. I smiled as I watched my son skip happily down the cement steps toward Matt's truck. He climbed inside to the rear bench seat, and we rode the three miles to the cemetery. Matt eased the truck over at the end of a row of headstones. "Here we are," he said. We followed as his walked down the row of graves until, near the end, he stopped and motioned at the final resting place of his mother. Christopher read aloud:

"Virginia Renee "Boots" Gray
B. March 1, 1934
D. January 27, 1962
Beloved Daughter, Sister and Mother
Rest In Peace Forever"

He stared at the headstone silently then looked up at me and said, "We sure have visited a lot of graves on this trip."

"Yes, we have," I replied and gently brushed his hair across his forehead.

Something seemed to disturb him and suddenly he stepped back. "Can they feel us?" His voice was anxious. He moved to the right of the grave, stacking his small feet perpendicularly on an imaginary line between it and the grave of the man buried next to Boots. "Standing up here above them. Can they feel us walking around, Mom?" His face full of worry.

"Oh Christopher, no. They are six feet down. Their souls are gone somewhere else, honey."

"It feels like they can," he said. He shivered. He cast an anxious look around the rows and rows of headstones. "I don't want to be in the ground after I die," he proclaimed. "When I die, I want to have my ashes spread over the ocean or something. I don't want to be in the ground."

I spread my arms open to him. "Christopher, I'm so sorry. This has been a lot for you, honey." But he did not come to me.

"No. It's okay, Mom. I don't like graveyards and I don't want to end up in one and I don't want people walking above me."

"Me either," Matt said, his voice clear and reassuring. "I don't want to be in the ground either." Christopher smiled.

I cast a look of thanks to Matt and then I stepped forward and knelt. I placed the bouquet of hydrangeas on Boots' grave. I wasn't sure what to say but finally settled on two simple words: "I'm sorry." Sorry, I thought silently, for all the awful things my mother and our family had wrongly assumed about her, who she was and what she had done.

Sighing heavily, I stood and regarded the headstones all around us. I thought about all the lives each represented. What were their stories? Who did they love? As they faced death, did they find meaning in the lives they had lived? Who mourned them? What was it was like to be dead? *Death can't be the end*, I thought. And if those who had passed and lay buried in the ground could not, as I told my son, feel us treading above their graves, could they at least hear us? Could they somehow know how we longed for them, how desperate we were to see them, to touch them and tell them all the things we didn't say when we had the chance?

Christopher's voice startled my thoughts. "Hey, Mom. It's going to get dark soon," he said uneasily. "I don't want to be here in the dark. I'm getting in the truck." He turned to walk away and said over his shoulder, "We need to get back . . . back to Second Chance."

Second Chance. My heart gushed with warmth and love for the town and for my family, our friends, our neighbors. Second Chance. Chance. No Chance. I smiled. The old town's name had at one time represented hope for anyone who was fleeing disappointment, failure, and pain. *And who wasn't*, I thought. Didn't we all long for a second chance at some point in our lives? Was a second chance just a random occurrence that only a few got? Was it something dependent upon fate or luck? Scanning the graves of all the old souls buried on the side of that ancient mountain, I thought, *no, a second chance was a choice; it was the conscious act of discarding the emotional layer of despair that weighed us down.* And how did we do this? I stared at the headstone of Virginia Boots Gray and realized it was quite simple and amounted to one simple act: forgiveness. Each time we forgave, we granted ourselves and the person we forgave, a second chance. But what about Mama and people like her who cannot accept and forgive? Does death provide the second chance to those who squandered it in life? I turned to look at Matt's truck and saw Christopher's little face as he peered at me anxiously from the front seat, his innocence squeezing my heart. No, I thought, I could not count on a second chance after I left this world. I would not carry the hurt in my heart to my grave. I would grant myself and the father of my son, a second chance. Phil's face came to me but now, instead of anger, I allowed myself to feel forgiveness. I closed my eyes and wished him peace.

Matt interrupted my thoughts, "I guess we should get going. I'm sure glad we came here. I hate to admit it, but it's been a while since I visited her. The last time was Mother's Day. But there's never a day that goes by that I don't think about her."

I smiled and again contemplated the near improbability that fate had brought us together and not just once, but twice. "I keep thinking about fate," I told him. "Of all the people to pass us on the road that day. And you didn't *have* to stop."

"Well, I sort of almost didn't," he said, playfully, laughing.

"Well, honestly, I don't know that I would have stopped."

"Yes, you would."

I shrugged, "I suppose I would have."

"Oh, I know you would have stopped. Based on what I've learned about you and your family." He paused, tilted his head to the side and said, "Yes, you would have stopped to help because you are your father's daughter."

I felt tears sting my eyes and wiped them away, feeling at once safe but vulnerable with this man who was still a stranger to me. "That means more to me than anything you could have said."

"Your dad helped my mom. The least I could do was help his daughter."

CHAPTER 23

It was time to say goodbye. The Suburban was packed with most of the boxes containing the belongings of my father. Jake had filled the gas tank, checked the oil and tires and, at my insistence, the radiator fluid, and given the okay for departure.

Claudia, Frank, Jake, Harrie and even old Mother the dog had assembled in the driveway to see us off. Hilda, Ruth and Margaret were not awake at this early hour, but I had said goodbye and hugged each of them the night before, promising to return soon. I had been surprised to see tears in Ruth's eyes and I hugged my aunt a second time, whispering in her ear that I loved her. I realized with a pang of sadness that I had never uttered these words to her in my entire life. In this family, love was something shown, not said. I was determined that that would change now.

The mountain air was fresh with a crispness that warned of the colder days to come. The sun was bright against the clear blue sky—perfect driving weather. I was eager to hit the road in order to get Christopher back to school. If we left now, I could get him there before ten o'clock.

"We're sure going to miss you," Claudia said, her voice cracking. She clutched her apron and pulled the corner up to dab her tears. "Oh! After so much excitement. It will be so quiet around here."

Frank laughed, "Are you forgetting your son is here? He's always cooking up something exciting."

We all laughed.

"We'll be back before you know it," I told them. I stepped over and embraced my aunt. "Thank you, Claudia, thank you for everything."

"Oh honey, I didn't do anything much. I'm just glad something so sad had such a happy ending."

Next, I turned to Frank, "Why don't you come down and see us sometime, Frank?" I reached up and rubbed his unshaven cheek gently. "It's been a long time since you've visited. I believe it was 1962."

Frank snorted, "Hell, what do I want to go and visit Virginia for? I've already seen it and I've got everything I need right here." He grinned but his face fell, "Except you." His voice broke and he took me into his arms and held me tightly. "You be careful driving," he whispered in my ear. He pulled back but kept a light hold on my shoulders. "You hear me?" I nodded solemnly.

I turned to Jake who grinned, stepped over, embraced me, and picked me up off the ground. I recalled him lifting me just days ago, a year ago, it seemed, when he had arrived at the house in the Pink Lady. *Why had I been so mean to him?*

"No need for goodbye tears," he said. "Only happy ones until we see you back up here!" He put me down.

"Jake, oh Jake." My eyes welled. "If it wasn't for you, I probably wouldn't have gone to Glad and I wouldn't learned about what really happened with my dad and about Matt and …. I know I was hard on you-" I focused on the burns on his face and saw they were almost healed, and I gently touched his face.

Tears in his eyes he said, "Well, I knew you had to go and find out. We all have to face our truths, even if we're scared of 'em, Laney Mae."

We held each other's eyes. "I promise I'll be back soon." I paused and grinning, said, "But God help me, it will never be behind a pink hearse again!"

"No," Jake said, arching his eyebrows, "you might be *in* it." He laughed so hard he bent over and slapped his knee.

"I think I'd rather . . . die." I said and we all laughed.

Harrie, who until now had been eagerly awaiting her turn to say goodbye, had worked herself up to the point where she was shaking with emotion. She pushed past Jake and grabbed me into a fierce hug. "I will miss you Laney Mae! I am sad you are leaving!"

I wrapped my arms around her and rocked back and forth. "Oh Harrie! Thank you, thank you," I murmured in her ear. "I'm so glad you kept my daddy's things safe."

Harrie planted a wet kiss on my cheek. "You are welcome. I am glad that you found me in the house when I was hiding. I am glad you were not mad at me. I am glad you have your daddy's things now. I don't have to keep them secret no more." She turned to Christopher and hugged him. "I will miss you, too, Christopher, but you have to go to school."

Christopher allowed himself to be hugged and kissed by Harrie. Then he moved away from the group and knelt down to Mother. I watched as he wrapped his arms around the dog and buried his face in her neck. "I'll miss you Mother," I heard him say. "Be a good girl. Take care of everyone and we'll come back soon." He rubbed behind the dog's ears then turned around and looked up at me, his face troubled, tears in his eyes. "Mom, how do we know?"

I cocked my head to the side, quizzically. "Know what, honey?"

"When it's the last time."

"The last time?"

"Yeah, the last time we're going to see someone or do something. Before . . . you know."

"Before dying?"

He nodded.

Frank spoke, "You don't. That's why every day you have to act like it is the last time, Christopher. Because one day, it will be. When we learn to accept death–and it's a mighty hard lesson–then we know to appreciate life, no matter how long or short it is." He paused. "At least that's what I have learned recently."

Christopher nodded. He gave the dog one last hug, patted her head, then stood.

"Are you ready to go home now?" I asked.

"Yes, I'm ready." He gave a quick wave to everyone, raced around to the front passenger seat and hopped in.

I gave everyone one final look. A sudden, odd feeling of unease filled me which gave me pause and made me shiver. "I'll call when I get home. And I will see you soon." I climbed into the Suburban and turned the key. I rolled down the window and stared at their faces. "I love you all very much."

Claudia began to cry. She blew me a kiss then turned and went up the steps and disappeared into the house with Harrie scurrying after her.

"Now don't get all sappy on us," Frank said, forcing a grin. He used the cuff of his shirt to dab his eyes.

"Love you too, cousin," Jake said exuberantly. "As high as the sky, as deep as the ocean!"

I grinned at him then turned to Christopher.

"Ready?"

"Ready."

I patted his leg. "Seatbelt on."

My mood lifted. The sound of the engine, the steering wheel in my hands, the road before me filled me with excitement and I exclaimed, "I can't wait to get home!" I thought of the little house on Custis Drive waiting for us, the yard, the tall trees, the fishpond, moving from the apartment, making a fresh start, going through every single item that had been my father's, and watching the home movies over and over. Turning to Christopher I said, "Now don't forget. We're playing the Beatles song game on the drive home."

He frowned and folded his arms across his chest. "I don't want to."

"Well, too bad little mister. You said you would and so you will!" I reached into the center cubby and pulled out a bag full of my collection of Beatles CDs. I handed them to Christopher. "Here you go. You get to choose the songs, any songs. Either I know the words—all the words—or you win that song. We'll keep track and see who wins!"

Christopher was glum. "You'll win. You know all the words to all of their songs. I've been hearing you sing Beatles songs all my life, Mom."

I laughed, "Now, come on. Even I can forget so you never know. And besides, I thought you liked games? Plus, you promised me you would. Remember?"

He shrugged, "Okay, I guess I did promise. We can play."

"We'll play for something good."

He grinned, "What?"

"Well, if I win, you have to take the trash out to the curb every week for . . . hmmm . . . six weeks."

He wrinkled his nose, "Gross! What do I win if you lose?"

"I don't know. What do you want?"

"No school for six weeks?"

"Come on . . ."

"Okay, if I win, I get to go to the tape store and rent a movie two times a week and I get to have a sleepover every Saturday for six weeks."

"Hmmm. You drive a hard bargain. But okay. It's a deal."

"When should we start?" He began to rummage through the bag of CDs.

"Let me get out on the main road and then we'll start."

I reached to the gearshift and lowered it to drive and began to roll forward, the gravel crunching under the weight of the tires. Looking at Christopher I said, "And you can mix up the songs, their early songs, their later songs. Any order you want—"

Christopher screamed, "Mom! Watch out!"

I turned my head forward and gasped. Harrie stood just a few feet in front of us, directly in the path of the Suburban. I slammed on the breaks and the tires screeched and the vehicle slid to a hard stop, thrusting us forward held tightly by our seatbelts. The car stopped one foot short of hitting Harrie. I gripped the steering wheel tightly in shock. My mouth hung open and my heart raced. "Oh my God!" I exclaimed. I stared at Harrie through the windshield where my aunt stood calmly, staring back at me, holding something. *What is that?* I squinted and realized Harrie held the large glass jar from my father's belongings, the one she had shown us the night before.

Recovering, I sprang from the Suburban and Christopher, along with Frank and Jake, rushed up to Harrie.

"You forgot this," Harrie said, thrusting the jar with both hands toward me. "It's Gil's jar of moonbeams. Remember? You need to take it home."

I stared at the jar, shaking my head. "Harrie!" I said sharply, "You shouldn't have gotten in front of me like that! I could have run over you!" I pointed at the jar and said, "I can get that the next time I come up."

"No," Harrie said firmly. "Take it now. These are Gil's moonbeams. He put them in there. They will keep you safe."

Jake, who had been listening, said, "Uh, Harrie, you sure about that? I mean Laney Mae almost ran over you and the jar." He chuckled.

Harrie turned to him. "Almost."

Jake arched an eyebrow. "Well, that's a fair point." He leaned over to me and said under his breath, "I think you better humor her and take the jar."

Still reeling from the shock of the moment, I pointed at the empty jar. "Harrie, no! You keep it for now and I'll get it next time. It was up here for over forty years. I think another couple of weeks won't matter plus–" I motioned toward the Suburban, "–we have everything packed and there's no room–"

"We have room," Christopher interrupted. He reached out and gently took the jar from Harrie.

"Don't open the jar," Harrie said with great seriousness. "Don't let the moonbeams out."

Christopher peered into the jar then stared solemnly into the eyes of his great aunt. "How come I can't see them, Harrie?"

"They don't shine all the time," she told him. "They only shine in the dark. They shine when you need them. Gil said, they could be a light when it got dark."

Christopher cast a quick glance at me. He knew what Harrie said was not possible but when he looked back into her eyes, he decided to believe her or, at least, believe that she believed the moonbeams were real. He said earnestly, "I won't open it. I won't let my grandpa's moonbeams out. I promise Harrie. I'll take good care of it."

Harrie nodded, satisfied.

An empty jar, I thought, *I almost ran over Harrie for an empty jar.* "Okay Harrie. We'll take the jar home."

I turned to Christopher as we walked back to the Suburban. Whispering under my breath, I told him, "Put it on the floor in the back against something. We don't want it to break and let the moonbeams out." I rolled my eyes at him and muffled a laugh as I turned to make sure Harrie hadn't heard.

MUSIC BY THE BEATLES FILLED THE SUBURBAN WHILE WE PLAYED the game and as my son correctly predicted, I knew all the words to the songs he selected. In between we talked about school, and moving from the apartment, and discussed getting another dog. When we approached River Mount, Christopher begged me to stop at the diner, but I refused. "I've got to get you to school."

He sulked and leaned his head against the window. "Mom," he said, "Are you still mad at Grandma? You know, for not telling you about your dad and all?"

"No, I'm not and I got to tell her that I wasn't, before she died. Not sure she heard me, but I hope so. I think so."

"You did?"

"Yes. And you know what? I realized something yesterday when we went with Matt to see his mom's grave."

"What?

"That I should have forgiven her a long time ago. We need to forgive people who hurt us. Because you know what? Everyone is walking around with a lot of pain, and it makes people so sad and so angry that sometimes they don't realize they're hurting others, even people they love. So, yeah, I forgave her, and I asked her to forgive me for not understanding her pain."

He considered this then asked, "But mom ...what about dad? Do we have to forgive him?"

I glanced at him and nodded. "Yes, we do. Especially him, I think. Because if we don't, how can we really get on with our lives with all that weighing us down? No, I am going to focus on all the things I have from now on; you, Neal, our family, our home—maybe a new puppy. What good is all of that if we're angry and hurt all the time? Forgiving gives us all a chance to start over ... a second chance." I winked at him.

He smiled. "Is that why they named the town that?"

"I like to think so."

"I like that." He paused and sighed heavily. "I miss my dad. I want to see him more." His voice cracked and he wiped away tears. "I want to forgive him. But mom . . . will he let me?"

"Oh, Christopher. He doesn't need to *let* you. It's something you can do all by yourself."

He nodded and let his head rest on the window and soon he fell asleep.

We crossed into Virginia and in no time, I was making the turn onto I-66 going east toward D.C. I glanced at the dashboard clock. It was just before nine o'clock and at this rate, I might get him there before ten. I drove onto the ramp leading to the highway and groaned when I caught sight of the heavy traffic ahead. I pumped the brakes to lower my speed and eased the vehicle across the highway to the left lane.

Christopher awoke. "Where are we? Back in Virginia?" He rubbed his eyes and shifted in his seat.

"Yep. We're back and we were making good time, but I forgot about rush hour. Look at this mess." I waved a hand at the road. "This could take a while."

He grinned. "Oh, that's too bad, Mom," he said with a laugh. "I'd hate to miss even more school."

"Well, at the rate we're going with this traffic you will. Let's listen to the news and get the traffic report. Maybe there's some accident or a broken-down car causing this."

I switched on the radio. The volume was turned up and perhaps that was why the announcer's voice seemed especially forceful as he reported something about an explosion. One of the Twin Towers in

New York City was in flames, he said. There appeared to be a ten-story high gaping hole from some sort of explosion. There were flames shooting out and so much smoke that the top of the building could barely be seen, he reported.

"Where did he say this was?" Christopher asked, fully alert.

"In New York." I turned up the volume.

The local station broke away to a CBS station in New York where an announcer told of reports that a commuter plane had hit the 110-story building. Christopher stared at the dashboard trying to comprehend the situation. "Have I ever seen the Twin Towers?"

"No honey, I've never taken you to New York City. Maybe you've seen pictures?"

He shook his head. He listened to more of the report and then said with sadness, "Everyone would have died on that plane, wouldn't they, Mom? How many people do you think work in such a tall building?"

"I'm not sure. Maybe thousands."

"How will they rescue the people who are still in the building up at the top? If it's such a tall building. Helicopters?"

"I—I guess." I knew the likely answer was that many could not be saved given the height let alone fire and smoke, but why tell him this? "It's very sad," I continued. "Sometimes awful accidents like this happen, Christopher. Let's hear the traffic report."

The local station began its regular line-up of headlines. I stared at the car in front of me as we slowly rolled forward and eyed the dashboard clock and tried to gauge what time I'd get him to school given the traffic. I figured at least an hour with I-66 being the worst part of the congestion as people headed into D.C. I was contemplating whether to get off onto the Beltway exit when the radio station's breaking news music blared. The anxiety in the announcer's voice caused me to lean over the steering wheel, closer to the dashboard. Another plane, he said, had crashed into the second of the Twin Towers. Both buildings. Each slammed by airplanes.

I reflexively hit the brakes. The Suburban stopped abruptly for the second time that morning. A woman driving a minivan behind me nearly rear-ended us and blew her horn. Shocked, I could only stare into the rearview mirror at the woman's angry face.

"What? Two planes in two buildings? How could that happen?" Christopher's voice rose.

We held each other's eyes. I found it impossible to comprehend what I was hearing. *Everything has changed now*, I thought. The woman in the minivan again blew her horn. The sound jolted me, and I accelerated too fast, nearly hitting the bumper of the car in front of me. The woman in the minivan accelerated and aggressively cut over to the right lane to pass us. Christopher and I stared at her as she waved her index finger in circles at her head to indicate I was crazy. "Learn to drive!" she yelled.

The traffic report aired, shorter than usual and the traffic reporter's voice was filled with strain and worry. There was, she reported, a broken-down truck on the Wilson Bridge. Hearing this, I decided to stick to I-66. The Beltway back-up from one truck would be a mess. I lightly pressed the accelerator and the Suburban inched forward as we listened intently to the unfolding horror. Eyewitness accounts were now being captured. One man told of coming into contact with a man on fire and, with a voice that sounded close to hysteria, recounted how he had tried to put the fire out on him and how the victim was screaming. This was too much. I turned the radio off.

"Hey! I want to hear that." Christopher turned the radio back on.

"No, you don't need to hear that," I switched it off again. "Let's just get home."

Again, he defied me. He turned the radio back on and said,

"Mom, there's something really bad happening. I want to know what it is. Turning the radio off won't change it from happening."

I glanced at him then back at the road as I considered how much my son had been forced to learn about death and sorrow and loss over the last few days and in the weeks leading up to Mama's passing. And here it was again; Death was back, in a most violent and horrific way, even if indirectly, claiming souls on this bright sunny day. I recalled the odd sense of foreboding I had felt earlier as we were saying our goodbyes and gripped the steering wheel more tightly.

The news announcers, their voices rising and filled with controlled urgency, continued to report updates. The planes were highjacked, according to the FBI, they said. Was the U.S. on high alert? Not yet. All flights to and from New York were shut down. What about D.C.? Not yet. President Bush said we would hunt those who did this down. Eyewitnesses recounted what they saw: people running, holding their hearts, lining up at public phones to call loved ones because cell phones weren't working. Reports that the White House was being evacuated. And, hideously, reports of bodies falling from the tall buildings in New York. Falling? Jumping? *Oh, dear God*, I thought. Again, I switched off the radio. I gripped the steering wheel so hard, my hands hurt.

Christopher turned the radio back on. "Mom. Stop turning it off!"

An announcer wondered aloud if other buildings in other cities may be targets by terrorists. Christopher leaned toward the dashboard. He placed his hand on my upper arm and squeezed it. "Mom, wouldn't *we* be a target? In Washington?" He looked at me, fear on his face, and added "What's a t—terrorist?"

I was considering how to answer when the local station breaking news music again blared causing us to jump and stare at the dashboard. It was as though we were watching, not listening to the news.

What in God's name is it now, I thought? The announcer provided the awful answer: fire and smoke at the Pentagon. A sickening feeling spread through my body and for the third time that morning I slammed the Suburban's brakes and again we fell forward and back, the seatbelts tightly restraining us and providing a peculiar sense of comfort. The car behind screeched to a halt but this time, the driver did not blow their horn. Perhaps they, too, had heard this news and in their shock, forgave me.

"Oh, Mom! The Pentagon–where Grandma worked!" Christopher pounded his leg with his fist. He began to cry. He rolled his window down and leaned out to look up, up to the sky to see if any planes were overhead.

"Christopher, roll-up your window. Keep inside the car. We need to focus on getting home."

"But Mom, the way we go, we're gonna drive right by the Pentagon like we always do." His eyes were wide with distress. "What if a plane comes?"

I stared at him dumbfounded, unable to reply. I had missed the opportunity to exit onto the Beltway and now we continued to inch along I-66 nearing Falls Church and a handful of exits before ours at Spout Run. My mind raced but I simply could not think clearly about an alternative route.

The news continued. The radio announcers betrayed frustration over numerous unconfirmed reports and issues with a phone line going dead as they eagerly awaited a live report. The announcer said that people were calling the station to report an aircraft had crashed into the Pentagon. Emergency response was underway.

"Mom! It was a plane! How many people work there?"

"Thousands." I said this in a voice so low it was more of a whisper. I forced myself to sit up straight. *Keep calm*, I told myself. *Reassure him.* "It's a huge place and it's a strong building. A very strong building. It's the Department of Defense, Christopher. I know this

is scary, I'm scared and upset, too, but we need to try to keep calm."
I reached and took his hand. "Let's turn the radio off for a while—"

"No! Mom, we have to be able to hear!"

I nodded and was about to offer him more words of assurance
when I heard the siren. I looked into my rearview mirror and saw
the fire truck about ten cars back, stuck, like we all were, in the
bumper-to-bumper traffic. I watched as cars stopped then struggled
to get out of the way on the crowded road. I put on my right turn
signal and tried get over but the car next to me ignored me. "Let me
over!" I raged. Christopher rolled his window down and motioned at
the next car to let us in. The driver, a man with sunglasses who
frowned deeply, kept his head tilted to the right, listening intently to
his radio. He did not acknowledge us. Lost in the news, he accelerated, closing the gap and blocking our way.

I looked into my side mirror and saw just three cars between us
and the ladder truck. "For Christ's sake! Why won't these people let
me over!" The sound of the siren blaring, the radio announcers'
voices continuing their awful reports, my son shaking his fist at the
car that would not let us over, it was too much. Overcome, I began
to weep. At last, a car eased to a stop to allow us over. "Mom, she's
letting you in!" Christopher waved at the woman who nodded. I
exhaled and eased the Suburban to the right. As the ladder truck
passed, I looked up, my face streaked with tears, into the face of the
fireman in the passenger seat. He glanced at me and it seemed to me
that he gave me a slight nod, as if he, I hoped, acknowledged how
desperately I had wanted to help by getting out of their way.

"I bet they're going to the Pentagon," I said, allowing my voice
to sound hopeful despite my tears. "See? They are going to help.
They will save people."

"But what if another plane comes, and another, and another?"
The panic in Christopher's voice alarmed me. What could I say to
calm him? I turned off the radio. He reached to turn it back on, but

I grabbed his hand firmly. "No! Leave it off! We'll turn it back on in a few minutes when we get off the highway. I have got to focus on driving now."

***

WE PULLED INTO THE DRIVEWAY AND SAT FOR A MOMENT IN dazed silence before allowing the unfolding terror its next act. There had been few words said after we had first caught sight of the large cloud of smoke billowing in the sky as we drove southbound on the GW Parkway toward the Pentagon. The smoke loomed before us like an evil entity in a horror film and, rather than drift away, it seemed that it was intentionally hanging above the destruction. It was as if the smoke hovered to mock the dazzling blue sky, mock what was left of that section of the building, mock the souls of those who had just perished or were injured and mock the light of the sun itself. As the smoke cloud grew wider and hovered, it also grew darker and more ominous as jet fuel fed the fire and it burned and burned below.

And now, at last we were home. There would be no school for Christopher today. He unfastened his seatbelt and opened the passenger door. "I want to get inside and watch the news."

I frowned. I wanted the news to stop. I stepped out of the Suburban and bent over at my waist, stretching my aching back. I rose and faced the front of the house and allowed a sense of comfort and relief to wash over me. At least we are home, I thought. Still, I cast a worried look up at the sky and did not allow myself to think we were safe. This day was too young.

Christopher came to stand in front of me, holding out his hand. "Where's the key? I'll open the door."

"In my purse." I opened the rear door of the Suburban and pulled out my purse. As I did, I glanced at the assorted boxes containing my father's possessions and allowed myself to smile and then immediately felt guilty. I thought of all the people—mothers and fathers, brothers and sisters—who would not be coming home to their families that day. My eyes filled and I raised my hand to cover my mouth, suddenly fearing I might be sick. I handed the house key to Christopher and followed him up the sidewalk to the front door.

The eerie quiet unnerved me.

"Christopher, wait."

He had opened the screen door and had the key poised. "Why? I want to get inside."

"Listen."

He frowned and shook his head. "Listen to what?"

"To the quiet." I slowly rotated around in a complete circle and took in the scene. I saw not one person, saw not one car drive by, heard not one dog bark, or a single door slam or engine start. I tilted my head back, my face turned upward, as I scanned the sky. The familiar roar of planes overhead that was so typical on a weekday morning was missing leaving the sky empty and silent.

"I'm glad it's quiet," Christopher responded. "I hope it stays quiet. If we don't hear airplanes with bad guys flying planning to crash, I'll be glad." He pushed open the door which jammed against a pile of mail on the floor in front of the mail slot. "There's a bunch of mail on the floor here, Mom." He stepped over it and repeated his plan to go and watch the news.

"Wait a second."

He stopped and pushed open the screen door, sticking his head out. "Now what?" He was impatient and edgy.

I motioned toward the Suburban. "Don't just go watch TV. We have to bring in all the stuff. You've got things to do. We need to check the fishpond, unpack and—"

"Mom!" he cried. "This is national emergency! We'll do that later."

৩%৩

WE SAT ON THE COUCH IN THE TV ROOM, WATCHING THE NEWS coverage, one audio and visual horror after the next. The dramatic collapse of both towers, the rumors of a fourth plane said to be another hijacked jet on the way to Washington, D.C. followed by the breaking news that a plane had crashed somewhere in Pennsylvania. Where had that been headed and what had been its target? Who did the terrorism experts think were behind such an attack? When would the President speak? This caused me to glance over at JFK. Was it my imagination or did his eyes look especially sad? A distinct memory came back of me standing beside Mama as we watched his funeral on TV. I recalled trying to comprehend that the man in the picture she had carried home from the Pentagon was now inside the flag-draped casket. *Is that the man in the picture,* I had asked. *Yes,* she replied sadly, *that's the man in the picture.* I looked at Christopher. He stared wide-eyed at the unfolding horror. I wondered what he would recall of this day when he grew up. What would he tell his children?

"Christopher, let's stop watching TV for a while." I clicked the set off and turned to see him shaking, tears streaming down his face. He rose, his fists clenched, his cheeks wet and flushed with what I realized was not just sadness, but raw anger. "So, Mom, are we supposed to forgive *them*?"

"What?"

He pointed at the TV. "Those bad guys that did this! Are we mom? Huh? You said we *had* to forgive! Well, I'm *not* going to forgive them for doing this. Ever!" He stomped his foot, seething.

I stared at him, my mind racing. *What should I say?* I moved to where he stood and gently took him by the shoulders. "No. It is not up to *us* to forgive them."

"But you said we had to forgive-"

"It is not up to *us* to forgive *them*," I repeated. "That is up to a higher authority than us."

He looked confused then said, "Up to God? But God let them do this! How could He? Is he going to forgive them?"

I shook my head. "I don't how to answer that, Christopher. I only this: we get to choose. We get to choose to go on despite the pain and the hurt and bad stuff. Even something as horrible as this. And no; we don't forget what they did, *ever*! But here's what we do: we carry on despite the bad stuff. There is good and evil in this world son and at the end of the day we decide if we're going to let it win by giving up hope. Because if we do, then the bad guys win. Do you understand that? I know it's hard."

He wiped his face roughly and bowed his head. "I'm not going to let the bad guys win, Mom," he raised his head. "But I'm glad they died, and I hope they are in hell."

I FINALLY REACHED NEAL ON THE PHONE. HE HAD BEEN LET OFF his job early and had attempted drive over to the house from Maryland, but traffic was so bad he had turned around and gone to his apartment. He had phoned earlier and left a voice message. Had I gotten it?

"I haven't even checked the machine," I told him.

"Do you want me to come over? It might take a while but-"

"No, we're alright. Come over tomorrow."

He told me he had reached Claudia and they had no idea about the attacks. "She doesn't even turn the set on until her soap opera in the afternoon, so she had no idea," Neal said. He added that Frank took the news the hardest. "He was beside himself and just dropped the phone to go turn on the TV."

"I tried to call earlier but there was no answer. I'll try again to let them know we're home ... safe." The word safe hung in the air as if it did not belong on this awful day.

***

THAT AFTERNOON, AS CHRISTOPHER AND I NIBBLED HALF-heartedly at grilled-cheese sandwiches, we heard the unmistakable roar of a fighter jet in the sky outside. We ran out to the backyard. Together we turned our faces upward and scanned the afternoon sky but did not catch a glimpse of the actual F16. I clapped my hands together excitedly. "Those are our U.S. fighter planes up there, Christopher!" I pointed to the sky. "They'll protect us. We'll be safe now!"

But he only stared at the sky, his face full of worry. He looked me in the eye. "Are you sure, Mom? Are you sure those were *our* pilots and not the . . . terrorists?"

I went over and hugged him and then promised him that yes, they were our pilots. The good guys. He looked warily at the sky. "I just wish they didn't have to fly over at all. I wish there was nothing they had to keep us safe from."

***

LATER, I SENT CHRISTOPHER TO HIS ROOM TO DO HIS HOMEWORK and reading assignment. With the house quiet, I allowed myself a moment to just breathe and then remembered the answering machine and went to Mama's bedroom. The door was open slightly and the shades were drawn. The muted light provided a respite of calm. I saw the red light of the answering machine blinking and stepped around the bed to where it sat on the nightstand. The first was from Neal. A second message was from Claudia, with Frank's voice in the background, asking me to phone to let them know we were home.

The last one, which greatly surprised me, was from Phil. "Hello Laney Mae, I am checking in on you," he said, haltingly. "It's Tuesday morning, the eleventh, and I don't really know where you all are." He paused then asked, "Has Faye passed?" Another pause. "Today has been so awful. I hope you and Christopher are safe. We're all okay up here." He paused again. "Things like this make you realize what's important. I'm so sorry I haven't been a good dad to Chris." His voice broke and he sobbed. He paused to compose himself. "I'll do better. I promise." I thought the message had ended but then he said, "Can you tell him I called? Can you have him call me when you get this?"

I sat on the bed and hugged my body. The sense of forgiveness that I had felt for him as I had stood at Boots Gray's grave just the day before, grew. "Thank you, Phil," I whispered. I would have Christopher phone him that evening.

❦

I KEPT THE TV OFF THE REST OF THE AFTERNOON BUT THE occasional roar of fighter jets above was a constant reminder of the day's events. To keep our minds on something else, we began unpacking the Suburban. The backseat and rear cargo area were full of the boxes. The ones containing the film projector and canisters of home movies were the heaviest. We unloaded those first. The rest were not too heavy and between the two of us, we had the Suburban emptied in a matter of minutes. I handed Christopher the last box then spied the jar on the floor behind the passenger seat where he had put it that morning. A decade ago, I thought.

"You need to bring in that jar Harrie gave us."

"Let me take this last box in and I'll come back and get it."

As I waited for him, an unexpected breeze blew. I closed my eyes and allowed myself to savor the feel of it on my face, such a simple thing, a warm breeze, was, like so many regular things, not to be taken for granted; not on this day. That's when I noticed an odd and annoying noise. I opened my eyes and looked around and then up as I realized where the source of the sound was coming from above. It was the brass snap hooks on Mama's flagpole. The snap hooks were being tossed about in the light wind, clanging against the pole. I stared at the flagpole, unadorned and stark, standing at attention in the center of the yard recalling Mama's order to fly the flag.

Christopher bounded down the steps and went to the other side of the Suburban. He lifted the jar gently and hugged it to his body. "Got it, Mom."

I pointed to the flagpole, "I think we should put up the flag. Can you help me?"

He gazed at the pole and grinned, the first real smile I had seen on his face since the morning. "Sure. Grandma would like that. Especially today."

"The flag's in the coat closet. Put the jar in the living room with the other things we brought home."

He carried the jar toward the house but paused before he reached the front steps. "Mom, I want to keep it in my room. The jar of moonbeams. Is that okay?"

"That's fine. Just don't drop it."

"Don't worry, I won't let it break. All moonbeams would fall out."

I scoffed, "Sure they will. I just don't want broken glass everywhere."

He frowned at me. "Mom, Harrie would be upset if it broke. She believes in the moonbeams you know."

"I know."

"I do too," he said defiantly. "Even if we can't see them."

I smiled at him. "That would make her very happy."

He returned, carrying the flag folded in a perfect triangle, the way Mama had taught me and I had taught my son. We stepped over to the flagpole. Christopher said, "Remember, we have to be careful. We can't let the flag touch the ground, Mom. If we do, we have to burn it."

"Honey, I know that. You know Grandma made sure I knew the rules."

He nodded and we held onto the flag and began to gently unfold it. Next, I carefully connected the top snap hook to the grommet closest to the blue field of stars on the flag. We hoisted the flag a bit then I let Christopher attach the other snap hook. Bit by bit, I pulled on the halyard until the flag was at the top of the pole. I then lowered it a couple of inches to allow the flag some space from the top pulley as Mama had taught me. I began to secure it in place by tying the halyard to the cleat in a figure eight when Christopher nudged my arm and whispered, "Mom, look." He pointed. "Across the street. It's that neighbor of Grandma's. The old grumpy guy."

I paused and turned to see Clive Anderson standing on the side-walk directly across the street, one hand holding his cane, the other hand on his hip, staring at me. I raised my hand and waved then lowered it quickly when he did not respond. Wearing a frown, he teetered slightly then and raised his cane and pointed at the flag and barked, "You need to lower it."

Confused, I tilted my head at him. "I'm sorry? What?" *Did he want me to take the flag down?*

"Half-mast," he said.

Of course! Half-mast. To honor those who had died. I nodded, gave him a thumbs-up. I undid the figure-eight tie and allowed the flag to lower to my best estimate of half-mast.

I looked back at him and watched as he carefully switched the cane to his left hand and worked to steady himself. Ever so slowly, and with obvious effort to maintain his balance, Clive Anderson began to raise his right hand, rigid in salute, inch-by-inch, past his stomach, past his chest, and past his neck until it reached and rested upon his brow. He held it there and managed to stand at attention for a brief moment, to be again the soldier he had once been, young, strong and alert. But suddenly his face crumpled, and his chest began to heave and he began to weep uncontrollably. He let tears roll down his clean-shaven face as his left hand, unaccustomed to managing the cane, shook slightly. Despite this, he continued to stand as straight, unwavering and erect as his old body would allow. With one quick motion, he brought his arm down by his side. We watched as he took a cloth from his back pocket and dabbed his eyes and wiped his face. We heard him give his nose a blow. He returned the cloth to his pocket, gave us a curt nod then turned slowly and ambled up his walk and went inside his house.

Christopher asked, "Mom, are we going to leave it up? All night?"

"I think we will. Tonight at least."

"Well, you have to shine a light on it then."

I nodded. "I know. Mama had a floodlight somewhere. I'll have to find it."

"Grandma told me once that you could only keep the flag flying at night if you keep a light on it when it's dark."

"That's right. A light has to shine on it when it's dark."

I thought, but did not say, what an especially dark night this would be.

***

BEFORE WE SAT DOWN TO DINNER, I HAD LED CHRISTOPHER TO stand before the answering machine. "I want you to hear this." I hit the play button and when my son heard his father's voice break and heard him sob, Christopher's face transformed from anxiety to surprise. When he heard his father say he promised to do better, my son's face transformed from resentment to forgiveness.

"You were right, mom. About forgiving. I mean, not the bad guys, but the people in our lives that sometimes hurt us." He wrapped his arms around me, and we stood holding each other for a moment. Then I dialed Phil's number, said a quick hello, and handed the phone to my son. I left him sitting on the side of his deceased grandmother's bed in the growing darkness of the awful day enjoying the first real conversation with his father that he had had in recent years.

They had much to talk about.

⊙⅏⊙

WE PULLED THE COVERS BACK AND GOT INTO BED. I READ TO HIM for only five minutes. My eyelids were so heavy I could barely keep them open. "Lights out," I told him.

He sat up. "Please, Mom, just tonight, let's leave the light on." He leapt from the bed and ran around to my side and switched it back on.

"Christopher, no. I can't sleep with the light on, honey. If you want a light on, go sleep in your room, okay?"

He pleaded but I would not give in. He stomped to his room, muttering to himself. He ran back and stood in the doorway. "Can I come back? If I get scared? To sleep with you?"

"Of course you can."

He nodded and ran back to his room. I cast my weary eyes at the digital clock on the nightstand and saw that it was 10:30 p.m. Would this day never end? I again switched off the lamp and my head fell back on to the pillow. A stream of images from the extraordinary day flashed in my mind but soon they were replaced with a blessed nothingness as I slept.

⚘

I BOLTED UPRIGHT AT THE SOUND OF CHRISTOPHER'S VOICE calling me. My heart raced. I struggled to wake up from the pull of sleep. I kicked off the covers as I glanced at the clock. My mouth dropped when I saw that it was just 11:45 p.m. and I moaned aloud at the realization that I had hardly slept, and that this day was not finished with us yet.

Christopher's voice, which seemed to be filled with excitement, summoned me. "Mom! Wake up! You have to come here! Hurry!" Had he had a nightmare? Had the fighter jets flown lower and been louder, causing him to panic? His voice did not reflect this; I expected his voice to be frightened and shrill. But instead, he sounded ecstatic.

I hurried across the short hallway and stood in his doorway. Christopher sat up on his knees in the bed, his hair a wild mess from tossing and turning. He was grinning ear-to-ear. He pointed at his desk.

"Look!"

I turned my head to see where he pointed. It was at the jar of moonbeams sitting atop his desk, aglow with what appeared to be small white lights, like Christmas tree lights.

"Harrie was right, Mom!" He jumped off the bed, rushing over to me. "The moonbeams are real! Just like she said!" He jumped up and down. "Your dad caught them and put them in there and they glow when we need them. When it's really dark and scary, like today."

I stood in the doorway, speechless, trying to make my overtired mind work to comprehend and address the phenomenon before me.

And then, I understood. My eyes told me what I was really

seeing. I looked up at the brightly lit overhead light on the ceiling and back again at the jar. I sighed. The light beams from the ceiling fixture were simply being reflected into the jar. There were no moonbeams, just regular old light beams bending as they hit the glass, retracting and glowing seemingly from within. It was an optical illusion.

But I could not tell him this. Instead, I smiled and hugged him. "Oh, my goodness! Look at that!" I lifted him off the ground and twirled him in my arms. "It's amazing, Christopher!"

Elated, he danced about the small bedroom, chanting, "*The moonbeams are real, the moonbeams are real, the moonbeams are real!*"

I clapped my hands joyfully and watched him. How far we have come today, I thought. The two extremes of sadness and joy. I told him it was wonderful but now time to go back to sleep. To my relief, he did not protest and jumped into his bed, fluffed his pillows and laid back, arms behind his head, "Good night, Mom!"

I blew him a kiss and turned to leave.

"Wait, Mom," he said, sitting up, resting on an elbow. "You can turn the light out."

I gasped. I tried to sound indifferent, "Oh, well, it's really okay to leave the light on."

"No, I have the moonbeams. I don't need that light on." He pointed to the ceiling fixture.

I paused, a pit in my stomach as I stared at him. "Christopher, if I turn out that light–"

"What?"

"The moonbeams will go away."

"What do you mean? They're right there, Mom."

I was too tired and drained to deal with this. Reluctantly, I raised my arm and, sighing, flipped the light switch off.

The room went dark. Only the light from the hallway shone.

"What the heck?" Christopher said. He jumped from the bed

and stomped across the room. "Turn the light back on," he demanded. I did and the jar again seemed to glow. He bent over and peered into it. I walked over to him and pulled out the desk chair and sat down.

"I thought they were real," he said.

"I know, Christopher. I wish the moonbeams were really real too, I do." I paused then had a thought. "But who says they aren't? Sometimes we have to believe in things we can't always see."

He frowned and shook his head as he stared sadly at the jar.

I said, "But you know what *is* real? What's real is that my dad, your grandpa, a long, long time ago, well, he captured the air and put the lid on that jar and it's still in there and to me, that means a part of him is still in there. That lid never came off. Harrie kept it safe. So, in a way, something that was part of him, is still in there. And I think, somehow, someway that we just can't understand, those moonbeams are in there and we saw them tonight. We saw them! See?" I pointed at the small, reflected lights. "So what if it's just a reflection of another light? They're still shining."

I put my hands on his shoulders and turned him to face me. He looked at me, a deep frown on his unhappy face, tears on his cheeks. "I guess so, Mom. I just . . . I just thought for a minute that it was real."

"But Christopher, don't you know?"

"Know what?"

I gently placed a hand over his heart and one over my own. "It's the light in here–the light inside all of us–that's what's real. The light of love, of courage, the light of hope. And you know what else?"

"What?" His eyebrow arched hopefully.

"This light inside of us, just like the little lights in the jar of moonbeams, it can't shine on its own. It needs us to make the light shine out."

He stared into my eyes. He sighed deeply then, a sound more

like one made by an old man than a ten-year-old boy. He stepped into my arms and wrapped his around my neck. I lifted him off the floor and carried him to the bed. My baby boy. My son. My hope. I laid him down and covered him with the blanket.

"Lights on or off?"

"On," he replied. "We have to let the moonbeams shine tonight, Mom. Especially tonight."

ACKNOWLEDGMENTS

As this is largely a story about motherhood, I want to first thank my children, Meredith, and John. You taught me more than you will ever know about love but also, how to see things from the innocent and honest perspective of a child. I thought about both of you as I developed the character, Christopher. I am grateful to you, Meredith, for reading early drafts and providing me the positive feedback I needed to keep going.

This is also a story about family and my heart is full and indebted to my family, both living and those who have passed, for loving me unconditionally and believing in me, even when I did not always believe in myself.

Writing was the one thing I knew I loved from early childhood. I remember one of my elementary school teachers sharing on my report card to my parents how much she and the other students "enjoyed Toni's creative stories." And so, to all the teachers, college professors, colleagues, editors, and other writers, thank you for sharing your enthusiasm and yes, constructive criticism and input with me over the years.

Many friends and colleagues kindly encouraged me as I wrote this novel, even when they had no idea about its subject or content. Your positivity got me past times I wanted to give up. Denise Benoit, Ellen McMackin, and Mary Lopez Schell, you three encouraged me when I needed it the most.

There were some very special people who helped me understand what I was writing about in this novel. To Cindy Orion, the most caring and thoughtful Hospice nurse we could have asked for at my father's death, thank you with all my heart for agreeing to read my early drafts and guide me about the dying process and the beauty and true gift that is Hospice care.

Melissa Thierry, my wonderful colleague, and friend, I am so grateful to you for reviewing my writing about my beloved character, Harriet, "Harrie" Hartman. Your input as the mother of a child with Down syndrome was invaluable to me and so helpful in ensuring my portrayal was accurate and respectful.

To novelist Angie Kim, I'm so lucky I got to meet you at a writer's conference in 2019. Your passion for writing is contagious and through you, I connected with a most wonderful writer and editor, Barbara Esstman. Barbara, your straightforward input, and thoughtful guidance helped turn this story around and your encouragement prevented me from giving up. You showed me how important it is to *do the work* of writing; that it isn't just words on paper. It is work. It is hard. It is humbling. But it is worth it.

To the helpful and brave individuals who responded to save lives and prevent more attacks on September 11, 2001, in Washington, D.C, thank you for sharing your unique stories with me. Arlington County Fire Captain Justin Tirelli, you made the horror and heroism of that awful day very real in a way I could not understand just by reading about those events. To Air Force Colonel (retired) Mark Valentine, I hope you know how much I appreciated you responding to me — someone you did not know - asking you to share how you and others bravely flew your fighter jets above Washington, D.C. to keep watch on us that frightening afternoon. And thank you to radio news reporter Neal Augenstein; my being able to reference your live broadcasts from that morning two decades later was incredibly helpful. Thank you for sharing and answering my questions about your experience so I could recount that morning accurately.

A special thanks to a young man who was once, a few years ago, my intern. Karl Diaz, when I met you, you had just self-published a novella. To say I was impressed is an understatement but what was even more meaningful was your encouragement to explore self-publishing, which I had not considered before. And to my dear cousin Catherine Pearce, I thank you for the generous guidance you shared after your own exciting publishing experience when you inspired me to look to independent publishers as a possible way forward.

I must also say a special thank you to those literary agents to whom I reached when pursuing a traditional publishing path and though not interested in my novel for various reasons, still took the time to personally write to me, acknowledge my effort and encourage me to keep writing.

This leads me to thanking the team at The Paper House from Luke White, who quickly responded and answered all my questions, to Tara Weniger who masterfully edited the manuscript and to Mo Raad, who worked with me to design this work's cover.

Thank you all.

ABOUT THE AUTHOR

Toni M. Andrews developed her love for creative writing in elementary school with the encouragement of teachers and classmates. In college, she shifted to journalism and is currently a communications and public relations professional working in higher education.

Her professional career has included work on a local newspaper, governmental affairs, as well as media relations at The White House. She owned and operated a full-service marketing, advertising, and public relations firm for over twelve years and served as vice president of communications for a community bank. She has served on a variety of business, educational and community organization boards.

She earned her Bachelor of Arts degree in Government & Politics from the University of Maryland, College Park, with a minor in journalism and contemporary U.S. History. She worked on a weekly newspaper and as a freelance writer for a magazine. Two of her creative works have been published in *The Washington Post*.

Toni is the founder of the Facebook Group, *The Baby Boomer Experience,* which explores the political, social, and cultural events of that era and their impact on the "coolest" generation.

She currently resides in Virginia where she has been active in the community while raising her two children. She loves sharing stories and songs from her youth with her new granddaughter, Tillie.

This is her first novel.

Printed in the USA
CPSIA information can be obtained
at www.ICGtesting.com
JSHW070022171023
50087JS00002B/2